Third Librarian

Detective Series

Bobby Cinema

PRISTINE
PRESS AND MEDIA

ISBN
978-1-96480-470-5 (Paperback)
978-1-96480-469-9 (eBook)
978-1-96480-471-2 (Hardback)

BOBBY CINEMA

Third Librarian

DETECTIVE Series

BOBBY CINEMA THIRD LIBRARIAN DETECTIVE SERIES

BY BOBBY CINEMA

SYNOPSIS:

I am telling two detective stories where they work in a library and help find a way to stop Criminal kingpins and their empires. This is my third librarian detective series that I am doing about another librarian crimefighters out there trying to stop Kingpins for their evil plans that a couple of librarian detectives and their teams to stop them before those criminal empires wreak havoc in the world or the USA. We have two stories one of them is a Dr and former green beret and part time CIA agent who comes out of retirement to help rescue a friend who is captured by terrorist. The new elected President of the United States assigns new CIA operatives that he picked to track down and stop an assassin who killed the first elected president, and the new vice president is now the new president to find this assassin who killed him and there is a bigger conspiracy, and this assassin was hired by someone to kill the president who didn't like his agenda. I am doing something different; it is writing a synopsis of a new detective story in the next book. So, enjoy the Bobby Cinema Third Librarian Detective series.

DR AND MAJOR
SUDARSAN CHAVALA

By Bobby Cinema

SYNOPSIS:

Dr Sudarsan Chavala is enjoying retirement who was born in India and grew up in India and worked as an Optometrist in Maryville Eye Clinic. He lives in a big house at 934 South Dunn in Maryville MO in the heart of Kansas City with his wife Girija. His son Sai needs his help as an Optometrist in Fort Hood in Dallas Texas. Just like his father he works as an optometrist in the military base there. Sudarsan and Sai both moonlight as Central Intelligence Agency operatives. Sudarsan Chavala went to Harvard University medical school and graduated in 1972. He also enrolled in ROTC training while he was at Medical School. He met his wife Girija with his brother-in-law Prakash who introduced them and got married after he graduated from medical school. He did his internship in Fort Leavenworth medical center as second lieutenant. After his first year in Fort Leavenworth, he wanted to join the green berets, the special forces and asked his superior to get him a recommendation to Fort Bragg. He told his wife about if he gets accepted to Fort Bragg and complete his training, he might have gone to Vietnam. Girija was shocked at first. But understood. Sudarsan got the recommendation to train in Fort Bragg by Colonel William Jameson, after a couple of months of training and Sudarsan shipped off to Vietnam and did some green beret missions. He did search and rescue missions on soldiers who were captured in north Vietnam Soldiers and become a war hero. He did three tours in Vietnam in three years and his wife living in Fort Leavenworth and writing as much as they can. He was awarded the distinguished service cross moved up to Major in three years. After returning home in Leavenworth, he worked with the CIA missions in Vietnam and know when his will be called up for a mission when they need him. Anyway, Sudarsan and Girija decided to stay as an army medical doctor and after he finished his residency and fellowship for four years in 1978 and their son Sai chavala was born in 1977 when he was doing his fellowship. Sudarsan decided to move to Maryville MO to begin his eye doctor practice from a medical school friend Kanthi Havaladar in Harvard. They both went to college in New Delhi and became friends. Both decided to join ROTC. Both were friends who decided to become green berets and worked for CIA part time operatives before heading back to the USA. Dr Havaladar got him a recommendation from the medical board as a new eye doctor. Sudarsan lived a quiet life in Maryville MO, until his son Sai followed in his footsteps as an eye doctor and joined ROTC in UMKC and became an eye doctor in Fort Hood. Sai moved up the ranks to Lieutenant Colonel. Anyway, he was recruited by the CIA last year and worked as an operative because the person who recruited Sai, is the guy who worked with his father as an operative and now is a deputy director. They both need them to save an old friend who used to be in the CIA and is captured by terrorist. The old friend they are talking about is Kanthi Havaladar, they both need them to rescue him. Sudarsan is reluctant to do this mission and since it is his best friend Kanthi, he will have to do it. Sai formed a team to help his father rescue his family friend. Can they do it and only time will tell.

The funeral of Dr Sudarsan Chavala is in Bram's funeral home in Maryville, Missouri in a part of Kansas City. Inside the funeral home everybody was listening to Dr Sudarsan Chavala son Sai, his only child giving out his father's eulogy. Dr Sudarsan Chavala wife Girija is crying and mourning her husband Dr Sudarsan Chavala. Sai speaks to a lot of mourners in Bram's funeral home. Sai has a wife Susmita and two children Lekha and Naveen. Lekha is 8 and Naveen 6 years old since the funeral is in October 1, 2022. Sai speaks to the mourners about his father Dr Sudarsan Chavala who are mourning some of are two Army Generals and five army colonels and three us senators and five congressmen who Sudarsan chavala examined their eyes and served with him before he left for private practice. Everyone spoke at his funeral and now it is Sai's turn to speak at his funeral. Sai is on the podium. Sai said to the mourners, "I am Sai Chavala, I am Dr Sudarsan Chavala son and his only son. Anyway, my father worked hard all his life and helped a lot of people and gave money to the less fortunate and was an honest worker. There was something I never told anyone about, but it may be fiction, and no one would believe me. But I got an okay from my father's former commanding officer to tell his story. That means, I have full clearance or authorization to tell the story. But it is fictional or real whichever you guys think it is. It was from my father's journal; about something no one ever knew about him. It all started when my father started his final year in medical school in UMKC. University of Missouri-Kansas City where it is six-year program and Dr Sudarsan Chavala getting his medical degree in the UMKC." Sudarsan was getting his medical degree and watches his family in the audience, his father came all the way from Tarangar where a small town in India is. Sail continues narrating and tells the mourners, "My father's graduation takes place in June 1, 1968 and Dr Sudarsan Sumanth Chavala was born in February 2, 1943 in Taranagar and grew up in New Delhi India where his father Ajay and his mother Lakhshmi died when Sudarsan was 2 years old and runs a very successful chain of market in New Delhi called Chavala. It was a family business, the chavala family had 7 sons and three daughters and Sudarsan was the final child being born in Taranagar before moving to New Delhi at age 2." After Sai telling the mourners. Dr. Sudarsan Chavala sees how proud of him when he got his medical degree. Sudarsan was speaking to his family in the hallway and Ajay tells his son, "I am proud of you, Son. You did it." Sudarsan tells his father, "Thanks father and you're not going to give me the lecture about me settling down speech again are you." Ajay tells his son, "No of course not I told your brothers go to college and make something in their lives. They did, they went to college and got master's degrees in engineering and medicine. Sairam wants to be a film maker, but I told him to go to college and learn the tricks of the trade first. That is what he is doing." Dr. Sudarsan Chavala tells his father, "You mean go to college or film school." Ajay told Sudarsan, "Yes, but I think he will fail and trust me he does not have the brain or will power to become a filmmaker. Why I wanted you and your siblings to get degrees in engineering and medicine. Those pay the bills, and I would not care if one of them gets a law degree. But filmmaking is a bad idea." Sudarsan tells Ajay, "I understand why you encouraged me go to medical school and Sai Ram did get into film school and graduated. The doors were not opening for him, so he decided to go back and get his engineering degree that pays the bills." Ajay tells Sudarsan, "SaiRam wanted me and my siblings to invest in this movie that he was making, and we told him no, because it will fail, and he has no brain or vision to get distribution or get into film festivals. That is why he decided to go back and get his engineering degree because it does not pay the bills and the odd jobs will not help him. I am proud he listens to me, and I am proud of you listening to me. Education and jobs are very important and just remember that." Sudarsan is upset about what his father said about his lack of encouragement, but he knew his father knew what he was best and maybe was right. Sudarsan tells his father, Father you were right and thanks for pointing SarRam to the right direction and me to the right direction." Ajay tells his son, "I am proud of you son." Ajay and Sudarsan hugged for a minute and let go. Sudarsan tells his father, "I am going to talk to Khanthi for a minute and he and I have to discuss our plans after graduation." Ajay tells his son, "Okay Sudarsan go ahead." Sudarsan exits in the middle of the hallway and sees Khanti Havaladar talking to his family. Sai narrating to the mourners and tell them, "My father had a childhood friend Dr Khanthi Havaladar who he knew in New Delhi and both of them got full scholarships to UMKC to become doctors. But that was not the scholarship they did not talk about. Mr father and Dr Havaladar took American citizenship classes and in India and both of them heard about ROTC. Reserves Officer Training School where college students go into military officer training while attending classes in college. Anyway, they say the brochure and their teacher said that you have to be American citizens to eligible to attend. But the teachers is friends United States Ambassador of India and he was a guest speaker here in this school and anyway he helped pull some strings get them into ROTC program in college in UMKC and help them pass the American citizenship test so they can be eligible to attend. They did and ROTC made an exception to let my father and Dr Havaladar take ROTC and medical school classes. Anyway, it was full workload, and they did it." Sudarsan taps Khanthi in the shoulder Khanthi turns around and sees Sudarsan and tells Sudarsan, "Hello Sudarsan, do you have a chance to say hello to my parents yet." Sudarsan tells Khanthi, I did before the ceremony started. Anyway, I wanted to tell you about our deployment, we have not told our parents about ROTC. We just got our commission as second lieutenants and not told them about we would be shipping out soon tomorrow and I don't know how they would take it, if we told them about ROTC." Khanthi told Sudarsan, "They would disown us if we told them, even if we told them before we left India do you think they would let us join the military and they may be worried they may send us off to war." Sudarsan tells Khanthi, "We wanted to go into ROTC and see the world and be part of the action. We were John Wayne fans, when we saw him in that war movie The Longest Day. He was a great war hero." Khanthi told Sudarsan, "He was a supporting actor in that movie." Sudarsan tells Khanthi, "Who cares he was in that movie whether he was lead or supporting actor. He was there and one of the main reasons why I wanted to join ROTC." Khanthi told Sudarsan, "Well they ship us off to Vietnam soon, because the war our there is bad. But we don't have to worry, Colonel Truman told us we won't have go to the front lines and let us work in the medical office. But they decide what medical office might ship is out soon. Since we have to be in Fort Riley tomorrow and tell us where we would be going." Sudarsan tells Khanthi, "I know how my father is going to react that I am in the army officer, he is a strict pacifist and did not want me and my brothers join the military. Not even the American military. But we have to tell them, where they like it or not." Khanthi tells Sudarsan, just better pray they won't disown us soon." Sudarsan tells Khanthi, "That's the least I am not worried about." After a few minutes, Sai narrates to the mourners, "My father and Dr Havaladar were about to bring in their family and tell them the truth. I am not going into details on how they took it." Sudarsan and Khanthi bring the family into an empty UMKC auditorium after the graduation ceremony is over. Everyone is seating in their seats and Sudarsan and Khanthi told them about them joining ROTC and being shipped out. Sai narrates to the mourners, "But they did not take it well at first." The Chavala and Havaldar family are upset and looking at them. Sudarsan told Khanthi, "They took it very well. But at least their still proud of us graduating medical school." Sai narrates to the Mourners, Dad and Dr Havaldar went to Fort Riley and get their shipping assignments and after my grandfather and the rest of my family and the Havaladar family cooled off for a few minutes and gives them their blessings to be in the military and finishing out their dreams of becoming doctors. Let them work in the medical office in the military base. The next day, my dad and Dr Havaladar went to Fort Riley and sees Colonel Truman in his office and is about to give them their assignments where they are being shipped." Colonel Truman is in his office working in his desk, the intercom buzz and Colonel Truman answers it and tells the person on the intercom, "What is it Sergeant?" Sergeant Thea Howard is the personal secretary of Colonel Truman, and he talks to Colonel Truman on the intercom, "Second Lieutenants Chavala and Havaladar are here to see you, Colonel Truman." Colonel Truman tells Sergeant Thea Howard, "Send them in." Sudarsan and Khanthi enters the office, they are standing up straight for attention and Colonel Truman tells them, "At ease gentlemen, good morning!" Sudarsan and Khanthi both tell Colonel Truman, "Good Morning to you sir!" Colonel Truman tells Sudarsan and Khanthi, "Have a seat, gentlemen." Sudarsan and Khanthi both sit down in their chairs and listen to what Colonel Truman tells them. Colonel Truman tells them, "Lieutenant Chavala and Lieutenant Havaladar, I look at your file, that you both did well in ROTC, the drills, the procedures, and Military procedures and took a full load in six years of medical school. Even after graduating from ROTC in UMKC to get your commission and we let you finish medical school there so it could look good on your resume. Now you guys are in full commissioned officers, you guys want to work in the medical field in our army base. Which I assigned to you. Is that true, Chavala." Sudarsan tells Colonel Truman, "Yes sir, even when I told our families that we went to ROTC. They were upset first, but after a few minutes they were proud of us serving our nation and protecting the citizens of the United

States of America. They also wanted us to become doctors, so we did both and they were thrilled. We were ready to serve the medical field here in the army." Colonel Truman tells them, "You guys can do your internship and residency in these army hospitals that I am shipping you too. But I am afraid you guys will be shipped off to different bases." Sudarsan tells Colonel Truman, "Different bases sir." Colonel Truman shipping orders paper to Sudarsan and Khanthi and both looked at it. Sudarsan and Khanthi both read where they are going to be stationed and they look upset that both are going to be separated. Colonel Truman tells them where they are going to be shipped," Lieutenant Havaladar, you will be stationed here at Fort Riley where you can do your internship and residency here where you are studying Primary care physicians and Lieutenant Chavala, you will be stationed at Fort Leavenworth at Leavenworth Kansas where you can start your internship and residency. You were studying Ophthalmology, and Fort Leavenworth can help you with that." Sudarsan tells Colonel Truman, "Sir, me and Khanthi do not want to be separated. We knew each other since childhood, and I thought we could be army soldiers and doctors together. Do you want to really want to separate us." Colonel Truman tells Sudarsan, "Chavala that is not a negotiation, it is about orders and what is best for you guys. The best thing for you guys starts your medical training in where you assigned to, once you guys are done in six years and maybe you can work full time in Fort Leavenworth, or any other army base you want to be assigned to and work with each other after training. In the meantime, you guys will start your medical training where you assigned to. Is that understood men." Both tell Colonel Truman, "Yes sir!" Colonel Truman and Sudarsan and Khanthi both get up on their chairs and all of them Salute. Colonel Truman gives them one final message, "Good luck gentlemen!" Both tell Colonel Truman, "Thank you, sir! After they were done saluting. Sudarsan and Khanthi both exit Colonel Truman's office and head to the hallway with transfer papers. Sudarsan tells Khanthi, "I'm going to miss you, Khanthi." Khanthi tells Sudarsan, I'm going to miss you too Buddy!" Sudarsan tells Khanthi, "Once we are done with our internships, residencies and it is possible if we finish our fellowship together in Fort Riley after I am done with my residency in

Fort Leavenworth. Maybe we can go into private practice together." Khanthi tells Sudarsan, "That sounds great, but maybe we can be private practice neighbors where we both working in different medical fields." Sudarsan tells Khanthi, "Sure thing. I will see you soon, once we are done. I have no idea if I could get leave anytime soon. I need to make a good impression." Khanthi tells Sudarsan, "So do I, Sudarsan I want to ask you something." Sudarsan tells Khanthi, "What is it?" Khanthi tells Sudarsan, "I want to ask you can you do something else in the military besides being a doctor. I always thought you wanted to be in the front lines. Since the war in Vietnam is ongoing, I thought you want to go out their fight to protect the people that we were serving for." Sudarsan tells Khanthi, "I don't know, my father was already cool with it when I joined ROTC and went to medical school in the same time. I do not think I am going into a battlefield exactly what he wants. I thought about going to Fort Bragg for special forces training. But I don't know if I can ask my commanding officer if I can train in Fort Bragg and be shipped off to Vietnam." Khanthi tells Sudarsan, "You never know if you try, I must report to Colonel John Thomas who is my medical superior but good luck Sudarsan and think about it. Besides, you always talk about being the next John Wayne, I don't think he would sit in a medical office and working in exam charts all day instead being in the field, bye!" Sudarsan tells Khanthi, "Bye." Sudarsan leaves the hallway and goes to Fort Leavenworth where he is reported to his medical training. Sai tells the mourners, "My father thought about being in the front lines and fighting for his country and not looking at eye charts all day. But right, he was concentrating his medical training." Inside AHC-Munson in Fort Leavenworth where Sudarsan changes into his medical scrubs in male Doctors locker room and make friends with some of the interns. He meets another Indian medical doctor and says hello to. Sudarsan tells this Indian doctor, "Hi, I'm Sudarsan Chavala." Sudarsan shakes this Indian doctor's hand and tells Sudarsan, "I'm Jaya Konajeti and I'm starting my internship here in Fort Leavenworth." Sudarsan tells Jaya, "So am I, I went to ROTC and UMKC medical school here for six years and now I am going to start my medical training here. What about you, how did you get here." Jaya tells Sudarsan, "I went to NYU Grossman School of Medicine and did my ROTC training five years after I got my commission and graduated from medical School. I was stationed here." Sudarsan tells Jaya, "What are you planning on to practice after you have done with intern and residency program." Jaya tells Sudarsan, "I'm going into General practitioner, I am always fascinated with helping patients and listening to their needs. I want to be that guy look up if they are hurt or injured or do what they can for my assistance." Sudarsan tells Jaya, "I want to specialize in Ophthalmology or Optometrist, I like helping people fix their eye sights or make they are seeing good or seeing well. If they cannot see at all, I must give them glasses to help them get their vision back. Besides an optometrist was a level to help patients see better." Jaya tells Sudarsan, "I guess we both have our work cut out for us. Our superior will be here to begin our training." Sudarsan tells Jaya, "I wish I can meet him, but I have to report to our commanding officer Colonel Ray Thomas." Jaya tells Sudarsan, "Colonel Thomas, he is the head of hospital why does he need to see you." Sudarsan tells Jaya, "He said, before I came here the nurse told me report to him at his office in an hour to speak with me before I begin my medical training. So, I must be in his office in twenty minutes. Wish me luck." Jaya tells Sudarsan, "Good luck." Sudarsan is done changing into his scrubs and exit the locker room and head to Colonel Thomas office. Colonel Thomas is working in his office and the door knocks. Colonel Thomas tells the person outside the door, "Come in.!" The door opens and it's Sudarsan. Colonel tells Sudarsan, "Hello Lieutenant Chavala." Sudarsan goes over to his desk and stands in attention. Colonel Thomas tells Sudarsan, "At ease Chavala." Sudarsan stands down. Colonel Thomas tells Sudarsan, "Have a seat, Lieutenant." Sudarsan tells Colonel Thomas, "Yes sir." Sudarsan sits down in his chair and tells Colonel Thomas, "You wanted to see me sir." Colonel Thomas tells Sudarsan, "Yes, I do. Lieutenant." Sudarsan tells Colonel Thomas, "It is odd, that the head of Military medical branch wanted to see on my first day. Mostly the whole first interns usually meet our supervisor Major John Rickford. But I am meeting you first sir, why is that." Colonel Thomas tells Sudarsan, "I been looking at your file, Sudarsan that you been asked if you can want go to Fort Bragg to train in the special forces after your fellowship. Is that true Chavala." Sudarsan tells Colonel Thomas, "Colonel Thomas, how did you know about me wanted to apply to Fort Bragg?" Colonel Thomas answered Sudarsan, "It's in the file that your superior Major Edward Bass who was your instructor in ROTC, that you requested that you want go to Medical school and after your fellowship here that you want to join the green berets." Sudarsan tells Colonel Thomas, yes sir. Major turned me down for that, he wanted me to pick one and he does not think that I cannot be a doctor and infantry soldier all at once. So I was in tough dilemma, because my father is a pacificist and he did not want me in the front lines that I would get killed their and wanted me go to Medical School. That is one of the main reasons why I did not tell him about ROTC. I told him after graduation, he was upset at first, but he calmed down a supported me for it. A military doctor would look good on a resume. I do not think he would approve of me being a fighting soldier." Colonel Thomas tells Sudarsan, "Why on earth asked go to Fort Bragg after fellowship and why do you want to fighting soldier." Sudarsan tells Colonel Thomas, "I don't want to serve my country. I want to protect the people that I am fighting for so they can feel safe or protected. Including my family. The war on Vietnam is getting worse, maybe I could be out there to help them. I do not want to be a war hero, but at least I can tell my children and grandchildren that I was out there in the front lines, and I wanted go out their make a difference for one day." Colonel Thomas tells Sudarsan, "Chavala I am going to level you, you do not look like Green Beret material, but you made it through ROTC training out of alive. But sending you out in the front lines is out of the question, the war might be over after you are done with your fellowship and sending you to fort bragg so you can fight in the front lines is not exactly a good move. The way I look at you, you barely made it through basic training even after the war is over before you go there will be other missions for green berets but not for you. Since you don't have the chops to be out in the front lines." Sudarsan tells Colonel Thomas, "Why is that sir, what chops are you talking about." Colonel Thomas tells Sudarsan, "Your body is very skinny, and you can barely fight and barely could fire a gun and you would be dead in seconds once you reach the front lines." Sudarsan tells Colonel Thomas, "I may not have six pack abs or good fight power or good speed. I can do it, even the worse soldiers can be the best. An underdog who has no chance winning, can win a title, or go the distance." Colonel Thomas tells Sudarsan, "What did you get that catchphrase." Sudarsan tells Colonel Thomas, "Kansas City movie theater had a showing of Pride of the Yankees, and I was a Gary Cooper fan. Lou Gehrig was my inspiration that he could make a difference from being a major league baseball star in New York Yankees and take them to a world series. That is what I want, to go out in the front lines to make a difference. Maybe I am not going to win a medal. At least I can do go in the front lines and protect the people I was sworn to do, and I would take a bullet for any of my guys, or you if it was life and death sir." Colonel Thomas tells Sudarsan, "That is touching, but I still won't recommend you go to Fort Bragg, I have some great pull there. I am friends with General Jackson McCarthy who's in charge of Fort Bragg, but I won't recommend you because I think you are going to make a great military doctor, but not as a soldier. I am sorry, but if you still want to think about going there after your fellowship, I will write a recommendation to General McCarthy if you want to go." Sudarsan tells Colonel Thomas, "Thank you sir, I won't be done in five years with my internship, residency, and my fellowship. So, I will probably work here in two years and after I am done, I will probably go into civilian private practice after I am done. But thanks for giving me the heads-up sir." Colonel Thomas tells Sudarsan, "I am just looking out for you soldier." Both get up from their chairs and salute each other. Sai narrating to the mourners, "Just like that my dad's other dream to become a special forces operative is over. But that does not mean he stops thinking about his dream to fight in the front lines or does not mean he has not given up. My father always found a way to make his dream come true, one door closes, and another door opens. Even if he can't get into Fort Bragg after fellowship, Colonel Thomas cannot get him in Fort Bragg. That does not mean he cannot pursue him, someday he will prove that he can do it. That is what he is going to do." Both stop saluting each other and Sudarsan exits Colonel Thomas office,

Sudarsan joins the rest of the interns, doctors lounge and sits back down in his chair and wait for his supervisor. Sudarsan's supervisor Major Rickford who is attending doctor in this hospital addresses the interns, "Welcome ACH-Munson Military Hospital, I like to welcome you interns. Let's get started and I will tell you where to start. Follow me!" Major Rickford is exiting the doctors lounge with the interns and Sudarsan. They are in the hallway of the hospital on the second floor. Major Rickford tells the interns what the interns' jobs are. Major Rickford tells the interns what they do here, "There are five things in your training you will have to do, Trauma protocol, phone lists, pagers. Nurses will page you; you answer every page at a run. You will be on call every day. Do not think about getting a drink while you are on call. When you guys run, I run and that's rule number two. Your first shift starts now and lasts forty-eight hours. You're interns, maggots, nobodies, just because you're miltary officers does not mean you have special privilege here, out here I outrank you and you want to be good doctors; you will have to prove it to me. If you can't go somewhere else. Anyway, you will run labs, write orders, work every second night till you drop and don't complain!" Majopr Rickford shows them bunk beds where doctors or nurses can rest for the day, Major Rickford tells the interns, "On call rooms. Attendings hog them, sleep when you can, where you can, which brings me to rule number three, if I'm sleeping, don't wake me, unless your patient is actually dying. Rule number four, the dying patient better not be dead when I get there, not only would you have k*ll someone, you would have also woken me for no good reason, we clear?" Sudarsan tells Major Rickford, "That's four rules sir, you said five rules." Major Rickford tells Sudarsan, "My mistake, when I move, you move. You Chavala!" Sudarsan tells Major Rickford, Yes Sir!" Major Rickford tells Sudarsan, drop, and give me twenty. Nobody talks until you are spoken to. Is that understood Chavala." Sudarsan tells Major Rickford, yes sir." Sudarsan goes down on the floor and does his twenty pushups. Major Rickford tells the Interns, Number five, when I move, you will move with me. Until then, we wait here until Private Chavala is done." Sudarsan continues doing his pushups and tells Major Rickford, Sir, I am first lieutenant." Major Rickford tells Sudarsan, "You are, in this hospital you start as a private and all you guys may be commissioned here, but here you guys are enlisted men who are privates and will start in the beginning. You interns have a nickname, Private. That is what you will start at. The reason why we are not moving, Private Chavala, is slowing us down. We are staying here to watch you laugh. Come on, soldiers laugh!" Everyone is laughing and Sudarsan feels humiliated. Sai tells the mourners, "In the military when you start out, they can make you or break you. That is how my father started out in ROTC. Not he has to do it again, as an intern. But it will not stop him, my father loved a challenge, and he is going to do it." Sudarsan finishes his pushups. Major Rickford tells Sudarsan, "On your feet, I hope you learn something Chavala if I were you. I would go home if you cannot do the job." Sudarsan tells Major Rickford, "Whatever you dish out sir, I can do it. ROTC was tough, but here is a piece of cake. I can do it." Major Rickford tells Sudarsan, "Let's see what you are made of, let's go Privates!" Major Rickford exited the hallway, and the interns followed him. Sai tells the mourners, "It was tough, but my father got through it. He is going to prove them wrong that my father can make it out there" Major Rickford shows the interns the surgical suits, where a patient is sick and needs surgery and the interns assist Major Rickford. Sudarsan listening to Major Rickford lecturing in the boardroom to his interns. Sudarsan is writing medical charts to some patients in the emergency room. Sudarsan is also helping Major Rickford in surgery in the surgical suite. Sudarsan is in his house outside the military base and reading medical books in his living room. Sudarsan is writing some notes about what he is doing. Sudarsan is with the interns and Major Rickford doing rounds in the hospital and seeing different patients, one has a broken leg, one is accidentally shot in the foot, and one gets stabbed in the knife training. Sudarsan helps the interns and Major Rickford out with their surgeries or cancer problems. Sai tells the mourners, after five years of learning, my father moved up the ranks and did examining patients, perform surgery and checkups. He also gives out vaccination shots for the patients. As five years went by, he made it through his internship, his residency and just finished his one-year fellowship on ophthalmology. My father is thinking about his other dream, but I think fate will come to him soon." Five years later Sudarsan is in the exam room, where he tests soldier eyesight. Sudarsan has a baton and shows the eye chart and soldier is sitting in the eye exam chair. Sudarsan tells the patient, "What letter is this?" Soldier looks at line 2 and Sudarsan is pointing at F. Soldier tells Sudarsan, "F, P." Sudarsan buts the baton in line 3. Soldier tells Sudarsan, "T O Z." Sudarsan moves the eye chart around. Soldier tells Sudarsan, "L P E D. Sudarsan moves to Line 9. Soldier tells Sudarsan, "L E F O D P C T." Sudarsan moves the last line 11, "P E Z O L C F T D." Sudarsan is done with the eye chart and tells the soldier, "Tanner, I can tell you, your eyesight is okay. You are cleared of active duty. I know you work in the army motor pool. I know grease hits your eyes well. But you are fine, after the examination you are fine, and you do need any glasses. Even if you do, they can still let you be a soldier. But not in aviation. Unless there is another way around it. But I can clear you, with or without glasses. But your eyes are fine and don't need any glasses. I will give you some eye drops to clear your eyes." Tanner tells Sudarsan, "Thanks Captain Chavala." Sudarsan tells Tanner, Sergeant, you can call me Dr Chavala here. Outside the base, you can call me Captain Chavala." Tanner tells Sudarsan, "Yes sir and thank you." Tanner gets up from his examining chair and salutes Sudarsan. Sudarsan tells Tanner, "At ease, Sergant. Your examination is done, and you can head back to the motorpool." Tanner tells Sudarsan, "Yes sir!" Tanner finishes saluting and exits the examining room. Nurse and Sergeant Lauren Wayne enter the examining room and tells Sudarsan, "Sir." Sudarsan tells Laura, "What is it Lauren?" Lauren tells Sudarsan, "Colonel Rickford needs to see you in his office right now." Sudarsan tells Lauren, "Okay, I am coming." Both exit the eye exam room and Sudarsan tells Lauren, "What is it Rickford need to see me, he just made Colonel?" Lauren tells Sudarsan, "He just got promoted yesterday. He wants to see you about an urgent matter." Sudarsan tells Lauren, I better pray I did not do anything wrong; I did everything right. I hope I did not violate any regulations that gets me court martialed and oh man, I am going to be kicked out of the military. Because I am close to be honorable discharge in a week." Colonel Rickford is working in his office and hears the door knocking. Colonel Rickford tells the person outside the door, "Come in." The door opens and it's Sudarsan. Colonel Rickford tells Sudarsan, "Captain Chavala, come in." Sudarsan enters Colonel Rickford office and closes the door. Sudarsan is now in attention. Sudarsan tells Colonel Rickford, "Sir, Sergeant Wayne told me you need to see an urgent matter." Colonel Rickford tells Sudarsan, "At ease Chavala and sit down." Sudarsan stops being in at attention and sits down in the chair and listens to Colonel Rickford wants to tell him. Colonel Rickford tells him, "Captain Chavala, I heard for the last five years you been mailing out memos to Fort Bragg to General Jackson McCarthy who runs fort bragg in North Carolina. That is where we train special forces there is that right Captain." Sudarsan tells Colonel Rickford, "Yes sir." Colonel Rickford tells Sudarsan, "Why are you sending memos to General McCarthy." Sudarsan tells Colonel Rickford, "I wanted to see if he can train me, and I want to join the green berets where I can go to the front lines." Colonel Rickford tells Sudarsan, "You are an excellent doctor and a good soldier, and you never given anyone trouble before. But you are about to be discharged in a week, but I think I can extend it for two more years and continue working with me as my military ophthalmologist since you completed your fellowship. But I want to ask you if you are still considering Fort Bragg. I can tell you do not look like green beret material." Sudarsan tells Colonel Rickford. "Sir I am good enough go to ROTC, I was good enough to get my american citizenship, complete medical school and good enough to complete my medical training here. I am good enough to join Fort Bragg. That is why I sent the memos and to see if they can give me a chance. If Colonel Thomas told me, I was not good enough to join the Green Berets. But I was good enough to join the army medical unit here. I was going into private practice in Kansas City since I kept in touch with my friend Kanthi who said I can go into practice with him. Since I am not interested in spending another couple year as an army medical doctor. I think I will go somewhere else, maybe I am going enough go into private practice as a civilian doctor but not as an army soldier. So, I am going to finish my service and head for Kansas City. My father set me up with a girl, I have to meet, and her name is Barthi Vokarra and I was supposed go to Srikalahasti and go on a date with her since her parents are friends and customers of his. So, sir if there is anything else it is an honor to work with you. So am I dismissed sir." Colonel Rickford tells Sudarsan, "No, you are not dismissed. I was going to ask you if you want to continue being in the military for two more years. I got a call from General McCarthy, and he's gotten your memos. Colonel Thomas transferred to Fort Bragg last week and I am taking over his duties. Colonel Thomas pulled some strings with McCarthy and if you want to stay in the military for two more years, you can report to Fort Bragg to begin your training. The war in Vietnam is getting worse and right now they are sending anyone who can join. So are you up for this Major Sudarsan Chavala." Sudarsan tells Colonel Rickford, "Major sir." Colonel Rickford tells Sudarsan, "You're up for a promotion and it came through and congratulations Major." Sudarsan tells Colonel Rickford, "Thank you, sir." Colonel Rickford tells Sudarsan, "Don't mess this up or if you fail you will be peeling potatoes for the mess hall for the rest of the two years, and I will make sure you won't return to the military hospital for the next two years. Is that clear, Major." Sudarsan tells Colonel Rickford, "Yes sir, I am clear." Colonel Rickford and Sudarsan get up from their chairs. Colonel Rickford tells Sudarsan, "You will be deployed tomorrow morning at 11 am at Fort Bragg and General McCarthy will help you begin your training. You should pack your bags Major and good luck in Fort Bragg and Major Chavala you are dismissed." Sudarsan is kind of happy that his dream has come true. Sudarsan tells Colonel Rickford, "Thank you, sir" Both of them salute each other and Sudarsan exits Colonel Rickford office. Sai tells the mourners, "Well my dad finally made his dream come true that he gets to join the green berets. But he has to tell his father about the bad news, and it is not exactly how my grandfather would take it." Sudarsan is finishing packing up his bags in his bedroom and his ride is going to take him to Fort Bragg. His telephone rings and answers his phone, Sudarsan tells the caller, "Hello? Hello father, I have something to tell you. I am being transferred. They gave me two years, because they need some doctors. You believe that, okay I am giving you the truth. I am going to Fort Bragg, and I am going to be trained for the Green Berets and after my training. I will be shipped off to Vietnam. I know you are scared, but this is for me. I want to do it. I am not going to meet Barthi at the end of the week, but I will go to Srikalahasti to meet her. I'm sorry, but I am doing this where you like it or not." Sudarsan hangs up the phone. Sai tells the mourners, "I have no idea how my grandfather took it. But it was not good, he was upset that my father joined ROTC behind his back and joining the Green Berets hurt him a lot worse. But my father wanted to be his own person. My grandfather has always been a strict pacifist. But my father wanted to go out in the front lines and make a difference. He will not win the medal of honor, at least he can be a team player and help fellow compatriots. That is what he did." Sudarsan grabs his two suitcases and leaves his house. Outside Sudarsan former house and sees Army driver and his jeep and takes him to the airport. After the plane landed in Fayetteville Airport and Sudarsan exits his gate and sees an army personnel greet him and sees his Major Sudarsan Chavala. Sudarsan tells the Army Personnel, "I'm Major Sudarsan Chavala." Army Personnel tells Sudarsan Chavala, "Come with me, Major Chavala. General McCarthy is waiting for you." Sudarsan and the Army Personall leaves the airport and heads to Fort Bragg. Inside Fort Bragg is General Jackson McCarthy working in his office, until his intercom starts buzzing. General McCarthy answers the intercom. Outside the intercom tells General McCarthy, "Sir, Major Sudarsan Chavala is here waiting for outside his office." General McCarthy answers to the person outside the intercom, "Send him in Sergeant." The door opens and it's Sudarsan. Sudarsan closes the door, and he is attention to General McCarthy. Sudarsan tells General McCarthy, Major Sudarsan Chavala reporting for duty sir." Sudarsan salutes to General McCarthy. General McCarthy tells Sudarsan, "At ease Major Chavala. Have a seat." Sudarsan tells General McCarthy, "Yes sir." Sudarsan sits down in his chair. General Mcarrthy will explain about what he will do here in Fort Bragg. General McCarthy tells Sudarsan about his training, "Major Chavala, Colonel Thomas sends me your recommendation five years ago and he wanted me to train you to be ready in the front lines in Vietnam since the war is going on. It is getting worse out there and we need more men we can get." Sudarsan tells General McCarthy, "Colonel Thomas sent me a recommendation five years ago. When I first reported to him, he told me that he was never going to send me the recommendation because I was not green beret material. I mailed in a few memos for five years and none of you guys write me back. I thought if you guys either rejected me, you would have sent me a letter to tell me that or probably threw it away after you read it." General McCarthy tells Sudarsan, "I kept it and each one of them." General McCarthy opens his right desk drawer is all the letters that he kept that Sudarsan to see if he can apply to Fort Bragg. Sudarsan tells General McCarthy, "You kept my letters and why!" General McCarthy tells Sudarsan, "After Colonel Thomas met with you five years ago and realized he does not want to spend a lot of time in the medical field. He wants to go back to the green berets. So, he transferred two weeks ago, while you were in medical training. He did send me a recommendation while he was stationed here and told him to wait for him when he finishes his fellowship training. Which I did and right now Colonel Thomas is with the troops in Vietnam, and he asked to train you for a few months and then you would be shipped off to Vietnam and right now we are here to get started. So, are you ready? Major Chavala." Sudarsan is smiling a bit and he told General McCarthy, "I am ready sir." General McCarthy tells Sudarsan, okay report to Platoon 9 and wait for Colonel Rosenberg and he will begin your training." Sudarsan tells General McCarthy, "Yes sir!" Both get up from their chairs and both start saluting. Sudarsan stops saluting and grabs his suitcases, exits the office and heads to Platoon 9. General McCarthy tells himself, "Good luck kid." Sudarsan reports to Platoon 9 and outside of Platoon 9 is where the rest of the soldiers begin their training. Colonel Rosenberg enters outside Platoon 9 and address the troops. Colonel Rosenberg tells the troops, "Fall in." Everybody falls in like Colonel Rosenberg told him too. Colonel Rosenberg told the troops, "Hello maggots, I'm Colonel Steven Rosenberg your instructor for the next three months. So, you guys want to be green berets huh and waste two or three years of my time. I can tell you it will not be easy; this will be a three-month training course and I will not go easy on you. I will be shipped off to Vietnam in three months to rejoin my troops with my colleague Colonel Ray Thomas and help him out with his missions. The next three months, I want to see what you guys are made of. After three months, I will pick five guys in this unit to come with me and the rest of the troops will go somewhere to do other missions. It is not negotiable. Is that understood!" Everybody who is in the troops tells Colonel Rosenberg, "Yes sir!" Colonel Rosenberg looks at Sudarsan and tells him, "Major Sudarsan Chavala, Colonel Thomas told me a lot about you, and he recommended to the General that you want to train and go to Vietnam. Is that true!" Sudarsan tells Colonel Rosenberg told, "Yes sir, General McCarthy after I complete my training, that I would be shipped off to Vietnam. I guess that's not going to happen. Since only five of us are going and the rest are going to different missions. The different missions will go to me is it, since I don't think I can impress you." Colonel Rosenberg tells Sudarsan, "Major do you want to go to Vietnam and serve your country to protect the people. Or you are doing it to impress women so you can get laid or look good in a uniform." Sudarsan tells Colonel Rosenberg, "No sir, I want to prove that I can do it. I am not here to get a medal or fame or glory. I just want to prove that I am out there protecting everyone from here and they know I can make one difference. I see the hippie movement and calling us a baby killer. But I am going to prove them wrong, maybe the war is wrong for them. It is not to me; we are trying to protect the people from evil dictators harassing the USA. That is why I am here to make a difference." Colonel Rosenberg tells Sudarsan and the rest of the troops, "Glad to hear it, like I said if you guys want to fight in Vietnam it will be different and tough. But you will have to prove it to me. You want it, everyone gets to your barracks we got a lot of work to do." Sai tells the mourners, "What Colonel Rosenberg told the troops, and my father is true, you want to go to Vietnam, and he is to prove it to him. That is what my father did." Sudarsan had gone through an Army obstacle course by crawling under barb wires, rope climb and going through a wall. It was not easy going through it. Sudarsan was shivering cold through an ice bath. Inside the Platoon 9 training center, he is learning martial arts, mostly the Colonel Rosenberg is usually flipping all the time. Everyone in the troops is learning to fire a gun in the artillery range outside Platoon 9. Sai address the mourners, "My dad is working hard, he had to crawl muddy obstacle course through barb wire, shooting bow and arrows, guns and hand to hand combat. He is really getting good." Sudarsan flips Colonel Rosenberg on the floor, makes it through the obstacle course alive, excellent in firing range and with excellent with bows and arrows in target areas and good at using a survival knife. Sai tells the mourners, "After three months, my father completed his training and Colonel Rosenberg the rest of the troops where they are being shipped off to." Outside Platoon 9 and where the troops see on the bulletin board where they are going. Sudarsan sees his name in the bulletin board, Sudarsan smiled a bit. Sudarsan tells himself, "Yes, I did it." Colonel Rosenberg sees Sudarsan and tells himself, "I knew you could do it kid." Colonel Rosenberg goes over to Sudarsan and tells him, "Well congratulations major pack your bags. Meet out here 0600 am, we are going to Vietnam. Sudarsan tells Colonel Rosenberg, "Thank you sir." Sai tells the mourners, "I was going to give out the four other names in the bulletin board that went with my dad in Vietnam. My dad barely knew them, and they were sent to another region in Vietnam and so it was just him and Colonel Rosenberg who was going to the front lines for this special mission." During six am outside the Platoon 9, the army airplane Fokker F27 Friendship that Sudarsan and Colonel Rosenberg sent them to Vietnam. The army personnel grab their bags and Sudarsan and Colonel Rosenberg inside the plane. After everyone was on board, the plane takes off for Vietnam. Sai tells the mourners, "I am not going into details about what my father did in Vietnam. But it was not pretty, he had to do rescue missions for the army and stops some missiles before it hits our command post in the US Army base in Vietnam. That is what my father did. Believe me, it was not easy." Sudarsan took out three bad guys with his AKM gun while hiding under the tree with two of his troops. Sudarsan and two of his troops are the only ones guarding the prison camp in the Vietnam jungle. Sudarsan fired his AKM gun with six bullets comes out of his gun and two of bullets hit the Vietnamese soldier 1 in the stomach in the chest and dies, the other two bullets hit second Vietnamese soldier 2 in the stomach again and dies and the third bullet hits the third Vietnamese soldier 3 in the neck and dies on the floor. All three of them are dead. The Vietnam soldiers are thrown grenades and firing at the Green Berets. Two of Sudarsan's compatriots are shooting at the Vietnamese soldiers, two bullets come out of his AKM gun of Sudarsan Chavala US army compatriot 2, three other bullets comes out of Sudarsan Chavala US army compatriot 3 AKM gun and hits the ground and misses Vietnamese soldiers. Their four more Vietnamese soldiers guarding the prison campy. Sudarsan keeps firing his gun and four bullets come out of his AKM gun. The three bullets hit Vietnamese soldier 4 in the head and falls down on the floor and dies. Vietnamese soldier is guarding the camp and being ambushed by the US army green berets. US army green beret 4 who is carrying a M1911A1 gun and the AN/PRC-25 pack that is phone and radio backpack behind his back. The US Army Green Beret 4 is crawling to the tree where Sudarsan is firing his gun and also misses Vietnamese Soldier. Sudarsan sees Us Green Beret 4 and tells him, "Sawyer, hurry up. They're ambushing us!" Sawyer tells Sudarsan and the rest of the troops, "Thanks for calling, I got the rest of the guns in in my backpack." Sudarsan tells Sawyer, "Thanks man, toss them to Abraham and Carmichael. I think they're out of bullets. Did the General tell us, how long they are going to send the chopper?" Sawyer tells Sudarsan, "Five minutes!" Sudarsan tells Sawyer, "We will be sitting ducks when that happens. We got the rescue of those POW's. They are locked in their two months, and we finally found a location." Sawyer sees Abraham and Carmichael about 40 feet near Sudarsan. Abraham sees Sawyer and tells him, "Sawyer We are out, man!" Carmichael tells Sawyer, "Hurry up, were the only four left. I do not think we can hold on much longer." Sawyer takes off his and gets three M1911A1 guns out of his backpack. Gives one of the guns to Sudarsan and grabs one since his AKM gun is out of bullets and throws it in the ground. Sudarsan grabs the M1911A1 gun that Sawyer gave to and fires two bullets out of his gun and hits the ground and misses them. Sudarsan sees his the AN/PRC-25 pack in the tree with him. He grabs the phone and tries to radio the General. Sudarsan tells the General on the phone, "Sir, we have three more Vietnemese soldiers guarding the gate. There is more, we tried to be sneaky, they knew we were coming and ambushed us. How much longer the helicopter arrives?" At US army base in the Thailand border and inside the army headquarter. General Roscoe Moses with Colonel Rosenberg and Colonel Thomas listening to Sudarsan report. General Moses is sitting down in his chair with Colonel Rosenberg and Colonel Thomas are their headsets. General radios Sudarsan and tells him, "The pilot informed on the speaker, The HH-3E "Jolly Green Giant chopper will arrive two more minutes to destroy the camp and nuke it. You guys have that M72 LAW rocket launcher, use it to destroy the gate. Remember you got three minutes before the chopper napalms the prison camp and destroys the missile before it hits our base." Sudarsan voiceover tells General Moses, "Roger General." Colonel Rosenberg tells General Moses, "Do you think they can make it?" General Moses tells Colonel Rosenberg, "Major Chavala informed ten of our men are dead when they ambushed them during prison camp." Colonel Thomas tells them, "I know Major Chavala, he is the one the best soldiers I know. If anyone can do it, he can. Since I never had a chance to tell him." Colonel Rosenberg tells Colonel Thomas, "Me neither. I did not want this go to his head." Colonel Thomas tells them, "God help us and make sure we get our troops back home alive." Back in the Vietnam jungle. Sudarsan and Sawyer sees the three POWs inside the prison campy. Mostly they are locked in a rope and Sudarsan had some grenades or guns to get him out. Three of the Vietnamese Soldiers is still guarding the gate. Another Vietnamese soldier comes out of nowhere from behind the bushes and sees Sudarsan and Sawyer hiding left side of the tree near the prison camp. Vietnamese Soldier 8 is wearing black gloves and carrying a Jerdon's pit viper and is near five feet to Sudarsan and Sawyer. Around 40 feet to the right is where Abraham and Carmichael who does not they see the other Vietnamese soldier carrying that snake and trying to use it to kill Sudarsan and Sawyer. Carmichael and Abraham are occupied being attacked by three other Vietnamese soldiers who is guarding the gate. Vietnamese soldier 8 stops and released the Jerdon's pit viper on the ground and points it to Sudarsan and Sawyer to attack them. Sudarsan squats a little and is tired and turns around a bit and sees the snake that Vietnamese soldier is releasing. Sudarsan is a scared seeing that snake and Vietnamese Soldiers 8 is looking by and luckily no one saw him. Sai tells the mourners, "When my dad saw that snake, he has to make a choice either he could run and takes his chances with those three Vietnamese soldiers that is guarding the gate that could easily get him killed or save his friend's life who is about to die from that snake and the other Vietnamese soldier who released it. My dad had to make one decision and he knows what he has to do." Sudarsan sees his M1911A1 gun on the ground and already make the quick decision. Sudarsan grabs the gun and does a roll up quietly and fire his gun two bullets comes out of his gun. The two bullets hits the snake and dies. Sudarsan also sees Vietnamese soldier 8 and he is about to fire his gun, since that snake failed and three bullets comes out of his gun and hits Vietnamese soldier 8 in the stomach and dies. Sawyer hears the gun shot and sees the Vietnamese soldier 8 and that snake were about to kill him or poison him first. Sawyer sees Sudarsan and tells him, "That snake or that Vietnamese soldier would either poison me or shoot me second. I owe you one Major." Sudarsan tells Sawyer, "I appreciate that, I was just doing my job Lieutenant. Sawyer, we are still distracted and that plane is going to arrive to nuke the camp if we don't get those soldiers out." Sawyer tells Sudarsan, "One of us will have to sacrifice ourselves to distract the guards, that will stall him long enough get into that camp to rescue those pow's!" Sudarsan tells Sawyer, "I will do it, if I am going to die, I am going to die for those POW's who deserved to be home." Sawyer tells Sudarsan one thing, "Sudarsan before you make the human sacrifice. I want to tell you tie your shoes before you do that." Sudarsan tells Sawyer, "Sure." Sudarsan sees his shoes are not untied and Sawyer tells Sudarsan, "I am sorry Sudarsan, but I have to do this." Sawyer punches Sudarsan in the stomach and Sawyer takes his helmet off and Sawyer hits M1911A1 gun in the head and is knocked out. Sudarsan is a little unconscious and sees Sawyer for a minute and tells him. Sudarsan tells him, "What are you doing?" Sawyer tells Sudarsan, "I owe you one and now is the time to return the favor." Sawyer exits the tree and runs as fast he can to tackle the Vietnamese Soldier 5 who is one of them guarding the gate. Sawyer is running as fast as he can and dodging bullets as fast as the Vietnamese soldiers are firing at him. Vietnamese Soldier 5 sees Sawyer; Vietnamese Soldier 5 fires his

M1911A1 gun and three bullet comes out of his gun and hits Sawyer in the stomach. Sawyer is almost dying, but he keeps running and takes a grenade and releases the pin. A dying Sawyer tackles the Vietnamese Soldier 5 on the ground. A dying Sawyer tells his buddies, "Gentlemen it's an honor to fight with you side by side." Sudarsan, Carmichael, and Abraham has been dodging bullets on the right side of the tree and sees Sawyer's sacrifice. All of them tell Sawyer, "Sawyer!" Sawyer and the Vietnamese soldier 5 both get exploded from the grenade and both died." Carmichael is upset now and fires two more bullets out of his gun that Sawyer gave him. The two bullets hits Vietnamese Soldier 6 in the chest and dies. Sudarsan takes out his M72 LAW with one rocket, while Carmichael and Abraham the final soldier guard the gate. Sudarsan sees the Abraham and Carmichael, "Stall him and I am going to destroy the gate!" Carmichael tells Sudarsan, "Gotcha!" Carmichael and Abraham fires their guns, and six bullets comes out of their gun. Three bullets from Carmichael and Three other bullets from Abraham's guns. One of the bullets hits the Vietnamese Soldier 7 in the left arm. The rest of the bullets hits the floor near Vietnamese Soldier 7 and misses him. The bullet that hit Vietnamese Soldier 7 is just a flesh wound. Sudarsan exits the tree with the M72 LAW and puts the small rocket near the Vietnamese Solider 7 and the gate." Sudarsan tells himself, "For you Sawyer." Surdarsan fires the M72LAW, and the rocket hits the Vietnamese Soldier 7 and the gate blowing them up. The gate is open and destroyed. Sudarsan drops M72 LAW from the ground and grabs his gun. Sudarsan tells Abraham and Carmichael, "Were going in. Let's go! Let's go!" Abraham and Carmichael exits the tree and joins Sudarsan and get into the prison camp. Six Vietnamese came are in the camp and sees Sudarsan, Carmichael, and Abraham. Sudarsan, Abraham, and Carmichael enter the prison camp and finds the POW's. But spots the six Vietnamese soldiers in the camp. The sixth Vietnamese soldier is guarding the POWs in the far right of the cage. Sudarsan, sees Vietnamese Soldier 9 and Sudarsan fires his gun and three bullets comes out of his gun and hits Vietnamese Soldier 9 in the chest and dies. Abraham fires his gun; two bullets comes out of his gun and hits Vietnamese Soldier 11 in the stomach and dies. Vietnamese soldiers are shotting their guns and ten bullets comes out of their guns and misses Sudarsan, Carmichael, and Abraham. Sai tells the mourners, "Sawyer made the ultimate sacrifice and my father, and the rest of his team also decide to honor First Lieutenant David Sawyer is to finish the mission and which they did." Sudarsan takes out two Vietnamese soldiers 10 and 12 and Abraham puts away his gun in the back of his pants and takes out knife from right pants pocket that has a knife holder. Sees Vietnamese soldier 13 and throws the knife fast in the Vietnamese Soldier 13 in the chest and falls down on the floor and dies. Carmichael shoots two other Vietnamese Soldiers 14 and 15 in the chest and dies from his gun. Sudarsan sees the POW"s cage and the Vietnamese Soldier 16 guarding the gate. Sudarsan aims his gun on Vietnamese Soldier 16 and fires his gun and two bullets comes out of his gun and hits Soldier 16 in the chest and dies. Sudarsan goes over to the POW's cage where the three POWs are and sees the lock in the cage. Sudarsan puts his gun behind his pants and takes out a grenade from his right pants packet and some black scotch tape. Sudarsan tapes the grenade to the lock and tells the POW's, "Get Back!" The POW's get back from the cage. The grenade explodes and the cage is open. Sudarsan tells the three POWs in the cage. "Everyone out! Hurry! Hurry! The rescue plane is going to arrive in a minute and nuke the camp before they fire that missile. The three POW's exit with Sudarsan and sees Carmichael and Abraham who also inspecting the prison camp. Carmichael and Abraham goes over to Sudarsan and talk to him and stop for a minute to breathe. Carmichael tells Sudarsan, You got'em." POW 1 tells them, "Thanks for getting us out, did you see the missile area?" Carmichael tells the POW 1, "Yes I saw it and that missile is going to be launched in 30 seconds, before the plane nukes the camp and the missile." POW 1 tells them, "That missile that I overhead is going to hit our base camp in Thailand." Sudarsan tells them, "Yeah, I know where it is, that is where our commanding officers General Moses, Colonel Thomas and Rosenberg are at and don't worry that plane knows the location of the missile since I have a tracking devince on my watch that the CIA built. All I have to do, is take off my watch and put it on the ground and knows where I am. So they can nuke the camp and missile." Sudarsan sees his tracking device on his watch in his right hand and takes it off and puts it on the ground. Abraham sees the HH-3E "Jolly Green Giant chopper flying here. Abraham tells them, "I see the chopper. We got a hurry before they nuke the prison camp." Sudarsan tells them, "We have to be miles straight ahead outside the camp where the chopper pick us up, Let's go!" Everyone exits the camp as fast as they can. The HH-3E dumps three kegs of explosives that came out of the plane and hits in the camp and destroys the camp and the missile before it was launched to hit military base in Thailand. Sai tells the mourners, "Luckily my father, Carmichael, Abraham who were his war buddies and the POW's exits that prison camp in time before the plane nuked the missile and prison camp and got out of there. My dad and his friends saved a lot of people that day. But he will not forget about First Lieutenant David Sawyer sacrifice to save their lives. Sudarsan, Carmichael, Abraham and the three other POW's sees the HH-3E "Jolly Green Giant chopper outside the prison and all of them hopped in the chopper and exited the war zone. Sai tells the mourners, "Like I said, my father and his friends were war heroes. They got back to the base and was commended for their services. The rest of the POW; s were treated in an Army hospital in Thailand before they head back to USA., General Moses with Colonel Thomas and Rosenberg awarded my father Major Sudarsan Chavala, Sgt's Bobby Carmichael and Floyd Abraham the Bronze star medal for their services and also awarded the medal to Posthumously to David Sawyer for his sacrifice to save the POW's." General Moses pins the medals to Sudarsan, Carmichael and Abraham and salute them. After they were done, General Moses gives the bronze medal in a case to Sudarsan that Colonel Thomas gave General Moses and to Sudarsan. Sai tells the mourners, "General Moses gives them two weeks leave and he wants Sudarsan to give this medal to Sawyer's wife. Which he did." After my father returned to the states and tells Sawyer's widow about what happened and about how much he sacrificed to save the POW's." Sudarsan return to America and goes to Sawyer's hometown where his wife lives and goes over to the front door and sees his beautiful wife opens the door. Sai tells the mourners, "It was tough for my dad to tell him what happened to her husband. Sawyer's wives ask Sudarsan, "Yes, can I help you." Sai tells the mourners, "I have no idea what my father had to say, but he had to tell her." Sawyer's wife heard about what Sudarsan told him about Sawyer and Sudarsan is carrying the fold out American flad and a case holding Sawyer's posthumous Bronze Star. Sawyer's wife starts crying. Sai tells the mourners, "Sawyer's took it hard. It is hard to lose somebody who is in the front lines in the military or in the life of fire if you are a cop. It is hard to lose anyone period no what the job is." Sudarsan gives her husband's American flag and bronze star medal in a case, and she grabs it and still sobbing. Sai tells the mourners, "After that, the army recovered Sawyer's body and gave him military honors in Arlington Cemetery." There are 1000 mourners in Arlington Cemetery and Sudarsan, Carmichael, Abraham, General Moses, Colonel Thomas and Rosenberg, Sawyer's widow and his five-year-old son and three-year-old daughter with the rest of the mourners watch Sawyer being buried. The soldiers are playing amazing grace and giving Sawyer the 21-gun salute. Sudarsan watches Sawyer being buried and tells himself, "I knew what it felt like to sacrifice yourself to save millions of people and I am going to keep doing that until I am done. I will do that for David." Sai tells the mourners, "That is what my father did. After the two weeks, my father and the rest of his army buddies went back to Vietnam to do other missions." In the Vietnam war, Sudarsan shoots at three Vietnamese soldiers in the rice field with his M60 gun. While Carmichael and Abraham are shooting at other Vietnamese soldiers too. Sai tells the mourners, "My father was taught how to fly the HH-3E "Jolly Green Giant helicopter and shoots down other three Vietnamese soldiers in the prison camp and drop a napalm keg on another prison camp after seeing US soldiers rescue other POWs in the camp. After the Napalm keg destroyed the prison camp after the US soldiers rescued the POW's. Sai tells the mourners, "My dad and his friends Carmichael and Abraham did other missions for two years while they were in the service. Also, the CIA recruited him and his team to take down a Vietnam warlord who is supplying new guns and rescue some American journalist who was on a big story. So that means my dad did another rescue mission and another prison camp in two years. Believe me this is the last one. Because he will be discharged in three days." The rest of US army soldiers rescued the American reporters. While Sudarsan took out Vietnam Warlord with his SIG-Sauer P226 gun and three bullets comes out of his gun and hits Vietnam Warlord in the stomach and dies. While the rescue mission is a success, another Vietnamese soldier comes out of nowhere and uses Sig-Sauer P226 gun and fires one bullet and hits Sudarsan in the butt. Sudarsan is aching that he was in the shot in the butt. Sai tells the mourners, "My dad never talk about any war wounders that he had while he was in Vietnam. But one war wound that he talk about being shot in the butt." Sudarsan tells himself, "Something bit me." Abraham sees Vietnamese soldier who shot Sudarsan in the butt, Sudarsan falls on the ground for a minute, but he is about to get up, the Vietnamese soldier was about to finish him. Until Abraham fires his gun, and two bullets comes out of his gun and hits the Vietnamese Soldier in the chest and dies. Abraham picks up Sudarsan. Sudarsan tells Abraham, "Was I shot in the buttocks." Abraham tells Sudarsan, "Yes, come on I going to get you out. They're going to nuke the camp in two minutes." The US soldiers with Abraham, Carmichael, Sudarsan and the rest of the American reporters they rescued out of the prison camp and run as fast as they can. The HH-3E "Jolly Green Giant helicopter flies through the prison and drops some napalm kegs on the prison camp and destroys the prison camp. Luckily everyone got out of them in time. Sai tells the mourners, "That was my last mission for my dad. After he was shot in the butt. Like Forrest Gump said it was a million-dollar wound. But the army must keep the money because we are never a quarter of the million dollars. Anyway, after they exited Vietnam. My father was treated in US Army hospital in Vietnam." Sudarsan is sleeping in a hospital bed in US Army hospital in Vietnam. Sudarsan hears the door knock. Sudarsan tells the person, "Come in." The door opens and it's a US Army messenger. A US army messenger goes over to Sudarsan and talks to him, and he is carrying a letter that is an important letter. US Army messenger tells Sudarsan, "Hello Major. How is it going?" Sudarsan tells US Army messenger, "I'm fine Andy." Andy ask Sudarsan, "What does the doctor say about your recovery?" Sudarsan tells Andy, "I've been here two days after he removed my bullet from my butt. He said I could leave in the day. I have no idea if I have to do another mission, I'm up for it. But right now, I could use a miller lite." Andy tells Sudarsan, "Actually I got one for you. Hospital cafeteria has a lot of beer and steaks for wounded veterans like yourself." Andy takes out Miller lite beer can out of his right pants pocket and the beer is still cold and tosses the beer to Sudarsan. Sudarsan grabs the beer and starts drinking it. Andy tells Sudarsan, "Actually you won't be doing any other missions. I have good news and bad news." Sudarsan tells Andy, "I hope the bad news is not me being court martialed. I followed every regulation and did what I was told. I took a bullet in the butt for Abraham when that Vietnamese Soldier was about to shoot him. I can't believe they are thinking about court martialing me." Andy tells Sudarsan, "Relax Sudarsan, the bad news is not going to be court martialing you. Did you forget you have two more days left in your service. That is the bad news for you, that your service will be over in two days unless you forgot." Sudarsan continues drinking his beer and forget about he is almost done with his service. Sudarsan tells Andy, "Oh I forgot about my discharge. It is bad news for me no more missions. But I always felt sometimes that this war is wrong. But those Vietnamese soldiers were evil and they were working for communist. Why were trying to stop it. But I had a job, I promise that I want to make a difference and I am." Andy tells Sudarsan, "Way to keep up the positive attitude and anyway I want to give you this." Sudarsan puts his beer in the nightstand and barely gets out of his bed. Andy gives Sudarsan the letter. Sudarsan grabs the letter and starts reading it. Andy tells Sudarsan, "The letter is the good news, you have been awarded the bronze star and you leave for Washington D.C. tomorrow. General Moses is returning to his office Fort McNair Army Base and he ask you go with him to award you the Bronze star and your discharge papers. Sai tells the mourners, "When my father heard those words that his service in the United States Army is over. He decided to live with that. So tomorrow my father left Vietnam and report back to the USA in Fort McNair to get his bronze star and his discharge papers." Outside the US Army hospital where Andy is in his Army Jeep waiting for Sudarsan and Sudarsan is carrying his army duffle bag and enters the jeep and both of them drive to the airport. The plane landed in Washington D.C. airport. Outside Fort McNair General Moses with Colonel Thomas and Rosenberg, while General Moses pin the bronze star to Sudarsan in his Army Uniform. After General Moses pins the medal to Sudarsan, he gives him his discharge papers and General Moses shakes Sudarsan's hand and salutes him. So does Colonel Thomas and Rosenberg. After they were done saluting, Sudarsan is thinking about what he will do next. Sai tells the mourners, "My father's days in the United Army is over. He has no idea what he will do next. He worked a long time as a doctor. His father and the rest of his family is in India. He thought about going to see them for a minute. But first, he decided to see his best friend Khanthi. That is what my dad did. After the awards ceremony Sudarsan looked at his discharge papers. Sudarsan took a greyhound bus that stops outside McDonald's. Mostly the bus usually stops there. Sudarsan exits the greyhound bus and gets his army dufflebag and sees Khanti Havaladar waiting for him. Sudarsan sees his best friend waiting for him. Sudarsan goes over to Khanthi and hugs him for a minute and stops. Sudarsan tells Khanthi, "It's good to see your old buddy." Khanthi tells Sudarsan, "I got your letters, I would have written you back it did not have a return address." Sudarsan tells Khanthi, "It's okay, I was on top secret missions. I could not tell you where I was. It would have jeopardized the missions. So, I heard you started your private practice here in Maryville." Khanthi tells Sudarsan, "It's the heart of Kansas City. After I was discharged, I married Cocula who went to Medical School with us in UMKC. We have a son Sunjay who is 3 and a daughter Abba who is 1." Sudarsan tells Khanthi, "That is what you told me in those letters. I am sorry I couldn't come to the wedding I couldn't get leave." Khanthi tells Sudarsan, "It's okay, I was in the Army too. Luckily they gave me and Cocula a military wedding. I couldn't get leave either to visit you." Sudarsan tells Khanthi, "I love to see your new house you talk to me about that you wanted me to see after I was done with the army." Khanthi tells Sudarsan, "Come one let's go I will show you the house." Sudarsan sees Khanti's Lexus and tells him, "That is an excellent car you have." Khanthi tells Sudarsan, "I just bought it last year when I decided go to private practice after I left the Army." Sudarsan and Khanthi gets inside the car and head to

Khanthi's house. Inside Khanthi's house where Abba is playing in her playpen while Cocula is watching tv and them. Sunjay is also playing with his toys under the couch. The door opens and it's Khanthi and Sudarsan. Cocula and Sunjay sees them and get up for a minute. Khanthi and Sudarsan enter the Havaladar house and Sudarsan is carrying his army dufflebag. Sudarsan puts his army dufflebag on the floor. Cocula and Sunjay greets Khanthi and both of them hug Khanthi for a minute and let's go. Sai tells the mourners, "It is been a while since my dad seen Khanthi both of them were stationed in different places. Khanthi's father gave his son money to pay for this house and started his private practice. He is doing really well with his life. My dad is trying to do what he is going to do with his life now." Khanthi tells his family, "Cocula, kids remember my friend in college and med school. This is Sudarsan Chavala." Cocula sees Sudarsan and tells him, "Hello Sudarsan it's been a long time." Cocula hugs Sudarsan for a minute and let's go. Sudarsan tells Cocula, "Yeah, me too. I am sorry I couldn't come to the wedding back then. I couldn't get any leave." Cocula tells Sudarsan, "I understand, you forget Khanthi couldn't get leave on the weekend either. But the Army was good helped paid for a military wedding." Khanti tells them, "Why do not have a seat in the kitchen table. So we can catch up." Sudarsan tells Khanti, "Sure thing." Cocula tells Sunjay, "Sunjay watch your sister for a minute. I am going to talk to Sudarsan for a minute." Sunjay tells his mother, "Okay mom, hello Major Chavala." Sudarsan tells Sunjay, "Sunjay you can call me Sudarsan or Dr Chavala. Which you ever like." Sunjay tells Sudarsan, "Can I call you Uncle. Because my dad told me when you call my parents friends like a surrogate Uncle or Aunty." Sudarsan tells Sunjay, "Sure thing that is what I called my parents friends when they visit or stay over." Sudarsan, Cocula and Khanthi went over to the kitchen table and sat down in their chairs and discuss about Sudarsan's future. Khanthi tells Sudarsan, "So Sudarsan what is your plan since you are out of the army?" Sdudarsan tells Khanthi, "I have not figured it out yet, my goal was to become a doctor like an optometrist or ophthalmologist. I joined ROTC which freaked out our parents for a minute when they calmed down a bit when they know having a military record would look good in a resume.

Khanthi you went to private practice after you left the army, I extended my army stay when I joined the green berets and fought in Vietnam. I am just luck I did not run into a crazy hippie who call me a baby killer." Khanthi tells Sudarsan, "The times changed back then. You knew back then you were protecting americans. We weren't we were protecting the government that was wrong." Sudarsan tells Khanthi, "I know we did not change anything after the war is over, the only reason why we fought in Vietnam was to end communism. But we made it worse." Cocula tells them, "Why Gerald Ford to decide to end the war after the fall of Saigon." Sudarsan tells them, "I'm sure Gerald Ford can find a way to end communism, if he can't there will be someone else." Khanthi tells Sudarsan, "We still haven't figure out what are you doing right now." Sudarsan tells them, "I forgot to tell you I was a war hero when I was awarded the bronze and silver star. My old man was not proud, when I told him I going to Fort Bragg for green beret training. After I was done, we were still on speaking terms. I wrote him a lot of letters, but he never wrote me back because I never had a forwarding address because my missions were top secret. Since I was done, I told him I am ready go back to being an optometrist full time. That is why I am here, Khanthi. I don't even know if you could put in a good word for me with the guys in the private practice to get me a job as an optometrist. If the position is filled, I understand." Khanthi tells Sudarsan, "Actually I have an opening. While you were coming to visit me. I pulled some strings with the medical board for you to go into private practice with me. In the meantime, you can stay with us until your new house is ready." Sudarsan tells Khanthi, "I appreciate that, but I was going to stay in a hotel until I find an apartment or a house and a job with it. But I guess I owe you one for getting me a job and letting me stay here until my house is built. You guys bought a house for me" Khanthi tells Sudarsan, "I didn't buy one, I built you one. It was in South Dunn Street. There were a few vacant lands and I put down a whole payment for the house for you. I was going to build the second house as my vacation home, but I decided to let my friend who needs a job and a house to live in. So not only you needed a job, I got you a house too." Sudarsan shakes Khanti's hand for a minute and let's go. Sudarsan tells Khanthi, "Thanks Khanthi, I owe you one. I will pay you back soon after I get my private practice gets off the ground." Khanthi tells Sudarsan, "You don't have to pay my back, but I will get an IOU someday for a favor no questions asked." Sudarsan tells Khanthi, "Sure thing." Khanti tells them, "Hang on a second." Khanti gets up from his chair and finds his notebook and pen. Khanthi tore a piece of paper and grabs a pen and wrote IOU. Khanti heads back to kitchen table and sits back down and hands the piece of paper to Sudarsan and Sudarsan grabs it and looks at it for a minute. Khanthi tells Sudarsan, "When I need a favor, keep the IOU and remember you will owe me one someday no questions asked." Sudarsan tells Khanthi, "Sure thing, but I cannot stay long." Cocula tells Sudarsan, "Why not." Sudarsan tells them, "When I called my father that I told him that I was done in the army. He still trying to fix me up with a woman I supposed to marry." Khanthi tells Sudarsan, "You mean Barthi Vokarra who he tried to fix you up after I graduated from Medical school." Sudarsan tells them, "Yeah, but a different Vokarra. Barthi could not wait around for me forever, so she married Prikash Jai, but he is using his wife's maided name Vokarra because it was good strong Indian name. Anyway, my father wants me to come to New Delhi and meet Barthi's sister Girija and go on a date with her. I think my father is planning an arranged marriage for us. Even if I meet her, I don't even know if I am in love with her." Cocula tells Sudarsan, "You never know if you don't meet her. You don't have to marry her. Just go on a date and see if something is there is not. You can find your own girlfriend whether your father likes it or not." Sudarsan tells Cocula, "You guys are right, but my father gave me the ticket to fly back home and meet her. By the way Khanthi, when do my new job starts?" Khanti tells Sudarsan, "That depends how long are you going to be in New Delhi?" Sudarsan tells Khanthi, "I will be in India in two weeks. I have no idea if the medical board would allow me to leave in two weeks when I have not started yet." Khanthi tells Sudarsan, "Well you work for me, I own the practice. So you can start anytime you want." Sudarsan tells Khanthi, "Okay, I guess I can start in two weeks and let's get his date with Girija over with. Sai tells the mourners, "Sudarsan looks at the IOU's. That was the day my father was going to meet my father. Mostly my dad was reluctant at first. But meeting my mom and them getting married was the best thing that ever happened to them. If they didn't, I would not be born. The airplane lands in New Delhi airport and Sudarsan exits the gate and carries his suitcases and sees his father waiting for him. Sudarsan goes over to his father and puts down his suitcase. Sudarsan starts hugging his father for a minute and let's go. Sudarsan's father tells Sudarsan, "Hello Sudarsan, how was the flight?" Sudarsan sarcastically tells his father, "If you like to change airplanes and airports three times and pass-through customs all night. Yeah, it was a smooth flight." Sudarsan's father tells Sudarsan, "Enough with the sarcasm, it was bad enough you broke my heart that you joined ROTC and trained to be a green beret and went to Vietnam is where you hurt me. That you went off to war and realize I would have been worried if something happened to you" Sudarsan tells his father, "Look father, I am sorry that you were worried that I would die out there. You are allowed to be scared for me, but it was my right to join the military and make a difference in my life. I know you would not approve of me joining ROTC and going off to war." Sudarsan's father tells Sudarsan, "I was okay with you joining ROTC, but going off to war without discussing or my consent was really hurtful." Sudarsan tells Sudarsan father, "I am sorry I broke your heart. But let's drop it for a minute and get home." Sudarsan's father tells Sduarsan, "Okay but we will talk about it later." Sudarsan grabs his suitcase and Sudarsan is very upset that his father put him down for making a choice to go off to war without asking him or going behind his back. While Sudarsan's father is driving his car with Sudarsan in the passenger seat. Sudarsan's father tells his son, "You could have still been killed there. I have no idea what you were thinking about when you went to the front lines. You went behind my back and fought out there and not thinking about your family." Sudarsan sarcastically tells his father, "Gee, I guess should have discussed it with you. But is this about losing a son or something else bothers you." Sudarsan father's tells Sudarsan, "You could have ruined my insurance if anything happens to you. You know getting killed in the front lines did not cover my insurance rates." Sudarsan tells Sudarsan's father, "I thought it was a suicide that does not cover your insurance not being killed in Vietnam. Don't worry, if anything did happen to me, I am sure US Veterans Affairs would love to give you a pension. Besides your insurance does cover death when somebody dies or being killed. Like a soldier in the front lines. This is not about me; it is about how to make it you look. When people talk about you behind your back." Sudarsan father tells Sudarsan, "Yes it does affect me. How people will look at me, if anything happens to you and how people will treat me. Some may feel sorry for me, and some will sneer at me behind my back when they see I could not control my son or stop him." Sudarssan tells his father, "That is why I never told you about me going to Vietnam you would never understand or approve. I probably get a disappointed or disown me look that I embarrassed you. It was not your decision, it was mine. Because I wanted to make my own decisions with or without approval. Maybe I could prove to you that I can do it. I did and that is why I was a war hero." Sudarsan father tells Sudarsan, "You could have been awarded the medal of honor and a war hero. You would still be nothing, you do not prove anything to me. You proved that you were lucky that you survived. Those medals that were awarded to you prove that you may save a couple of lives but the war did not change anything, because communism is still here. I wanted you to become a doctor or an engineer and marry a nice girl that I arranged for you and have a couple kids. Which is what I want, not going crazy in one of your stupid stunts that could have embarrassed me. Right now, I want you to do is meet Girija and hit it off with her and someday I hope you marry her and have a child and forget about this one mistake that could have gotten you killed and embarrass in front of my friends." Sai tells the mourners, "Dad wanted to tell my grandfather off and told him where to stick it. Because he is not going to be pushed around and try turning into something he isn't. So my Dad did one thing that he told his father would never do." Sudarsan tells his father, "I'm sorry father that I embarrassed from your friends and joined the Green Berets and fought in Vietnam behind your back without discussing you. So I will make it up to you, I will meet Girija and go on a date with her and see where it goes. I will propose to her in a week. If she says yes." Sudarsan father tells Sudarsan, "Okay I am proud of you admitting your mistakes and you and Girija will make a great couple. When you meet her." Sudarsan tells his father, "I can hardly wait." Which Sudarsan looks at himself in the rearview mirror and is reluctant to do what his father told him to do. Sai tells the mourners, "My Dad always cave in when his father yells at him for making mistakes and he lies there and take it. That is what he did for a long time." Inside the Chavala home where Sudarsan and his father enter the Chavala home and Six of Sudarsans brothers and three of Sudarsan's three sisters are here to visit Sudarsan. Sudarsan puts his duffle bag down and starts hugging his brothers and sisters. Sudarsan tells his siblings, "Hey guys!" Sudarsan siblings tell Sudarsan. "Hello Sudarsan, it's good to see you." All of them enter the living room and sits down in the couch. Sai tells the mourners, "My dad had a lot of siblings, I barely remember their names or their children's names. But my dad wrote had a list in the library. Dad's oldest or first brother is Ajay Jr, he got married in 1950 to his wife and has one son and he works with Grandpa running the market together. Dad's second brother Ajay the third and people call him by his middle name Ravi is also married with two sons and also runs the market with Ravi in the second store that my grandfather owns. Dad's third, foruth and fifth brothers were named Kanan, Dhruv and Tenzin all married and all three other siblings have two kids each of their own. All of them went to college and got engineering degrees and all three of them work as Electrical Engineers. I skipped to the parts because I want to finish my story. Because I don't want to bore you guys, anyway Dad's sixth brother Sai who he named me after also went to medical school here and runs his own successful private practice as an optometrist and is happily married and has one son. My father's sisters Ambar, Marjane and Artha married doctors and two children of their own. Anyway this is all my father's siblings." Ajay Jr tells Sudarsan, "So Sudarsan what is your plan now since you are out of the army?" Sudarsan tells his older brother Ajay Jr, "You know I went to medical school in America. I graduated nine years ago, I did my medical training as an optometrist in Fort Leavenworth. Since I am a full fledge doctor, after my stint in Vietnam, I decided go into practice with Khanthi Havaladar." Ravi tells them, "I remember Khanthi, he was a smart kid. You two always played tag in the back yard. But Khanti was really fast, you barely can catch him." Sudarsan tells them, "Since he was married and has two children and he got me the job working in private practice as an optometrist and also put a lot of money to build me a house for me. He said I could stay with until the house is built." Ambar tells Sudarsan, "Thas was nice of them." Ambar tells Sudarsan, "I just want to know if you are hungry. I can make some Chippati for you." Sudarsan tells Ambar, "No thank you. I have to save my meal, because I have to meet Girija Vokarra. Dad set me up with her. Mom and Dad were old friends with her parents. He's been trying to fix me with her oldest daughter Barthi." Tenzin tells Sudarsan, "Weren't you supposed to go on a date with her after graduation." Sudarsan tells them, "Dad was disappointed that I told them, that I had to report for my medical training in Fort Leavenworth. Instead of coming back to India and go on a date with her. Dad already set up a wedding date. In his mind, he wanted me to marry after one week of dating. But I had decline, because I had gone to medical training in Leavenworth. So, Barthi married Prikash who was a friend of their family after I left for Fort Leavenworth. I heard they have three kids, but I am not going into details about it. But I wanted to complete my medical training, my internship, residency, and fellowship. So, I can have enough money to support my family. But the truth is, maybe I am glad I did not go through after medical school. But first, I have to pass all through my medical training before I become a doctor. I work 24 hours a day and I was on call all day. I did Barthi a favor and I am very happy for them." Marjane ask Sudarsan, "So when do you meet Girija?" Sudarsan tells Marjane, I must meet her in an hour in Ishani's." Ajay jr tells Sudarsan, "That is very a expensive restaurant. It takes a week to get a reservation in that place." Sudardsan tells them, "Dad made the reservation two weeks ago. I know Girija is reluctant to have dinner with me. So am I, at least I could do get this dinner over with. If she and I are not the right people together. I could find another girlfriend. Excuse me, I must get up from my room and go change." Dhruv tells Sudarsan, "Sure thing. Hey good luck little brother!" Sudarsan tells them, "I am going to need it." Sudarsan gets up from his chair and grabs his army duffle bag. Dhruv tells the siblings, "He's definitely going to need it." The siblings tell Dhruv, "Yeah!" Sudarsan gets up from his chair and heads upstairs. Sudarsan is in his room and getting dressed wearing a suit for his date. The door knocks and Sudarsan tells the person outside the door, "Come in." The door opens and it's Sudarsan's father. Sudarsan's father goes over to Sudarsan putting on his tie. Sudarsan tells his father, "Hello father, are you here to chew me out again." Sudarsan's father tells his son, "No, not this time. I am sorry about what I said to you." Sudarsan tells his father, "Do you always had to be hard on me all the time. I know I was too young to remember when Mom died. I barely remember her. I was only two years old when she passed away. When I was growing up, we never talked. The only thing we talk about is to do this and do that. So, I did that, it was never enough for you." Sudarsan's father tells Sudarsan," I was in mourning. I am sorry I took it out in you. But I had to, I want you to do great in life and be a better man. Your mom and I never had a chance to see the world. She wanted one of your siblings to see the world or go to America and make a difference. She did not want any of us to settle for a life that we were stuck with. I was happier where we were, but she wanted one of us to go out in the world and do something in your life. When you decided to go to college in America. Your mother was proud of you." Sudarsan finishes putting on this tie. Sudarsan tells his father, "You never say anything, I used to lie there and take it if I made a mistake. I still lied there and take it when you told me about how you plan my entire life for me." Sudarsan's father tells Sudarsan, "I was right about that. Because I want you to have a good job as a doctor and settle down so you can have a child and a good place to stay. I did not want a raise a dreamer." Sudarsan is still upset with his father and cannot hear what he said. Sudarsan tells his father, "Don't worry, my whole life I will not embarrass you. I Still won't and don't worry my dreaming days are over. If you excuse me, I have gone meet my date in Ishani's." Sudarsan is still upset and exits his room. Outside Ishani's parking lot, Sudarsan drives his father's car and parks outside the front door from the Valet. Sudarsan exits the car carrying some flowers and gives the keys to the Valet. Sudarsan tells the Valet, "Park it next to the BMW." Valet tells Sudarsan, "Yes sir!" Valet got Sudarsan's car keys and got into the car and starts to park the car in the parking lot. Sudarsan sees outside Ishani's and tells himself, "This is going to be a long night." Inside Ishani's where the Maitre'd is waiting. Sudarsan goes over to the Maitre'd and tells the Maitre'd, "Excuse me." Maitre'd tells Sudarsan, "Hi, can I help?" Sudarsan tells the Maitre'd, "Excuse me, I am meeting someone here, her name is Girija Vokarra. Is she here?" Maitre'd tells Sudarsan, "Yes, she is, sir. You are Sudarsan Chavala?" Sudarsan tells Maitre'd, "Yes, I am. It is Dr. Sudarsan Chavala." Maitre'd tells Sudarsan, "Sorry about that Dr. Chavala. This way please, Dr. Chavala." Sudarsan tells the Maitre'd, "Thank you." Maitre'd shows Sudarsan his table where Girija is at. Girija is sitting at her table waiting for Sudarsan. Girija is very young and pretty. She looks like she is in her early twenties. The Maitre'd takes Sudarsan to Girija's table, Sudarsan sees Girija for a minute and sees how pretty she is. Sai tells the mourners, "When my father looked at my mother the first time, it was love at first sight. She looked like a model. My dad saw how attractive my mom is." Sudarsan tells the Maitre'd, "Excuse me, am I in the right table. She looks a super model and I think she is expecting her ruggedly handsome boyfriend who might multi-millionaire or a professional cricket player." Maitre'd tells Sudarsan, "That is the right table, Dr. Chavala." Sudarsan tells Maitre'd, "Okay thank you." Maitre'd tells Girija, "Miss Vokarra, Dr Chavala is here to see you." Girjia tells Maitre'd, "Thank you, Kabar!" Kabar tells Girija, "Sure thing, Girija. Say hello to Auntie for me." Girija tells Kabar, "Sure thing." Sudarsan sits down in his chair and Kabar hands him a menu. Kabar asks them, "What would you two like to drink?" Sudarsan tells Kabar, "I take a miller lite." Kabar asks Sudarsan, "Miller Lite!" Sudarsan tells Kabar, "Miller Lite aka beer, unless you do not serve american alcohol here?" Kabar tells Sudarsan, "We do serve American alcohol, but we don't have any Miller Lite, we have Coors and Budweiser." Sudarsan tells Kabar, "I'll take a Bud Light." Girija tells Kabar, "I'll take a diet coke." Kabar tells them, "Sure thing, coming right up." Kabar leaves the table and Sudarsan ask Girija a question, "You know that guy?" Girija tells Sudarsan, "Around!" Sudarsan looks at Girjia for a minute and Girija tells Sudarsan, "My auntie owns the restaurant. That is my cousin Kabar, he is working as a waiter top to the bottom." Sudarsan tells Girija, "It's a pleasure to meet him. It's good to see you, Giirja. I haven't seen you since you were five years old. Girija tells Sudarsan, "Yeah, it's been a long time since I saw you. By the way how old are you again?" Sudarsan tells Girija, "How old are you first?" Girija answers that question and tells Sudarsan, "I'm twenty years old." Sudarsan tells Girija, "Wow, twenty years old. I was 17 years old when I saw you. I was about to go away to college when your mom brought you and Barthi to my house. Your parents were friends with my parents and your mom wanted to visit my aunt and my father. Your father was busy ruinning the store, he wanted your mother to meet my family. I never heard what they were saying, when I said hello to him. I went out to hang out with my friend Khanthi and saw a John Wayne movie together." Girija tells Sudarsan, "You may not hear them, but I did. Before I had to play with Barthi in the backyard. My mother was trying to send you with my sister Barthi in the near future. They would have hoped that you guys would start dating and getting married after a week." Sudarsan tells Girija, "My father was hinting about it for a long time when he visited me in UMKC. He always already tried to push me go on a date with her after I graduated from medical school." Girija tells Sudarsan, "Well, I heard you are now a doctor. What is that like?" Sduarsan tells Girija, "Sometimes it is not easy job. You must work 24 hours a day, trying to cure people from cancer or save them from injuries. Worse, you must be on call every day. Believe that was the toughest job in the world." Girija tells Sudarsan, "Any speciality that you are practicing in?" Sudarsan tells Girija, "I am practicing Ophthalmology and Optometrist. I am going into practice with my friend Khanthi Havaladar. He is letting me work as an Optometrist in Maryville Missouri." Girija tells Sudarsan, "Sounds great. I heard of the U.S.A., but I always wanted to go there and go to school there. I'm attending the University of New Delhi and I live with my aunt and Uncle who owns this restaurant. So, I go to classes during the day and go home to my aunt after classes." Sudarsan tells Girija, "So, you don't live in the dorms. Man, that must be cool." Girija tells Sudarsan, "My mom did not want me to go far away to school. We both decided it was best that I live with my Aunt Ambar and my cousin Kabar that you just met to go to school here." Sudarsan tells Girija, "So your aunt owns this restaurant. This place is like an Indian Russian Tea Room in New York City. Which I never went to, I never left Kansas City when I went to medical school." Girija tells Sudarsan, "I've heard of Kansas City, but not Maryville where is that." Sudarsan tells Girija, "It's the heart of Kansas City. Mostly Kansas City has other towns merged in Kansas City. Big cities have that." Girija tells Sudarsan, "Sounds great. I wish I could leave India and go to America. It's my kind of dream." Sudarsan tells Girija, "What do you want to do there when you get to America. Because any foreigner who comes to the USA, must have goal and purpose to go there." Girja tells Sudarsan, "I always wanted to be a college professor or be a computer programmer. I have a thing for electronics. Computer programming is something I always love." Sudarsan tells Girija, "Did you ever tell your mom you want to transfer from University of New Delhi to University of Missouri-Kansas City. Because all you must do is tell her you want to go see the world. Even if it doesn't not work out at least you chance to see what is out there. Besides, I am sure she would understand that and that she wants you to be happy about living out your dream." Girija tells Sudarsan, "I do not that think that is very simple. I just can't tell her what I want." Sudarsan tells Girija, "Why not?" Girija tells Sudarsan," Because she is old school. That she lives in the 1950's that women don't have a choice. We do what are told. She doesn't want me to go far away like 1000 miles to another country." Sudarsan tells Girija, "Sounds like my dad, he never lets me decide all the time. But he did let me go to college and med school in America. But he was upset that I went behind his back when I joined ROTC." Girija tells Sudarsan, "ROTC, what is that?" Sudarsan tells Girija, "Reserve Officers' Training Corps, where guys join military training program that helps you become commissioned and military officers after you graduate from college and the program. After I graduated, I was commissioned as second lieutenant. I was in the army full time." Girija tells Sudarsan, "Are you still in the army full time. Because I know about the military. Because I read it all the time." Sudarsan tells Girija, "Not anymore. I finished my ten-year service. I also fought in Vietnam, the war ended a few months ago. That is when

I got my discharged and I came to see my friend Khanti to see if he could find me a job in Maryville. He did and found me a place to stay." Girija tells Sudarsan," So where are you staying in Maryville MO. Since you are working as an optometrist with Khanthi Havaladar practice." Sudarsan tells Girija, "I am staying with Khanti until my house being built. Khanti paid for my new house that is in South Dunn. So, I am going to be in New Delhi for two Reserve Officers' Training Corps weeks." Girija tells Sudarsan, "You're going to be here in two weeks. Boy, do I envied you Sudarsan. I wish my mom could let go to America." Sudarsan tells Girija, "Man, that bites. I wish their was a way for you to convince your mom come to America, like I did." Girija tells Sudarsan, "The only way, I could go to another country a thousand miles away unless I take someone with me. If I was married, I don't think that happened." Sudarsan got an idea and thinking about it. Sudarsan is in love with Girija, the first time he saw her. Sudarsan tells Girija, "So why does your mom need you to get married." Girija tells Sudarsan, "She is worried about me going far away. I think she is protecting me. But sometimes she does drive me crazy." Sudarsan tells Girija, "A lot of parents do that to kids. Drive them crazy, so is my father. I have an idea why don't we get married. Because my father is pushing me to get married, he was mad at me that I was supposed to marry your sister after I graduated from medical school. Marrying you make up for pissing off my father." Girija tells Sudarsan, "We just met. I am not that desperate to leave India and go America." Sudarsan tells Girija, "I know that, I know you have a lot of big plans. You can still keep your dreams. I fell in love with you when I first met you. I know I am way out of your league. I am really in love with you." Girija tells Sudarsan, "I don't know, it feels like an arrange marriage. I usually against it." Sudarsan tells Girija, "You don't have feeling for me. Hey, I understand. Look, I did not go through this date in the beginning. My Dad tried to push me into going on a date with you and thinks it would lead to marriage. But I thought if we get married, it would get your mother off your back and stop fixing you up. Maybe you can live out your dream of going to college where I am living and your dream career." Girija tells Sudarsan, "I do have a lot of reasons why I would say no and not go through with this. But after meeting you and realize I can talk to you about anything. I did fall in love with you when I first saw you. I would want to do it." Sudarsan tells Girija, "Okay, I can call my father and tell him the good news. You can call your Mom and tell her the good news too." Girija tells Sudarsan, "Wait, how am I going to get to America. Mostly it would takes a few weeks to do the paper work and get a Visa." Sudarsan tells Girija, "Don't worry, I have a friend who is General in the army that I served for in Vietnam. He can make some calls from the American Embassy who is friends with the President of the United States. So, he can get you that Visa or a green card in a minute. All he has to do is make a call to the President and the American Embassy in India." Girija tells Sudarsan, "Sudarsan, I have one thing to say to you. I love you." Sudarsan tells Girija, "I love you too. Before we call our parents and tells them the news and my General friend to make the arrangements. I want to propose to you. Because I want to tell our kid, where I met you and proposed to you." Girija tells Sudarsan, "I can tell him, we fell in love here in my Auntie's restaurant and we decided after knowing each other for an hour. We decided to get married right after we proposed." Sudarsan tells Girija, "Sounds like a great story we should tell our kid. If it's a boy, I want to name him Sai. Like in Sai Baba, if it's a girl what would you name her?" Girija tells Sudarsan, "Well, it is kind of too soon, to talk about baby names. Since you are about to propose to me. But I would say, Lekha if we had a girl." Sudarsan tells Girija, "Okay, Lekha it is." Sudarsan gets up from his chair and so does girija. Sudarsan goes on one knee and starts proposing to Girija. Sudarsan tells Girija, "Girija when I first saw you, I knew I would love to spend my eternity with you now and forever. When I saw the movie, Jaws. I was scared of that shark. If I face that evil shark in the silver screen. I can face anything that comes at me. Even especially Vietnamese military bastards who tried to kill me and my friends. I have no idea who won that war. Because I think it was a lost cause. Anyway!" Sudarsan takes out his ring box and opens an engagement ring outside of it. Sudarsan continues telling Girija, "Anyway, I love you when I first saw you. I know you are right person for me. You now you were missing part of my life when I first saw you. I know I am the missing part of your life too. I wanted to say, I love you. Girija Sudarsan Vokarra will you marry me, I know I can do whatever it takes to make you happy and live out your goals. I would give anything to make sure you get anything you need. So, what do you say. Will you marry me?" Girija smiled at Sudarsan for a minute. Sai tells the mourners, "My mom heard my dad proposing to her. She thought about what her answers is. Either she says yes or no. Where people are watching her if she says no, the people would not care if she says no. My dad would understand and he would have wait for her and find a way for my mom come to America. But the answer my Mom gave the answer to my Dad is…? Girija tells Sudarsan, "Yes! Yes! Yes Sudarsan of course I would marry you." Everyone cheered for them. Sudarsan puts the engagement ring on Girija right ring finger. Before Sudarsan was about to get up and Girija ask Sudarsan something, "Where did you get the engagement ring, we just met. We just started dating right now." Sudarsan tells Girija, "My father gave me my mother's ring before I left to UMKC. Any time I was about to propose for my true love. That I would use it and told me to guard it with my life." Girija tells Sudarsan, "Okay, I was just asking." Sudarsan gets up from the floor and kisses Girija for a minute and let's go." Sai tells the mourners, "My parents were officially engaged. First what they did they called their parents and tell them announcement in the morning." Sudarsan and Girija tells their family in Sudarsan's father's house that they are getting married. Sudarsan's father and Girija's mother were excited for the news. So is Sudarsan's siblings, Girija's sister Barthi and her husband Prikash. They went over to hug Girija and Sudarsa for a minute and let's go. Sai tells the mourners, "My parents family were thrilled they got married. Dad was supposed go back to America in two weeks. Grandpa and my Grandmother from my mom's side arranged the wedding in a week. The wedding is in Srikalahasti in a hindu temple. She runs a clothing shop inside her house." The Indian wedding where Girija is wearing a Sari and Sudarsan is wearing an Indian garment. The Swami is performing the ceremony and marrying Sudarsan and Girija. After the wedding ceremony is over. Sudarsan and Girija kissed each other where everybody is cheering them on with Girija's mom, Sudarsan's father, Girija's sister and brother in law with their three children Raju, Ravi and Bindica who are nearly toddlers. Sai tells the mourners, "After the wedding, after my parents were officially married. They had their wedding reception in my Grandmother's house from my Mom's side of the family." Everyone is celebrating the wedding reception and both of them ride on Wedding elephant around the town. Sai tells the mourners, "My parents had their honeymoon upstairs in Grandmother's house. After the honeymoon was over. My dad's former army superior pull some strings with American embassy and the President to have my Mom an American Visa so she can come to America. She can also get a green card when she gets there. My Grandfather from my father's side and my mother's side and the rest of their siblings said goodbye to them after a week when my Grandfather arranged a car for them to take them to the Airport in New Delhi." A van drives off outside of Girja's mom's house and everybody is watching them go. Everyone cried watching them go. Sai tells the mourners, "I used to visit my grandparents every three years during Christmas. Mostly my parents wanted to get away from the cold once in a while. So that is when I visited my grandparents in India. Once in a while my grandparents usually visit us in America every two years. Before we visit them. So, this is my first time my Mom got to see America." The plane landed KCI airport aka Kansas City Airport. Everybody exits the gate and Girija and Sudarsan also exits the gate too and Girija sees America the first time. Sai tells the mourners, "My mother was very excited when she saw America. My parents stayed with Sudarsan's childhood friend Khanti Havaladar and his family for a year, before my parents' house was built. My Mom made friends with the Havaladars when she first came to Maryville to stay with them." Inside the Havaladar's house, Khanti and Cocula greeted Sudarsan and Girija and so is Sunjay and Abba. Sai tells the mourners, "My mom felt like she was part of the family when she met the Havaladars. They were friends for a long time." Inside the private practice where Khanti and Sudarsan works. Sduarsan got to work with patients five of them are waiting for his service in the waiting room. Sudarsan ask Patient number 1 come to the exam room and check on his eyes. Sai tells the mourners, "My dad started working with patients in his first day in private practice with Dr Havaladar. He was really good at it." Inside the eye exam room Sudarsan is examing his patients eyes on Phoropter. After the patient was done, Sudarsan wrote down his prescription on his eyes to get his glasses. The patient grabs the prescription and exams it for a minute. Sai tells the mourners, "My parents' house was finished after a year. They moved in 1976 and another year is that I was born." Inside the O.R. in St Francis Hospital in Wichita Kansas, Girija just gave birth to a baby boy where Sudarsan and the two doctors, two nurses and one orderly wearing scrubs and is helping cleaning up the baby boy that came out of Girija. Sudarsan was happy that he has a son and after Girija was carrying his son and gives their son to Sudarsan. Sudarsan looks thrilled to see his son. Sai tells the mourners, "That was me, Sai Hemanth Chavala born in January 3, 1977 in Wichita Kansas at St Francis Hospital. I bet you are going to ask what parents were doing in Wichita. My dad had a medical conference and he took my Mom with me. I wasn't supposed to be due until another week. So, my mom went into labor with me way early. Luckily they were prepared for me. Anyway that is when I was born." Girija and Sudarsan exits the O.R. and Sudarsan's father and Girija's mother and two of my Sudarsan's brothers are their in the waiting room and seeing Sai being born. They are in awe of him. Sai tells the mourners, "My grandparents and some of Dad's siblings arrive to see me born. After one year later, my dad ran his private practice and named it Maryville Eye Clinic and my Mom transferred to college at Northwest Missouri State University and she got a bachelors in Computer Science and two masters degrees in finance. One is in Northwest Missouri State University and the other one is in my dad's alma mater University of Missouri-Kansas City. She worked as a college professor in computer science and as a Computer Programmer manager in 1982 and retired 35 years later. My dad worked in Maryville Eye Clinic for a long time. He had two other medical offices in Bethany and Mount Ayr." Inside the Northwest Missouri State University graduation ceremony where Girija got her master's degree in business. Where Sudarsan and three-year-old Sai watches the graduation in 1981 and they are proud of Girija. Sudarsan works in the exam office with patients in Bethany and Mount Ayr. Sai tells the mourners, "My grandfather died when I was five, I barely remembered him. Because I went to India to visit him twice when I was a infant and I was 3 and my father went to his funeral in India. My Grandmother from my Mom's side of the family and she watched me grow up. I used to visit every three years when I was born. I forgot I told you that, but I wanted to remind you. Anyway, moving on after my Mom's retirement party. She got to stay in India for a couple of weeks. Some say, that my grandmother was really sick. So my mom spend a couple of weeks to help her. After two weeks she passed away and she was their at her funeral. After that she came home. As for me, I went to boarding school in Middleton Delaware called St Andrews. My parents were proud of me when I graduated from St Andrews." Outside the St Andrews front yard is where teenage Sai's graduation is at and gets his high school diploma. Sudarsan and Girija watched Sai get his high school diploma. Sai tells the mourners, "They also see me get medical school degree in UMKC. Yes, I went to my parents alma mater. I met my love of my life in college is Susmita Utukuri. We did not get married until I started my fellowship. First I started my internship in NYU medical hospital. Where I was saving lives and what you call it 9/11 the worse day when the terrorist hi-jacked four airplanes and crashed the Twin towers that was a worse day in anyone's life. I finished my residency in Cleveland and started my fellowship in Duke University. After I completed my residency me and Susmita got married in Toronto Canada." Inside Sai's medical school graduation where he gets his medical degree where his parents Sudarsan and Girija are watching. Sudarsan and Girija's nephew Ravi and Raju moved to USA when Sai was 18 when Raja come to America and Ravi come to America when Sai was 23 years old also attended. Sai and Sumita wedding was at the Hilton in Toronto. Inside the wedding where Swami marries Sai and Susmita got married and Sai's parents Sudarsan and Girija were watching, Ravi and Raju aka Sai's cousins, Susmita parents and her brother and his wife there. All of Sai's friends were there. Sai tells the mourners, "In my wedding, my friends Krishna Konijetti and his brother Rama that my father was friends with in the Army in Fort Leavenworth. After Rama and Krishna's father was done as an Army medical doctor he worked. He also married

Jayprada that he knew when there were medical school and moved to Leavenworth for him. Anyway after he was done with the Army, they moved and start their private practice in Terre Haute Indiana. We visited them a couple of times a year and sometimes they visited us there. My friend Lonnie Brazier and Adam Teale who I knew when we were kids also attended my wedding. There were others, but I am not going into details about it. After my wedding. I worked on my fellowship and started my practice in Raleigh North Carolina. I would tell you what my wife does for a living while we were in college. I had two kids, my daughter Lekha and my son Naveen. We moved to Dallas Texas to start my private practice a year before my Mom's retirement party. I was not their when my father had his retirement party last year. All the years, my parents worked really hard running a very successful business and life. Why my parents also earned a six figure salary when they started from the bottom and work their way up to the top. That is what I did. The story I wanted to tell you about what an amazing adventure that me and my father did together and it was six years ago in 2016 after my father's retirement party." Sai and Susmita sees outside the house in Raleigh-Durham North Carolina they moved in and wanted to see it for a minute. Inside North west Missouri State University, Sai and Susmita, young Lekha and Naveen and Sudarsan were there to see Girija retirement party in Student Union building with Sudarsan watching Girija party. Sudarsan was 72 years old when he sees his wife's retirement party and is proud of her. After one year later in 2016. Inside the Maryville Eye Clinic where the employees and Kanthi and Cocula and Girija celebrated his retirement. Khanti tells Sudarsan, "You did it. After 40 years, you did it Sudarsan. You run a great practice for a long time." Sudarsan tells Khanthi, "So did you Khanti. You retired last year and it was time for me to retire too. All our children are grown and married and having children of our own. I keep thinking about my father, I wasn't their when he died. I was here running my private practice. Before he died, he and I had a falling out. He and I said some things we regret. It was before I was leaving back to Kansas City." Khanti tells Sudarsan, "What is it you guys said that made have a falling out." It was in January 2, 1981 before me and Girija left." Sai tells the mourners, "I remember what my father told me, that him and grandpa before he passed away." Flashback in January 2, 1981 in New Delhi, India in the Chavala house. Inside the Chavala house at the front door, Sudarsan was about to grab his suitcase and his father goes over to Sudarsan and talk to him. Sudarsan's father tells his son, "Okay Son, do you have everything?" Sudarsan tells his father, "Yes, I have everything." Sudarsan's father tells his son, "I know I only visited you one time in the hospital when Sai was born. You only visited me three years later after me and Girija's mother threw you that wedding. I want to ask, why you never visited more often." Sudarsan tells Sudarsan's father, "Because I am running my own practice in Missouri. I barely have time for you. Besides I am here now. I promised Girija that we visited the family every three years to catch up. Well, I am here now." Sudarsan's father tells Sudarsan, "Now, you are. But I always think there was another reason why you never come often. Mostly you stayed at Srikalahasti with Girija's family first and spent one week there and you only one day here in my house." Sudarsan tells his father, "First of all, I promised Girija, that I spend a couple of weeks at her home and we spend one day here before we head back to Kansas City and visit you and the rest of my family." Sudarsan's father is upset and can tell his son is lying. Sudarsan's father tells him, "I can tell, that you are lying." Sudarsan tries to deny it for a minute and tells his father, "Father, I am not lying." Sudarsan's father is not buying it and tells his son, "I'm not buying it and I want the truth, why you never visited me more often. Last time, I was their when Sai was born. I only saw twice, one he was born and next when he is a toddler. Why is that!" Sudarsan is upset and tells his father, "Did you forget how you criticize, how I was going to raise my son and you tried to take over the whole thing. You were never going to give me advice. You wanted me to raise him that way you wanted to. To tell him, what to eat, what to do and where to live and how to behave. You been doing that to me when I was young. After mother died, you barely talk to me. You treated me like a total stranger back then. I always think way deep down, I am not going to hear the end of it when I joined ROTC while I was in medical school and also trained in the Green Berets and went to Vietnam. Deep down you were upset with me that I was being shipped off to Vietnam and fought in the war behind your back without discussing with me." Sudarsan's father tells his son, "Well I am upset with you. You could have been killed out there and do you ever think about your family and how they felt and do you ever thought about me how would you embarrass me in front of the people that I knew. That people would feel sorry for me and talk bad about me behind my back. That I let my son go off to war." Sudarsan is still upset and sarcastically tells his father, "Well, I'm sorry that I embarrassed you in front of your friends or my family. I didn't think about them. I was thinking about myself and how this looks to you." Sudarsan's father slaps Sudarsan in the face. Sudarsan's father tells his son, "Don't get smart with me. You know what you deserve that and you know I raised you to be a pacifist. Not some army military nut that goes off half cock when there are bullets and explosion out there that could have gotten you killed. You should know better than that." Sudarsan tells his father, "You were embarrassed by me that I went behind your back when I fought in the war. I wanted to make a difference and do something for myself and maybe help the people I was sworn to protect. I read about Ghandi and he was a pacifist and so was I. But in life and death situations, I would do anything save lives or I definitely a bullet for anyone who fought out there. I did and I wanted to prove that I could change things and end this war. I thought I would go out their protect those people in America that I was fighting for. But guess what I did not make a difference, I didn't change anything and neither did anyone else who fought in Vietnam. I remember the Fall of Saigon that ended the war and guess what nobody won. But guess what nobody won, father. I had no regret going there and fighting in that war. You know before I married Girija, you never let it go about what I did. You were happy with me when I went to medical school and became a doctor. You were upset with me. It was in America, and I joined ROTC that would look good on my resume and decide to fight in a war that you opposed. Guess what, I am a pacifist too. But in life and death situations, I would go out their fight and stand up for the people that I was sworn to protect in America. Those decisions behind your back were my decision and not yours. Because I am a grown man, who needs to make decision whether my father likes it or not." Sudarsan's father tells his son, "Well, you never made a good decision in your life, that I would never be proud of. Sometimes, I just wish you would follow the rules and listen to me. Instead of being stubborn and rigid all the time. You always must get your own way." Sudarsan's father tells Sudarsan, "So what, you always get your way too. Yeah, I am stubborn and rigid sometimes. But I am a good guy and I care about people. I did everything you told me too, it was still not enough, you wanted me to run the business with you. It was not for me, when I told you to become a doctor. You were happy, but you were miserable, it was a thousand miles away from you. I wanted to get away from you or India. Because I wanted to see the world and not here all the time. I wanted to go into ROTC and fight in the war, I thought I could make a difference. I did everything you said, and you still got your own way. You wanted me to marry Barthi, Girija's sister. But I wanted to finish my medical training, like my internship, residency, and fellowship. I did that you still pushed me into going on a date with Barthi's sister. I did that and I married her. Somewhere down the line, I loved her, and we both wanted to be different people and be our own individual. But I never wanted to come here first, without you criticizing me or tell me how to behave." Sudarsan's father tells his son, "Wow, I am now disappointed in you. You know what I am still going to criticize you and never let you live this down. A lot of times, you really embarrassed me and my communication. Sometimes I wish you were never my son. You are no longer my son." Sudarsan is still upset with his father and tells him, "You know in America where I lived, you embarrassed me with my community. You had never disappointed me; you were upset that you could never do what I could do. Go to medical school, fight in the military, save lives, and marry a great girl like Girija like I did. But you know what I have done with you. You are no longer my father and don't worry next, I visit it will just be Girija's family from now on. At least they appreciate that. Good day, father. I can say that my father is an asshole, you are an asshole and I hope I have a better relationship with my son. Then we ever have each other. Goodbye father!" Sudarsan grabs his suitcase and opens the door. Sudarsan exits his father's door for the last time. Sudarsan's father looks at his son leaving, and he is upset about what he said to him. Back in the present in Bram's funeral home where Sai is on the podium. Sai tells his mourners, "That was the last time my dad seen my grandfather. I was four years old when the last time saw him. My grandpa died ten months later in November before my fifth birthday. My dad and never had a chance to pick up a phone and apologized together. Maybe it was the hurtful stuff they said to each other and worse about disowning each other. Anyway, after my grandfather died, I made it to the funeral, but he and grandpa never had a chance to reconcile. So, he felt like an orphan for the first time. Now he spent every three years in India visiting Mom's family. My grandmother, my aunt Barthi who I call Pethama and Prakash with my three cousins Raju, Ravi and Bindica who I was really close to. To feel like he still has family and make them feel not alone." The flashback is over and back to 2016, where Sudarsan and Khanti conversing. Sudarsan tells Khanthi, that was that. That was the last time I spoke to before he died." Sudarsan was almost crying and tells Khanthi, "I always felt bad what we said to each other, sometimes I wish I could take it back about what I said to him. Mostly I never did, at first, he should have apologized to me. But none of us were man enough to pick up the phone. He had a will left to me and a letter that my borther Ajay gave me after he died. But I kept it. I never had a chance to open it." Khanti tells Sudarsan, "It's been 35 years, don't you think it is time to make peace with it and read your father's will and letter." Sudarsan tells Khanthi, "Maybe someday I will when the time is right. Like when I am dying, and I will have a chance to read it." Khanthi tells Sudarsan, "When you are ready to read it and let me know." Sudarsan tells Khanthi, "Sure thing." Khanthi tells Sudarsan, "What are you going to do now since we both retired. You are goanna to sleep in, watch tv all day and eat in Mcdonald's like two double cheeseburgers with ketchup and mustard only and a small fry and a large diet coke." Sudarsan tells Khanthi, "I do that every day when I was working, you're right I can sleep in anytime I want. Girija and I went everywhere, Russia, England, France, Germany, Ireland, China, and Mexico. We got to see San Francisco, Graceland, Washington D.C., Los Angeles, Fresno, Chicago, Dallas, and New York

City. We see everything even in our vacation when we have time off." Khanti tells Sudarsan, "I heard you have another house in Dallas Texas." Sudarsan tells Khanthi, "I built it last year, so me and Girija will be close to Sai and Susmita and our grandchildren. It's been a year since my Mother-in-law passed away. But Girija is okay now. My mother-in-law always regrets that she never got to spend a lot of time with us. Mostly Barthi and Prikash took care of her and ran the business. Mostly their sons Raju and Ravi came to America, I helped them out. They got married and have children on their own." Khanthi tells Sudarsan, "How come your niece Bindica did not come?" Sudarsan tells Khanthi, "Going to America is not for her, mostly India is her home and that is where she belongs. A lot of times we go over to India to see her and her family every three years. They love it when they visit us. Me and Girija are going to see Sai and Susmita and Lekha and Naveen in two days." Khanti tells Sudarsan, "That sounds great. I hope you have a good retirement." Khanthi pats him on the left arm and leaves to mingle with the rest of the guests. Sudarsan tells himself, "Sometimes I wish I had one more adventure before I die." Back to Bram's funeral home and Sai is back on his podium and tells the mourners, "My dad told me that before he died. That he wished that he had one more adventure before he dies. That is when fate came in and told you the story about me and my father's adventure that I want to tell you about. Guess who gave him his final adventure and it was me. Like I said, my father wanted to tell you guys. Here is the reason why I wanted to speak about this. Back in 2016 after Sudarsan's retirement and inside his house in 934 South Dunn. Sudarsan is upstairs in his den where he has a home theater, two guest rooms, Sai's room the master bedroom upstair and the den that is close to six room upstairs. They have a pool table, fountain and a gym in their basement and have seven bathrooms. Sudarsan is in his den wearing his pajamas and sees the file box. Sudarsan opens the file box and in the third drawer and takes out yellow envelope and opens it. He takes out a white envelope that is sealed that Sudarsan never opened after his father's will and letter when he died in 1981. Sudarsan tells himself, "I wish I could open this up. But I don't think it would happen because I know what it is going to say. So, forget it father!" Sudarsan sees the desk and computer and office chair and sits down on the office chair. The door knocks and Sudarsan tells the person on the other side of the door, "Come in." The door opens and it's Girija. Sduarsan tells Girija, "Hello Girija." Girija tells Sudarsan, "Hi, honey. What are you reading?" Sudarsan tells Girija, "The letter that I always look at, that I never had a chance to open. Girija closes the door and goes over to Sudarsan and sits down on the couch. Girija tells Sudarsan, "You still haven't read it yet?" Sudarsan tells Girija, "It's been 35 years since my father passed away. After the funeral my brother gave me this yellow that was a letter, he wrote to me before he died and will that be in it. A lot of times, I think Ajay is playing me. That the letter is probably blank, and he is trying to play a prank on me." Girija tells Sudarsan, "I don't think Ajay would ever do that to you. Besides it was your father's funeral, I don't think there was any time to joke around. When I look at you and the envelope, I think it is more than Ajay playing a joke on you." Sudarsan tells Girija, "You are right about that. Part of me thinks it is not about Ajay playing a joke on me and part of me thinks that my father's letter is about how much more he is disappointed in me. We practically disowned each other after I left. I never had the chance to pick up the phone to call him and tell him I'm sorry." Girija tells Sudarsan, "You think it is another letter tell you, you don't know how to live your life and I am still disappointed in you for all the decisions you make." Sudarsan tells Girija, "That is one of the main reasons why I never opened it. Do you think I want another letter where chews me out aka where he yells at me how much of a disappointment I am. That is one reason why I can't do it. I even told Khanthi that I would have a chance to read this letter until I am dying or when the time is right. The time is not right for me, and I think I changed my mind not to read it when I am dying." Girija tells Sudarsan, "You don't mean that do you Sudarsan." Sudarsan tells Girija, "Well I guess I really don't mean it. Because I promised Khanthi that I would read it when I am dying or when the time is right. Besides I did promise him. A promise is a promise." Girija tells Sudarsan, "Since you and Khanthi are retiring. I know where we are going. Did Khanti ever tell you where he is going? Sudarsan tells Girija, "Cocula is visiting her relatives in a month in

India. Because it is her niece's wedding and she wanted to be there for her. So Khanthi needed something else to do, while Cocula is in India. So, he decided to sign up for doctors without borders program for a month. He will be gone in a month. I guess we are all booked up for a month. That is how long we are staying in Dallas for a month." Girija tells Sudarsan, "Did Khanti tell you where he is going?" Sudarsan tells Khanthi, "Khanthi told me he is going to Congo to help out the sick there." Girija tells Sudarsan, "Well, it is very thoughtful for him. To help the native country of Congo, there are a lot of sick refugees there." Sudarsan tells Girija, "Me too, I wish I could help him out there. But this mission is for him. He wanted to help the refugees himself and concentrate on helping them. So that is what he is doing?" Girija looks at Sudarsan for a minute and tells him, "You sound like you wanted to help. Nah, I been helping a lot of people all my life not just for charities. Everyone who never had insurance or the money to pay me, I gave them a free pass and helped them get jobs so they can keep on working. I had good contacts with the state department and my friend in the state department always knows when someone is looking for a job and he needs one. He has the political connections to get it for him. So, I think I can take a vacation for a while." Girija tells Sudarsan, "That sounds like full of crap to me. You want to help. But it is not just being a doctor. It is something else you want to help them with." Sudarsan tells Girija, "I would have helped the sick if I wanted to. They have enough doctors and Khanthi is the only one that asked for. But you are right, Girija. If they need me, it won't just being a doctor. They probably need me for something else. I hope someday, Khanthi pull some strings to help them out with something." Sudarsan gets up from his office chair and gets up from his chair and goes over to Girija and starts hugging him. Girija tells Sudarsan, "Don't worry, honey. I am sure you will find a way to help them. I am sure you can." Outside the Congo African village in the medical area where he Khanti gives a booster shot to a young African village refugee. Khanthi is done, giving the young African village refugee his booster shot. Khanthi tells the young African village refugee, "Okay, that's it." The young African village refugee tells Khanthi, "Thank you, Dr Havaladar." Dr Havaladar high fives the kid and he leave. Another doctor from Doctors without Borders sees Khanthi and goes over to talk to him. Doctor from Doctors without Borders talks to Khanthi, "Hey Khanthi?" Khanthi tells the other doctor, "Hello Walter, how are you doing? Walter tells Khanthi, "I'm fine. Listen Khanthi I got an email from General Roberts." Khanthi tells Walter, "You're contact from the army. My superior Colonel Jacob Styles used to serve General Roberts in Vietnam and desert storm when I was an army doctor in Fort Riley. Colonel Styles always hated General Roberts yelling at him all the time. But it is part of the army. You make one mistake you get yelled at. I made a couple of mistakes that got me yelled at." Walter tells Khanthi, "I hope it wasn't something big." Khanthi tells Walter, "Not much, I accidentally spilled some coffee on his lap, and he yelled at me for it." Walter laughs for a minute and tells Khanthi, "Oh boy, I guess why he yelled at you. I hope he was mad at you." Walter tells Khanthi, "Not much, after I got a towel and tried to wipe off the coffee from his shirt and pants and some of his coffee got on his dick. I thought about wiping the coffee from his Dick and he said no. Believe me that is one place I never want to wipe. Trust me, he cleaned himself up and told me to get out." Walter tells Khanthi, "I hope he did not give you a hard time after that. Mostly for me, he probably gives you the worse punishment or make your life hell all week." Khanti tells Walter, "No, he did make my life hell. For the whole week, I owe him fifty pushups. When he comes to see me. Luckily, he only sees me a few minutes a day. I had to 350 pushups all week for him. Believe me, I learned my lesson and never spilled anything again." Walter tells Khanthi,: Man, that bites." Khanthi tells Walter, "Tell me about it. So, what was it General Roberts called you about." Walter tells Khanthi, "There might be reports some aftrican warlord and his troops might be invading this village. Mostly African warlords are terrorist who usually invades places to terrorize and pillage and kill anyone who is in their way." Khanthi tells Walter, "Look Walter, I'm sure there is a misunderstanding. There are no such thing African warlords, mostly if they were terrorist, they usually get weapons from the black market and mostly they need money to fund it. Mostly terrorist usually don't attack if they want something or want to take over. We are in Congo remote village. We have nothing here they want and terrorizing and killing people in this village is not going to make them fear them anymore. Walter tells Khanthi, "Well, I think you are wrong about that. Because General Roberts informed me that they were about to arrive in ten minutes and starts attacking the village." Khanthi tells Walter, "Walter, I think you drank too much water in that reservoir that we drank at, or I think the way I look at you." Walter looks worried for a minute and Khanthi tells Walter, "I think you are not lying. I can tell when someone is lying, not all the time. But I can tell, you are telling the truth. We need to get the villagers out of here." There is one problem, there is a Zastava M57 gun behind his pants. A couple of miles outside the village there are two jeeps that carry M60E3guns in their jeep. One of them is an African Warlord and two jeeps carried six African terrorist in it. African warlod is in the passenger seat, with his African Warlord solider 1 driving the jeep with two of his guys in the back seat. While the other three are driving the other van. In the village Khanti is panicking for a minute and tells Walter, "Should we tell everyone to evacuate the village. Because they are arriving. They can attack the village but not the people, we have some time to get everyone to safety. How far is the border aka safety from here." Walter tells Khanthi, "Goma, it's about eight miles there. There is no way, the African warlord would cross that path because their us military base in Goma they would not cross since the villagers are protected by them." Khanti looks at the villagers they are not panicking since the African Warlord is not here. Khanthi tells Walter, "Why everyone is not panicking. You did tell the villagers that the African Warlord is coming. How come you told me first; I thought if there was a life and death emergency you would have told the African Village Chief." Walter tells Khanthi, "I did tell him. Khanthi, I did tell him. We are about to evacuate right now. Tell me, can you say my full name for a minute." Khanthi tells Walter, "Walter, why do you need me to tell you, your full name. We have to get out of here and get everyone to safety." Walter tells Khanthi, "Tell me my full name." Khanthi is about to leave and Khanthi tells Walter, "Walter I don't have time for this. We have to get everyone to safety." Walter is about to take his Zastava M57 gun behind his pants, aims the gun on Khanthi and yells at Khanthi, "Tell me my full name you son of a bitch!" Khanthi is little bit confused and tells Walter, "What are you nuts…?" Walter takes out his gun from back of his pants and African Warlord just arrive with his troops in their jeeps throwing grenades in the african huts and they are exploding. Everyone from the village starts panicking and trying to exit the village. African Warlord soldier 2 and 3 gets the machine guns out and starts firing at the villager. Three villagers are shot but six bullets come out of Warlord Soldier 2 and 3 guns and two bullets' hits Afircian villager 1 in the chest and dies, two other bullets hit African Villagers 2 in stomach and dies and two more bullets hits African Villager in the head and dies. The jeep stops and the rest of the rest of the soldiers start attacking the villagers. Walter is still angry and Khanti starts being scared and tells Walter, "Walter Eugene Chong. There are you happy now!" Walter tells Khanti, "Wrong Asshole!" Walter punches Khanti in the stomach and still aims his gun on Khanthi and tells him, "Like I said, I did warn the African Village Chief about the African Warlord. I also told him he was working for me; I am leading this attack to find you. Right after I killed the Chief first before I found you. Khanthi is still groaning for a minute and stops and tells Walter, "So Walter if that is your real name. You are leading this invasion and killed the African tribe chief when you told him who you are, and you were about to warn me. Why haven't you killed me yet!" Walter tells Khanthi, "Let me explain, my name is Anh Lan Jr that is my birth name. Who is the father my North Vietnam Cong General Lan Sr who was an excellent drug lord and terrorist who would do anything to win the war against USA that stuck their noses in a place where they don't belong. Luckily nobody won the war, that is good. Because North Vietnam still hates USA, and we still do. I been planning my revenge when my father is killed by a soldier who is a friend of yours and I want him dead to avenge my father. My mother Sun Lee Chong runs the triad in Dallas Texas in China Town. That is where we are going to lure him here and make a huge drug deal with my clients. African Warlord and his soldiers are killing African villagers. Six of the the African villagers escape the village, but another military jeep with three more African warlords use their machine gun attached to the jeep and starts firing their gun. Ten bullets come out of the gun, two bullets hit the African villager in the chest and dies, young African American kid who is about ten is killed when three bullets hit the chest and dies, two bullets hits female villager in the head and dies. This female African villager who saw her husband and son dies. Two bullets hit the African villager 4 in the stomach and dies. One more bullet hits the head of African Villager 5. Five more bullets were fired from that gun and two more bullets hits African Villager 5 in the chest and dies finishing him off. Two more bullets hit the African Villager 6 in the stomach and dies. African Warlord soldiers are continuing killing off villagers. More of the African huts are exploding and One of the African Warlord throws another grenade in another African hut and kills another African Villager. Lan tells Khanthi, "Who is my friend that killed your father and why are you letting me live and come to Dallas so you can kill him." Lan tells Khanthi, "Because he is your friend and if he knows I captured you. He will come to look for you. I want to see his face when I kill you first and then him." Lan kicks Khanthi in the stomach and takes out a beating rod from his right jacket pocket and takes it out. Lan uses the beating rod to hit Khanti on the head and his back. Khanthi falls on the floor hurting. African Warlord goes over to Lan and talk to him. African Warlord tells Lan, "Dr Lan, we captured some of the villagers and some doctors here, what do you think you want to do with them sir?" Lan tells African Warlord, "We are taking them with us and by the way Kovu. You know why I hired you. Since my mother died, I had to take over her empire. She met my father in Vietnam in the bar in North Vietnam and drug dealing with them. It was love at first sight. But they had to go their separate ways, she ran her drug empire in Dallas in Chinatown, but she always kept a low profile. She always found a way to cover her tracks from Law enforcement. She always has a guy inside to inform her where the shipments are going to hit. Anyway, she was pregnant with me, my father decided to invade Vietnam and take down the American scum. I never knew my father, because he was busy invading South Vietnam and making Americans suffer and give them to surrender to us. But that backfired in him, and he was killed when I was young, and I didn't even chance to meet him. After my mother died last year, I took over and wait for the right time to get my revenge of the guy who killed him." Kovu tells Lan, "Why are you telling me this life story anyway. Because we have a lot of work to do anyway sir." Lan tells Kovu, "You know why I am telling you this story?" Kovu tells Lan, "Why sir!" Lan tells Kovu, "I can't tell people when they are lying or bluffing. Or somebody is about to double cross me when they tried to take over some gang or crew like you are about to point that gun at me. Lan aims the gun at first and tells Kovu, "Your crew thinks they're loyal to you, they are loyal to me." Kovu also aims his gun at Lan. Kovu tells Lan, "My crew is loyal to me. They always have. They would never work for you. Not some Chinese punk who is way over their head running his mother's empire to the ground. Because like I told my crew, no witnesses" Lan tells Kovu, "You're right Kovu, no witnesses. But one thing you forget when you terrorist crew. First you need to play the fear card which you have. You must beat them up to keep them in line and there. You know what three is Kovu?" Kovu tells Lan, "No, what is number three?" Lan tells Kovu, "Three is the golden rule, whoever has the most gold control the crew. Gold makes anyone walk in water. Guys kill him." Two African warlords goes over to Kovu and kills Kovu when they fired their guns, and six bullets comes out of their guns and hits Kovu in the chest and almost dies. Lan tells Kovu, "Final Lesson Kovu, when you control a crew always have the gold to back them up. Since I have all the gold, they're backing me up." Kovu is almost dying and tells Lan, "You are a sick bastard, Lan." Lan tells Kovu, "I know." Kovu is dead and Lan tells his crew, "Take the doctors, Havaladar and the rest of the villagers in the van. We got a plane to catch. Abebi take me to the radio room; I got a message to Colonel Rosenberg." Abebi tells Lan, "Yes sir." Abebi and Khanthi exit the medical area and head to the radio room in the village that is not damaged. The rest of African warlords' soldiers takes Khanthi and the rest of the doctors and African villagers to the van outside the village. Inside the radio room in the hut of an African village where Abebi and Lan enter the radio room and sees the radio and communicator. Abebi tells Lan, you are going to radio the Defense department, Mr Lan!" Lan tells Abebi, "Yes, I need to get his attention." Abebi and Lan head to their chairs and use the radio and transmitter to call in the Defense or any US military involved. Lan makes a call to someone from the defense department and tells someone from the radio, "Wolfdeck, anyone there! Wolfdeck anyone there!" The radio transmitter already responded and the person on the radio, "Wolfdeck identify yourself?" Lan tells the person on the radio, "You first, because my name is not important right now, but right now I am here to inform you we have prisoners for us that we captured, and I know you want them back. We took in African Village tribe and some American doctors and wipe out their village. But my message will explain it to you! Abebi play the message on the DVD." Abebi tells Lan, "Yes sir!" Abebi is wearing a jacket and takes out the DVD from his right pants pocket that DVD is on a case and gives the DVD to Lan. Lan grabs the DVD and opens the CD-DVD player on the laptop and puts the DVD on the slot and starts playing the recording. The person that Lan and Abebi are contacting is a communication room listening to in and he is from the Pentagon. The person in the Pentagon is listening in and Lan voiceover tells him, "I have doctors and African Villagers hostages. We are not here for money and no prisoner exchange. Their names are not important, but I want to give you one name which is Dr Khanthi Havaladar. I want you to contact your superior and your superior is a friend of his. I want your superior to send out a message to his friend Major Sudarsan Chavala. That I have his friend Dr Khanthi Havaladar held hostage. Tell your superior, give his friend Chavala the message and come find me and I will release his friend and the rest of the hostages. Don't even think about sending in reinforcement. Don't even think about looking for me, because I blocked out all the areas of tracing devices to find me, but I can give you a clue Lan. Tell him to find me, once he finds me, I will release the hostages and his friends. Where I can capture him and let him face his own execution. Chavala got one week to find me. Good day." The person from the Pentagon already copied the voice from his laptop and it was recorded on DVD and takes out the recording device from his hard drive." The person from the pentagon tells himself, "Luckily, I am good at recording things. My superior does not know who Major Sudarsan Chavala is. But I better to look him up." After Abebi and Lan finish the recording on the DVD and take out the DVD from the laptop. Lan tells Abebi, "We're done now, let's go and begin the mission." Abebi tells Lan, "You think Chavala will find us and luckily the pentagon does not know what we are doing. Once we finish this plan and execute my enemy I despise. We will begin our next mission." Abebi and Lan stats laughing for a minute and exit. General Rosenberg who is working in his office in the Pentagon. The door knocks and General Rosenberg tells the person on the other side of the door, "Come in." The person from the communication room in the Pentagon enters the office and carrying a DVD and tells General Rosenberg, "Hello General Rosenberg, I think you need to listen to this." General Rosenberg tells the person from the communication room in the Pentagon, "What is it, Lieutenant Wallace?" Lieutenant Wallace tells General Rosenberg, "There is this recording in the DVD sir. We just radio distressed signal from Republic of Congo African Village and this recording from this DVD you should listen to sir." General Rosenberg tells Lieutenant Wallace, "Let's hear it and what tribe from Congo is calling us?" Lieutenant Wallace, "The Luba Tribe, sir. Pentagon has contacts with African Chief who is friends with our current African President. We also sent in the Army to protect the tribe from terrorist or Warlords who is out to attack the Tribe." General Rosenberg tells Lieutenant Wallace, why hasn't the army stopped them before they attacked," Lieutenant Wallace tells General Rosenberg, "I checked it out, sir. They were about ambushed by some African Warlord; we don't know about. Their military weapons are usually from the black market. So that means somebody is funding terrorism. We never knew who is funding them and who this African Warlord is." General Rosenberg tells Lieutenant Wallace, "How come we find anything about these guys. How did that army got ambushed by those guys?" Lieutenant Wallace tells General Rosenberg, "I have no idea, but they must block out the signals and find a way to make them invisible so they can ambush them. But I did some checking that a company that built some stealth explosive devices and some alarm devices that can block out tracing signals from any tracking device that was stolen three weeks ago." Lieutenant Wallace gives the DVD to General Rosenberg and grabs the DVD and plays it on the laptop. Lieutenant Wallace sits down in his chair. General Rosenberg tells Lieutenant Wallace, "Any idea what the company name that the stolen equipment that they were going to build for us?" Lieutenant Wallace tells General Rosenberg, "I have the file in my office sir. But I can't give the company's name. Somebody might be bugging this office. It's better I give you the file of the name of company after you listen to his recording General." General Rosenberg tells Lieutenant Wallace, "Let's hear it." General Rosenberg opens the slot of DVD and CD player to start the laptop and starts listening to it. Sudarsan and Girija arrive at their second home in 12985 Averi Lane in Farmers Branch Texas when they open the door. They are carrying their suitcases, dropping them off the floor and Sudarsan turns on the light. Sudarsan tells Girija, "We are home." Girija tells Sudarsan, "I can't believe it took us six months to build this house and get everything ready after your retirement so we can spend our vacation here." Sudarsan tells Girija, "Let's put our luggage in the master bedroom and start unpacking before Sai and Susmita arrives in two hours." Girija tells Sudarsan, "What is the rush to unpack we can do something else before we unpack." Sudarsan tells Girija, "You mean we can get laid before two hours before they arrive." Girija tells Sudarsan, "I thought we order some pizza and some miller lites before they arrive." Sudarsn tells Girija, "You read my mind. But you were serious about holding off sex for today." Girija tells Sudarsan, "Nope, we can do that tomorrow or now!" Girija starts making out with Sudarsan and stops. Sudarsan tells Girija, "Now is good. We got two hours left, let's go." Sudarsan grabs Girija hand and head to the couch and starts making out and getting laid. In General Rosenberg office finishes listening to Lan recording device and is still unaware who he is. General Rosenberg turns off the recording from the DVD. General Rosenberg tells Lieutenant Wallace, "I see enough what I heard Harry." Lieutenant Wallace tells General Rosenberg, "This unknown guy who is working for this African warlord took hostages some doctors and some African tribe people hostages just to get to Major Sudarsan Chavala. I checked him out, he was an army doctor in Fort Leavenworth and ex green beret. The recording said you know him." General Rosenberg tells Lieutenant Wallace, "I know him, I was his commanding officer in Vietnam and trained him in Fort Bragg. He was an excellent soldier and one of my best men I knew. He was awarded the bronze star for his action in Vietnam." Lieutenant Wallace tells General Rosenberg, "Our kidnappers is not asking for money or prisoner trade. He is not asking to flee the country. He only wants Major Chavala to find him and he will release the hostages. I know why the kidnappers want with Sudarsan, just for him to find him and kill him so they can release the hostages. I have no idea why this kidnapper wants to find him. Unless there is something else going on that we don't know about." General Rosenberg tells Lieutenant Wallace, "I know but I need to call him. But until then, we can't investigate this. But we will have to leave the investigation for the CIA." Lieutenant Wallace tells General Rosenberg, "Why are we not investigating this and why we are letting the CIA investigate this?" General Rosenberg tells Lieutenant Wallace, "Somebody might be listening in. They might be bugging the system; we need to go outside the defense department and leave it to law enforcement like the CIA. They know how to make themselves invisible." Lieutenant Wallace tells General Rosenberg, "The CIA might be in danger too, because the terrorist could be listening in and may have some inside guys listening in. Neither is this place; they may have some inside guys who might be moles for the kidnappers." General Rosenberg tells Lieutenant Wallace exactly why none of us should investigate. So, we need somebody to go off the grid and investigate and luckily I know someone who is a liaison between the Pentagon and the CIA." Lieutenant Wallace tells General Rosenberg, "Who is that sir?' General Rosenberg tells Lieutenant Wallace, "I can't tell you, but I must keep this off the record. You're dismissed Lieutenant Wallace." Lieutenant Wallace tells General Rosenberg, "Yes sir." Lieutenant Wallace gets up from his chair and heads to the door and opens it. Lieutenant Wallace exits General Rosenberg office and closes the door. General Rosenberg picks up the phone and makes a call. The person on the end of the phone voice tells General Rosenberg, "Hello this Sergeant Nicholas Jones from Fort Hood Texas, how can I help you sir." General Rosenberg tells Sergeant Jones from the phone, "Yes this is General Rupert Rosenberg from the Pentagon. I need you to get me General Victor Stone and I need to ask him to give a message to his liaison Lieutenant Colonel Chavala." Sergeant Jones from the phone and tells General Rosenberg, "Yes sir, I transfer you to General Stone now sir." General Rosenberg tells Sergeant Stone, "Thank you." In Sai's house while he is watching tv with his children Lekha and Naveen on the couch while Susmita is cooking dinner. She is making spaghetti. The phone rang and Susmita put the stove button on low and answers the phone. Susmita tells the person on the phone who she is answering to, "Hello!" The person on the phone tells Susmita, "Hey Mrs Chavala. This is Josh Wentz from the office." Susmita tells Josh from the phone, "Hey Josh, you don't have to call me Mrs Chavala. We're being friends for three years, I told you to call me Susmita." Josh tells Susmita, "I know, I just want to make you squirm." Susmita laughs for a minute and tells Josh from the phone, "Funny, cute but funny." Josh tells tells Susmita, "Anyway, the reason why I am calling is Sai home?" Susmita tells John from the phone, "Yes, he is home. He is watching tv with the kids." Josh tells Susmita, "Can you call him, I need to talk to him for a minute." Susmita tells Josh on the phone, "Sure thing. I called him. Sai! Sai!" Sai hears Susmita calling him and tells the kids, "I'm coming!" Sai exits the couch and goes over to the kitchen and talks to Susmita. Sai goes over to Susmita and ask here, "What is it, honey?" Susmita tells Sai, "John is on the phone, it must be urgent that he wants to talk to you about." Sai tells Susmita, "I better take the call. I take it in the den aka my office." Susmita looks at Sai for a minute and tells her, "Oh our office. My mistake, we both forgot we both work." Sai exits the kitchen and heads to the den to take Josh's call. Susmita tells Josh on the phone, "He'll be right with you, Josh." Sai is in his den and sits down in his chair and picks up the phone and tells Josh, "Josh, you still there?" Josh who's on the other phone tells Sai, "Yes, I'm here Sai." Sai tells Josh, "What is it?" Josh tells Sai, "Domino's Pizza has two large pepperoni pizza's with buy one and get one free." Sai recognizes that tone and tells Josh, "Thanks for the offer, my wife is a vegetarian, but I am not. I can eat it. But I think she can start eating meat today. I'll pick it up, where can I meet you?" Josh on the other side of the phone, "Meet me at 1253 Grey Street." Josh hangs up the phone and so does Sai. Sai tells himself, "1253 Grey Street that is Domino's Pizza, Josh is slipping. But I must meet him. Susmita! I ordered some pizza at Dominos, one with Vegetarian for you and me and the kids who like pepperoni. I going to pick it up, since all the drivers are out today and I going to pick it up." Susmita voiceover tells Sai, "Okay Sai. Thanks for ordering. Because I burnt the food again." Sai gets up from his chair and heads to the garage. Sai's car, a BMW M4 exits the garage and heads to 1253 Grey Street, that is Domino's Pizza. Inside Domino's Pizza where Josh is waiting for his Pizza. Josh is in his late thirties and waiting for Sai. Josh is carrying a briefcase. The door opens and it's Sai. Sai enters Domino's Pizza and goes over talk to Josh. Sai talks to Josh, "Hey Josh. What's the emergency." Josh tells Sai, "Not here, everyone's watching." Josh and Sai exit outside Domino's Pizza when they open the doors and head outside. Now they are outside Domino's Pizza and Josh explains why Sai called him here and tells him, "We have an emergency. I got a call from the Pentagon. They have an important mission for us." Sai tells Josh, "What mission, look me and Susmita are done being CIA analyst. Why did you recruit us in college in the first place. You know I went to my father's alma mater, and he was proud of me when I joined ROTC and after I graduated from medical school and became an army doctor and optometrist there. The Army allowed me to work in NYU medical hospital and when I heard about 9/11 and trying to save a lot of people from that incident about terrorist attack. I thought about joining the green berets like my dad, but my grandfather and my father had a fallout because of it because he wanted to join the green berets. But you recruited me to become an analyst, which I did and I ask you recruit my wife with me. Which you did, I did a lot of missions for you and the Army while I was finishing my internship, residency in Cleveland and my fellowship to Durham North Carolina. Me and Susmita were planning on leaving the agency soon. Right now, I work as an eye doctor in Fort Hood and Susmita had a cover story where she works as a pharmaceutical rep Rental Pharmaceuticals. Thanks to the CIA making it happen, Rental Pharmaceuticals is a cover story. So whatever mission is, I have to decline, because me and my wife are planning our careers full times and spend more time with the kids. Josh tells Sai, "Okay if you want to give this up. I understand maybe you and Susmita can do one more mission and then you guys can retire." Sai is thinking about it and tells Josh, "What is the mission?" Josh tells Sai, "I got a call from General Victor Stone, he told us some African Villagers Tribe and some doctors were kidnapped by some terrorist team in the Congo of Africa. This terrorist team might be an African Warlord who is been terrorizing the local villagers in Africa. But they don't know who he is, but the African Warlord is not the calling the shots. I think he is working for somebody who is calling the shots and this person is funding their terrorist organization by building weapons for them." Sai tells Josh, "Man, that is bad. You don't know who is funding them. If this African Warlord is working for someone and someone funding the operation. It might be some defense company who is funding money to the terrorist. Do you know who might be funding them?" Josh tells Sai, "I have a company's name in the file, but I don't think they have anything to do with the funding. Because the company who built those guns and grenades for the US military and was supposed to deliver it to the Pentagon in Washington D.C. for weapons testing? But some terrorist team might stole the weapons and hijack the phane and was delivered in the Congo to some terrorist team in the Congo." Sai tells Josh, "I think this company is the victim and not the perpetrator. But you think this company who is running the show, might fake the hijacking and deliver the weapons to the Warlord themselves. I don't think so. But even if I want to do it. This will be my last one. Before I do this, why are you coming to me. Me and Susmita are retiring in two weeks." Josh tells Sai, "Because the doctor who was kidnapped is a friend of your father's. He was in the Doctors without borders in the African Tribe. Dr Khanthi Havaladar." Sai is shocked to hear that his father's friend is kidnapped and tells Josh, "Dr Khanthi Havaladar, he is one of the doctors who got kidnapped in the Congo. Man, this is going to hurt my Dad. Don't worry, I will do whatever I can to help you guys out." Josh tells Sai, "Are you going to reassemble the team." Sai tells Josh, "I may have a cover story as a doctor. I was more than a Analyst in the CIA. I was highly trained as a field agent. I picked my team really well to help me out. I call them and we can get started tomorrow. But my father is in town for two weeks and he wants to spend time with me and my family. They are already here and I supposed to meet them in an hour." Josh tells Sai, "The reason why I called you out here is not just by calling your team to do this mission. I wondered if you could recruit your father to join the team. He could be a big help to find his friend and the rest of the doctors and the African tribe. We are doing this off the books, so no one can know about this mission. Because their might spied or leaks anywhere to blab about our plan." Sai tells Josh, "You want me to recruit my father in this. My dad maybe an army doctor in Vietnam. But he was not much of man of action guy. Besides if I want to do this rescue mission, I would have recruited Chuck Norris." Josh opens his briefcase and gives out the file to Sai. Sai grabs the file and looks at it for a minute." Josh tells Sai, "Actually your father was not in Vietnam for being a medical doctor." Sai ask Josh, "I beg your pardon." Josh tells Sai, "He was an ex green beret aka Special Forces. He did a lot of mission for the army and for us. He was a war hero over there. Anyway, we need your father in this. Because this lead kidnapper ask for him. He wants him and you guys to find him. But he did give us a clue Lan. That is why you need your father on board for this. Sai is upset that his father lied about what he was doing all the time, but the mission is important. Josh tells Sai, "Since Sudarsan is in town and you were expecting him to meet you in an hour. Find him and tell him what's going on." Sai tells Josh, "What if I don't want to work with him. My father and I don't see eye to eye that much. He always criticize everything I do." Josh tells Sai, "This is not a request, it's an order. This is you and Susmita last mission together and make it good. The ransom demand from the kidnapper ask for him. He might know about Lan and what it is. He is the key to get the hostages back." Sai tells Josh, Okay, I'll him. By the way why are we meeting at Domino's Pizza. I always meet you in your office in Fort Hood. That is where the CIA assigned you for a year when I meet you for missions." Josh tells Sai, "I always gave you the code of Domino's Pizza, when I tell you what Pizza is half off and make an excuse for your kids and your friends when you go over to pick it up and when you come up with nothing and find out they close. I decided to make it real, you pick up the pizzas for real because sooner or later somebody might find out about your secret. So I got two pizzas for you one is pepperoni and one is vegetarian. That is why I was waiting to pick up the pizzas." Sai tells Josh, "Good thinking Josh." Josh tells Sai, "We better get inside and get your pizzas." Sai tells Josh, "I don't want the kids disappointed in me for going empty handed again." Sai and Josh goes back inside the Dominos to pick up the pizzas. Sai goes inside the house with the two pizzas in the front door. Sai is carrying his file on the right hand. Sai tells everyone, "Guys, I'm home. I got pizza." Lekha and Naveen enters the front door and goes over to Sai and talk to him. Lekha tells Sai, "Thanks dad. I always thought you always forget. But you always told us that the place closes in different hours." Naveen tells Sai, "Sometimes, you might get lost because the GPS system does not work." Sai tells his kids, "Not this time. Lekha grab the pizzas and take it in the kitchen." Lekha tells Sai, "Okay Dad." Sai tells the kids, "I'll be with guys in a minute in the kitchen to eat with you guys. I have to be in the Den for a minute and drops this file in my desk." Naveen tells Sai, "Dad what kind of file is that you're carrying." Sai tells Naveen, "Naveen it's a patient that I working within a few days for cataract surgery. I have to look for a minute on my patient." Naveen tells Sai, "Okay dad." Naveen and Lekha grabs the pizzas and take it to the kitchen. Sai tells Susmita where he is, "Susmita, I'm going to the den to drop off my file. Can you join me for a minute and I need to talk to you about my patient that I about to do surgery for." Susmita voiceover tells Sai, "I'm coming." Sai is sitting down in his chair and reading the file in his den. Susmita enters the den and closes the door. Susmita goes over to Sai and sits down in her chair and discuss the file that he is reading. Susmita tells Sai, "I thought we talked about this. That you and I are going to retire. We are always out of town in missions like Prague, Paris and London. Or Tokyo when we had to go around the world to do dangerous missions to stop terrorist stealing stolen items from the military and government and retrieving it. Mostly we barely had time for our children or our friends." Sai tells Susmita, "We had Lucy who is our nanny to look after Lekha and Naveen while we were gone. It was tough to explain to our friends about why we never went to dinner in our place or have time to see them. Because we were busy. Josh knows that we are retiring in two weeks. But he gave us one more mission we have to do. It involves my father." Susmita tells Sai, "You're father what does he have to do with this?" Sai tells Susmita, "Josh told me we need him to join the team to help us out on our mission. Some doctors and African villagers were kidnapped in the Congo tribe. They gave a recording to the pentagon and to us that they need my father to find them or the kidnapper will kill the hostages. They want my father to find them." Susmita tells Sai, "Why do they need your father to find them. So the kidnappers are not asking for money or a plane out of the country. They just want them to find your father." Sai tells Susmita, "Exactly! Mostly the CIA or the US government would never negotiate with terrorist. But the hostages are important and do whatever it takes to save them. That is why Josh needs me to recruit my father and get the team together to find the hostages and track down the kidnappers and bring them to justice." Susmita tells Sai, "Or take them out whichever comes first. So what are you going to do?" Sai tells Susmita, "Josh tells me that this is not a negotiation and they need my father on board with this. Because he is the key to find the hostages. I usually reluctant to let him in my team." Susmita tells Sai, "Look, I know he is an army doctor in Vietnam. But he doesn't have to be field with us. We are the ones doing the heavy lifting. So maybe he can help us a bit. But one thing I want to ask. Why do they need your father in this mission?" Sai tells Susmita, "Because my dad's friend Dr Khanthi Havaladar is one of the doctors who was kidnapped. That is why they need him and they gave us a clue how my father can find the kidnappers, is Lan." Susmita tells Sai, "Lan what is that. Is that a person or a place. What is it?" Sai tells Susmita, "I don't know but my father is the only one who knows about it. So, we have to meet him and my Mom in twenty minutes and maybe he can help us." Susmita tells Sai, "Whatever Lan is, I hope he knows." Sai tells Susmita, "I hope so too." Back in the 12985 Averi Lane inside Sudarsan and Girja's house and inside the house where Sudarsan shirt and pants are untucked when he hears a doorbell when he goes to the front door to answer it. Sudarsan opens the door and it's Sai, Susmita and Lekha and Naveen to greet their grandparents. Sai tells Sudarsan, "Hi, Dad!" Sudarsan tells Sai, "Hey son." Sai hugs his father for a minute and lets go. Susmita hugs his father-in-law for a minute and tells Sudarsan, "Hi Dad!" Sai tells Sudarsan, "Dad, why are you clothes untucked." Sudarsan tells Sai, "Let's just say, don't ask and don't tell." Sai figures that out that his parents had sex and Sai is grossed out for a minute and tells his father, "I'm not planning on it." Sudarsan tells Susmita, "Hi Susmita how is my favorite daughter." Susmita tells Sudarsan, "I'm your only daughter-in-law." Susmita let's go of her father for a minute. Naveen and Lekha also gaves hugs to Sudarsan and let's go. Naveen tells Sudarsan, "Hey grandpa got any candy for us." Sudarsan tells Naveen, "I got some Hershey bars for you guys. It's in the kitchen. I let grandma give it to you." Sai tells Sudarsan, "Dad, you always spoiled those kids a lot." Sudarsan tells Sai, "I'm a grandfather it is my job to spoil them. I spoiled you a lot. I got you that Hershey bars that you guys love." Sai tells Sudarsan, "That is why I love you about that." Girija enters the front door and Lekha and Naveen hugs their grandmother. Naveen and Lekha tells Girija, "Hi Grandma." Girija tells them, "Hi guys." Girija let's go of their grandkids and Girija tells them, "You guys want some candy, I'm sure your grandfather that we have some Hershey bars here. We do, come with me in the kitchen." Lekha and Naveen are pleased. Girija, Lekha and Naveen exits the front door and exits the kitchen. Sudarsan tells them, "Are you guys here for dinner. Girija makes a great lasagna. But it's microwavable." Sai tells Sudarsan, "No dad, we already ate. Listen Dad, there is something I need talk to you about. Can we talk in the den." Sduarsan tells Sai, "Sure what is it?" Sai tells Sudarsan, "I will tell you in the Den." Sudarsan tells Sai, "Okay, I just hope he is not dying or broke. I can help you with both of them if you are in trouble." Sai tells Sudarsan, "No it isn't." Sudarsan heads to the den and waiting for Sai. Sai is about to meet his father in the den. Sai tells Susmita, "Wish me luck." Susmita tells Sai, "Good luck honey." Sai kisses Susmita in the lips for a minute and stops. In the den where the door opens and it's Sai and Sudarsan enters the den. Sai sits down in his chair and Sudarsan sits down in his office chair. Sudarson tells Sai, "What is you want to talk to me about?" Sai tells Sudarsan, "Look Dad, I don't you would believe if I told you. But I work with the CIA and I need your help with an important mission." Sudarsan laughs for a minute and tells Sai, "You work for the CIA, yeah I'm Ethan Hunt from Mission Impossible." Sai tells Sudarsan, "Dad, I am not kidding." Sai takes out his wallet from his right pants pocket and shows his father his CIA badge." Sudarsan tells Sai, "Looks fake, I can get this online on Ebay for 12.00." Sai tells Sudarsan, "I am not kidding. That badge is real. So is this!" Sai gets up from his chair and takes out a beretta 92x gun from his back of his pants. Shows it to his father. Sudarsan looks convinced that he is a CIA agent and Sia puts his gun on the desk. Sudarsan tells Sai, "You're CIA, central intelligence agency. That CIA who are government spies that...?" Sai stops his father for a minute and tells him, "The one that one you see in James Bond movies." Sudarsan tells Sai, "How do you become a CIA agent, I thought you were a doctor like me. I work really hard to put you through medical school and that is a lie." Sai tells Sudarsan, "It's not a lie dad, "I am a doctor for a real, my medical id is in wallet their too. You did put me through medical school and I joined ROTC when I was there. After I graduated from medical school and got my commissioned from ROTC. I was assigned in Fort Hamilton, but the army allowed me to start my internship in NYU medical hospital. After 9/11, I was recruited to join the CIA and still commissioned in the army. I realize I can help. So I did, I became a CIA analyst while I was stationed in New York for a year finish my registry, three years in Cleveland to finish my residency and one year in my fellowship while I was continuing doing missions as a CIA analyst figuring out terrorist attacks while I was there as a part timer while I was working in different army bases. I did my CIA analyst job full time and traveled around in Japan, Africa, Afghanistan Australia, Iraq and South Korea. While my cover story is an eye doctor." Sudarsan tells Sai, "So, you don't have an private practice like you said you have." Sai tells Sudarsan, "I still have my private practice it is still in five miles from Fort Hood when they usually call me for analyst job." Sudarsan is disappointed that his son lied about who he is and tells Sai, "I am disappointed in you Sai. That you lied to me about this. That you work on dangerous that could've gotten you killed. Did you ever thought about your wife and your kids. Think about how you put them through."

Sai tells Sudarsan, "Susmita knows about me, that I am a CIA analyst and mostly my job is to get information on possible terrorist attacks. But my kids don't know I working as a spy and so does my other friends so I can protect them from safety from terrorist or international crime boss. Before they know about us or attack us." Sudarsan is not upset anymore and starts to understand since his father put him through the same thing. Sudarsan tells Sai, "How did Susmita take it, when you told her you were a CIA analyst." Sai tells Sudarsan, "She took it really well, since she works with me. Because when I was recruited by the CIA, I asked them to make an exception to work with me. They did, we travelled together and we have a live in nanny Lucy to watch the kids. So we are okay and yes Susmita does work as a pharmaceutical rep and the CIA creates a cover for her company as a traveling Pharmaceutical Rep where she sales FDA pills around the world for new accounts." Sudarsan tells Sai, "Why are you telling me now. I know the m.o. that you are not allowed to tell you who I am to protect me terrorist attacks. Why are you telling me now." Sai tells Sudarsan, "Because I need your help. Me and Susmita are retiring from the agency. I know you told me that you were an army medical doctor and you went to Vietnam as a medic there. But I found out you were green beret doing missions for them. I was upset that you lied to me about that you were an ex green beret and that you fought in missions that could have gotten you killed. I never asked why you and grandpa had a falling out. But I think it had to do with you taking out Vietnamese Congs soldiers out there and rescuing people who were held hostage out there. But you were a war hero. How come you never told me." Sudarsan tells Sai, "I'm not a guy who brags about my success. But I just wanted to be a regular guy. Yes, that is why me and your grandfather had a falling out. He was a strict pacifist, but I was a regular pacifist. In life and death situations, I would go out there and take a bullet for a little guy. I would take a bullet for you." Sai is really touched for a minute and Sudarsan continues telling Sai, "But my dad did not see that. I did everything I was told back then, but he never gave me any options or ask me what I wanted. He was okay with me going to medical school in America, but he did not want me to get killed in the Army. But I needed to make my own decisions and be my own person. So, I joined the green berets and I wanted to make a difference and help people. Which I did. I was upset too, you went behind my back too that you went to ROTC and joined the CIA. But you wanted to be your own person and make your own choices. Which I was supportive of and which I am now. I'm proud of you Son." Sai tells Sudarsan, "Thanks dad. But you wanted to ask why I told you now about who we are. Here's why." Sai takes out his cellphone from right pants pocket and go to email account and opens the photo of Khanthi Havaladar. Sai gives he cell phone to Sudarsan and grabs the cellphone from Sai. Sudarsan looks at the phone and sees his friend Khanthi being captured by terrorist. Sai tells Sudarsan, "Josh Wentz who is my CIA handler aka my boss has a dangerous mission for me and Susmita. He asked for your help us out." Sudarsan tells Sai, "This is a picture of Khanthi, he looks like he was being captured by terrorist." Sai tells Sudarsan, "Did you know he was in African somewhere in Congo." Sudarsan tells Sai, "Yes, he was their for Doctors with borders programs to help heal the sick. That he was going to be their for three weeks after our retirement." Sai tells Sudarsan, "He was captured by an terrorist who was led by an African warlord who was raided an African village. He was captured and so is the rest of the doctors and African villagers while they were their. This African warlord did not work alone, he was working for somebody above they ask for you." Sudarsan tells Sai, "Because of Dr Havaladar. They would not draw you out of the open if he was not their and I know you would rescue those villagers and those doctors too if they had ask for you." Sudarsan tells Sai, "They got Khanthi and man those poor villagers and those doctors. I want to help you guys, but I don't' know where to start. I been out of the green berets for a long time. But I want to ask did they ask my any ranson demands." Sai tells Sudarsan, "Just you, they sent this recording in the Pentagon to your old commanding officer General Rupert Rosenberg. He sent to my superior who works in the CIA too General Victor Stone so I can get it. They ask you find you and look for them. He will release the hostages. But the person on that recording did give out a time limit. But what I heard from his tone, we might start now and look for them. If we find them they release the hostages including Dr Havaladar."

Sudarsan tells Sai, "Mostly the CIA or the US government don't usually negotiate with terrorist. We don't ever negotiate with those bastards." Sai tells Sudarsan, "But I think we will have to make an exception. Besides they are not asking for money or plane out of the country. Even if we do find them and they release the hostages. It is more like a prisoner trade where you take their place so they can take someplace to execute you." Sudarsan tells Sai, "That is true, somebody who is working for that African Warlord wants me dead for something that I made him angry about. Now, he wants to kill me, and I wish I have my army records with me so I can figure out what missions I did." Sai tells Sudarsan, "Dad, I'm in the CIA, I can get you any records I need. But the guy on recording to find them." Sudarsan tells Sai, "What's the clue?" Sai tells Sudarsan, "Lan. That was the clue." Sudarsan remembers Lan and tells Sai, "I think I know what Lan is. It is not a place, it's a who. But I think I can tell you tomorrow. You said you have a team that can help us find Khanti and the rest of the hostages." Sai tells Sudarsan, "Yes, I do. Mostly we have a place where we can meet. Some place no one ever looks at." Sudarsan tells Sai, "Sai, tomorrow morning I will meet you at the place to meet your team and get my army records. I think I might know who Lan is." Sai tells Sudarsan, "Sure thing dad. I called my team before I got here, and Susmita is also going to meet us their tomorrow in our meeting?" Sudarsan tells Sai, "So where is this meeting place where you guys go at?" Sai tells Sudarsan, give me my phone number and I'll text you were to meet. Come on, the whole family is waiting for us. Remember not to say a word to mom, this is a top-secret mission. She can be in danger." Sudarrsan tells Sai, "Sure thing, do you always bring your gun with you everywhere you go." Sai tells Sudarsan, "No, I do not bring my gun everywhere I go. Only on missions and me and my team store our weapons in our secret place in the meeting. Me and Susmita would never bring our guns at home, that is where the kids would find it." Sudarsan tells Sai, "That sounds right." Sai gets up from his chair and Sudarsan gives him his phone. Sai texted Sudarsan the secret meeting place on his cell phone and when they have to meet them. Sai puts his wallet and cell phone back in their pockets and grabs his gun on the desk and puts it back on his pants. Sai opens the door and eixts the den. Sudarsan takes out his cell phone from his right pants pocket and looks at the text when and where to meet them. Sudarsan looks at the text and tells himself, "No way." In the morning Sudarsan parks his SUV van in the parking lot and exits the SUV and closes the door. Sudarsan sees the Outside entrance of the Dallas Public Library right across the parking lot. Sudarsan tells himself, "Interesting place to do a CIA meeting." Sudarsan heads to the entrance of the Dallas Public Library. Inside the library where Sudarsan enters the library and sees the elevator. Sudarsan heads to the elevator and goes inside the elevator. Sudarsan tells himself, Push the first-floor button five times." Sudarsan pushes the first-floor button five times. The elevator went down to the first floor and the elevator door opens when heads to the first floor. The elevator door opens and it's Sudarsan. Sudarsan exits the elevator and heads to the first floor and sees the door. On the other side the door is a top-secret CIA room where a table is with Sai, Susmita and two members of his team. The two members of the team are Lonnie Brazier who is a childhood friend of Sai. Both of went to ROTC together and recruited to the CIA together. Krishna Konijetti who is also a childhood friend of Sai that their parents are friends too. The door opens and it's Sudarsan. Sudarsan enters the first floor and sees Sai, Krishna, Lonnie and Susmita at the meeting table. Sai sees his father and tells him, "Hey Dad." Sudarsasn sees them and tells them, "Hi, son." Where Sai, Susmita, Krishna and Lonnie see him and they all wave at them. Sudarsan tells Sai, "How did you guys put this CIA headquarters in this library does the head librarian knows about this place." Sai tells Sudarsan, "CIA funded the library and asked me to run the librarian. But during my private practice, Jenny Ryan who is my second-in-command and assistant head librarian runs the library when I am not working. We kept the first floor under constructions so no one can get it." All of them tell Sudarsan, "Hello Dr Chavala." Sudarsan recognizes Sai's team and tells them, "Hey guys. Lonnie, Krishna is that you." Krishna tells Sudarsan, "Yes, it's me. Dr Chavala." All of them get up from their chairs and greet Sudarsan. Sudarsan tells Krishna, "Hey Krishna it's good to see you. I didn't know you were in the CIA. Lonnie, it's also good to see you. Sai, your friends are CIA agents. How did that happen. Susmita, Sai told me that you are also a CIA analyst too." Susmita tells Sudarsan, "Yes, I am Sudarsan. You were also a green beret and used to fought in Vietnam." Sudarsan tells Susmita, "Yes, I did." Susmita tells Sudarsan, "You've been out of the field for a long time. Can you still fight." Sudarsan tells Susmita, "I don't know, I been out of the field for a long time. I am kind of rusty. Maybe, a little training will help me with that." Lonnie tells Sudarsan, "I hope so." Sudarsan tells Lonnie, "Lonnie, Krishna, I haven't seen you guys since you graduated from medical school." Sudarsan hugs Lonnie for a minute and let's go. Lonnie tells Sudarsan, "Me, Sai and Krishna all went to ROTC. Mostly my parents and Krishna's parents supported us when we went to ROTC and when we got our commission." Krishna tells Sudarsan, "It's good to see you, Dr. Chavala." Sudarsan tells Krishna and Lonnie, "it's good to see you guys too. So, Krishna how is Missy and the kids." Krishna tells Sudarsan, "They're fine and doing well in Lexington Kentucky." Sudarsan tells Lonnie, "So Lonnie, how is your wife and the kids in St Louis." Lonnie tells Sudarsan," They're doing well." Sudarsan tells Lonnie, "That's great." Suduarsan hugs Krishna and let's go. Sudarsan tells Krishna, So, Krishna how is your father?" Krishna tells Sudarsan, "He's fine. He retired last year, and my parents went to London England for the summer." Sudarsan tells Krishna, "Your parents supported you for being in ROTC and did they know you guys are in the CIA?" Krishna tells Sudarsan, "No, they don't know we're in the agency. We are trying to protect our family. Rama is the only one who didn't go to ROTC when he attended UMKC medical school with us. My parents were still proud of my little brother and since he is practicing in L.A." Sudarsan tells them, "I guess me and Khanthi did the same thing when we joined ROTC. He became an army doctor and after he was discharged, he went to Maryville to run his private practice full time after he was done. So did Jaya when he left Army doctor behind too. I joined the green berets after I was done with my fellowship. Anyway, you guys know why I'm here." Krishna tells Sudarsan, "We're sorry about Dr Havaladar. That is the reason why we all are here." Sai tells Sudarsan, "Does Mrs Havaladar know about her husband being kidnapped and why she is not called the police or the national guard about this?" Sai tells Sudarsan, "She is India for a month visiting relatives. I don't think she doesn't know that her husband is been kidnapped by terrorist. Besides, even if she knew and called the Pentagon or the FBI there is nothing they can do about it. So, Lonnie, Krishna what did tell your wives?" Krishna tells Sudarsan, "I told Missy, I was going to medical conference in Dallas and staying with Sai's family. She understood and she and the kids are visiting their grandparents for two weeks." Lonnie tells Sudarsan, "Same thing I told my wife, that I also went to a medical conference here Mostly the guys who kidnapped him are like ghost." Lonnie tells Sudarsan, "Like mercenaries, that is why African warlords are mercenaries or crime bosses in Africa when they invade villages." Sudarsan tells them, "Exactly, it's time we get to work. Since you guys are grown up now. You can call me Sudarsan." Everyone told Sudarsan, "Okay." Sudarsan tells Sai, "Sai, you're the only one can call me Dad." Sai tells Sudarsan, "Okay, Pop!" Sudarsan tells them, "Okay guys, let's get to work. Sai, you have the file and the army records." Sai tells Sudarsan, "It's on the table." Sduarsan tells them, "Let's go." Sudarsan, Sai, Susmita, Krishna and Lonnie head to the table and sit down in their chairs and Sudarsan sees the files on the table and grabs it. Sudarsan starts reading the file and army records. Sudarsan tells them, "Nothing yet. I'm still looking." Sudarsan is still looking at his army recorders and still hasn't found anything. Sai tells Sudarsan, "Dad, you found him yet?" Sudarsan is still looking in the file and hasn't found anything yet. Susmita tells them, "What happens if Sudarsan doesn't find anything about this Lan guy. Mostly the army records are usually classified." Sai tells Susmita, "Those files we are reading are classified. But since the army is desperate to take down this unknown terrorist, since we are CIA, they are giving us whatever we need." Lonnie tells them, "Then we are back at square one." Sudarsan looks at the name Lan. Sudarsan was shocked to see who this Lan was. Sudarsan tells himself, "Oh no, that was him." Sai tells Sudarsan, "Dad, you okay. It's looks like you seen a ghost right in front of you, it's not Sam Wheat from Ghost." Sudarsan tells Sai, "It's worse than a ghost. I know who he is." Sudarsan flashes back in Vietnam, where Sudarsan was tied up like Clark Kent was in the pilot episode of Smallville like a scarecrow. General Lan used his sword to slash Sudarsan's stomach like an X and he was aching. Back in the present and Sudarsan tells them, "It was more than a ghost, more like I was in hell. It was my fifth mission in Vietnam War, where me and my crew rescued some missionaries who were captured Vietnam Military Congs while they were help the sick in Vietnam. They were captured by the cogs and tortured them and made them as slaves. Anyway, my crew went over to rescue them, they found us and captured us. We were only there for two weeks for being tortured. Sai the scars you have seen in my chest that look like an X." Sai tells Sudarsan, "You told me that was a birthmark." Sudarsan tells Sai, "Those were torture scars that I got from the Prison Camp Leader who wanted to spill where the military camp is at. I told them no; they tortured me for three weeks when me and my crew were captured in that prison camp. But I never spilled anything, they would have had to kill me if I could spill where the rest of the army is. Anyway, the Vietnam Congs were tired of torturing us, so they decided to execute us. I think we were about to done for, but General Rosenberg brought in the cavalry to save us. Lucky, I had a tracking device that the CIA built as a comb so it could be used as a tracking device. Anyway, I got out. But I found the leader of the comb, who tortured me. We started fighting for a minute, there was a gun right next to me on the floor after he beat the snot out of me for three minutes, so I blocked the kick and kneed him in the stomach. I distracted long enough to grab the gun on the ground that was dropped and pick it up and shot before he took out his gun. I helped get the rest of the crew and the missionaries out on time before any of us spilled. Part of our mission wasn't just to rescue the missionaries but take down their weapon that were rocket launches to attack our military base. That is why they needed it and destroyed it. Anyway, the mission was a successful. But I never did let go of the guy who tortured me and killed." Sai tells Sudarsan, "Who was the guy?" Sudarsan tells them, "General Anh Lan is the guy who tried to be killed me." Sai tells Sudarsan, "Wow, I can't believe those were battle scars, not a birthmark. I'm sorry that happened to you." Sudarsan tells Sai, "It's okay, I was fine. It took three months of therapy with the Army shrink to work on my PSTD." Susmita tells Sudarsan, "Are you sure he's dead. What if he's still alive." Sudarsan tells Susmita, "Trust me, he's dead. The army sent a couple of planes to nuke the camp while he was still in there. Trust me, he is dead." Lonnie tells them, "Okay, suppose he's dead. Did General Lan had children or a family." Krishna tells them, "Possibly, mostly I think Lan probably hid his family off the grid to protect them from any harm. Even if he did have a family, they're family probably be classified to keep them low key so no one can find them." Sai tells them, "Too us, nothing here is classified. I'll get my laptop." Sai gets up from his chair and exits the table and gets his laptop from the computer room. Sudarsan tells them, "If Lan does have any family, he probably will be out here planning their revenge. Explains why you guys need me and hired you guys. The CIA and the government want to keep it low key, so no one knows that they exist. It would be bad press if anyone knew about Lan. It could start another war if they knew he was around and terrorize our country." Lonnie tells them, "Guys, I don't Lan relative wouldn't just kidnap Dr Havaladar just to lure you out of the shadows so he can kill you to justice for General Lan. I think there is something else." Sudarsan tells them, "I think the only way Lan's relative is covering his tracks, he has a rogue CIA on his payroll to cover his tracks and he's planning on something big. Not just to kill me, but something bigger. It's like he's killing two birds in one stone." Sai gets back from the computer room and brings his laptop on the table with a battery that is connecting to an outlet. Sai tells Susmita, "Susmita can you plug the laptop for me." Susmita tells Sai, "Sure thing." Susmita sees the plug on the floor and grabs the plug on the floor. Susmita gets up from her chair and sees the outlet and starts pluging the laptop. Sai turns on the helicopter and looks up at General Danh Lan. Sai found him and tells them, "Sai, I found him." Lonnie tells Sai, "What's its Sai?" Sai tells them, "General Anh Lan was in Hong Kong for R and R with his Vietnam Congs buddies in 1950, where he met the daughter Sun Lee, whose father runs the Chinese Triad in Hong Kong that in a nightclub and hotel where he stayed and fell in love with. Mostly the Chongs, were practically feared in Hong Kong. Anyway, Sun Lee Chong and Lan went back and forth in Hong Kong to Vietnam seeing each other. Mostly Sun Lee was pro North Vietnamese and a communist who hated the South Vietnamese, and they think they were weak. In 1974, during the Vietnam war the Chong triads smuggled weapons for the North Vietnamese and Sun Lee was pregnant at that time. General Lan was killed during the prison camp war riot where his crew captured missionaries until the US Army rescued and took down Lin and nuke the camp after rescuing the missionaries. That was all in the classified files, some say Sui Lin gave birth to Lan's child and left China for a long time. No one knows where they are. Since Sun Lee Chong wanted Lan to destroy the US military base so America can surrender, and Sui Lan can control America with an iron fist. But that's just a theory. But the other stuff is true." Sudarsan tells them, "Well, I think I know how Sun Lee has been smuggling military weapons for the North Vietnamese, is by having a rogue CIA agent in their payroll." Krishna tells them, "We don't know who this rogue CIA agent is, they could be anyone. Besides that, is why the CIA wants to keep it low key. It could be headline and might ruin their reputation if they found out one of their own is working for Chinese Triad Leader and selling weapons to the enemy in Vietnam." Sudarsan looks at the file, "I don't think our rogue CIA agent didn't just sell weapons to North Vietnamese Congs, but the rogue agent also sold weapons to Al-Qaeda." Sai tells Sudarsan, "Al-Qaeda, thee Al-Qaeda that Osama Bin Laden ran back then." Sudarsan tells them, "CIA never had any proof, neither did defense department had any proof to link our rogue CIA agent for selling weapons to terrorist." Sai tells them, "Luckily we won that war and stopped Al-Qaeda from terrorizing our troops and before they came to our country to invade it." Sudarsan keeps looking at the files and tells them, "I think they might be rumors that the rogue CIA agent might be selling weapons to an Iraq terrorist team who used to fight in Al-Qaeda." Lonnie tells them, "If there is an Iraq terrorist team who is getting buy stolen weapons and use it to resurrect Al-Qaeda." Sai looks at his laptop and did some research on Lin. Sai tells them, "Good news I think I found a Sun Lee Chong here in Dallas. I don't know if it's the right person, but we must find out." Susmita tells them, "Sui Lin here, you know what that means?" Krishna tells them, "What is that?" Susmita tells them, "That means Sui Lin might be alive and might be running some illegal operation somewhere in Dallas." Sai tells Susmita, "I don't think so, honey this Sun Lee runs a nightclub and restaurant called the Black Dragon in China Town. She passed away two years ago and left it to his son Walter. Walter Chong's father is unknown or out of the picture and graduated from the Unicersity of Texas medical school and enrolled in ROTC and got his commission their and worked his way up to Major Walter Chong as an army medical doctor. There are rumors that he is M.I.A when he went to Doctors without Borders in Congo." Sudarsan tells them, "Congo, that is where Khanthi is at. Are you sure this Sun Lee Chong has no connections to Triads in Hong Kong." Lonnie looks at the file and tells them, "There were rumors that Dallas P.D. was investigating a heroin operation five years ago and that Sun Lee's ran the operation. But Dallas P.D. had any proof that Sun Lee never linked to heroin dealing that the cops tried to bust Dallas Harbor five years ago. So, Dallas P.D. has nothing when everything in that harbor was gone." Sudarsan tells Lonnie, "I think this might be our Sun Lee Chong, besides she may be dead. But her son might be running the show. I don't think it is no coincidence, that Khanthi and Walter did run into each other in the Congo just like that. I know Walter might be working for an African Warlord. Anything about those guys." Sai looks at his laptop, "Not yet, just like Sun Lee and his son, they are not connected to any arms deal or working with an African Warlord. Since all of them are off the grid." Sudarsan tells them, "If Walter was the mastermind behind the kidnapping and he might be the guy who might selling guns and weapons to a terrorist team in Iraq." Susmita tells Sai, "Sai, can you find anything about this Iraqi and that the CIA is trying to look for." Sai trying to research them on the internet and cannot find anything. Sai tells them, "I can't find anything in him, the way I look. I think they maybe a rumor that a rogue CIA agent was trying to sell weapons an Iraqi and terrorist team who used to fought in Al Q Qaeda. Trying to resurrect it. But I don't think this Chong is selling military weapons to an Iraqi and terrorist team. But I think he might be selling weapons to an African Warlord and his team to raid African villages and trying to be the new Al Qaeda. But I could be wrong." Sudarsan is thinking and tells Sai, "Sai, I think you might be right. I think the hostages might be here in Dallas. We don't have any proof of that. But Chong does need me to be out in the open. He's not MIA, he's keeping himself off the grid so we can't find him. But if the Black Dragon in Chinatown is still running. I think we should pay a visit someone who is running the show in the Black Dragon if it's still running and maybe we should go over to piss them for a minute." Sai tells Sudarsan, "You're right Dad, but one problem?" Sudarsan tells Sai, "What's that?" Sai tells himself, "Whatever we do, they are not going to talk to CIA team who are posing as doctors. So, if someone is running the Black Dragon in Walter's Place, I think we should go talk to the person. Maybe make them angry, so that way Walter can come out and hiding." Sudarsan tells Sai, "I think I like that idea, but I think whoever is running the black dragon is going to talk to some doctors. Since we are going in master in disguise." Sai tells them, "I think we should talk to the new boss who is taking Walter's place in the Black Dragon. I think the weapons that the Chong is selling must be stolen. So, they must have hi-jacked it. Here's the plan. Dad, you, and I are going to Black Dragon talk to new boss and ask him about the arms deal with African Warlord. Susmita, Krishna, and Lonnie, I need you to find any companies that are building military weapons for the army and see if they were anything stolen for a couple. Susmita tells Sai, "Okay, no problemo." Sudarsan tells them, "That's it for the day, will meet back here and see if we can find anything." All of them tell Sudarsan, "Okay!" Sudarsan, Susmita, Sai, Lonnie, and Krishna get up from the chairs and exit the CIA room on the first floor in the Dallas Public Library. Outside the Black Dragon night club where Sudarsan's car is parked in the parking lot across the Black Dragon in Chinatown. Sai and Sudarsan exit the car wearing suits and Sudarsan is carrying a briefcase. Sai and Sudarsan go inside the Black Dragon nightclub. Sai and Sudarsan enter the nightclub and see the club empty during the day. Sai and Sudarsan seeing the bartender cleaning up the bar table. Sai and Sudarsan go over talk to bartender. The bartender sees them and tells them, "Hi, can I help you?" Sudarsan tells the bartender, "It's kind of slow today." The bartender tells Sudarsan, "We don't open the place in 10 minutes. So, what can I do for you gentlemen,, since you guys did not come all the way early to have a drink. Sudarsan tells the bartender, "We were here to meet Mr Walter Chong, he called us two months ago, if he wants to donate money for our charity." The bartender tells Sudarsan, "Mr Chang is out of town, he went to volunteer as a missionary in Congo in Africa. Mostly, I heard on the news that he was missing and nobody knows where he is. There were rumors that he was being kidnapped by some terrorist, but that was just rumor. I think he got lost somewhere in Africa." Sai tells the bartender, "Is he is missing, did they call a search party to find him." The bartender tells them, "They did, but they are still looking for him. Anyway, what is the charity you wanted Mr Chong to donate?" Sudarsan tells the bartender, "Mr Chong called us two months ago, to see if he wants to donate money to help the kids from Congo who is sick and needs medical supplies. The Red Cross has a new fund called Congo Cancer Relief and they want to donate money and medicine to African tribes in the Congo." The bartender tells Sudarsan, "I did not remember, Mr Chong wanted to donate money Congo Cancer Relief." Sudarsan tells the bartender, He called us two months ago and wanted to donate money to the charity anonymous. Mr Chong wants to keep a low profile. Since he is not here, I guess we can come back when Mr Chong returns from the Congo when the search party finds him." The bartender tells Sudarsan,, "Mr Chong maybe gone, but his bar manager Mr Abebi is here" Sai tells the bartender, "We wanted to speak to Mr Chong, since he is not here, I guess we can come back later when he is found." The bartender tells them, "Mr. Abebi was in the missionary with him, he got out safety and Mr. Chong sacrificed himself so Mr. Abebi can come to Dallas, and he asked him to manage his company while he was away and he Mr Abebi would love to donate money for your charity in Mr. Chong's absence." Sudarsan tells the bartender, "That is great, is Mr. Abebi here or he hasn't arrived yet?" The bartender tells them, "Mr. Abebi is here in the club, I'll call him in his office and let him know you're here." Abebi is working in his office and Sudarsan and Sai does not know that he is leader of the African terrorist team, until he hears the phone ring. Abebi answers the phone and tells the bartender on the other side of the phone, "What is it Cal?" Cal voiceover tells Abebi,

"There are two men who wanted to see Mr. Chong, but I told them you are running the business in his absence since he is missing in Congo during the missionary." Abebi tells Cal on the phone, "That's good, what do you want to see Mr. Chong about or me since I'm managing the business." Cal tells Abebi on the phone, "These two men are from the charity called Congo Cancer Relief and Mr. Chong called them about two months ago and about donating money for their charity drive. So, what do you want to do, Mr. Abebi?" Abebi is considering tossing them out, but since they said from Congo Cancer Relief, that does feel strange and wants to know about them. Cal on the phone tells Abebi, "So Mr Abebi should I throw them out and tell them to never come back." Abebi tells Cal, "Send them in, I need a word with him." Back in the bar where Cal tells Sai and Sudarsan, "Mr Abebi will see you now." Sudarsan tells Cal, "Thanks buddy, maybe after we meet Abebi, we can come down here and get some beer." Cal tells them, "Hey, no problemo. What kind of beer you guys want before you see Mr. Abebi." Sai tells Cal, "We'll take two miller lites." Cal goes over to the fridge behind the bar table and takes out two bottles of Miller Lites and puts them on the table. Sai tells Cal, "How much?" Cal tells them, "The beer is on me, guys." Sai tells Cal, "Thanks, I appreciate that." Sai and Sudarsan grabs miller lite bottles and open them and Sai and Sudarsan start drinking their beer and stops. Sudarsan tells Cal, "Where's Mr. Abebi's office, anyway?" Cal tells Sudarsan, "It's upstairs." Sudarsan tells Cal, "Thank you." Sudarsan and Sai put the Miller Lite bottles down and exited the bar table and head upstairs. Abebi is still working in his office and hears the door knock. Abebi tells the person on the other side of the door, "Come in." The door opens and Sudarsan and Sai enter Abebi's office. Sudarsan and Sai go over talk to Abebi. Abebi gets up from his chair and goes over to Sudarsan and Sai and talks to them. Abebi tells Sudarsan and Sai, So, you guys are from the Congo Cancer Relief program. Sudarsan tells Abebi, "Yes sir, "Dr Sudarsan Chavala and this is my son Dr Sai Chavala." Abebi tells them, "It's pleasure to meet you gentlemen, I'm Joffe Abebi, I'm the club owner of the Black Dragon." Abebi shakes their hands and let's go. Abebi tells them, why don't you gentlemen have a seat and let's talk about this charity that Mr

Chong wanted to donate money from Congo Cancer Relief." Sudarsan tells Abebi, "Sure thing." Abebi goes back to his chair and sits down. Sai and Sudarsan sit down in their chairs. Sudarsan puts down his briefcase on the floor. Abebi tells them, "So, gentlemen tell me about that Congo Cancer Relief." Sudarsan tells Abebi, "Mr Abebi, before I start how does an African American guy runs a nightclub in Chinatown." Abebi tells Sudarsan, "Well Dr Chavala, I'm just an acting Club Owner while Mr Chong gets back from the Congo and still M.I.A. and runs his club until his return. We formed a huge search party for him in Africa and trust me he is not easy to find." Sai tells Abebi, "So, Mr Abebi how did you end up running Mr Chong club in his absence." Abebi tells Sai, "I came to America two years ago and my Uncle Abeeku lives in Dallas and let me stay with him. He's the one who paid and sponsored me to come to America. I got a job here as a bartender in Black Dragon when they had an opening. Mr Chong mother used to own the place and she passed away two years ago and Mr Chong needed some help. He gave me the job and I worked there for six months and knew I did a good job and he promoted me to bar manager. We were like best friends, and he was a surrogate brother to me." Sai tells Abebi, "Your bartender said that you went to the Congo in a missionary with Mr Chong." Abebi tells Sai, "Yeah, Mr Chong has always been a good humanitarian. I asked him if I come with him and help him out. I was from Congo, and I knew the area forwards and backwards. So, he let me come." Sudarsan grabs his briefcase and takes a brochure of Congo Cancer Relief program. Sudarsan closes the briefcase and puts his briefcase down on the floor. Sudarsan shows Abebi the brochure of Congo Cancer Relief and gives it to Abebi. Abebi grabs the brochure and looks at it for a minute. Sudarsan tells Abebi, "Congo Cancer Relief charity has to do with an African Tribe that the natives are getting sick. Some of it, mostly some of it usually brain, throat, and ovary cancer. The worse disease they have Hodgkin's in that tribe. My friend formed this charity two years ago, he was raising a lot of money to help the sick and find a cure for a lot of cancers. If there was a cure for cancers any scientist or doctor would find it. My friend who started this company really wanted to raise a lot of money to help this African tribe." Abebi tells Sudarsan, So what is the name of this African tribe that the charity is helping raising money to cure the cancers from?" Sudarsan tells Abebi, "I think it was called Luba." Sai tells Abebi, "A week ago, I heard there were terrorist or what do you call outlaws called in Africa. We call it an African Warlord who loves to terrorize villages and tried to make tribes or countries to surrender to them. This African Warlord was terrorizing the Luba village and I don't think they were not just ransacking or robbing the place. I think they were looking for someone to kidnap and needed to lure someone out of the open. But hey it was just a rumor. So, Abebi, you family must have been members of the Luba tribe and I bet you saved a lot of money and get a lot of pull to immigrate America. Good thing, your uncle got you in. You probably be stuck in the border all day." Abebi laughs for a minute and Abebi tells Sai, "Yeah, lucky me." Sudarsan tells Abebi, "It must have been cool to volunteer with Mr Chong. When those African terrorists terrorizing the Luba village, I always think about where they get their weapons. Like those machine guns or those grenades, I don't think you get those on the black market, I bet you somebody was funding the operation and probably stole those weapons from a defense company that was building weapons for the Army. I sure that company is going to lose a lot of money and probably out of business if those weapons were not delivered and the worse part that the guy who is funding the African Warlord is probably a rival company. Do you know Mr Chong, just owns this night club. He also owns a multinational company called Chong Industries that runs a high-tech company and builds weapons for the military. I guess that rival company beat Chong Industries from building new weapons that would made the company billions. It's just my theory." Abebi laughs for a minute and gets suspicious. Abebi tells Sai, "Really how about that. Mr Chong family does own a multinational company in Hong Kong and I'm sure Mr Chongs family is upset they lost a billion-dollar account from the US army. But Mr Chong just runs the nightclub here and his family manages the billion-dollar company in Hong Kong." Sai tells Mr Abebi, "Yeah, I guess they must build some new weapons or build another computer or website for their company. Besides I'm sure Chong Industries is not connected to the Triads who are the Black

Dragons who are vicious criminals who is not running a drug or arms dealing empire in Hong Kong and no way they would steal their rivals' weapons and sell it to a terrorist team who might the African Warlord who might need it to take down African tribes and Army bases with it. I'm sure Mr Chong is not arms leader Kingpin who was working with an African Warlord to terrorize an African village and kidnap someone to lure someone out in the open who is the friend of the guy who killed his father who was the leader of North Vietnamese Cong like Anh Lan, who held some missionaries hostage in Vietnam in 1975 and some green beret who was doctor at the time who killed his father while rescuing hostages from that prison camp and nuked it to save everyone. The worst part is that this General might have a family who might out for revenge against this ex green beret and this doctor like a nephew or a son. But that's not going to happen. So anyway, Mr Abebi I want to know if you're club wants to donate some money for Congo Cancer Relief. It is a good cause to help that Luba tribe get all the medicine they need." Mr. Abebi tells them, "Mr. Chong sacrificed himself from that African Warlord and his posse from terrorizing you and risked his life to save me and other missionaries in that village to save us. I owed him my life, so I would do whatever it too took to save those missionaries and Mr Chong. He left me in charge while he is missing in action, and he said that he was going to donate money to your charity." Sudarsan tells Abebi, "That's right." Abebi tells them, "Well, I guess in Mr Chong's place, I will donate 30 million dollars for your cause. I will mail the check to your charity organization in a few days." Sudarsan tells Abebi, "Well thank you Mr. Abebi, I appreciate that, I'm going to make sure that the 30 million dollars will go into name of Mr Chong. I want to thank you for donating money for the Congo Cancer Relief and on behalf of the Luba tribe is proud to have a great guy like Mr. Chong and you helping the tribe out. There are a lot of sick people out their tribe who love your generosity and saving their lives so thank you and Mr Chong in the bottom of our heart." Abebi tells them, "Hey, no problemo." Sai and Sudarsan shake Abebi shakes hands with them for a minute and let's go. Abebi tells them, "Like I said the check will be mailed to you in three days to your organization." Sudarsan tells Abebi,

"Thank you." Sai and Sudarsan get up from their chairs and Sudarsan grabs his briefcase from the floor. Sudarsan tells Abebi, "It was nice talking to you, Mr Abebi." Abebi tells them, "It was nice talking to guys too." Sai and Sudarsan head to the door and open it and exits the Abebi's office and closes the door. Abebi smiles for a minute and stops when he gets suspicious about who those guys are. Outside the Black Dragon nightclub Sai and Sudarsan head to the car. Sudarsan tells Sai, "You think he bought it?" Sai tells Sudarsan, "Well, I don't know, Dad. I think one or two days, he might figure out who we are and send in a couple of guys to kill us." Sudarsan tells Sai, "Just hope it does not come to that." Back in Abebi's office and getting very suspicious Sai and Sudarsan and picks up the phone and makes a call. Abebi tells the person from the other phone, "Cal, do you have a security camera in my office. You do, get the DVD out of the camera. We must go see Chong." Back in the Dallas Public Library in the CIA room where Susmita is playing video games in the laptop. Krishna and Lonnie arrive in the CIA room. Krishna is carrying two pepperoni pizzas and one vegetarian pizza in Pizza Hut. Lonnie is carrying a case of 24oz diet pepsi and five miller lite beers. Krishna tells Susmita, "Hey Susmita!" Susmita turns around and sees Krishna and Lonnie carrying the food. Krishna tells Susmita, "We've got the pizzas and beer and diet pepsi for us." Susmita tells them, "All right, I'm hungry. We got to save some food for Sai and Sudarsan." Krishna tells Susmita, "Don't worry, I have one pepperoni pizza for me and Lonnie and another pepperoni pizza for Sudarsan and Sai." Susmita tells Krishna, "So Krishna, you have my pizza too?" Krishna tells Susmita, "One vegetarian pizza for you and some 24oz diet pepsi and beer for us." Susmita tells them, "Good, I'm hungry." Susmita gets up from his chair and sits down on the table where Krishna and Lonnie join her where all three of them sits down in their chairs and put their food on the table. Krishna opens the pizza box where the pepperoni is at, and Susmita opens her pizza box that has vegetarian pizza that she wanted. Susmita grabs a miller lite bottle and opens and starts drinking the beer. While Lonnie and Krishna are eating their pizzas. Krishna tells Susmita, "You found any defense companies that their weapons were stolen or carjacked anytime this week." Susmita tells Krishna, "I found a few companies that build weapons for the military. But I did find one company that had weapons was being delivered to US army to the pentagon about a week ago. But the delivery van was carjacked, and the weapons were also stolen and two of the drivers were dead after they were carjacked by their van by some unknown assailants that the Dallas Police Department couldn't identify." Lonnie tells Susmita, "What was that name of the company that was carjacked?" Susmita tells Lonnie, "It was Ryantech Industries that was carjacked Lonnie." Lonnie tells Susmita, "Susmita, any idea what Ryantech was building?" Susmita tells Lonnie, "Mostly the weapons they were building were top secret, because they're being corporate might steal their ideas, after the van was carjacked. I got a hold of the company, they said they were building new USAF M16 rifle guns and grenades for the US army. They beat out a rival company for a military contract for those guns and grenades. Mostly the US army paid them 500 million dollars to build those weapons." Krishna tells them, "With that military contract, the stocks would hit the roof and made Ryantech billions of dollars." Susmita tells them, "Exactly, so I think Chong company might be the rival company that stole those weapons and puts them out of business and use it to sell those weapons that Ryantech would build to that African warlord to invade those African villages and make them surrender." Susmita tells them, "They may connect Ryantech weapons to those invasions and worse the media will blame those weapons were used for terrorism. The media won't care if those weapons were stolen." Lonnie tells them, "I bet the US army is going to cancel their military contract since those weapons are not going to be delivered on time." Krishna tells Susmita, "How long does the US army are going to hold that military contract to Ryantech before they cancel it?" Susmita tells Krishna, "They're going to hold the contract until Sunday, if those weapons they are going to delivered during the due date, they will send the contract to their rival company Chong industries." Krishna tells them, "It's going to bankrupt the company without those military contracts." Susmita tells them, "I'm going to call Sai and Sudarsan and tells them what's going on. But what worse part is if they were going to hide the weapons and hostages. Chong must have an operation somewhere to hide Ryantech weapons and hostages before they sell it to those African Warlords. First, we have to find their operation and the meet where they going to sell those weapons and the hostages for their execution to make an example if those villagers don't surrender." Lonnie tells Susmita, "Chong operation and his drop could be anywhere. So, it would take a miracle to find them." Susmita tells Lonnie, "Lonnie, we have a unknown source aka a friend that can help us find Chong's operation and the drop. But first, I must contact Sai and let him know what's going on first." Back in downtown Dallas where Sai is driving Sudarsan's car and Sudarsan is in the passenger seat in Dallas traffic. Sudarsan's phone rings and tells Sai, "It's mine." Sudarsan grabs his phone out of his right pants pocket and answers the phone. Sudarsan tells the person who is on the other end of the phone, "Hello, hey Susmita." Sudarsan looks at Sai and tells him, "It's Susmita, she found the company that Chong Industries was rivals with and the weapons they stole from?" Sai tells Sudarsan, "What was the name of the company that the weapons were stolen from?" Sudarsan tells Susmita on the phone, "What was the name of the company? Oh man, okay. Thanks a lot Susmita. Will be back in the library in an hour." Sudarsan hangs up his phone and tells Sai, "The name of the company that built those USAF M16 rifle guns and grenades for the US army is Ryantech Industries. Their van was carjacked a week ago and killed the drivers who was delivering the weapons to the Army by some unknown assailant." Sai tells Sudarsan, "I bet it was Chong's company. His company is in Hong Kong. Mostly I know Chong calls the shots here in Dallas Nightclub while his billion dollar is in Hong Kong. We know Chong is the biggest Triad guy in Dallas that people fear of." Sudarsan tells Sai, "Let me guess, Dallas P.D. has no proof that anyone in Chong's company is connected to the driver's death and the stolen weapons." Sai tells Sudarsan, "Exactly, we were going to head back to the library and figure out our next plan." Sudarsan tells Sai, "Well first, we got a bigger problem." Sai tells Sudarsan, "What's that?" Sudarsan tells Sai, "First the Dallas P.D. or the FBI has no proof that Chongs company is connected to the robberies or the kidnappings. Since they want me, and they want me to find them. The ransom demand and clue are just a trap to find them to ambush me and kill me. Chong would never leave that clue behind of Lan, unless he wants to find him, so he can kill me." Sai tells Sudarsan, "Dad, trap or no trap. Dr Havaladar been kidnapped, Mrs Havaladar is going to get worried what happened to her husband. We owe it to Dr Havaladar to find him." Sudarsan tells Sai, "I know Sai. Khanthi did a lot for me. So, I owe him a lot. We are going to find him. I don't care what Chong does to me. We will find him, and I will stop Chong. Because his father was a war criminal that hurt innocent people. I am not going to let scumbags like Chong get away with it." Sai tells Sudarsan, "So don't we should head back to the library and head back to the library and figure out our next move." Sudarsan tells Sai, "Not yet. Susmita asked me if they were hiding the hostages and the stolen weapons somewhere. Chong must have an operation somewhere. But I don't have any sources that can help me in Dallas." Sai tells Sudarsan, "I know a guy, who can help us." Sudarsan tells Sai, "Who's that. I'll tell you on the way." Inside the warehouse where Chong's men are hiding guns in crates and filling it with yellow mustard. The garage door opens, and a limousine enters the warehouse where Chong's men are inside hiding weapons for their meeting with their clients the African Warlords. The limousine stops and the door opens and it's Abebi and Cal exiting the limousine and Cal closes the limousine door. Abebi is carrying a dvd in his left hand. These see the warehouse office upstairs where Chong and his CIA inside guy are at. Abebi tells Cal, "Come on. Let's go, the boss is waiting for us." Cal and Abebi heads upstairs and goes over to see Chong and his CIA inside guy." Inside Chong's office where he's working in his desk and his CIA inside guy is sitting down in his chair." Chong tells his CIA inside guy, "All right, Nate you got the arrangements with Bobo?" Nate tells Chong, "Yes sir, everything is ready for their arrival. I pulled a lot of strings to get Bobo here to make the drop." Chong tells Nate, "Excellent." The door knocks and Chong tells the person on the other side of the door. Chong tells the person on the other side of the door, "Come in." The door opens and it's Abebi and Cal who enter the warehouse office. Cal closes the door and Chong tells Abebi, "What is it Abebi?" Abebi tells Chong, "I got a dvd to show you, there were two guys in my office who asked the questions about you. I told them that you were MIA and lost in the Congo." Chong tells Abebi, "Who are these two guys?" Abebi tells Chong, "There were two Indian guys, I'll show you." Abebi has the dvd on his left hand. Abebi goes over to the laptop and opens the DVD slot and plays the DVD where Sudarsan and Sai are asking questions to Abebi. Abebi tells Chong, "That's the one who asked me about it and knows about us stealing stolen weapons from our rival Ryantech and put them out of business. He knows about the hostages we stole and our main hostage Dr Khanthi Havaladar to lure out his friend Dr. Sudarsan Chavala." Cal tells Chong, "Mr Chong, do you think that old guy, might be Sudarsan Chavala. The guy you wanted to kill." Chong gets up from his chair and goes to Cal and tells him, "Cal, do you know the two main characters from toy story?" Chong tells Cal, "Yeah, it's Buzz Lightyear and…? Oh, no." Chong tells Cal, "Woody!" Chong punches Cal in the penis. Cal is moaning and Chong gives Cal a roundhouse kick to the face. Cal falls down on the floor moaning. Abebi laughs for a minute and Chong is upset and Chong gives Abebi a roundhouse kicks in the stomach and grabs his shirt and toss him into the floor. Both Abebi and Cal are moaning on the floor. Cal tells Chong, "What was that for?" Chong tells Cal, "Nobody speaks until they are spoken for you little shit. Next time, it'll be a lot worse shitface." Abebi tells Chong, "Why did I do it? I didn't say anything?" Chong tells Abebi, "To give you a warning next time you question my authority or do not speak until you are spoken too. Now get up. We got a lot of work to do." Chong heads back to his chair and sits down. Abebi and Cal get up from the floor and they are still moaning. Chong tells them, "We got to find out if this is Sudarsan Chavala and I don't know who this guy is. Nate, call some of your CIA contacts and find out who these two gentlemen are." Nate tells Chong, "Yes sir boss!" Nate sees the phone and grabs it. Nate picks up the phone and makes a call. Nate tells his CIA contact, "Hello Rudy, listen I need a favor." Nate continues to call Rudy on the phone and stops for a minute. Nate tells Chong, "Mr. Chong it would take twenty minutes to id the two guys and they'll fax us the information us when they are done." Chong tells Nate, "Tell them to get started." Nate is still calling Rudy. Inside TK's Place where

Sai and Sudarsan enter the comedy club and sees TK sitting down in his chair in his bar. Sudarsan tells Sai, "Who is this TK guy?" Sai tells Sudarsan, "He's the guy who owns the comedy club here in Dallas. It's the most popular comedy club and most of the top comics play here like David Spade and Chris Rock." Sudarsan tells Sai, "How's the comedy club owner is going to help us find Chong's operation and his drop?" Sai tells Sudarsan, "His father used to be CIA agent and is also promoted to CIA deputy director. TK can get access to anything he needs or any information that he can find. Mostly his father has friends in the DOJ and the FBI. Any CIA agent need anything or find anything, TK is your guy." Sudarsan tells Sai, "Around." Sudarsan looks at Sai for a minute and tells Sudarsan, "He was my patient two years ago. He figured out I was CIA when I recommend Laser eye surgery if he does not wear glasses full time. He didn't want to, because glasses makes him more smarter. So, he told me about his father and I told him that I work as a CIA analyst and gave him anything he needs and wants. Someday, I owe him a favor. The favor was the advice that he should continue wearing glasses to make him smarter. So, he owes me one." Sudarsan tells Sai, "By the way, what does TK stand for?" Sai tells Sudarsan, "Tommy Knox, Tommy is his first name and Knox is his last name." Sudarsan tells Sai, "Interesting." Sai and Sudarsan goes over to the bar and talks to TK. TK sees Sai and Sudarsan. Sai and Sudarsan headed to the bar and talks to TK. TK tells Sai, "Hey Sai, it's good to see you." TK shakes Sai's hand for a minute and let's go. Sai tells TK, "It's good to see you too, TK." TK tells Sai, "So Sai, who is your friend?" Sai sarcastically tells TK, "Oh, did I tell you that I am gay. I was in the closet for a long time. I decided it is time to come out. I am going to tell Susmita the truth and I think we will be getting divorced soon and marry my boyfriend Sudarsan after me and Susmita divorce is final. But it will be devasted to the kids." Tk starts laughing for a minute and stops. TK tells Sai, "Funny, cute but funny. You should use that in Open mic night on Tuesday." Sai tells TK, "This is my father Dr Sudarsan Chavala." TK shakes Sudarsan hand and tells Sudarsan, "It's a pleasure to meet you Sudarsan. You're son is really funny." Sudarsan tells TK, "I'm sure he could be the next Kal Penn if his private practice didn't get in the way. Anyway, we need your help?" TK tells them, "What do you need?" Sai tells TK, "You've heard of Walter Chong?" TK tells Sai, "He owns a huge nightclub in Chinatown called the Black Dragon. Sudarsan tells TK, "I think the nightclub is run by Black Dragon triad that is run by him. We figure out he is running an arms deals that he stole the weapons from his competitor called Ryantech and he is going to use to sell the weapons to a terrorist team who leader is an African Warlord. They are goanna arrive in a week to sell the weapons to them." Sai tells TK, "It's another thing about Walter Chong, Walter Chong is an alias called Anh Lan Jr. Whose father is North Vietnamese Cong General named Anh Lan Jr who was a general of that army, he led a prison camp in Vietnam. His son took hostages from an African village from the Congo called Luba to lure my father out here." TK tells them, "Why would Chong to lure you out here?" Sudarsan tells TK, "One of the main hostages is a friend of mine called Dr Khanthi Havaladar. We were childhood friends in India. He was in Luba African village to volunteer for the Doctors without Borders for a few weeks an African Warlords gang invaded the village. The main reason why the African Warlords men were there to capture Khanthi and we find out they were working is Walter Chong who was actually their as a missionary. But the missionary was fake, he was planning on going there to get his men ready to kidnap some doctors, African natives and my friend to get me out of hiding. So he can find me and kill me. This was part of his vengeance to kill me and avenge his father." TK tells Sudarsan, "Why does Chong want to kill you?" Sudarsan tells TK, "I was an ex-green beret and one of my mission was to rescue some missionaries who were in Vietnam village to help the sick. North Vietnamese Congs raided the village and capture the missionaries and they were planning to execute them and they were led Chong's father Anh Lan Sr who was the general of the army. My green beret team went there to rescue the hostages, but we were ambushed and I was captured there for two weeks in that prison camp until my general send out another rescue team. I got out and rescued the hostages and took out Chong's father after a huge beatdown. After I rescued the hostages, the mission was a success. But I still battle scars from it when Lan tortured me for two weeks before he killed me." TK tells Sudarsan, "That must have been." Sudarsan tells TK, "I got through it after a couple of months therapy and I was ready to do another mission." Sai tells TK, "Anyway we need you help us find the Dr Havaladar and the hostages. Chong has an operation somewhere where he's keeping the hostages and storing Ryantech weapons so he can sell it to African Warlord who will be in town this week to buy the weapons to raid other villages in Africa to surrender. The worse part once the deal is completed they are going to kill the hostages before the African warlord to start the invasion. So, that is why were here, we need you to help us find Chong's operation and his drop where the deal is going to be at. I know Chong didn't work alone, since the only way he covered his tracks. I think he is working for a rogue CIA agent. Can you help us find the rogue CIA agent and find his operation and his drop." TK tells them, "Sure, no problemo. It will take my day to call my father and get the information you need. I will give you guys a call tomorrow, when my father call my for the information." Sai tells TK, "Thank you, any information you find. You can call my wife Susmita or email the information you need when you get it from your father. You have my wife's cell phone number." TK tells them, "I have her number. I give her a call tomorrow when my father emails the information about Chong's operation and his drop." Sudarsan tells TK, "Thanks a lot TK. We appreciate it what you're doing for us." TK tells them, "Hey no problemo. Bye guys!" Sudarsan and Sai tells TK, "Bye TK!" Sudarsan and Sai leaves the comedy club and TK takes out his cell phone and makes a call to his father. TK tells his father on his cell phone, "Dad, listen I need a favor." Outside the comedy club where Sai and Sudarsan exit the comedy club and head to their car. Sai tells Sudarsan, "I hope TK can find Chong's operation and his deal before the week is over. I think Dr Havaladar time will run out soon and so is the rest of the hostages." Sudarsan tells Sai, "I'm sure TK will find them, you told me yourself. If anyone finds anything or get any information on anything. TK is your guy." Sai tells Sudarsan, "Well Dad, I hope so. Come on, 'let's head back to the library. The others are expecting us." Sudarsan tells Sai, "I hope they save us pizza before we get there." Sai tells Sudarsan, "Yeah, me too." Back in the warehouse office where Chong, Cal and Abebi are sitting down in their chairs and waiting for the fax machine. The fax machine rang, and the fax machine printed out information about Sai and Sudarsan. Cal gets up from his chair and grabs the information about them in the fax machine. Chong tells them, "It arrived and Cal who are those bastards try to interfere on my arms deal." Cal looks at the information on Sudarsan and Sai and tells Chong, "It's true, they are who they are?" Chong tells Cal, "Who are they?" Cal tells Chong, "Mr Chong, they are doctors and that is Sudarsan Chavala. The one you wanted to kill and the guy who killed your father. His son Sai is also a doctor too. There is something about his son and how easy was for them to find you." Abebi tells Chong, "We know Sudarsan is an ex-green beret and he does have a military contact to find anything." Cal tells Chong, "His son Sai, has the real power. I found out he's a CIA analyst and so is his wife. That's how they got information on us. No wonder I didn't recognize them before." Abebi tells Chong, "We found Chavala and his son. Should we go find them and kill them. That way you can avenge your father." Chong gets up from his chair and tells Abebi, "Abebi get up for a minute." Abebi tells Chong, "Yes sir." Abebi gets up from his chair and Chong goes over to Abebi and stops for a minute. Chong punches Abebi in the neck and the face. Chong gives him a roundhouse kick in the stomach. Abebi is soaring hard, and Chong tells him, "I decide when Chavala and his son die. I want to kill him to avenge him. But I am not stupid to get my hands dirty. Besides I have people to do it for me. Abebi, you are going to lead the attack. I want you and your men to find them tomorrow and kill them. We are going to ambush them and take them out one by one. That way my father would have been proud of me avenging him. Get the troops ready and after their dead and we will make arms deal with your boss who is going to be in town for a little business deal in a few days." Abebi tells Chong, "Yes sir." Abebi body is stop soaring and Chong tells Abebi, "Make the call." Abebi tells Chong, "Yes sir." Abebi sees the office phone and picks up the phone and makes a call. Inside the CIA room inside the Dallas Public Library. Where Krishna, Susmita and Lonnie are eating pizza and drinking beer and diet pepsi. Sai and Sudarsan enter the CIA room and Susmita tells them, "How did it go with Chong?" Sai tells Susmita, "Well it well. I think Chong bought it. But I do think sooner or later, he's going to find out about us and gets us troops to find us and kill us." Sudarsan and Sai sit down in their chairs and they start eating pizza. Sai is drinking his Miller Lite Beer bottle and so is Sudarsan. Sudarsan tells them, "Did you find anything more about Ryantech?" Lonnie tells Sudarsan, "The company is run by Thomas Ryan, but people call him. He built that company five years ago. We got a hold of Ryan and he told us about some weapons that he built for the army. Like USAF M16 rifle guns and grenades. They had 10 boxes of those weapons they were going to deliver to the army a week ago in Dallas Love Airport that were going to be transported to the pentagon. The army was expecting those guns and grenades for a test launch they need for three weeks ago. But five days ago, it was carjacked by some unknown assailants that killed the drivers and took the van and the weapons with them." Let me guess, that van went to Chong industries and since Chong has a warehouse somewhere in Dallas that he's storing the weapons at for his deal with African Warlord." Sai tells them, "While we were at the Black Dragon night club, we met a bartender who has African accent. I know he might not be the African warlord that Chong selling the weapons too and going to kill hostages after the drop. He just works for the African Warlord and I know he will be in town for a week to make the arms deal with Chong." Sudarsan tells them, "Susmita, TK will call you tomorrow and give you the information about Chongs operation and his drop soon. So, there is nothing we can do now. So we will come back tomorrow and wait for TK to call us." All of them tells Sudarsan, "Sure, no problemo." Krishna tells them, "I have to head back to hotel, I promise Missy that I call her today." Lonnie tells them, "Yeah, me too." Susmita tells them, "Me and Sai have to head back home and check on Lucy and see if the kids are okay." Sai tells them, "Actually, I'm going to stay for an hour. I got a lot of training to do." Sudarsan tells Sai, "Well, I'm going to stay with Sai and train with him. You never know when Chong's men might attack us. So we have to keep our A game." Susmita tells them, "All right, bye guys." Susmita, Krishna and Lonnie gets up from their chairs and exits the CIA room. Sai tells Sudarsan, "Dad, is mom expecting you back."

Sudarsan tells Sai, "She went shopping with her friend Anisha, so she will be busy all day and all week with Anisha. So, we have plenty of time to get started." Sai tells Sudarsan, "What did you tell Mom, when we work together in this. She might get suspicious about who we are and we do not want to put her in danger." Sudarsan tells Sai, "I told her I was spending time with you guys all week. Having Anisha will keep her busy for a week, before we finish this mission. Come on, let's train." In the training room, Sai and Sudarsan have workout gear. Sudarsan tells Sai, "Where did you get the workout gear anyway. I never expected to come here in the first place when I visited you guys." Sai tells Sudarsan, "Before I recruited you, in case you were going to say yes. I had some workout clothes for you in your size." Sudarsan tells Sai, "Let the training begin." Sudarsan is wearing boxing gloves and punches out the boxing bag. Sai is kicking the practice dummy. Sai and Sudarsan are using video game guns and using the live action screen on the computer to shoot bad guys. Sudarsan still his green beret power going and shoots five bad guys in the construction site. Sai shot down three bad guys in the construction site. Sudarsan flips his son in the ground. Sai punches Sudarsan in the face, but Sudarsan blocks the punch and knees Sai in the stomach and flips him again. Sai uses the speed bag where he does his punching. Sudarsan kills seven more bad guys in the video game computer with his video game gun. Sai starts boxing really hard on the boxing bag. Sai also flips Sudarsan in the ground. Sudarsan continues boxing in the boxing bag. Sai also takes out six more bad guys with a video game gun. Sudarsan is also kicking the attack dummy really hard. Sai flips Sudarsan in the floor one more time. Sudarsan is tired right now and tells Sai, "I think that's it for today. Why don't we call it a day." Sai tells Sudarsan, "Are you sure, we still have some more training to do." Sudarsan tells Sai, "Trust me, Sai. I want to save my strength and what's left of my dignity for the rest of the day." Sai tells Sudarsan, "Okay dad, I will pick you up in the morning and see what we can do." Sudarsan gets up from the mat and is a little tired today. Sudarsan tells Sai, "I'm in my 70's and I'm still in good shape. What's ever left of me." Sai tells Sudarsan, "I'm tired too. Come on, Dad. Let's go home." Sudarsan tells Sai, "Yeah, I'm ready too. Let's hit the showers before we leave. I don't want to come home smelly." Sai tells Sudarsan, "Yeah, me too." In the morning in Sudarsan's car where Sai is driving his father's car and Sudarsan is in the passenger seat. Sudarsan tells Sai, "Do you think yesterday, when we spoke to this Abebi guy, do you think he called Chong and spoke about us. I have a feeling; they didn't buy our story." Sai tells Sudarsan, "Whether they didn't buy it or not. Sooner or later, they would find out about us. If they figured out who you are. They would try to kill us soon." Sudarsan tells Sai, "I know they wouldn't just get to my family to get to me to lure me out of hiding. The only person they needed to get me out of hiding was Khanthi. I know the recording, I heard to come find them and they would release the hostages. I know bad guys don't keep their word, like I said no witnesses. They would kill Khanthi and the rest of the hostages when I find them." Sai slows down for a minute in his father's car and sees Abebi and five guys in another SUV van driving right behind us. Sai tells Sudarsan, "I think if Abebi told Chong about us and figure out what we were doing, they were planning on ambushing us when we park somewhere." Sudarsan tells Sai, "Why do you think that is son?" Sai tells Sudarsan, "Because I saw Abebi right behind me and he must have told Chong about us. Now he's planning on killing us. The recording said, come find them. We did, but Chong is not stupid to kill us himself. He is not stupid to get his hands dirty and ordered Abebi to kill us. So, I think they are planning on ambushing us when we park somewhere. I think they been following us for ten minutes when we were about to head back to the library." Sudarsan tells Sai, "Do you have any guns?" Sai tells Sudarsan, "I got some in the glove compartment and in the back." Sudarsan tells Sai, "I just hope you're kids never found any guys or weapons in the back or the glove compartment." Sai tells Sudarsan, "This is a company car, I don't even take this car at home. Me and Susmita, parks this car in the library parking lot. If they are going to ambush us, I know a place. Follow me." Sudarsan tells Sai, "Where's that?" Sai tells Sudarsan, "You're about to find out Dad." Outside an abandoned parking lot where Sai's SUV van is parked right outside the parking lot. The car is practically vacant, and no one is inside. Abebi SUV van sees Sai's car parked right outside the parking lot where it is abandoned. Abebi SUV stops and parks the car. Abebi and five of Chong's men exits the van and closes the door and all of them are carrying All of them are carrying berretta 92X rdo guns in their left hands and heads to Sai's car for a minute and stops. Abebi tells them, "Where are they, we followed them here." Chong's Man 1 tells Abebi, "They ditched us a couple of minutes ago, lucky we figured out where they were turning and spotted their car here." Abebi tells them, "Well, where are they? They wouldn't leave their car unattended." Chong Man 3 tells Abebi, "Let's give them a warning shot in their car, to send a message wherever you are we will find you." Abebi tells Chong Man 3, "Good idea. Let's do that." Abebi and five of Chong's men aims their gun on Sai's car until a lot of marbles comes out on the other end of Sai's car. Abebi tells them, "What the…?" What are these marbles from?' Sudarsan comes out back of Sai's car with a Berreta 92X Performance Carry Optic gun and comes out of hiding and tells Abebi and Chong's men, "From me. Tell Chong, I found you." Sudarsan dives down on the floor and fires his gun and three bullets comes out of his gun and hits Chong's Man 5 in the chest and dies." Chong's four other men and Abebi fires their guns, and six bullets comes out of their guns and hits the floor near Sudarsan and misses him. Sudarsan rolls to the road to the right and Abebi fires his gun and three more bullets hit the road near Sudarsan and misses him. Sai who is in back of the car and also carries a Berreta 92X Performance Carry Optic gun and squats a little. Sai aims the gun on Chong's Man 4 and fires one bullet out of his gun. The bullet hits Chong's Man 3 in the left leg. Chong's Man 4 is aching. Sai fires his gun again and three more bullets comes out of his gun and hits Chong's Man 4 in the stomach and dies. Sudarsan gets up from the road and dives down back on Sai's other end of the car. Sudarsang gets up from the floor and squats a little and aims his gun at Abebi. Abebi fires his gun, and three bullets come out of his gun and hits the front door of Sai's car. Sai tells them, "Hey, I just got this car detailed." Sudarsan fires his gun, two bullets come out of his gun and hits Abebi in the chest and dies. Sai fires his gun, four more bullets come out of his gun and hits Chong's Man 2 in the chest and dies. Chong's Man 1 fires his gun and five bullets come out of his gun and hits the back door of Sai's car and misses Sai and Sudarsan. Sai fires his gun, and three bullets comes out of his gun and hits the road near Chong Man 1 and misses him. Chong Man 1 jumps a little when he was almost shot. Sudarsan fires his gun, three bullets come out of his gun and Chong's Man 2 in the chest and dies. Sai fires his gun and two more bullets comes out of his gun and hits the road and misses Chong"s Man 1 again. Chong's Man 1 jumps a little. Chong's Man 1 is upset and fires his gun, and four more bullets comes out of his gun and hits the back of Sai's car again and misses Sudarsan and Sai. Sudarsan tells Sai, "We can't do this all day, I have an idea. I need you to stall him, do you still have more marbles in your pocket." Sai tells Sudarsan, "Yeah, I got some in my pocket." Sudarsan tells Sai, "Give it to me, I'll stall him and you fire." Sai tells Sudarsan, "We're going to do the pick and roll." Sudarsan tells Sai, "We are going to call this the alley oop." Chong Man 1 is about to fire his gun and still upset that his crew is dead. Sudarsan comes out back of Sai's car and gets his hands up. Sudarsan is carrying his gun in his right hand. Sudarsan goes over to Chong Man 1 and tells him, "Look, I'll come quietly. I surrender." Chong Man 1 tells Sudarsan, "I'm not buying it Chavala. Where's your son. Sudarsan tells Chong Man 1, "He's dead. You shot him quickly because one of your bullets came out of nowhere and shot him. I was going to show you. But since I have nothing to live for and since he is dead. I decided to come quietly. If Chong's wants to avenge his father. I'm right here. He did send you here to kill me. So, I can join my son when we both go into the light. My wife can manage without me. She'll grieve, but she will get over it. But I can't, so kill me." Chong's Man 1 tells Sudarsan, "Drop the gun first. So, I know you are not faking before I kill you." Sudarsan tells Chong Man 1, "Okay." Sudarsan drops his gun, and his gun falls down on the road. Chong's Man 1 tells Sudarsan, "I think I'm going to get a raise and a promotion. So long, asshole." Chong's Man 1 is about to fire his gun, until Sudarsan tells Chong Man 1, "There is one last words. I want to tell you." Chong's Man 1 tells Sudarsan, "I don't have time for last words Chavala. I'm going to kill you right now." Sudarsan tells Chong Man 1, "Please one last word. That will be it and you can kill me." Chong Man 1 thought about it and wants to give it to him. Since Sudarsan is begging hard. Chong Man 1 tells Sudarsan, "Okay, what is your last word." Sudarsan puts his hands down and takes out a few marbles out of his right pants pocket and tells Chong Man 1, "I wondered if you want to play marbles with me. Guess what it's your turn." Chong Man 1 tells Sudarsan, "What the…?" Sudarsan throws the marbles at Chong's Man 1 in the face and Chong's Man 1 is blinded a little and Sai squats down on the right of his car and aims his gun on Chong's Man 1 and Sai fires his gun. Three bullets come out of his gun and hits Chong Man 1 in the chest and dies. Sai comes out of the car and talks to Sudarsan. Sudarsan tells Sai, "I knew it would work." Sai tells Sudarsan, "Dad where did you learn that alley opp trick anyway." Sudarsan tells Sai, "A little trick in the army and the army got NBA finals 1974 in Vietnam. Believe that was important game everyone wants to watch." Sai tells Sudarsan, "I better call this in. I call my friend from Fort Hood to take care of this." Sudarsan tells Sai, "Well, I'm proud of you son. At least you were sharp and keen, and you knew when and where they were going to ambush us. That is smart thinking." Sai tells Sudarsan, "Thanks Pop." Sudarsan tells Sai, "Let's get back to the library. I hope TK calls us and give us the information to Sumita." Sai tells Sudarsan, "I hope TK found something." Sudarsan tells Sai, "Yeah, me too." Back in the library where Krishna, Susmita and Lonnie are drinking their 20oz diet pepsi in their CIA room in Dallas Public Library. The phone rings and Susmita tells them, "It's mine." Susmita takes her cell phone from her left pants pocket and answers the phone. Susmita tells the person on the other side of the phone, "Hello. Hey TK. You got it. Alright, I wait for the fax machine and get the information that you gave me. Thanks TK, me and Sai will catch your comedy show in two weeks. Okay, bye." Susmita hangs up her cell phone and tells them, "It was TK, he's got the information about our African Warlord and Chong's operation and about Chong's CIA contact that's been covering his tracks." Krishna tells Susmita, "That's great. When is TK fax us the information about Chong?" Susmita tells Krishna, "In five minutes. I'll head to the fax machine and pick up the information on Chong. We'll have to wait for Sai and Sudarsan, until I read out the information what we're dealing with." Lonnie tells Susmita, "When are they getting back?" Susmita tells Lonnie, "Lonnie, I already text them, they text me back. So, they'll be here 20 minutes." Lonnie tells Susmita, "I guess will have a lot of time to look at the information before they get here." Susmita tells them, "I'll going to head to the fax machine and wait for the fax arrive." Lonnie and Krishna tell Susmita, "Good luck." Susmita tells them, "I'm going to need it." Susmita gets up from her chair and head to the fax machine." Back in the warehouse office where Cal and Chong are sitting down in their chairs waiting for Abebi for the results. The door opens and it's one of Chong's men. Chong tells one of his men, "What is it, Newton?" Newton tells Chong, "Sir, we have a problem?" Chong tells Newton, "Where's Abebi and why isn't he giving me good news. Instead of bad news." Newton tells Chong, "Chavala and his son are still alive. They took out the crew and Abebi too." Chong is very upset right now and gets up from his chair and goes over to Newton. Cal gets up from his chair and tries to calm Chong for a minute. Cal tells Chong, "Mr Chong. You should calm yourself. So, it's a little set back, we will try again and kill those shitfaces." Chong stops and calms down for a minute. Chong tells Cal, "You know what, Cal I am calm. When I am calm. I thought I was going to Deck Newton. Because he's the messenger. Mostly I don't kill the messenger. Mostly I would have punched Newton in the face. But guess what. I'm not going to punch Newton in the face." Cal is thrilled he wasn't going to punch Newton in the face. Chong tells Cal, "I'm going to punch your face Cal." Chong punches Cal in the face and knees him in the stomach. Chong gives Newton a round house kick in the face. Newton falls on the floor." Chong tells Cal, "I said I wasn't going to punch Newton in the face. That doesn't mean I can't give him a roundhouse kick and you punch in the face." Newton and Cal are soaring right now. Chong sits back down in his chair. Newton gets up from the floor and he is still soaring. Cal is soaring a little, but he is okay. Chong tells them, "You're right Cal it is setback. Besides we are going to try it again. I don't have time; the deal is going to start in three days. We have a lot of work to do. We must move the hostages in our drop in three days." Cal tells Chong, "We put the hostages in the storage room. Mostly Abebi was supposed to watch them today. Since he is dead, it will be Newton turn to watch them. Before we move." Chong tells them, "I don't have time to kill Chavala and his stupid son. They already made me angry. But I will find them, after we finish the deal and then will kill the hostages. After they are done, we will find Chavala and his son and kill them. Once the deal is complete." Newton tells Chong, "What if they come looking for us or find the drop?" Sudarsan tells Newton, "They we kill them. We will not have to wait until the deal is complete if they find us or drop us. If they show up, they will be dead. Until then once we finish the deal. We will find them and kill them. Newton goes check on the hostages and make sure to keep them in line after we execute them." Newton tells Chong, "Yes sir." Newton heads to the door and opens and closes the door. Newton is heading to the storage room. Chong tells Cal, "Let's go check on the weapons. We must make sure everything is stored before the drop. When we meet our African Warlord." Cal tells Chong, "Yes sir." Chong gets up from his chair and heads to the door and opens it. Chong and Cal exit the office and Cal closes the door. In the huge storage room, Khanthi is sitting down in his chair tied up and has tape in his mouth. Six of the Congo villagers and three doctors are also tied up and taped with their mouth. The door opens and it's Newton. Newton closes the door and sees Khanthi. Khanti is struggling a bit, being tied up to a chair. Newton goes over to Khanthi and tells him, "Three more days, that will be it for you guys. Even if you're friend Chavala, doesn't arrive on the deal to watch us kill you and the rest of you guys right in front of you. We won't have to worry; we will still kill you anyway. Even if he's here or not, you guys will watch us kill Chavala first if we want to. Or maybe after we are done with you. We will still find him and kill him anyway." Newton slaps Khanthi in the face and gives Khanthi a round house kick in the face and Khanti falls on the chair on the floor. Newton tells Khanthi, "My job is to keep you in the line. I am going to make sure you stay in line." Khanthi is hurt and feels like he lost hope if Sudarsan cannot find him or the rest of the hostages. Inside the warehouse where Chong's men are storing weapons with mustard to keep the smell to throw the customs agents off the track. Cal and Chong supervise the operation. Chong tells Cal, "We got a lot of work to do in three days. Let's get started." Cal tells Chong, "Yes sir." Back in the CIA headquarters in the Dallas Public Library. Susmita, Krishna, and Lonnie are sitting down in their chairs and looking at the information that TK gave them. Sai and Sudarsan enter the CIA headquarters and Susmita tells them, "Are you guys, okay?" Sudarsan tells them, "We're fine. I guess Chong found out about us. Send a crew to give us a message." Lonnie tells them, "What was the message?" Sai tells them, "We asked him questions about kidnapping my father's best friend and the rest of the doctors and African tribe that he took and about his weapons deal that he made with an African Warlord that he is going to use attack African villages. I think those questions were a soar subject to him and why he sends his associates to kill us." Sudarsan tells them, "I think he was trying to set an example to us when you ask him personal questions we die by your men. Luckily, we got out their alive." Sudarsan and Sai head to their chairs and sit down. Lonnie tells Sudarsan, "You think Chong will send another crew to kill us." Sai tells Lonnie, "I don't think so Lonnie. Chong's is busy with his arms deal. I think he has other plans than just trying to find us and kill us." Sudarsan tells Lonnie, "Besides Lonnie, I think Chong is busy with something else than killing me to avenge his father. He is busy with this arm deal with this African Warlord. Once he is done and he will kill the hostages and Khanthi after the deal is done. After he is done with the hostages, he'll find me and Sai and kill us." Krishna tells them, "We're not going to let that happen. If we can find his operation and where the drop is. We can bust them and get Khanthi and the hostages back from them." Lonnie tells them, "Even if we find the operation and inform the FBI or Dallas P.D. They'll probably be gone and so will the weapons and hostages since Chong has a CIA informant that will tip before they arrive. Mostly I don't think they're search warrant is enough to put them behind bars." Sai tells them, "The only way we can bust them is to find the drop. We find the drop, we find Chong, his CIA informant, the African Warlord and the hostages and Khanti will put him behind bars permanently." Susmita tells them, "Luckily TK faxed me and got me the information we need to find Chong's operation and his CIA informant and his client the African warlord he is selling the weapons too." Sudarsan tells

Susmita, "Susmita what did you find out from TK?" Susmita looks at the file and tells them, "Chong's operation is at 156 Valley Road that is owned by Chong's Industries. Mostly it's an abandoned warehouse and it looks practically like a ghost town. Nobody is there since the warehouse is vacant." Sudarsan tells them, "That makes perfect sense. Using a vacant and abandoned warehouse will be perfect way to hide his weapons and the hostages. That is the last place law enforcement will find them." Susmita tells them, "The only reason why the FBI and Dallas P.D. never checked out that warehouse even though was suspicious of Chong's drug operation and which he is not running. Since they have no proof that he's not running a drug dealing operation or an arms deal is because of Chong's CIA informant who is covering his tracks." Sai tells Susmita, "Susmita, any idea who this is CIA informant who is covering Chong's tracks." Susmita tells them, "His name is Calvin Yensin, he left the CIA two years ago. They're being rumors he was a corrupt agent working as a mole for an African Warlord named Bello Mufasa. Capitan Bello Mufasa was a rogue Congo Army special forces who wanted to take over the Congo. He left the army and went rogue to terrorize the Congo African villages, mostly the Congo usually stops them before they attack. Until they had a rogue CIA agent to hand out weapons from the black market to Mufasa's men to take down Congo Army that is…?" Sudarsan interrupts Susmita for a minute and tells her, "Calvin Yensin. Our rogue CIA agent." Susmita tells them, "I think I know where to locate him." Lonnie tells Susmita, "Where is that?" Susmita tells them, "I know there were rumors that Mufasa will be in Dallas in three days and since Yensin is covering Mufasa tracks so he can get to the city. I found out Yensin manages a club called Club Black that is owned by Chong. He'll be at the club in three days at 6:00pm. Good news at least we know who we are dealing with and where the operations is at. The bad news we don't even know where the drop is." Sai tells Susmita, "But Yensin does. We will go to Club Black in three days at 6:00 pm and make him tell us where the drop is." Krishna tells Sai, "If it doesn't?" Sudarsan tells them, "We will go to plan B." Lonnie tells Sudarsan, "What's Plan B Sudarsan?" Sudarsan tells Lonnie, "Lonnie, we will go to his operation. Before they leave we will put a tracking device in one of their cars. We can track down where their deal is and stop them." Sai tells them, "I have a tracking device that can do that." Sudarsan tells Sai, "What is that?" Sai takes out a watch from his right pocket and puts it on the table. Sudarsan tells Sai, "Sai, it looks like an ordinary watch." Sai tells Sudarsan, "Dad, this is no ordinary watch. This watch has a tracking device. If you press the button two times, the tracking device will start whoever holds it. You can track them down on the laptop once the device is on. So, just in case if Yensin didn't work out. We can use this watch as a tracking device. One of you guys will have go to the operation in the evening in three days to tape the tracking device and monitor it in the laptop. Whatever you do, tape the watch in the back of one of Chong's cars and get out of there quickly and head back to the car and hide. Once they leave monitor the tracking device in the laptop and we will follow them wherever the opcration is at?" Sudarsan tells them, "I know exactly what to do? Sai, Krishna! You guys will be coming with me at Club Black at 6:00 in the evening in three days." Krishna tells Sudarsan, "Check Sudarsan." Sudarsan tells Lonnie and Susmita, "Lonnie, Susmita you guys will go to 156 Valley Road and find Chong's car and tape the watch aka tracking device in back of his car and get out quickly and head back to the car and hide before he leaves. Once they leave, use the laptop and track him down. Then call in the FBI or Dallas P.D. and tell them where the deal is at and they can arrest them" Susmita and Lonnie tells Sudarsan, "Got it!" Sudarsan tells them, "We got three days to find that deal and stop Chong from killing the hostages and selling those weapons to Mufasa. We have a lot of work to do. So let's begin our training. Lonnie, Susmita practice the tracking device on that watch before you guys start. We got three days to complete or we're dead. Everybody ready." Sai, Krishna, Susmita and Lonnie tells Sudarsan, "Ready." Everybody gets up from their chairs and put their fist together and shake. Sudarsan tells them, "Let's get ready." In the training room, Krishna and Sai are practicing their video game gun and doing a live action computer game where they shoot five bad guys in a harbor. Sai kicks the practice dummy really hard. Susmita flips Sudarsan from the mat. Lonnie uses the laptop on the watch to track Krishna who is in the second floor of the library. Krishna is holding the watch with a tracking device and he on in the second floor of the library gives Lonnie a thumbs up when he is in the CIA room. Sudarsan who is wearing his boxing gloves is boxing really hard. Susmita is kicking the practice dummy. Sudarsan and Lonnie is shooting six bad guys in construction site with their video game gun in a live action screen. Susmita is practicing the tracking device on the laptop with Lonnie who is outside the library. Lonnie is outside the library wearing the tracking device watch and gives Susmita a thumbs up. Sudarsan is flipping Sai on the training mat. Sai is wearing his boxing gloves and hitting the punching bag. Lonnie is kicking the practice dummy really hard. Susmita is on the laptop again and is also checking to see if the tracking device works on the watch again. Lonnie is on the first floor and gives Susmita a thumbs up. Sudarsan and Sai kills five more bad guys inside a warehouse with their video game guns. Lonnie is also practicing on the laptop with Susmita using the watch that has a tracking device. Susmita is on the third floor wearing the tracking device watch and gives Lonnie a thumbs up. Sudarsan is kicking the dummy really hard. Sai is wearing his boxing gloves and hitting the punching bag. Sai keeps hitting the punching bag. Sai is done hitting the punching bag and he is ready. Lonnie is using the laptop to practice the tracking device on the watch again where Susmita is on the second floor. Susmita is on the second floor and gives Lonnie a thumbs up. Back in the CIA Room where Sudarsan, Sai, Lonnie and Krishna are sitting down in their chairs and finish their meeting before their mission starts. Sudarsan tells them, "It's 5:30, we got a lot of work to do. If you guys don't want to do it, I understand. But you guys are here for one reason is to save the hostages and my friend Khanthi. He is depending on us to save him. We got to make sure Chong and Mufasa arms deal doesn't go through. Everyone knows their position." Sai, Susmita, Krishna and Lonnie tells Sudarsan, "Let's get to work. Sai, Sudarsan, Krishna, Lonnie and Susmita gets up from their chairs and go over to each other and puts their fist together as a hand shake. Sudarsan tells them, "We got a mission to do. Let's get started." They put their fist down and let's go. Outside the Club Black where Sudarsan parks Sai's SUV in front of Club Black entrance. Sai,

Sudarsan and Krishna exits the car and closes their doors. Sudarsan looks at Club Black and sees the entrance. Sudarsan tells them, "You guys know what to do?" Krishna tells Sudaran, "We find Yensin and make him tell us where Chong's drop is at." Sai tells Sudarsan, "Dad, what would happen if Yensin recognize us and he doesn't say anything." Sudarsan tells Sai, "Two options, that we make him tell us where Chong's drop is at or we go to Plan B." Sai tells them, "Just hope Yensin doesn't recognize us." Inside Club Black where is really crowded and sees the waitress. Sudarsan, Sai and Krishna goes over to talk to her. Sudarsan tells the waitress, "Excuse me waitress, you know if Calvin Yensin is in his club today?" Waitress tells Sudarsan, "Yes, he's here today." Sai tells the waitress, "You know where to find him?" Waitress tells them, "Yes, he is in the VIP room in the first floor to the right. I want to ask why do you want to see Mr Yensin about?" Sudarsan tells the Waitress, "Mr Chong sent us, we wanted to ask Yensin if the club is doing okay and if he needed any help. If the club it's too much for him." Waitress tells them, "Well, I'm sure the club is doing okay." Sudarsan tells the Waitress, "Mr Chong did sent us to make sure Yensin is doing okay." Waitress tells them, "Like I said, I'm sure he is fine. But you want to check on him. He's in the VIP room to the first floor to the right." Sudarsan tells the Waitress, "Thank you for helping us. We will put in a good word with Mr Chong." Waitress tells them, "Hey, no problemo." Sudarsan, Sai and Krishna the front entrance and head to the VIP room to the right where Yensin is at. Yensin is sitting down in his booth with five of Chong's men drinking bud lights. Sudarsan, Sai and Krishna enters the VIP room and sees Yensin and five of Chong's men in the VIP room and Sudarsan, Sai and Krishna goes over to the VIP booth to talk to Yensin and they stop. Sudarsan tells Yensin, "Hi, Yensin. I hope I didn't catch in a bad time." Yensin sees Sudarsan, Sai and Krishna and recognizes them. Yensin tells his men, "It's them, kill those bastards!" Yensin and five of Chong's men takes out their Beretta 85BB guns from their right jacket pocket and aims their guns on Sudarsan, Sai and Krishna. Sudarsan tells Sai and Krishna, "Get down." Sudarsan, Krishna and Sai dives down on the floor to the right and takes out their Beretta 92X Compact W/Rail guns out of back of their pants. Chong's Man 4 fires his gun and two bullets comes out of Chong's Man 4 gun and hits the wall on the right side of the club. Sudarsan, Sai and Krishna rolls downs to the right side of the VIP booth. Three bullets comes out of nowhere near Sudarsan and misses him. Sudardan, Sai and Krishna reaches the right side of the VIP booth and hides in the table. Yensin fires his gun, three bullets comes out of his gun and hits the wall again near the right side of the VIP booth near Sudarsan, Sai and Krishna and misses them. Sudarsan aims his gun on Chong's Man 3 and fires his gun. Two bullets comes out of his gun and hits Chong's Man 3 in the chest and dies. Sai fires his gun, two bullets comes out of his gun and beer bottle on the table and misses Yensin. Yensin fires his gun three bullets comes out of his gun and hits the floor near Sai and misses him. Krishna fires his gun, two bullets comes out of his gun and hits Chong's Man 1 in the stomach and dies. Sudarsan fires his gun, one bullet comes out of his gun and hits the picture frame near Yensin and misses him. Sai fires his gun and one bullet comes out of his gun and hits the table and misses Yensin. Sai fires his gun again and two bullets comes out of his gun and hits Chong's Man 4 in the stomach and dies. Yensin tells his men, "Come on kill them. We almost have them." Sai aims his gun on Chong's Man 5 and he has a good shot. Chong's Man 5 fires his gun and one bullet comes out of his gun and hits the wall near Sai and misses him. Sai fires his gun, three bullets comes out of his gun and hits Chong's Man 5 in the chest and dies. Sudarsan tells Sai and Krishna, "We've got to get out of here, we can't hold them off!" Krishna tells them, "I'll stall them before we get away." Sai tells Krishna, "Do it!" Krishna aims on the floor near Yensin and Krishna fires his gun. One bullet comes out of his gun and hits the floor near Krishna and misses him. Yensin jumps a little when the bullet almost hit him. Sai, Sudarsan and Krishna gets up from the table and exits the VIP room away from Yensin and Chong's Man 2. Chong's Man 2 sees Sudarsan, Sai and Krishna exiting the club. Chong's Man 2 tells Yensin, "Yensin, they're leaving." Yensin tells Chong's Man 2, "Let's follow them, we cannot let them get away." Outside Club Black, where everybody is panicking from gunshots. Sudarsan, Sai and Krishna exits the club and goes inside Sai's cair. Sudarsan is driving the car, while Sai is in the passenger seat and Krishna is in the back. Sai tells them, "We've got to get out of here. They're catching up on us." Sudarsan starts the car and exits Club Black. Yensin and Chong's Man 2 sees Sudarsan, Sai and Krishna car's leaving the club. Chong's Man 2 tells Yensin, "They're getting away. Man, we lost them." Yensin tells Chong's Man 2, "No, we haven't I know where they are going. Let's get to the van." Sai's van reaches the Dallas highway and loses Yensin and the rest of Chong's crew." Sudarsan is still driving Sai's car while is Sai in the passenger seat and Krishna is in the back seat. Sudarsan tells Sai and Krishna, "Do you think we lost them." Krishna tells them, "I don't know we got out in the hurry. I don't think they see us." Sai tells them, "If we did see us, they would have attack us right now." Sai hears a bullet hitting back of the van. Sudarsan and Krishna also hears two more bullets hitting the back of the van too. Sudarsan sarcastically tells them, "Nope I don't think we lost them. Because they found us." They see a black SVU van where Yensin is driving the car and Chong's Man 2 is the passenger seat where the car window is open and carrying Winchester 1300 "Defender" gun and fires his gun again, three bullets come out of his gun and hits Sai's taillight. Back in Sai's car, Sai tells them, "Oh great now Yensin is shooting at us now." Krishna tells them, "We've got to lose them." Sai takes out his Beretta 92FS gun out of his glove compartment and opens the passenger car window while Chong's Man 2 continues shooting at them. Three more bullets come out of nowhere from Chong's Man 2 gun and hits the road near Sai's car and misses them. Sai turns around a little and fires his gun. Three bullets come out of his gun and hit the road near Yensin's car and misses him. Chong's Man 2 fires his gun and two more bullets come out of his gun and hits the back of Sai's car and misses them. Sai fires his gun too and two more bullets comes out of his gun and hits the road again and misses Yensin's Car." Sudarsan sees a road closed where they are doing construction in the highway and Sudarsan turns around and hits the Road Closed sign and is heading to road closed bridge. Sai tells Sudarsan, "Of all god damn roads in this highway, you had to pick this one!" Sudarsan tells Sai, "It's the only way to lose them! I have an idea." Sai tells Sudarsan, "Whatever it is Dad, we're going to be sitting ducks for a minute!" Sudarsan tells Sai, "There are three watches in those glove compartments. Press the button and throw it to them!" Krishna tells Sudarsan, "Are you nuts. We are going to tasting bullets in a few seconds and we are going to lose them throwing three watches." Sai takes out of the three and presses the button and it's ticking thirty seconds. Sai tells Krishan, "These are no ordinary watches. Just watch the show!" Sai turns around again. Chong's Man 2 fires his gun and two more bullets come out of his gun and the road near Sai's car and misses them. Sai throws three watches on Yensin's windshields on his car and the thirty seconds is almost up. Sudarsan slows down a little and breaks. Krishna tells them, we're not going to make it!" Thirty seconds watch is, and the watches explodes and so is Yensin's car and both of Yensin and Chong's Man 2 is dead. Sudarsan stops the car and parks it. Sudarsan, Sai and Krishna get out of the car and sees Yensin and Chong's Man 2 dead from that explosion. Sudarsan tells them, "Hey guys, what would you like in your barbeque steak, burgers or hot dogs." Krishna tells Sudarsan, "I'm in a mood for hot dogs. Too bad, I forgot to bring the mustard and the buns. Sai, what kind of watches were they anyway that made them explode?" Sai tells Krishna, "They were explosive watches that were more powerful than a grenade. Those are grenade watches; I always use them for emergencies." Sudarsan tells Krishna, "Sai told me about those watches that exploded yesterday. Since we have a grenade watch and now, we have a tracking device watch." Sai tells Sudarsan, "I guess Plan A didn't work because Plan A went up to smoke. I just hope Plan B works." Krishna tells them, "I just hope Susmita and Lonnie gets that tracking device on Chong's car on time." Sudarsan tells them, "I hope so too. Come on, let's get back in the van." Sai, Sudarsan and Krishna head back to the car. Outside of Chong's warehouse where his operation is at. Susmita's car, a Ford Taurus, is parked right across Chong's warehouse. Susmita and Lonnie are inside the car and see Chong's RANGE ROVER SPORT V6 HSE 4WD V6 HSE 6 parked outside the warehouse. Susmita is carrying the watch with a tracking device and black tape. Susmta is in the driver's seat and tells Lonnie, "I better hurry up before Chong arrives." Lonnie tells Susmita, "Whatever you do, get in and get out quickly." Susmita opens the car door gently and exits her car and closes the door. Susmita is carrying black scotch tape and the watch with a tracking device. She hustles quickly across the street near Chong's van. Susmita is in the back of Chong's van and Susmita presses the watch button to turn on the tracking device. Susmita tapes the watch is back of Chong's van and exits quickly. Susmita gets back into her car and gets back in the driver's seat and closes the door. Lonnie tells Susmita, "You made it. Did you, do it?" Susmita tells Lonnie, "I got it. Lonnie turns on the laptop and start the tracking device. Susmita sees Chong and three of his men getting into his van and exiting the warehouse. Another Range Rover also exits the warehouse from the garage door and one big truck where the hostages and Khanthi are at. Susmita sees them leaving and tells Lonnie, "I see them leaving and that big rig must be where Chong is holding Khanthi and the rest of the hostages. Lonnie, you got the tracking device on?" Lonnie tells Susmita, "It's on. They are about to head northwest." Susmita tells Lonnie, "Lonnie makes the call to Sudarsan, Sai and Krishna." Lonnie tells Sumita, "Sure thing Susmita." Susmita starts the car and follows Chong and his men. Back on the highway where Sudarsan is driving Sai's car with Sai in the passenger seat and Krishna in the back seat. Sai's cell phone rings and tells them, "It's mine." Sai takes out his cell from his pants pocket and answers the cell phone. Sai tells the person on other side of the cell phone, "Hello! Hey Lonnie. Hold on." Sai is about to tell Sudarsan and Lonnie where they are and tells them, "They got the tracking device on." Sudarsan tells Sai, "That's great, where are they going?" Sai tells Lonnie on the cellphone, "Okay!" Sai tells Sudarsan, "Go northwest and make right." Sudarsan tells Sai, "Got it!" Chong's two vans and his big rig is on the highway. Sudarsan is driving Sai's car on the highway with Sai and Krishna. Sai tells Sudarsan, "Three more miles and make a left." Sudarsan tells Sai, "Got It!" Sudarsan is driving Sai's car in that direction. Lonnie is still looking at the laptop in Susmita's Car where Susmita in the driver's seat on her cell phone with Sai and tells Susmita, "Go three miles and make a right." Sai tells Sudarsan, "Go three miles and make a right." Sudarsan drives to the right after driving three miles in Sai's car." Chong and his are driving Two Range Rovers and one big truck is also driving on the highway. Lonnie is still on his laptop in Susmita's car and Susmita's is still on her cell phone with Sai and tells Susmita, "I found the drop, go two more miles, and make a right. It's on an abandoned construction site. That's where the deal is at." Susmita tells Sai on the cellphone, "Sai we found the drop. Tell Sudarsan…?" Sudarsan is still driving Sai's car and Sai who is on the cellphone with Susmita tells Sudarsan, "Dad, they found the drop." Sudarsan tells Sai, "Where is it?" Sai tells Sudarsan, "Two more miles and make a right. The drop is at an abandoned construction site." Sudarsan tells Sai, "Got it!" Sai tells Susmita on his cellphone, "Okay, I will meet you guys in the construction site in a few minutes." Susmita's car is driving on the highway where Susmita is driving her car and Lonnie is on the passenger seat. Susmita is calling Josh on her cellphone and tells him, "Josh, I found the hostages and I found out Walter Chong is running the show. He's a big Dallas kingpin in Chinatown and is about to make arms deal with an African Warlord Bello Mufasa. I need a favor, send in two SWAT vans and one helicopter to the construction site. Hurry up, alright bye!" Susmita hangs up the phone. Outside the construction site where Susmita's car is parked right across the construction site where Susmita and Lonnie are waiting for Sudarsan, Sai, and Krishna. Sai's SUV van arrives and parks right next to Susmita's car." The car door opens, and Sai, Sudarsan and Krishna exit the car and closes the door. They can't make a sound and they would be spotted. Sudarsan, Sai, and Krishna go over to Susmita and Lonnie. Sudarsan tells them, "That is where the deal is." Sai tells Sumita, "Susmita, you called Josh?" Susmita tells Sai, "Yeah, he's going to send in a few agents and SWAT in ten minutes." Sudarsan tells Sumita, "We don't have ten minutes. Chong and Mufasa will be gone by then after the arms deal is over. We're going must stop them ourselves before they arrive." Krishna tells Sudarsan, "How are we going to do that Sudarsan?" Sudarsan tells Krishna, "We'll Krishna in football we call this the statue of liberty play. I know what to do, Sai, do you have another exploding watch?" Sai tells Sudarsan, "Yeah, I have another one in the glove compartment." Sudarsan tells Sai, "Go get it. Time to gear up." Sai goes to his car in the passenger seat to get another exploding watch in the glove compartment. Sudarsan opens the back on the trunk and takes out six beretta 92X Performance Carry Optic guns out of the back of the car, gives the guns to Susmita, Krishna, and Lonnie. Susmita, Krishna, and Lonnie grabbed the guns and Sudarsan put the gun in the back of the van for Sai. Sudarsan tells them, "Gentlemen, it's time to play. We got the ball." Inside the construction site where Chong, nine of his men including Newton and Mufasa and five of his men are the deal. Chong puts two crates on the table and opens one of the crates for Mufasa and there are stolen guns and grenades inside the crate covered with mustard when Chong pulls two guns and one grenade. Chong wipes the mustard off his hands with a rag that is on the table. Chong puts the crates down on the floor and Mufasa sees the two briefcases on the floor next to him and carries the two briefcases and puts them on the table. He opens and it's five million dollars each in one briefcase. Chong likes the money that he saw. In the back of the rig that is right across Mufasa and his men. Chong nods on Chong Man 1 to open the back of the truck. Chong Man 1 heads to the back of the truck and opens it. There is Khanthi, Six of the Congo villagers and three doctors are also tied up and taped with their mouth behind the truck sitting down. Chong nods his head and looks like they are going to make a deal, until a watch comes out of nowhere and hits the floor. Chong and his men saw the watch. The watch is practically harmless, until the watch explodes. They all had a knee jerk reaction. All of them took out their Beretta 92X Performance guns from their right jacket pocket and aimed the gun at someone, since no one was there. Sudarsan is hiding behind the barrel and comes out of the barrel and tells them, "Surprise Assholes!" Sudarsan is carrying his gun and fires his gun. Three bullets come out of his gun and hit Newton in the chest and dies. Chong is angry right now and tells them, "Kill that bastard!" Chong fires his gun, and two bullets come out of his gun and hits the floor near Sudarsan and misses him. Sudarsan dives down the barrel to the right and makes it to the barrel before two more bullets come out of nowhere and hit the floor near Sudarsan again and misses him. Sudarsan dives down the barrel on time. Chong Man 2 fires his gun and one bullet come out of his gun and hits the beam. Mufasa Man 4 fires his gun and three more bullets come out of his gun and hits the box to the right. Sai, Susmita, Krishna, and Lonnie enter the construction site. Sai fires his gun, two bullets come out of his gun and hits Mufasas Man 4 in the chest and dies. Krishna, Lonnie, and Susmita hide behind the boxes to the left and Sai hides behind the barrels to the right next to Sudarsan. Susmita aims her gun on Chong Man 5 and fires her gun. Three bullets come out of her gun and hits Chong Man 5 in the stomach and dies. Chong's Man 9 fires his gun and three bullets come out of his gun and hits the barrels near Sai and Sudarsan and misses them. Krishna fires his gun, two bullets come out of his gun and Chong Man 9 in the chest and dies. Lonnie fires his gun, three bullets come out of his gun and hits Chong Man 1 in the chest and dies. Sai also fires his gun, three bullets come out of his gun and hits Chong Man 3 in the chest and dies. Lonnie fires his gun again and two more bullets comes out of his gun and hits Chong Man 4 in the stomach and dies. Chong fires his gun and two more bullets come out of his gun and hits the floor near the box where Susmita is at and misses her. Susmita fires her gun, two bullets come out of her gun and hits Chong Man 3 in the chest and dies. Sudarsan fires his gun and two bullets come out of his gun and hits Mufasa in the chest and dies. Mufasa Man 2 fires his gun, two more bullets come out of the gun and hits the construction beam. Sai fires his gun, three bullets come out of his gun and hits Mufasa Man 1 in the chest and dies. Lonnie also fires his gun, two more bullets come out of his gun and hits Chong Man 3 in the chest and dies. Susmita fires her gun, and two bullets comes out of her gun and hits Chong Man 4 in the chest and dies. Chong Man 2 fires his gun, four bullets come out of his gun and hits the floor near Sudarsan and misses him. Sudarsan is upset and fires his gun. Two bullets come out of his gun and hits Chong Man 2 in the chest and dies. Krishna fires his gun and two bullets come out of his gun and hits Chong Man 7 in the chest and dies. Lonnie fires his gun and two bullets come out of his gun and Mufasa Man 2 in the stomach and dies. Chong's Man 6 fires his gun and three bullets come out of his gun and hits the barrel near Sudarsan and Sai are hiding at. The three bullets missed them. Sai fires his gun, two bullets come out of his gun and hits Mufasa Man 3 in the chest and dies. Sudarsan tells Sai, "Cover me, I'm going in." Sai tells Sudarsan,

"You've got it." Sai sees Chong Man 7 and aim the gun on the floor and one bullet come out of his gun and hits the floor near Chong Man 7 and missed him. Chong Man 7 jumps a little. Sudarsan comes out of the barrel and is about to make a tackle on Chong. Sudarsan runs as fast as he can, and three bullets come out of nowhere and hit the floor near Sudarsan and missed him. Sudarsan tackles Chong right to the table where the briefcases with ten million dollars in it. Sudarsan and Chong hit the table, and both dropped their guns. Chong gets up and he is angry. Chong grabs Sudarsan from the shirt and drags him to the right of the construction site to finish him off. Chong sees his gun and grabs the gun. Chong sees Sudarsan's gun and kicks to the left, so he will not reach it. Chong goes over to Sudarsan who is soar and Chong is about to aim his gun at Sudarsan. Sudarsan sees his groin and kicks his groin with a left kick. Chong is soaring for a minute. Sudarsan knees Chong in the stomach and grabs him by the shirt and tosses him to the floor. Mufasas Man 3 fires his gun, two bullets come out of the gun and hits floor near Susmita and miss her. Susmita fires her gun, and two bullets comes out of her gun and hits the floor near Mufasa Man 3 and missed him. Sai fires his gun, and two bullets comes out of his gun and hits Chong Man 8 in hits his chest and dies. Chong gets up from the floor and Sudarsan goes over to Chong and punches him in the face and gives him a roundhouse kick to the stomach. Chong is soar and Sudarsan punches Chong in the face again and falls on the floor. Chong is still soaring, and Sudarsan goes over to Chong again. But Chong kicks Sudarsan in the groin. Sudarsan is hurting. Chong gets up from the floor and punches Sudarsan in the face and gives him a roundhouse kick in the face. Sudarsan falls on the floor and he is hurt. Chong kicks Sudarsan in the stomach twice and Sudarsan is still soar. Lonnie fires his gun, two bullets come out of his gun and hits Chong Man 6 in the chest and dies. Sai fires his gun and three bullets come out of his gun and hits Chong Man 7 in the chest and dies. Mufasas Man 3 tells Mufasa Man 4, "Let's retreat, it's a lost cause." Mufasa Man 4 tells Mufasa Man 3, "Let's go in the back. We can slip out without anyone seeing us." Mufasa Man 3 and 4 exits the construction site in the back area where no one is there. Lonnie sees the rest of Mufasa's

Men leaving the construction site and tells them, "Their getting away, we got to stop them." Susmita tells Lonnie, "We don't have to, I have another surprise for them." Lonnie tells Susmita, "What is that?" Susmita tells Lonnie, "You'll see." Back of the construction site where five CIA SWAT members are carrying M16A1 rife guns and sees Mufuas Man 3 and 4 exiting the construction carrying guns and they stop. Mufasa Man 3 and 4 aims their guns on the five CIA SWAT and about to kill them to get out of the construction site. CIA SWAT 1 tells his crew, "Fire!" CIA SWAT fires their guns, and ten bullets comes out of their guns and hits Mufasa Man 3 and 4 in the chests and dies. Sudarsan gets up from the floor and Chong punches Sudarsan in the face and the stomach hard. Chong gives Sudarsan and roundhouse kick in the face and falls on the floor. Sai, Lonnie, Krishna, and Susmita come out of the boxes and barrels from the construction site. Sai tells them, "I'm going to help my dad. Stay here!" Susmita tells Sai, "Sure thing, Sai." Sai goes over to the right side of the construction site where Chong and Sudarsan are at. Chong kicks Sudarsan in the stomach. Chong sees his gun and goes over there to grab it. Chong grabs his gun and aims his gun at Sudarsan. Chong tells Sudarsan, "I been waiting to kill you all my life Chavala. My father always sees when a soldier is weak and pathetic, they always need to be put down. I guess this time I will put you down. Sudarsan gets up from the floor and Chong aims gun on Sudarsan's left leg and fires his gun and one bullet come out of his gun hits Sudarsan in the right left. Sudarsan is hurting. Chong tells Sudarsan, "You think that bullet hurts and wait until three more bullets hurt. Like I said, Chavala. When a soldier is practically useless, it is time to put them out of pasture. You are way past your pasture, bye-bye Chavala. This is for you father." Sai sees Sudarsan and gives him a nod. Sudarsan nods back for a minute. Chong is about to fire his gun, until Sudarsan takes out a few marbles out of his left pants pocket and throws the marbles into Chong's face. Chong is blinded a little since the marbles were thrown into his face and cannot see anything. Sudarsan tries to get up from the floor and takes out his spare gun from the back of his pants and aims the gun at Chong. Sudarsan tells Chong, "Guess what Chong, I am not weak and pathetic. But your father is and say hello to him for me." Chong sees a little and tells Sudarsan, "What the…?" Sudarsan fires his gun and two bullets come out of his gun and hits Chong in the chest and dies. Sudarsan leg is hurting after getting shot and Sai goes over to Sudarsan and holds him. Sai tells Sudarsan, "Dad, you, okay?" Sudarsan tells Sai, "Yeah, I'm okay. But I am a little soar." Sai tells Sudarsan, "Josh called, he told me all the weapons are retrieved and will be back to Ryantech in no time to make the deliveries to the Pentagon on time to save his company going bankrupt and all the hostages are freed including Dr Havaladar. We are going to be awarded CIA Distinguished Intelligence Cross and Dad, you also will be awarded the Medal of honor for your excellent service to the army and rescuing the hostages." Sudarsan tells Sai, "Sounds great. You got an amazing team out there; I am proud to have you as my son Sai." Sai tells Sudarsan, "Thanks Dad." Sudarsan tells Sai, "We should get some donuts. I know one that is open 24 hours." Sai tells Sudarsan, "We should get the glaze. We always love glaze." Outside the construction site where Sudarsan is back of the ambulance van where one paramedic is bandaging Sudarsan's left leg. Sai, Susmita, Krishna, and Lonnie to check on Sudarsan's leg if he's okay. Khanti who is untied, and the rest of the hostages are now free from Chong. The rest of the CIA are unloading the stolen weapons from Ryantech. Khanthi goes over to Sudaran in the ambulance van and tells him, "Sudarsan, I want to tell you I owe you one." Sudarsan tells Khanthi, "You were there for me Khanthi. So, I decided to repay the favor. You know Khanthi, I almost died today. I never had a chance to read my father's letter. As soon as I get healed up. I will read my father's letter." Khanthi tells Sudarsan," You should, but maybe save it when the time is right or someday when you are in your deathbed and read it." Sudarsan tells Khanthi, "I will, it's going to be tough explaining this to Girija. But I think I can come up with something. But what are you going tell Cocula where you were?" Khanthi tells Cocula, "I think I'm going to tell her about what and give her a huge story. If she doesn't believe me or not." Sudarsan tells Khanthi, "I think I would just tell her that I was touring other villages in Africa. But when the time is right, I will tell her or I can tell her, don't ask, and don't tell." Sudarsan tells Khanthi, "I think sounds a lot better. I will see you in the hospital soon and maybe we can get together to have a beer sometimes when I get checked out of the hospital." Khanthi tells Sudarsan, "Sure, I love that too. You're buying." Sudarsan laughs a little and Sudarsan gets up from the back of the ambulance and sits down on the stretcher where two paramedics join him in the back of the ambulance and closes the door. Sai sees Sudarsan behind the ambulance and tells the mourners, "That was one time me and my father had one last adventure together and he came up with an excuse to tell my mom. That he got shot in the leg of a mugging that went wrong. It is unknow if she bought it. She never asked questions if he was okay. That's all that matters right now." Back at Bram's funeral home in Maryville Missouri where Sai finishes the story to the mourners in the podium. Sai tells the mourners, "My father continues living his life six more years, until he passed away in October and we are here. Before my father died, he did read the letter that my grandfather wrote to him before he passed away. I'm going to read it to you, "Dear Sudarsan, I am sorry about the fallout that we had together last time before I died. I never tell you a lot of times I was proud of you. I should have. I was upset that you joined ROTC and wanted to go to Fort Bragg and serve your country. You didn't go to Fort Bragg to serve your country; you wanted to make a difference and protect all your loved ones and total strangers that he was sworn to protect. I did read about your accomplishment, and you did everything right. You got a good education, you got an excellent job, a beautiful wife and son and everyone was proud of you. You were also a war hero and that saved a lot of people that you risked your life for. I just want to tell you before I go. I am proud of you, son! Grandpa was right, he is proud of him. So are we, I love you dad. We will honor your commitment and what you stand for." The mourners are crying about reading that story, where Girija, Lonnie, Susmita, Lekha, Naveen, Krishna, Khanthi, Cocula and all the mourners are crying a little. Outside Bram's funeral home everyone including Sai, Girija, Lonnie, Susmita, Lekha, Naveen, Krishan, Khanthi, Cocula and all his friends are outside seeing five soldiers doing a 21-gun salute. Sai is crying a little and he is proud of his father. Sai tells himself, "I love you, Dad!"

The End

PRESIDENT ROBERT CHAVALA BOOK GUYS

By Bobby Cinema

Synopsis:

Srinivas Robert Chavala is Indian American who was the youngest vice president of the at age 40. His predecessor Joe Robinette is the current elected President of the United States. Mr. Chavala is an open function with the president while he was assassinated by a sniper on the roof across the street was at. Bobby Chavala will be sworn in as President in a week. Until then the President Robinette is in a coma, does not have a chance to make it So right now, as acting president he will launch an investigation to find out who assassinated the president. It would take years and Mr Robinette doesn't have a chance to make it. But what we can do is find the assassin or he is next. The open investigation to find out who this assassin is teaming up with and who hired this assassin. President Chavala formed an investigating team to find this assassin and make sure it does not happen to him. The team he formed to find the assassin and who hired him. He picked three out of the lineup, one of them is Detective Sergeant Billy Wallace from the Los Angeles Police Department is a lazy and fat cop who is does not follow police procedures and protocol, but he a great narcotics and counterfeiting detective who solved 500 cases in drug dealings and shut down drug empires. The next one is Gary Rodriguez, a campus security guard in University of Southern California and was Billy's partner. Both were friends in college, and both went to the army and served in Green Berets and fought in Iraq. After the army they went to the police academy together, both worked their way up as detectives. Gary left the force after a messing up a case and chose to resign instead of being suspended. He has a friend in campus security that got him a job working in USC. Mostly it is his cushiest job in the world. His friend is Brian Scott who was also selected to join the team to find the assassin. They're being assigned Laura Wilkerson as the President's senior advisor and a liaison to a new CIA team called the Book Guys. Laura addressed the men that Laura will be team leader and was an ex-green beret who served with Billy and Gary, and she was the one who pulled the strings to recruit them. Their job is to find the assassin and who this assassin is working for and stop their evil scheme. They got two weeks before the president lets the FBI takes over the investigation. They have no clue how to find him. Can the Book Guys find this assassin and the guy who was hired by him and whoever they are it will be up to the Book Guys to stop them. Can they, only time will tell.

Inside the banquet hall in the Ritz Carlton where the President Elect Joe Robinette is at the podium with a lot of people who were invited to watch the President's victory speech. Right next to Joe Robinette who is sitting left of the podium is his Vice President elect Srinivas Robert Chavala aka Bobby Chavala is an Asian-American guy whose family immigrated from India is their watch the president makes his victory speech before his inauguration in two weeks. Everybody is listening to what Joe is saying. Joe tells the audience, "My fellow Americans thank you for electing me in office. I promise you that I want to help every American citizen I can. But I will do my best to see what I can do. I will not make any promises. But I will do what I can to help you guys out. Everyone gets up from their chairs and starts clapping. Joe, Bobby and two of his senior advisors exit the tables and podium. Outside the Banquet Hall in Bellevue Conference and Event Center. Everyone outside is greeting the president-elect Joe Robinette and Vice President elect Bobby Chavala. They are exiting the banquet hall where Joe and Bobby gave the victory speech, and they will be ready for the inauguration in two weeks. With the secret service and president's advisors who are their entourage escorts Joe and Bobby to the presidential limo. Bobby tells Joe, "I think that victory speech inspired a lot of people Joe." Joe tells Bobby, "I hope so. I want to make a good impression. I want to change the world someday." Bobby tells Joe, "That this new bill we are working on, could help a lot of people. The economy is the toilet right now. These new jobs bill can help them get jobs for everyone." Joe tells

Bobby, "Once we get sworn in, we can get to work on this new works bill. Before that, we are busy making a peace treaty with his unknown country that was declaring war with us ten years ago. Right now, this new bill can help this country and make peace with them." Bobby tells Joe, "That this country is not just trying to invade us, they were also trying to invade South Korea, I heard they were working with North Korea." Joe tells Bobby, "That is why we are doing this peace treaty so they can switch sides and maybe team up with South Korea to protect them and not just us." Bobby tells Joe, "I hope so, Joe." A bullet comes out of nowhere and hits Joe in the chest and he falls on the floor. Joe is hurting and the secret service are on the walkie-talkies. Secret Service Agent 1 tells everyone, "Stay back! Stay Back! POTUS has been shot." Across the street in a building where a sniper is carrying a Remington Model 700 rifle and sees everyone panicking. The sniper takes out his cell phone and makes the call. The sniper who is the presidential assassin tells the person on his cell phone, "POTUS is down! Mission accomplished. Send a chopper right away." The secret service 2 sees the assassin and tells his boss, "Marcus, I found the assassin, he's on the roof." Marcus tells the rest of the secret service on their walkie talkies, "I spot the shooter. The shooter is at 156 Hannah Avenue on the roof! Get up the roof now!" Three of the secret service members are heading to 156 Hannah Avenue on the roof where they see the shooter. Joe is dying and Bobby is holding him until the ambulance arrives. The ambulance arrives and stops where the President-elect is at. The two paramedics exit the ambulance and Paramedic is carrying his medical bag while Paramedic 1 is opening the back of the ambulance door and gets the stretcher. Bobby looks at Joe and tells him, "Hang on, Joe. You can do this. Just don't die on me will you." Paramedic 1 tells Bobby, "Mr. Vice President can you step back, and we need to get the president on the gurney. Bobby tells the paramedic, "Okay!" Bobby lets go of Joe and gets up from the road and the two paramedics pick up Joe and put him on the stretcher. The two paramedics brought him inside the ambulance. Inside 156 Hannah Avenue the three secret service agents are carrying their SIG-Sauer P228 guns. They are on the stairs trying to get to the sniper before he exits the roof. The roof door opens and it's three secret service agents. The three secret service agents enter the roof and see the assassin picked up by a Bell 427 helicopter. The helicopter already exited the roof before the secret service got there. The three secret service agents try to shoot the helicopter and the assassin. Ten bullets came out of three secret service agents' guns. Three of them come out of Secret Service agents 1 gun, three other bullets come out of Secret Service Agent 2 gun and three other bullets come out of the Secret Service 3 gun and the ten bullets hit the helicopter and misses the assassin. The assassin aims his Remington Model 700 rifle at the three secret service agents. The assassin fires his gun, five bullets hit the Secret Service Agents 1 in the chest and almost dies. The Assassin fires ten more bullets, five bullets hit Secret Service Agent 2 in the chest and dies and the five other bullets hit Secret Service Agents 3 in the chest and his head and dies. The first secret service agent 1 is still alive and the assassin sees that the first Secret Service Agent is still alive. The Assassin fires his gun and three more bullets come out of his gun and hits Secret Service Agent 1 in the head and dies too. The pilot sees that the assassin is going to be a problem and is going to be bad for the team if they find them. The pilot sees his berretta 92x gun in the passenger seat and grabs it and aims the gun at the assassin. The pilot aims his gun on the assassin and tells the assassin, "Hey, Reynolds you know you are a casualty of the war." Reynolds turns around before the rest of the secret service gets up on the roof. Reynolds tells the pilot, "What are you talking about. What do you mean I'm a casualty of war. Come on, let's get the chopper moving. The rest of the Secret Service is coming." The pilot tells Reynolds who is the assassin, "You know what happens to soldiers who are in the capacity of the war. The military always thinks of the weakest soldiers when they outlive their usefulness. Reynolds your usefulness is up." Reynolds tells the helicopter pilot, "Look I don't know how much coffee you've been drinking. Come on, let's get the chopper out of here." The pilot tells the assassin, "Time to take out weak." The helicopter pilot fires his gun, four bullets come out of his gun and hits the assassin. The assassin fells out of the helicopter and hits the roof and drops his rifle gun. The assassin is dying. The helicopter leaves the roof before the rest of the secret service agents arrive. The assassin is almost dying. Five other secret service agents carrying their guns and entering the roof and see three of the crew dead. Secret Service Agent 5 sees the assassin and on the floor dying. Secret Service Agent 5 tells the crew, "Go check out to see the rest of the crew if they are okay. I go check out the assassin." Secret Service Agent 5 heads to the assassin, who is dying, and the rest of the secret service team checks out the rest of the crew to see if they are still alive. Secret Service Agent sees the assassin aims his gun on him and tells him, "Why did you try to kill the president." Reynolds tells the Secret Service Agent 5, "Our new president is weak and practically useless to run the country. The way I look at him, I don't think he has time left." Secret Service Agent 5 tells Reynolds, "Give me one reason why I shouldn't shoot you now." Reynolds tells Secret Service Agent 5, "Because I'm dying. My lifeline will expire in 20 seconds. Before I die, I didn't plan this assassination. I was hired to do it. You'll never find the guy who hired me to kill the president. I guess one good thing, I dodged a bullet not going to jail." Secret Service Agent 5 tells Reynolds, "You may dodge a bullet, you will be heading to hell." Reynolds tells Secret Service Agent 5, There is no heaven or hell for me. Just eternal light for me. I am going to see the light and like I said good luck finding that guy who shot your beloved president elect." Reynolds is dead and Secret Service 5 checks to see if he is dead and he is. The rest of the crew checks on the dead three secret service agents. Secret Service Agent 6 goes over to Secret Service Agent 5 and tells him, "Cooper, they're dead." Cooper tells Secret Service Agent 6, "So, is our assassin." Outside the street where the president is shot. The ambulance exits the street and heads to the hospital. George Washington University Hospital where two secret service agents are guarding the president-elect in his hospital room and inside the president's hospital room where the president is a coma. The door opens and it's Bobby. Bobby enters the president's hospital room and closes the door. Bobby sees a chair and puts the chair next to Joe where he is in a coma. Bobby sits down in his chair and holds Joe's hand for a minute. Bobby tells himself, "Hey Joe, how are you doing. I miss you. You were a great president. You were a top prosecutor in New York, was elected to Congress for ten years and the US Senator for 15 years and chose me as your running mate. I was a bestselling book author in Missouri. I was born in Wichita Kansas and was raised in Maryville Missouri where my dad moved his private practice as an Eye Doctor. But I am not going into details about that. Anyway, I was a top book author who wrote a princess series books where the princess are heroines. They were best sellers and box office hits. I had an associate degree in business in Northwest Missouri State University and a bachelor's degree in English. Because I was a good writer and I always wanted to be a screenwriter or a book author. I sold my book to a publishing company in Random House and my book The Princess School was a best seller. The rest was history, but I was famous enough to run for Governor of Missouri, since a political consultant was a fan of mine, and I was elected Governor in 2018 and you made me your running mate in 2020. How does a guy who has a college degree from a smalltime university to become Vice President elect. But Joe, you were practically qualified to be president. Because you had a bachelor's degree in criminology and Juris Doctor from Yale. I wish you could wake up because this country needs you. I was damn lucky, I was elected Governor of Missouri, because I was a famous bestselling book author. My father Sudarsan died five years ago, and my mother passed away a year ago. My brother Sai and my sister-in-law Susmita are doctors in Dallas with their kids, my niece Lekha and my nephew Naveen. I can barely run the state of Missouri, then running the country. That was your job, I would have helped you run the country. You know how to run and figure out what to do. I don't know what I'm doing. I just hope you wake up soon." The doctor enters Joe's hospital room and talks to Bobby. The Doctor tells Bobby, "Hello Mr. Vice President." Bobby tells the doctor, "Look Doctor, you don't have to call me Mr. Vice President. Just call me Bobby. Will you because I won't answer if you call me Mr. Vice President. Just call me Mr. Chavala or Bobby." Doctor tells Bobby, "Okay Bobby, I have some bad news sir." Bobby tells the Doctor, "Doctor the President is going to be okay. Is he because the country needs him. He's about to be sworn in a week. Mostly the current President right now is already leaving office and so I am going to be taking Joe's place while he recovers, or he wakes up. So, we can find out who killed him." Doctor tells Bobby, "Mr.

Chavala the President is not going to make it. The bullet dodged all the way to my heart. The president had heart problems for a long time, we removed the bullet, but his heart is not working anymore. He's got one more week left, then we must unplug the machines. His wife, the current first lady-elect is going asked us to pull the plug since she gave us her consent to pull the plug, since the president is going to die. He has only a week left." Bobby tells the doctor, "How is his wife, the current first lady-elect." Doctor tells Bobby, "In a week she will be the former first lady after we pull the plug. She is not doing well, trying to pull it together." Bobby tells the doctor, "Where is she now?" Doctor tells Bobby, "She is in the waiting room, she didn't want to leave her husband side. I'm going to check on the president for a minute" Bobby tells the Doctor, "I'll go check to see if she is okay. Thanks doctor, doing what you can to take care of the president." Doctor tells Bobby, "Hey, no problem Mr Chavala." Bobby exits Joe's hospital room and heads to the waiting room where Joe's wife is sitting down in her chair and sobbing that she is losing her husband. Bobby tells the First Lady-elect, "Hey Joan. I'm sorry about your husband." Bobby sits down in the waiting room chair and hugs Joan for a minute and let's go. Joan is still crying and tells Bobby, "I can't believe it that Joe was shot. I always worry they would be trying to kill him while he was president, not after being elected. I have known why they want to kill him. He wasn't sworn in yet and I don't even know what to do." Bobby tells Joan, "Don't worry, you still get your presidential pension even after he was elected president." Joan tells Bobby, "I wish I know who this assassin is and why they want to kill him." Bobby tells Joan, "We're about to investigate soon who is trying to kill your husband." Joan tells Bobby, "How's he doing?" Bobby tells Joan, "He's not doing good and is still in coma and waiting to die. Since he only has one week left to live. Since you guys already pulled the plug after the week." Joan tells Bobby, "The doctor told me, he doesn't have much time. After he was shot, the bullet dodged from the heart. They removed the bullet they can't fix his heart and the way I look he only has one week left." Bobby tells Joan, "Is there anything I could do for you?" Joan tells Bobby, "No, I want to be alone right now. I'll probably stay in for the night here or head back to the hotel. I haven't thought this through. My kids, it is going to be tough on them losing their father." Bobby tells Joan, "I'm like their surrogate Uncle to them. You guys treated me like family when Joe asked me to be his running mate. I didn't think we would make the front runner area or win the general election. But we did. But now, I'm just counting the days he has left. I know I must fill in for him, since the current president and first lady already left the white house and I'm going must stay there until I get sworn as president soon. Right now, before I get sworn in, I will be the acting president. I have no idea what I will do. But I will tell the public to give condolences to Joe." Joan tells Bobby, "Bobby, I know you can do the job. If anyone could run the country, it would have been you. At least right now, you must protect the citizens of the United States. America needs a guy like you to protect them." Bobby tells Joan, "Truth is Joan, I don't even know where to start." Joan tells Bobby, "You will know when the time comes." Bobby's head of the secret service enters the hospital waiting room and goes over talk to Bobby. Head of the Secret Service tells Bobby, "Excuse me, Mr. President. I wanted to tell you that the assassin who killed the president elect is dead. But I think this assassin did not do this alone, I think he was working for someone. Bobby tells the head of the secret service, "How do you know that Woody?" Woody tells Bobby, "The assassin was escaping from a helicopter, but he was shot at by the pilot. I think the pilot and this assassin was working for someone to kill the president elect." Bobby tells Woody, "This assassin and the pilot are just minions aka means they're just mercenaries hired to kill the president. We have no idea who hired this assassin to kill Joe. It could be anyone. Woody, did your id the assassin who it is.?" Woody tells Bobby, "Not yet, sir." Bobby tells Woody, "Find out who he is, is this assassin sent to kill Joe, I could be next and the person who hired this assassin could kill me too. So, get on with it, we will start this investigation soon. Call the FBI and tell them to start investigating. Woody tells Bobby, "I'll get right on it, Mr. President. Mr. President I was going to tell you, the reason why I'm here is the press is outside and waiting for your statement." Bobby tells Woody, "I guess I better tell the country what is going on and give them a heads up what we're dealing with. Tell the press I'll be out there giving them a statement. I need a couple of minutes to think." Woody tells Bobby, "Yes, sir." Woody exits the waiting room and heads to the front door of the hospital to inform the press that Bobby is coming outside for a press conference. Bobby tells Joan, "I guess it's better late than ever." Joan tells Bobby, "Good luck Bobby." Bobby tells Joan, "I'm going to need it." Outside George Washington University Hospital where Bobby is the acting president and is on the podium where he is addressing the press with two Secret Service agents are protecting him from the podium. Bobby exits outside the hospital and heads to the podium where the press is waiting for his statement. Bobby is at the podium and ready to talk to the press. "Bobby tells the press, "Hello I am Srinivas Robert Chavala, the acting president of the United States. I can give the condition to the President-elect Joseph Robinette, according to the doctors that President Joseph Robinette is in a coma, and he has one week left to live. Since, I am the Vice President and the President in now in a coma. I am the new acting President and right now we will begin an investigation on this unknown assailant who shot and killed President Robinette. Unknown reporter tells Bobby, "Excuse me, Mr President. Lou Harper from the Washington Post, has the assassin been identified?" Bobby tells Lou, "We have not identified who this unknown assassin is, and the Medical Examiner will identify the man who shot him." Another unknown reporter asked Bobby, "Excuse me, Mr President. Charlotte Cooper from New York times, did the assassin worked alone when he shot the President Robinette?" Bobby tells Charlotte, "No the assassin did not work alone, this assassin to take out the president and we are going to open investigation who this assassin was working for." Lou Harper tells the President, "Is this going to open investigation and when will the FBI start this investigation?" Bobby tells Lou, "This will be a closed investigation for the FBI and the FBI will start this investigation into who this dead assassin is working for. Until then, that's all the information I can give you. Right now, the former president has vacated the White House today and he will attend the presidential Inauguration in a week. So, I will be moving to the White House in an hour. Until then, I am acting President Srinivas Robert Chavala signing off." Bobby and the two secret service agents exit the podium and the rest of the press wanted to ask more questions, but they never had a chance since Bobby and the rest of the secret service agents are leaving George Washington University hospital. Bobby and the two secret service agents head to the presidential limo. Bobby and the two secret service agents reached the presidential limo and Secret Service Agent 1 opens the limo door where Bobby, Secret Service Agent 1 and 2 go inside the limo and Secret Service Agent 2 closes the limo door. The limo exits the hospital, and the limo is heading to the white house. Inside the limo, Bobby, the two secret service agents and Joe's presidential advisor are in the back of the limo. The Presidential advisor tells Bobby, "Mr. President, I will inform the director to begin the investigation?" Bobby tells the Presidential Advisor, "Tell him not to begin the investigation until tomorrow and get him to identify the unknown assassin. If this assassin works for someone. I could be next. I have no idea why this assassin took out Joe before inauguration. Waldo can tell me what's today on my schedule?" Waldo tells Bobby, "Well Mr. President there is nothing in your schedule today. So, all you can do go to the white house and make yourself home and the rest of the movers will get your stuff from the hotel tomorrow." Bobby tells Waldo, "Thanks Waldo, the director will find out who this assassin is and what he is up to. Since Joe will be dead soon, my inauguration is not going to start after his funeral. Until then, Waldo, I need you to tell you not to make any funeral arrangements until this investigation is over and tell John to double up security in the hospital and Joan. The person might go after her too." Waldo tells Bobby, "Sure thing, Mr. President." Bobby tells Waldo, "Waldo, you can call me Bobby. Because I won't answer if you call me Mr. President. Only the public or my fans can call me Mr. President." Waldo tells Bobby, "Sure thing, Bobby." Bobby tells them, "I going to get some sleep and we will figure out our plan tomorrow." The Bell 427 lands on the warehouse roof and the helicopter stops and the helicopter door opens and it's the pilot who killed the assassin. The pilot exits the roof and closes the door. He heads to the warehouse door and opens the door and enters the warehouse. Inside the office a man is calling his boss in his phone and the person on the phone tells his boss on the other side of the phone, "Yes boss, Mr.

Alexander, it was a success. The President elect is dead. The mission is complete and don't worry we covered our tracks well. Okay, we will begin the mission soon and don't worry our clients are waiting for us in a week. Okay, bye." The door knocks and Alexander tells the person on the other side of the door, "Come in." The door opens and it's the helicopter pilot. The helicopter pilot enters the office and closes the door. Alexander tells the Helicopter pilot, "Hello Ernie, did the mission was a success?" Ernie tells Alexander, "Yes, Mr. Alexander the mission was a success and we promised Rufus that we would pay until the mission was done. He killed the president elect and now his mission was complete. His services were no longer needed, and we don't have to pay him. Our clients hired him to kill the president and they knew he was a good assassin, but he was weak and useless. When his useless is up and we take him out. It's our clients' orders." Rufus sits down in his chair and Alexander tells Ernie, "The boss is happy with us that the president is dead. Cooper industries is building new guns and grenades for our clients. Our boss's clients is going to pay them 800 million dollars for them and double our money for our company when we begin our mission. When our clients get our weapons, they can invade their enemy's country and take over for them. The stocks will hit the roof for all of us that will make us billions of dollars." Ernie tells Alexander, "Well Mr. Alexander, what happens if they identify our assassin, and they could connect us and our boss from this assassination." Alexander tells Ernie, "I wouldn't have to worry about it. Our assassin is a ghost, and they will never connect us with the presidential assassination. Besides their new acting President Srinivas Robert Chavala is practically incompetent for the job. That is why our boss wanted Robinette dead. Because Robinette would figure out that our boss is making arms deals with our clients. He needed to go, and we did. Now we can watch this idiot mess up this country. So, we got nothing to worry about, come on we got to check the inventory." Ernie tells Alexander, "Yes sir." Alexander and Ernie got up from his chair and headed to the door. Ernie opens the door and Alexander, and Ernie exits the office. Ernie closes the door. Inside the warehouse Alexander's guys are hiding guns and grenades inside the creates and covering it with flour. Alexander and Ernie look at the crew hiding the weapons. Alexander tells Ernie, keep an eye on them. Make sure they don't lose anything, and make sure nothing is taken. Because our clients are paying a lot of money for us to start their invasion in their country." Ernie tells Alexander, "Yes sir." Alexander tells Ernie, "I'm going to head back to the office and tell the boss that nothing is taken. Make sure all our men don't lose any of the weapons or we are in big trouble." Ernie tells Alexander, "Yes sir." Alexander exits the warehouse and heads back to his office. In the morning inside the oval office in the warehouse. Bobby is looking at information about the whereabouts of this assassin. Waldo enters the oval office and closes the door and goes over talk to Bobby. Waldo stops and tells Bobby, "Bobby, I got an id on our assassin." Bobby tells Waldo, "Who is he Waldo?" Waldo tells Bobby, "I have the name of the assassin who killed Mr. Robinette yesterday." Bobby tells Waldo, "Who is he?" Waldo tells Bobby, "His name is Rufus Stonewalk, he was a military sniper for the US marines. He was an excellent sniper who made 500 kills for the Iraq and Afghanistan war. But there is one problem." Bobby tells Waldo, "What's that?" Waldo tells Bobby, "He's dead." Bobby tells Waldo, "I know he died assassinated Joe while trying to get away at a helicopter when the pilot shot him." Waldo tells Bobby, "He died in Iraq war on January 10, 2007. He was killed by a grenade explosion by some Afghan soldiers." Bobby tells Waldo, "That this is no coincidence the guy who killed Joe. might be a doppelganger who looks like the guy who was killed in the Afghan war. Unless this guy was a mercenary and faked his death. This mercenary must be working for some top Intelligence agency." Waldo sits down in his chair and hands out the information to Bobby. Bobby grabs the information and looks at it for a minute. Waldo tells Bobby, "If he is working for an intelligence company, it must be someone who has top resources to fake someone death and use it for some unofficial missions that the agency never sanctions." Bobby tells Waldo, "I know National Security Agency has the resources to fake someone's death to recruit agents who are ex-military guys so they can do important missions like the CIA does." Waldo tells Bobby, "Do you think someone in the NSA is involved in this assassination?" Bobby tells Waldo, "I think so. But it could be anyone in the agency that could have been involved. Mostly everyone respected Joe. Besides the only reason why they want to kill him unless he knows something or trying to keep him away from something." Waldo tells Bobby, "Do you think anything has to do with works bill that he was lobbying for." Bobby tells Waldo, "He was lobbying with the President to build a new works bill that can help a lot of jobs in the country. Mostly he was working with a peace treaty with an unknown country that we were trying to end the war with. Joe never told me what country we were trying to make peace with. They said they were going to declare war on us ten years ago and I think that the assassin was trying to stop the peace treaty with Joe on board. This peace treaty could help us prevent the war against our country. Waldo finds nothing about this country that was trying to declare war on us. If we can find the country, what Joe was planning to prevent this war." Waldo tells Bobby, "Sure thing, Bobby." Waldo gets up from his chair and exits the oval office. Bobby grabs his telephone and makes a call to his secretary. Bobby tells his secretary on the phone, "Hello Cindy, can you call the NSA director and tell him I would like to see him in my office in twenty minutes. Thank you." In Mcdonald's in Los Angeles California, Detective Sergeant Billy Wallace is eating a cheeseburger and French friends and drinking his diet coke. Mostly Billy is a fat and lazy cop who is taking his lunch break right now. Mostly his friend Gary Rodriguez who is campus security cop in USC goes over to Billy and talks to him. Gary tells Billy, "Hey Billy!" Billy tells Gary, "Hey Gary, how's USC." Gary tells Billy, "It's great." Gary sits down in his chair and joins Billy. Gary tells Billy, "It's fun and it's great." Billy tells Gary, "Mostly the job must suck." Gary tells Billy, "The job is not bad, mostly it is kind of boring. Mostly I just hand out parking tickets to college students when they usually park in a no parking zone. I escort students to their cars or places, so they don't get mugged. Billy tells Gary, "So you don't miss the police force and the action." Gary tells Billy, "I do miss it sometimes. But LAPD is not well liked, mostly a lot of people hate us and don't trust us. Mostly we were not ordinary cops, we cared about people, and we only had one job in the LAPD to serve and protect the people. Mostly a drug bust gone wrong, I got shot in the line of fire. You took out the drug lord and shut down his empire." Billy tells Gary, "You got shot and they made you take a desk job." Gary tells Billy, "I didn't want a desk job, either I retire, or I take the desk job. I didn't want to spend the rest of my pushing papers. I chose retirement. Good thing, our friend from alma mater got me a job in USC campus security." Billy tells Gary, "Our friend in college Brian Scott is the new dean of students pulled some strings with the Board of Regents to get me the job. Can you believe it? Two nerdy and lazy guys like us become cops after we graduated from college, and we became cops. How did we do that and why did we want to become cops." Billy tells Gary, "Gary, we wanted to make a difference. We loved those dirty harry movies. Dirty Harry is a cop people look up to. He did not care about protocol and procedure. All he cared about was protecting the people that he was sworn to. Mostly cops only care about law and order. I only cared about one thing Serve and Protect. I wanted to serve and protect the people." Gary tells Billy, "I never did ask how we got into the academy, mostly we were practically unqualified to get in." Billy tells Gary, "A long time ago, there was a police shortage and right now the academy is accepting all willing recruits. Plus, my father is a police captain, and he pulled a lot of strings to get us into the academy." Gary tells Billy, "I usually forgot about that. I can't believe he suspended you on that drug bust. We took down that drug cartel and their leader. But we did not get commendations and we get is reprimands from your father." Billy tells Gary, "I've been suspended for two weeks, and you end up working as a campus security. How low is that. My dad always gave me a hard time and I did everything I was told; he still gives me crap." Gary tells Billy, "My dad died when I was five years old, and my mom took care of me. Luckily my parents were corporate lawyers and they both had busy schedules and they were never home. But I love my mom taking care of me. I wanted her to make her proud. She was proud of me; she was disappointed in me that I didn't go to Law School and went to the police academy with you. But she was okay with it after a few months I told her." Billy tells Gary, "I told you I was going to join the army to pay for college and maybe I could be a green beret. But you went with me, even though your mother is very wealthy and can pay your tuition for school. But you joined anyway."

Gary tells Billy, "I didn't want you to go alone, even after basic training. The sergeant sends us to Fort Bragg to train with the green berets. Even though we were lousy at training, but it was good enough to send us to Iraq to fight. But we were war heroes when we rescued the POWs in Iraq and prison camp. After we left and went to college and got degrees for communication and English" Billy tells Gary, "I wanted to be a book author, I have nothing to write about right now. Even our exciting lapd job made it boring since we only do research and we have never been in the field. Until one time, we went off the books to catch the drug lord. We did, until that drug lord tipped us off. Luckily, we stopped it and shut down his empire." Gary tells Billy, "Too bad, your father chewed us out for that. Even without a warrant, our drug lord would find a guy in the inside and move his drug operation somewhere else before the LAPD arrive." Billy tells Gary, "Luckily we were the ones to help stop that drug deal before it hit the streets." Gary tells Billy, "Too bad we can't do a good job like that again. Besides Billy even after your suspension, I think your dad is going to move you into a desk job to keep you out of trouble." Billy tells Gary, "I know. I give anything to prove to my father that I can be a field cop and work as a great detective. But he always knows I like a lazy cop who doesn't follow orders or protocol or procedure. I wish I can prove him wrong." Gary tells Billy, "You never know maybe someday we can catch a break." Billy tells Gary, "You never know." Gary tells Billy, "I must get back to work before Brian starts a search party. I'll see you later Billy." Billy tells Gary, "I'll see you later too, Gary." Gary gets up from his chair and exits McDonald's. Back in the oval office where Bobby is working in his office. The intercom button rings and Bobby answers it. Bobby tells his secretary on the intercom, "What is it, Laura?" Laura tells Bobby on the intercom, "I wondered if I could come into your office, I need to tell you something important. If it's okay with you, sir?" Bobby tells Laura on the intercom, "Okay, come in." Laura opens the oval office door and enters the oval office. Laura is a very attractive secretary who is in her late 20's. Laura closes the door and goes over and talks to Bobby. Laura stops for a minute when she reaches Bobby's desk and tells him, "Mr. Chavala, I want to inform you that your senior presidential advisor

Waldo Carter is going to be out for the week. So, he can't help advising you for a week." Bobby tells Laura, "What happened to him." Laura tells Bobby, "His mother had a heart attack. So, he went to Phoenix to visit her mother who is in the hospital. He called me and sent you a message that he will be gone in a week since his mother had a heart attack and cannot help you out." Bobby tells Laura, "Man, I felt bad about his mother. I wish I could help him and his mother. I am going to give him his condolences to his mother. If there are any medical bills, I'll pay for them. At least I can do is help Waldo out. He was loyal to me and Joe. Joe always trusted Waldo when he was a US Senator and helped him go through tough times and decisions. So, did I. But right now, I need to find a senior advisor to help me out. So, Laura I know you're just the white house secretary. I read your file, that you worked as a secretary in this white house for 10 years. So, I never did this before. I'm going to start now. Laura, I am appointing you, my new senior advisor, for a week. So, I need you to fill in for Waldo when he gets back." Laura is really touched that she gets to be Bobby's advisor for a week. Laura doesn't know if she can handle the responsibility and tells Bobby, "I'm very touched Mr. Chavala. That you are appointing me as your new senior advisor. But I never advised anyone before. I barely don't even know what to do?" Bobby tells Laura, "Neither do I. I'm president of the United States. I don't even have any experience running the country. I can barely run in the state of Missouri. But I figured out how to do it. I know how to be a vice president. I think I know how to figure out how to be president if I have the right people to help me. So that is why I need you as my advisor." Laura tells Bobby, "I appreciate the honor. I will do my best to fill in for Mr. Carter for a week." Bobby tells Laura, "I know you can." Laura tells Bobby, "Sir, there is something else I wanted to tell you, before I came here." Bobby tells Laura, "What's that Laura?" Laura tells Bobby, "Logan Roberts, the director of the NSA is here to see you sir." Bobby tells Laura, "Send him in. I've been expecting him." Laura tells Bobby, "Yes sir." Laura heads to the door. Laura opens the oval office door and closes the door while she exits the oval office. The oval office door opens and it's Logan Roberts who is the Director of the NSA. Logan enters the oval office and closes the door and goes over to Bobby's desk and stops. Logan tells Bobby, "Hello Mr President, you said you needed to see me." Bobby tells Logan, "Have a seat, Logan." Logan sits down in his chair near Bobby's desk. Bobby tells Logan, "Logan, I'm not going to beat around the bush. I think they might be a rogue NSA agent that might be responsible for Joe Robinette assassination." Logan tells Bobby, "You don't really believe that sir. That one of my own had something to do with the president elect assassination. I'm appalled sir. I do a lot of background checks on my men. They have all passed with flying colors and none of them went rogue." Bobby tells Logan, "You're right General Roberts, I don't think it would be any of your men. Because the assassin that we id is Rufus Stonewalk. He used to be a sniper for the marines. I found out, he was an excellent sniper who made 500 kills for the Iraq and Afghanistan war and was killed in Iraq war on January 10, 2007. He was killed by a grenade explosion by some Afghan soldiers. It is no coincidence that this assassin looks like the guy who should have been dead 15 years ago." Logan tells Bobby, "What is that have to do with one of my NSA soldiers." Bobby tells Logan, "I don't know how NSA agents get recruited. But the only way I know is to fake their deaths and join the organization and use an alias. Since our assassin that looks like the dead solider who died in 2007 is the same guy who killed President elect Robinette and himself. Mostly since Stonewalk is dead, I don't think he worked alone since the weapon he used to kill Robinette might be connected to NSA guns." Logan tells Bobby, "Is Stonewalk is one of mine. I threw him out of the agency five weeks ago, when I questioned some stolen weapons that were in a warehouse in a top-secret area in 167 Robin Lane in Arlington. We had no leads on who took the weapons, I thought it might be a rogue NSA agent who knows that warehouse inside and out." Bobby tells Logan, "Did anyone investigate it?" Stonewalk tells Bobby, "We investigated it, and we couldn't find anything about who stole those weapons and the unknown assailant who stole them. These guys who stole those weapons are usually ghost." Bobby tells Stonewalk, "Mostly the guys are usually ex-military. Mostly I would inform the FBI about this and call the director about the missing weapons. These missing weapons from the NSA warehouse may be tied to Stonewalk since you guys questioned the stolen weapons. He is the only one you trusted to give him access to the warehouse." Logan tells Bobby, "I'm a peaceful guy. I usually accept all willing recruits. Even if they didn't pass a background check. I still give them second chances even if they did pass the requirements." Bobby tells Logan, "So do I. Until then, we got locate those missing guns from the NSA before it goes in the wrong hands." Logan tells Bobby, "So, Mr Chavala. Should we call the FBI and inform them about what's going on. They can investigate the mission guns and maybe find out who hired Stonewalk to kill the President-elect." Bobby tells Logan, "I don't think so if we informed the FBI or anyone else. Those weapons will be long gone. Since we have a rogue NSA agent who might be listening in and tried to move the weapons somewhere else. Stonewalk's boss might be selling weapons to terrorist, and we got to find out who they are." Logan tells Bobby, "So if we can't get the FBI to investigate this and how are we going to find the stolen weapons and the mastermind behind the president's assassination." Bobby tells Logan, "We are going have go to take off the books in this one. That means we are going to hire someone outside to help us find the missing weapons and the mastermind behind this assassination." Logan tells Bobby, "Were going to find some outsiders who can help us find the stolen weapons and mastermind behind this assassination." Bobby tells Logan, "Of course." Logan tells Bobby, "I think you lost your mind Mr. Chavala. I think we should find real professionals who are in law enforcement to handle this job and not some outsiders." Bobby tells Logan, "Like I said, Logan. If we are going to find our guy and the missing weapons. We are going to need all the help we can get." Logan tells Bobby, "How are you going to find them?" Bobby tells Logan, "I'm not going to find them, that will be Laura's job. So, I going to let her find them." Logan laughs a little and stops. Logan tells Bobby, "Laura, you're Secretary Laura." Bobby tells Logan, "Yes, my secretary." Logan tells Bobby, "You're going to let your secretary find these men to locate the stolen weapons and our mastermind." Bobby tells Logan, "First of all, I appointed her as my temporary senior advisor for the week while Waldo is visiting her mother in the hospital who just had a heart attack. If anyone can find these guys. It will be her." Bobby turns on the intercom and tells Laura,

"Laura can you come in. I need to speak to you for a minute." Laura's voiceover on the intercom tells Bobby, "Yes, Mr. Chavala." Bobby turns off the intercom. The oval office door opens and it's Laura. Laura closes the door and goes over to Bobby's desk and stops. Laura tells Bobby, "Yes Mr. Chavala is there anything you need?" Bobby tells Laura, "Listen Laura, I need a favor." Back inside the warehouse office where Mr. Alexander is answering the phone to his boss. Mr. Alexander tells his boss on the phone, "Yes sir, it was a success." The dark office where Alexander and Ernie's office is lurking in the shadow and using raspy voice tells Alexander on the phone, "The weapons are they in check." Alexander's voiceover on the phone, "Yes sir, the weapons are ready for the week. Should we worry if the FBI or any law enforcement is investigating about us." Alexander and Ernie's boss in the shadows tells Alexander on the phone, "We have nothing to worry about. I have the connections to cover our tracks. So far, law enforcement is investigating us. Stonewalk is their only suspect who acted alone in this assassination. We can begin our arms deal with our important clients. I'll be there two days to check on you guys, remember I don't want you and Ernie to mess this up. Or else you guys will be joining Robinette in a minute if anything happens to weapons deal." Back in the warehouse office where Alexander is talking to his boss on his phone and tells him, "Don't worry sir, nothing is going to happen sir. I'll see you in two days." Laura is in her desk that is right across the oval office entrance where Bobby is at. Laura is looking at some files on anyone who can help Bobby find those missing weapons and the mastermind behind this assassination. Laura tells herself, "Nope, I have not found it yet." Laura kept looking and couldn't find any guys who could do the job. Laura tells herself, "These guys are way overqualified to do the job and it would take a miracle to find anyone who could do this mission. Somebody that nobody would suspect in a million years. But it is kind of hard to find someone like that." Laura got an idea and snapped her fingers. Laura tells herself, "I got it. I think I have found someone who can help us?" Laura picks up her phone and makes a call. Laura tells the person on the other side of the phone, "Hello Rudy, Listen I need a favor. I need a file on a couple of friends of mine. Okay, thank you."

Back in the Oval Office where Bobby is working at his desk. The door knocks and Bobby tells the person on the other side of the Oval Office, "Come in." The door opens and it's Laura. Laura enters the Oval Office carrying two files in her left hand. Laura closes the door and goes over to Bobby and talks to him. Laura tells Bobby, "Mr. Chavala, I found two guys that can help us find our mastermind who ordered Stonewalk who killed the President elect." Bobby tells Laura, "Who are they?" Laura puts down the files of Laura that has on Billy Wallace and Gary Rodriguez on his desk. Laura tells Bobby, "One of them William Wallace, people call him Billy Wallace. He is a detective sergeant in the Los Angeles Police Department in Narcotics. Gary Rodriguez was also an ex-LAPD detective sergeant who was Billy's partner in a drug bust that had gone wrong. They shut down the drug empire and took down the Cartel leader. Billy was suspended and Gary was reassigned to desk duty. But he declined and chose to resign from the force. He works as a campus security in University of Southern California whose friends with Brian Scott who is the Dean of Students in that university got him a job. He's been working as a campus Security guard for two weeks." Bobby looks at their files and sees reads about them. Bobby tells Laura, "It says here Billy and Gary only got into the academy because Billy's a legacy in the police force since his father is a Captain in their precinct and pulled some strings to get in. How about that then both graduated from USC and were theater and communication majors and joined the army and were in special forces. But they usually get a lot of reprimands from the superiors and almost court martialed when they disobeyed when they rescued POWs from a prison camp in Iraq. These guys did three tours of duty of Iraq for three years before they joined the force." Laura tells Bobby, "They were awarded silver stars for the rescues. But they lack authority and disobey orders just to save lives and stop a crime. I think these guys don't look like the ones I would pick to find the mastermind behind Robinette assassination and the missing weapons from the NSA." Bobby tells Laura, "If they are useless, why are you recommending them." Laura tells Bobby, "Because they are war heroes and have 98% percent of a case closure rate and shut down 10 drug empires on the force for ten years." Bobby tells Laura, "They do have an excellent record on the force and have lack of authority. That is why I like them; I want them on my team. By the way, Laura how do you find these guys anyway?" Laura tells Bobby, "I used to serve with them when I was in Iraq. I was there commanding officer." Bobby tells Laura, "Didn't you work as a secretary for 10 years here in the white house. How long were you in the army?" Laura tells Bobby, "I was an army brat, and my father was a colonel in the US army, I was born in Washington D.C., and I traveled around with for five years and we moved back to D.C. when my father got a job working in the Pentagon full time. I attended George Washington University and majored in world history. I also joined ROTC and after I graduated from college and got my commission as Second Lieutenant. I was in the reserves after 9/11, when I was trained at Fort Bragg and shipped off to Afghanistan and Iraq for ten years and was ranked as a major." Bobby tells Laura, "How did you end as a secretary here in the white house." Laura tells Bobby, "I got shot in the line of fire in a mission in Iraq. My commanding officer gave me a desk job back in D.C. and I worked as a secretary for the rest of the two weeks during my discharge and my commanding officer had a friend in the white house who is looking for a secretary for the president of the United States and the rest is history." Bobby tells Laura, "I can see you deserve better job than working as a secretary for me." Laura tells Bobby, "It's okay Mr. Chavala. I like working here, this is a great job where I can meet a lot of interesting people and I got work with two different presidents in ten years. My father was happy, that I got a good job working here than being out on the field." Bobby tells Laura, "Whatever makes you happy. At least you can tell your father that you were my senior advisor for a week. No secretary from here ever had that opportunity. Anyway, make the call and bring them in here. I know a place where they can work. You and I will be leading them for a week." Laura tells Bobby, "Where is this special place that we can work at to investigate the missing weapons and the mastermind behind Robinette assassination?" Bobby tells Laura, "The last place on earth that no one will suspect. All right, Laura makes the arrangements." Laura tells Bobby, "Sure thing, Mr. Chavala." Laura heads to the door and opens and closes the door to the oval Office door." Billy is sleeping in his bed wearing his pajamas in his apartment. Billy's cell phone rings and Billy answers it. Billy is a little bit groggy and when he answers the phone. Billy tells the person on the other end of his cell phone, "Hello, hi Captain. Look, I am already suspended. You already chewed me out last week about that drug bust. What...? I don't believe it. Okay, I'll be in your office in thirty minutes." Billy hangs up his cell phone and tells himself, "Oh, great not only I messed up a drug bust that I closed now the feds wants to speak to me. Oh, man I hate my life." Billy gets up from his bed and tells himself, "I better get this over with." Billy heads to the bathroom door and opens the bathroom door. Billy enters the bathroom and closes the bathroom door." Inside LAPD headquarters where Billy enters the headquarters and is about to head to his captain's office. Billy sees his fellow police officers and detectives. Billy's fellow detective goes over to Billy and tells him, "Hey Billy, what are you doing here. I thought you were suspended?" Billy tells his fellow detective, "I was Rice, but the captain needs to see me and guess what not only he was done chewing me out that drug bust. He's going to chew me out again and this time he brought in a fed with him as a witness." Rice tells Billy, "A fed, man this must be serious business. If the feds are here. What do they want?" Billy tells Rice, "I don't even know, I barely didn't do anything. I did stop a drug bust and retrieve a lot of heroin and took down a drug lord. But instead of commendation, I got a reprimand and a suspension. I better pray that this fed is not here to arrest me for because I stepped on their turf. The feds would never bring down this drug lord, without me and Gary. We knew that area inside and out. Warrants, protocol, and procedure would never bring him down and not even in court could convict or his posse. I better get this over with." Inside the police Captain's office where the captain is working in his desk and the Secret Service Agent is standing right next to the captain. Mostly Gary and Brian are sitting down in their chairs waiting for Billy. The door knocks and the police captain hears the door knock. The police captain tells the person on the other side of the door, "Come in." The door opens and it's Billy. Billy enters the captain's office and closes the door. Billy tells the captain, "Look sir if you here to chew me out again. I am tired, I already respected my suspension. I do need another ass chewing." Captain tells Billy, "Relax Wallace, I'm not here to yell at you again. You know why you are here?" Billy tells the captain, "Something tells me, it has something with this Fed guy here about stepping into his turf. Look, you would never bring down Gonzales, he covered all his tracks. Not even you guys could link him to the heroin. But I did, I got suspended for it." Captain tells Billy, "Billy has a seat. There is something I need tell you, Gary, and Brian about." Billy sits down in his chair and sees Gary and Brian with them. Billy tells the captain, "Sir, what are Gary and Brian doing here. I know you reassigned Gary and suspended me. That is why Gary quit. But Brian did not work on that case with Gonzales with us, why is here." Brian tells Billy, "I've been trying to figure out that myself." Captain tells Billy, "Billy, I have known you for a long time. You don't respect my authority, you don't respect protocols, procedures, and warrants. I yelled at you a lot of times. I threatened to fire you or suspend you for ten years. Why haven't I fired you or Gary from the force." Billy tells the captain, "A lot of reasons, maybe because we have 99% case closure rate and we do have a few medals and commendations for closing those cases and the main reason is Mom won't let you fire me." Captain tells Billy, "Sometimes, I have no reason why I always put up with you." Billy tells the captain, "I don't know Dad, because maybe you weren't around that much when I was growing up. All you cared about was your job." Billy's father tells Billy, "I'm sorry about that, my cases kept me away from you and your mother for a long time. I should be around more. Even after your mother died last year. I have been trying to keep busy. Anyway, about this fed who wants to see you guys. He is not here about the drug bust last week. This fed wanted to congratulate you in person." Billy tells the fed, "Thank you, I appreciate that. By the way who are you and why are you here?" Billy's father tells the Fed about why is here, "Agent Simpson, you can state your business why you are here?" Agent tells Billy, Gary, and Brian why he is here, "Billy Wallace, Gary Rodriguez, Brian Scott, I am Agent Ronald Simpson from the United States Secret Service from Washington D.C." Agent Simpson takes out his US secret service badge from his right pants pocket and shows it to them. Gary tells Agent Simpson, "You're a long way from Washington to commend us for a drug bust that we took down last week. But mostly narcotic bust are not usually Secret Service turfs." Agent Simpson puts his badge back in his right pants pocket. Billy tells Agent Simpson, "At least you can do is give us recognition like a medal or a recognition letter to my father and that way he can reinstate me back in the force and my best friend Gary." Agent Simpson tells them, "That is not why I am here, you three been selected to work on a top case for the current president of the United States elect." Billy is excited and tells Agent Simpson, "The president-elect called us for help. The current president-elect." Agent Simpson tells Billy, "That's right, but the current acting president elect is Mr. Srinivas Robert Chavala is running the show now. Since if you guys heard the news about President elect Joe Robinette is in a coma, he only has one week left to live. Until then the President-elect Chavala needs your help on an important matter." Billy tells Agent Simpson, "Me, you need my help?" Agent Simpson tells Billy, "Not just you, but Mr. Rodriguez and Mr. Simpson will be assisting you in the important matter. If you guys want this case the President wants my plane will leave in two hours. I'll let you men talk it out." Agent Simpson heads to the door and opens the door and closes the door to Captain Wallace's Office." Captain Wallace tells them, "It's up to you, gentlemen if you guys want this job." Billy tells Captain Wallace, "Dad, even if we want this job. What is the case that the president called us for. Doesn't he have a lot of law enforcement agencies to do this job?" Captain Wallace, "Look Billy, I am now allowed to tell you what the case is about. But if you guys do this case, the person who selected you will tell you when you get there. If you guys do take the case and solve it. I'll reinstate you guys both back in the force and give you guys' commendations that I stiffed you guys from." Brian tells Captain Wallace, "I never did ask the why the president called me, I was friends with Billy and Gary in college and I never did join ROTC or the police force. So, why did the president picked me to join you guys since these two have military experience and have law enforcement credits?" Captain Wallace tells Brian, "I don't know why they picked you to join them. Since you are friends with them and maybe you can help them out with the files. I know you guys come to Brian for help a lot of times in your cases, so the President think of you as an asset. I don't think he would get Billy and Gary without your help. So, it is up to you guys if you want the job." Billy tells Gary and Brian, "This case can give us good recognition and maybe get us our jobs back in the field." Gary tells Brian, "No offense Brian, it's good pay and I get to hang out with a lot of cool college kids when they ask me to hang out with them. But this job could help me get back in the field." Brian tells Billy and Gary, "None taken, Gary. But I did miss you guys working on the field. I helped you guys out a lot. I always have great contacts to help you guys out. So, I want to be in the field with you guys. So, I am in. I want to join you guys." Billy tells them, "So do I, I want to take this case too. Not just to give me my job back and Gary's. But I always wanted to way to serve my country again and this is my chance to do it again." Gary tells them, "Yeah, me too. I'm in." Billy tells his father, "We're in Dad. We want to take the case." Captain Wallace tells them, "Good, you guys go home and pack your bags. The limousine will pick you up and take you to the airport." Billy tells them, "All right guys it's time we get started." Billy, Gary, and Brian get up from their chairs and put their first together and fist bump together and stops. Outside the LAX airport gate where the presidential limousine heads to the Private jet and stops the limousine. The door opens and it's Agent Simpson, Billy, Gary, and Brian exiting the limousine and Agent Simpson closes the door. Billy looks at the private jet and tells them, "I guess the president is going all out for us." Gary tells them, "At least he knows how to treat a VIP." Agent Simpson takes out Billy, Gary, and Brian's luggage out of the limousine trunk and puts it on the floor. Billy, Gary, and Brian see their suitcases and grab their suitcases. Billy, Gary, Brian, and Agent Simpson exit the runaway and head to the private jet. The Private Jet takes off from LAX airport and heads to Washington D.C. Inside the private jet, Billy, Gary, Brian, Agent Simpson is drinking miller lite beer bottles and Agent Simpson drinks his can of dr. pepper. Billy looks at the window and sees a lot of clouds in the sky. Billy tells them, "Welcome to first class." Gary, Brian and Agent Simpson tell Billy, "First Class." Gary tells Agent Simpson, "Ron are you sure you don't want to drink a beer with us." Agent Simpson tells them, "Sorry guys, I am still on duty.

So, I can't drink any beer until I'm off duty." Billy tells Ron, "When do you get off-duty?" Ron tells Billy, "Until I take you to meet the president and he will brief you on the case." Brian tells Ron, "Are you sure you can't tell us what the case is about Ron?" Ron tells Brian, "Yes, I'm sure. If you want to know about the case, you must wait for the president, and he will tell you." Billy tells Gary and Brian, "Whatever this case is, must be really hard if the FBI or Homeland Security if they can't solve this." Brian tells Billy and Gary, "Whatever it is, it must be important that the president called us here for a reason." The private jet landed at Dulles International Airport and the private jet stopped on the runway and the plane door opened. Billy, Gary, Brian, and Agent Simpson exit the private jet and go down the stairs. All of them are in the runway of Dulles International Airport. Billy looks at Dulles International Airport and tells them, "This airport was a lot different than I seen in Die Hard 2." Ron tells Billy, "That movie was filmed in Stapleton International Airport, Denver, Colorado." Billy, Gary, and Brian look at Agent Simpson for a minute. Agent Simpson tells them, "I've seen die hard 2 million times. Come on, let's go." All of them see their luggage outside the plane when the baggage carrier takes them out and all four of them grab their luggage and head to the limousine. The limousine drives them downtown Washington D.C. and heads to the DC Public Library and the limousine stops in front of the DC Public Library. The back of the limo door opens and it's Billy, Gary, Brian, and Ron exiting the limousine and Ron closes the door. All of them see the front of the DC Public Library. Billy tells Ron, "Ron, what are we doing in a public library?" Ron tells Billy, "This is where you will be working at Billy?" Billy tells Ron, "I beg your pardon." Ron tells Billy, "If you guys are going to work on the case. This is the last place on earth no one knows about the top-secret case that we are working on. Come on, gentlemen the president is waiting for us." Billy tells Gary and Brian, "This is one weird to work on a top-secret case with the president." Gary's tells Billy and Brian, "I wondered if they have any Stephen king books here?" Brian tells Gary, "They do, but we are not here to read. We must work." Ron tells Billy, Brian, and Gary, "Come on, gentlemen let's get inside the president is waiting for us." Billy, Gary, Brian, and Ron enter the

DC Public Library. Inside the public library is the main entrance where Billy, Gary, Brian, and Ron are at in the library. Ron tells them, "Follow me." Billy, Gary, Brian, and Ron head to the elevator and Ron presses the elevator button. The elevator door opens, and Billy, Gary, Brian, and Ron enter the elevator. The elevator closes the door and inside the elevator Ron turns on the elevator button on the third floor. The elevator reaches the third floor, and the elevator door opens. Billy, Gary, Brian, and Ron enter the third floor and the elevator door opens. Billy, Gary, Brian, and Ron are in the third-floor computer room and see Bobby and Laura waiting at the table waiting for them. Billy, Gary, Brian, and Ron go over talking to Bobby and Laura and they stop. Billy recognizes Laura and tells her, "Laura, is that you?" Laura tells Billy, "Hi Billy is good to see you." Billy tells Laura, "How do you know the president and what are you doing here?" Bobby greets Billy, Gary, Brian and Ron and shakes their hands. Bobby tells them, Mr. Wallace, Mr. Rodriguez, Mr. Scott, and I am Srinivas Robert Chavala the acting president-elect and welcome to the Book guys headquarters. After Bobby stops shaking their hands and Billy tells Bobby, "The book guys, Mr. President." Bobby tells Billy, "That is what I am calling this team and since we are in a library. I needed a name for this team, Book Guys makes more sense." Billy tells Bobby, "Yes sir, I think that makes more sense to call this team." Bobby tells Billy, "First don't call me president, you guys call me Bobby or Mr. Chavala. I suggest you call me Bobby." Billy tells Bobby, "Okay, Bobby." Bobby tells them, "Mr. Wallace and the rest of you gentlemen, and I will begin the meeting and explain why Miss. Wilkerson is here. Billy, Gary, Brian, and Ron sit down in their chairs. Billy looks at the file and grabs and starts reading it for a minute before Bobby addresses the team. Bobby tells the team, "You gentlemen have been selected investigate assassination of your former president-elect Joe Robinette. Right after the banquet hall in the Ritz Carlton two days ago, President-elect Joe Robinette was shot by an unknown assassin that was also killed when he tried to get away at a helicopter before the secret service arrive. The man who we identified who assassinated President Robinette is Rufus Stonewalk was an ex-marine sniper who was killed in action January 10, 2007, by a grenade explosion that was orchestrated by Afghan soldier. But the guy who killed Robinette is not a doppelganger it is the same guy who was supposed to same guy who died in that grenade explosion fifteen years ago." Billy looks at the file and tells Bobby, "Bobby, this is no coincidence that this is the same guy." Bobby tells Billy, "Since Stonewalk is dead, I don't he planned this assassination himself. I think he was hired to kill Robinette, even though he wasn't going to be sworn in a week." Gary tells Bobby, "So this guy faked his death and now he is a murder for hire business. Stonewalk knows that killing the president would present red flags any major law enforcement. Who will do anything to find him." Brian tells Gary, "Well Gary since Stonewalk and the current president are dead there will be no need for an investigation. But the way I look at the Law Enforcement, I guess they will have to figure out if Stonewalk acted alone or somebody hired him to kill him." Billy tells them, "If Stonewalk faked his death, it had to somebody hire up to cover his tracks and someone who has the resources to make them dead. Since Stonewalk was a marine sniper, I think he was an NSA agent who was recruited by the organization. By why someone from the NSA would want to kill Robinette." Bobby tells them, "Anyway Robinette has one week left before his wife pulls the plug on his deathbed and right now, I will be sworn in as a week. So, we got six days to investigate who hired Stonewalk and why they want to kill him." Billy tells Bobby, "Bobby, do you think the head librarian is going to let us stay over hours and how did you convince him to run the meeting here?" Bobby tells Billy, "I told the head librarian, we need this place for National Security, and we can stay as long as you want?" Gary tells Bobby, "That actually works?" Bobby tells them, "No, we have a lot of funds raising for the library for a long time and they gave us access to use the library anytime we want. But one thing, we cannot tell anyone what we are doing. Because the book guys are doing the case off the books." Billy tells Bobby, "Why are we keeping this secret?" Bobby tells Billy, "Because they're a lot of spies around and we cannot tell anyone the guy who was responsible for Robinette may come after me or tried to kill us or anyone close to us. So, we are keeping this top-secret mission." Billy tells Bobby, "Okay, I understand. It sounds cool and awesome like secret agents."

Bobby tells them, "Anyway, but the first clue has something to do with the stolen weapons that were in a top-secret warehouse in 167 Robin Lane in Arlington. My director of the NSA General Roberts told me Stonewalk had access to the warehouse and knows the place inside and out. Roberts fired him five weeks after he questioned him about the missing weapons. But Roberts never had any proof that Stonewalk was ever linked to the stolen weapons." Gary tells Bobby, "What was inside those stolen weapons?" Bobby tells Gary, "There were three boxes, and the two boxes carry 20 Remington Model 700 rifle guns and one box that has grenades for a test launch six weeks ago. Mostly the company who built these weapons for the military is Cooper Industries. Jackson Tech had a huge 600-million-dollar contract for the NSA and the army to build them 20 Remington Model 700 rifle guns and grenades for them." Billy tells Bobby, "600 million dollars, if this military contract goes through, the stocks will hit the roof for and make them more money." Bobby tells Billy, "Correct Billy, the weapons were supposed to be delivered to the army in Cambodia at Fort Conway. Mostly the army was going to use those weapons for a test launch and use it to protect the people in Cambodia against Armenian terrorist team that is trying to invade the country. Robinette was going to make a peace treaty with the Armenia and Cambodia. But the Armenian terrorist team is not going to make peace but to invade the country. Why the us Army needs those weapons protect them." Brian tells them, without the weapons for the army, Cambodia is practically defenseless with the Armenian Terrorist team. They could probably make Cambodia surrender and Armenia would take over and worse the peace treaty will fall through and probably blame Cambodia and America for it." Bobby tells them, "Exactly why Robinette was planning on helping Cambodia giving out those weapons to stop the invasion and would help get a peace treaty with Armenia. I do know that Stonewalk used the 20 Remington Model 700 rifle that killed Robinette so that way they can block the peace treaty and without the missing weapons, Cambodia is practically defenseless. Agent Simpson was here to bring you guys here and I appointed him as my head of my presidential unit, and I also appointed Laura Wilkins my secretary as my acting senior presidential advisor for a week until my current advisor Waldo Carter is taking care of his sick mother for a week, and I appointed Laura to advise me for a week. She is the main reason why she recommends me to you guys. Until then, me, Agent Simpson and Laura are going to help you guys with this investigation and don't worry, I took a week off from running the country for a week to help you guys out in that matter. So, me, Laura and Ron will help you guys out. So, gentlemen are there any questions." Billy tells Bobby, "Bobby where are we going to stay?" Bobby tells them, "You guys can stay with me in the white house. I have a lot of room for you guys. So, after we begin this case, we're all going back to the white house where you guys can stay. Ron will show you to the rooms, until then let's get started." Billy asks one more question before Bobby starts and tells them, "One more question Bobby, before we start?" Bobby tells Billy, "Sure thing, Billy. What is it?" Billy tells Bobby, "Are you guys going to be in the field with us?" Bobby tells Billy, "No, I am going to help you guys here since I am president of the United States and Ron can't protect me all the time when I with you guys. Besides I am lousy fighter and I hate guns; I probably will hold you back in the field. Besides, Laura will be in the field with you guys since she has special forces training. Any more questions before we get started." All of them nod their heads to say no. Bobby tells them, "Okay, let's get started." Bobby and Laura sit down in their chairs and begin the meeting. Billy looks at the file, "Cooper Industries built these 20 Remington Model 700 rifle guns and grenades. They delivered it to the NSA for safe keeping and it was stolen a few weeks ago and it was on Stonewalk watch. NSA even questioned Stonewalk if he had anything to do with it. But he denied and chose to resign since they didn't trust him." Ron tells them, "I guess he had a lot to do with it, since he had access to that warehouse and knew it inside and out. I think we figured it out that he used one of the stolen Remington Model 700 rifle guns and use it to kill President Robinette." Laura tells them, "I know Stonewalk was the assassin and I know he was a rogue NSA agent. But I don't think he can do this by himself." Gary tells them, "Mostly Stonewalk was just hired help and they killed him to silence him if he ever got caught and knew that who ordered the hit on Robinette." Bobby tells them, "If Stonewalk was involved with theft of stolen weapons, someone ordered him to steal the weapons and assassinate Joe." Laura tells them, "We don't know who ordered Stonewalk anyway to steal the weapons since he had access to the stolen weapons. Besides, I bet it had to be someone Cooper Industries who hired Stonewalk to steal the weapons and kill Robinette." Billy snaps his fingers, and he's got it. Billy tells Laura, "You're right Laura, I think someone from Cooper Industries is involved with the theft. But it could be anyone?" Bobby tells them, "It could be someone who runs the company like the CEO and chairman of Coopers Industries." Ron tells them, "I did some checking on Cooper Industries, they have a mysterious CEO and Chairman of the company that never showed his face. Supposed this mysterious CEO and Chairman of the company not only ran the company, but he must also have ties with NSA." Bobby tells Ron, "I think you're right Ron, it would just take more than cash to buy it. But it had to be someone else who knows the ins and outs of the NSA. The mysterious arms dealer who is about to sell weapons to Armenians terrorist they could use to invade Cambodia and break the treaty." Laura tells them, "Robinette was trying to make a peace treaty with Cambodia and Armenian. If it happens the war will continue and make it worse." Bobby tells them, "We must check on ex-nsa agents who must have worked for Cooper Industries." Billy tells Bobby, "He might be unlisted, since our mysterious CEO would wipe off name in the NSA so they would not suspect him." Bobby tells Billy, "I think you have a point, Billy. He wouldn't just put his name on the list, but we must check anyway, and Ron go to the NSA website and print out a list of Ex-NSA agents and let's see if any of them are connected to Cooper Industries." Ron tells Bobby, "Sure thing, Bobby." Ron gets up from his chair and heads to the computer and finds the NSA website. Bobby tells them, "There has to be someone who is an Ex-NSA agent who is connected to Cooper Industries." Brian tells them, "It's going to take us all day to find him." Bobby tells them "I guess so. I'll order it in. What kind of Pizza, you guys like?" Billy, Brian, Gary, and Ron tell Bobby, "Beef and Pepperoni." Bobby tells them, "So do I. I'll order a Pizza Hut." Gary tells Bobby, "Me, Brian and Gary would like two bud lights and a 20oz diet Pepsi." Ron tells them, "Since you're here Bobby,

I'll take a bud light too." Laura tells Bobby, "Me too." Bobby tells them, "Okay then, I'll take a 20oz diet Pepsi too. Laura after I make the call, wait for the pizza guy in the front door to pick up the food and drinks and bring it back here." Laura tells Bobby, "Sure thing, Bobby." Bobby takes out his cell phone from his right pants pocket and makes a call to Pizza Hut. Bobby tells the person on the cell phone, "Hello Pizza Hut. Yeah, I would like to order Three Large beef and pepperoni pan pizza and five bud lights beer bottles and five 20oz Diet Pepsi's." While everyone is waiting for Bobby to make the order and looking at ex-nsa agents who is connected to Cooper Industries after Ron prints out the list." Back in the warehouse office where Alexander is calling his mysterious boss on the phone, "Yes sir. We will be on schedule for Saturday Night. We have everything under control and don't worry Mr. Acting President-elect is too incompetent to find us and track down our stolen weapons. Okay, boss where do you want to deal to go down at?" Back in the Book Guys headquarters in D.C. Public Library on the third floor. Where Bobby, Billy, Laura, Gary, and Ron are eating their pizzas and drinking beer and diet Pepsi. Billy is looking at the ex-nsa agents on the list and can't find anything who is connected to Cooper Industries." Gary tells them, "We check every ex-NSA agent on the list and none of them are connected to Cooper Industries." Ron tells them, "I wondered if Cooper guy is real, and when he founded the company or any of his family members are still running the company." Bobby tells them, "I did some checking on Cooper Industries that it was founded by Jonathan Cooper in 1980. Jonathan had a wife Maisy who they married in 1990 and had a daughter named Carrie who was born in 1993. Carrie was the sole heir to the company. Since her parents both died an airplane crash 2013 and Carrie would have been nineteen years old, and she passed away last year while she was out doing charity work for Cambodia when she caught Malaria while she was there and passed away last year." Gary tells them, "Since they are all dead, I have no idea who is taking over the company now." Bobby tells Gary, "Gary, there is something you should know that Carrie had a husband that she married two years ago." Gary tells Bobby, "Any idea what his name is?" Bobby tells Gary, "It's not much of a name, but it's an alias named

Waldo Cooper. I think this Waldo took his wife's last name and use it as an alias." Billy tells Bobby, "Didn't you tell me you had a presidential advisor, Waldo Carter. Do you think our weapons kingpin and the guy who was the mastermind behind Joe Robinette assassination must be him. I don't think it was any coincidence Waldo might be the same guy who is running Cooper Industries and being the presidential advisor at the same time. While planning out his assassination of President Robinette." Bobby is thinking for a minute, I don't think it is a coincidence, Waldo was in his hotel room when Joe got shot. I don't think he could have ordered Stonewalk to kill Robinette and get one of his associates to kill Stonewalk to cover their tracks in case if he ever got caught and spill the beans on Carter. Besides Joe trusted him with all his life. He was practically overqualified to be his advisor when Joe appointed him after he was elected." Brian tells Bobby, "Did you ever check his resume about his qualifications?" Bobby tells Brian, "No, it wasn't my job, because joe was the one who appointed him and his job to check his resume to hire him. Besides, I owe Waldo everything. He was the one that Waldo encouraged Joe to pick me as his running mate. Joe listens to him and how do you think we got elected, because Joe was a shoo-in to win the election because of Joe." Billy tells Bobby, "But keep in mind, do you think he picked you as a running mate just to help Joe win or he was just using you guys just to win the election. So, he can control the white house within." Bobby tells Billy, "I don't think so, mostly all decisions go by Joe or me after we were sworn in. But let's just say for argument sakes that Waldo might be the mastermind behind this and why we he wants to kill Robinette and I have no idea if he was an ex-NSA agent." Billy tells Bobby, "Bobby, do you know Waldo's middle name?" Bobby tells Billy, "No, he never told me his middle name. Even Joe does not know his middle name. Why do you ask?" Laura tells Billy, "I think I know his middle name; I took a look at his file once after Joe was elected and he asked me to put Waldo's personal file in the file box." Billy tells Laura, "Laura what is Waldo's middle name?" Laura tells Billy, "Rudy, Waldo Rudy Carter?" Billy looks at the file and sees Waldo Rudy on the ex-nsa agents list. Billy tells them, "I think I am right, that Waldo maybe the mastermind behind the assassination of Robinette." Gary tells Billy, "Why is that, Billy?" Billy tells them, "Because I think Waldo has another alias and that is Waldo Rudy. Because he was an ex-NSA agent who left the agency last year while Joe and Bobby were running for president." Bobby tells Billy, "I don't think you are lying Billy. I think you are telling the truth, but we must look more at his information. Let's get to the computer and check it out." All of them get up from their chairs and head to the laptop. Bobby opens the laptop and goes to the NSA website and types in the information about Waldo Rudy. The NSA has the file on Waldo Rudy, and they read about it. Billy tells them, "Waldo doesn't have a picture, but it said here that he got a bachelor's degree in political science and a law degree from that university in 1997. He was in Marines ROTC in his freshmen year and got commissioned as a second lieutenant and did six tours in Iraq and Afghanistan. He was in the marines for ten years and ranked as a major. He was recruited to the NSA while he was in the marines, and he faked his death as he stepped into a detonator in his tenth year and faked his death. Mostly Waldo's real name Waldo Albert Carter before they changed it to Waldo Rudy as his NSA name." Bobby tells Billy, "Anything about him leaving the NSA to run his father-in-law's company." Billy tells Bobby, "No, it doesn't say anything about him running his father-in-law's company or being Joe's presidential advisor. But I do know that he left the NSA three years ago because he fell in love with a woman he met while he was doing political business in China." Bobby tells them, "It is unknown if that is Waldo Carter. But if it was him, he probably met Carrie in China while he was doing NSA business and gave up his career to be with her. But I think the only reason why he married her is because her company builds the weapons for the NSA and has political strings to give anyone elected. But Carrie and her family run an honest company, until he married Waldo to assassinate Joe, steal their weapons from the NSA warehouse and sell those weapons to Armenians terrorist so they can invade Cambodia to make them surrender and make a huge fortune for his company." Gary tells Bobby, "I think you are right Bobby. But I think we should pay a visit to Cooper Industries and see if Waldo is there. Bobby tells Billy, "Waldo told me that he was going to visit his mother who was sick in the hospital and was going to be gone all week. I hardly doubt if his mother is sick, and he is Cooper Industries running the company." Billy tells Bobby, "If he was going to visit his sick mother for a week, then her mother would have gotten sick and died in 1997 the day Waldo Rudy graduated from Law School. I think Waldo visited his mother in the hospital a little bit late 25 years ago and I think he would probably have been a little late for his mother's funeral. So, I think he played us because he was up to something big. Why he killed Robinette because he has a bigger plan after Robinette assassination, and he is planning on getting bigger power after his arms deal with Armenian terrorist and use it start invading Cambodia and break the treatment to make his defense company a fortune and kill you so he can control the Speaker of the house who is probably afraid of him." Bobby tells Billy, "I think you are right Billy, but until then we don't know if this is the same guy. Until then, we should go to Cooper Industries to pay our CEO a visit." Brian tells Bobby, "You mean were going to piss the guy off when we question him." Bobby tells Brian, "Exactly, but I cannot go with you guys if it is Waldo. He might recognize me, so Billy, Gary. You guys go to Cooper's Industries and talk to the CEO. Find out if he knows anything and leave the place. Ron will take you there and I have a good cover to get you in." Billy tells Bobby, "Okay, no problem." Bobby tells them, "Brian, Laura you guys will stay here with me and find some more information on Waldo and find anything about Armenian Terrorist that our mastermind assassin is going to make a deal with soon. We must find their operation and where they are going to make the drop. So, we're going to look at the files and information on the computer. Everyone knows what to do?" All of them tell Bobby, "Yes!" Bobby tells them, "Let's get started." Billy, Gary, and Ron exit the Book Guys headquarters and head to Cooper Industries. Outside Cooper Industries where the limousine is parked right in front of Cooper Industries. The limo door opens and it's Billy, Gary, and Ron and all three of them exit the limousine. Billy and Gary are wearing suits and Billy is carrying a briefcase. Billy tells Ron, "Thanks for the suits and briefcase Ron." Ron tells Billy, "Well Bobby arranged everything for you guys to be the master of disguise. Luckily Bobby made the arrangements and delivered it to the first floor before you guys arrived." Gary tells Ron, "What is our cover?" Ron tells them, "You guys are posing as Insurance salesman. I made the appointment that two insurance agents are here to the CEO if he wants to buy insurance for your company Simpson Insurance. I used the fake website and brochures to handle my cover identity. So, all you must do is pretend you guys are insurance salesman, tried to sale him some insurance and then when you get close to the CEO and ask him questions. After that exit the office right now." Billy tells Ron, "That is practically awesome that is what we do, every time we talk to a drug dealer or drug kingpin so that way we don't have to arrest him and haul his ass of interrogation room where his high price lawyer to bail him out and find ways to cover his tracks before the search warrant arrives before he covers his tracks and gets away Scott free and were back at square one. So, the only way to take down a kingpin is to go master of disguise." Gary tells Ron, "That is what we are doing. Okay, wish you us luck Ron." Ron tells Billy and Ron, "Good luck, gentlemen. Remember to get in and get out quickly. I'll be waiting for you guys." Billy tells Ron, "Thanks Ron, we will see you soon, bye!" Ron tells them, "Bye" Billy and Gary goes inside Cooper Industries. Inside Cooper Industries Billy and Gary head to the elevator and Gary presses the elevator button. The elevator door open and Billy and Gary go inside the elevator and the elevator door closes. Inside the elevator Billy and Gary are little bit nervous if they could pull this off. Billy tells Gary, "Do you really think Waldo would show up in his office." Gary tells Billy, "I don't think he would show up in his office if he was lying to the president that he was going to visit his already sick dead mother for a week so he can work in his dead wife's company and make arms deal with Armenian terrorist in the same week while working as the presidential advisor." Billy tells Gary, "It's good thing the secretary from the front desk bought our act. Or we had to come up with our own second act." Gary tells Billy, "Mostly I would tell her that we are investors and that way she would let us go see him." Billy tells Gary, "I think it would have worked if she didn't buy the insurance salesman act first." The elevator stops and the elevator door opens. Billy tells Gary, "That's our floor, it's showtime." Billy and Gary exit the elevator.

Alexander is working in his office, until he hears an intercom button buzzing. Alexander answers the intercom and tells the person on the other end of the intercom. "Alexander tells the person on the other end of the intercom, "What is it, Sherry?" Sherry, who is Mr. Alexander's secretary on the intercom tells Mr. Alexander, "Mr. Alexander there are two gentlemen who are here to see you, sir?" Alexander tells Sherry from the intercom, "Who are they?" Sherry from the intercom tells Mr. Alexander, "They are from Simpson Insurance and wants to sell you some life insurance." Alexander tells Sherry from the intercom, "Who are they?" Sherry from the intercom tells Alexander, "Mr. William Wallace and Gary Rodriguez who are from Simpson Insurance." Alexander tells Sherry from the intercom, "Tell them, to leave because I already have life insurance." Sherry tells Mr. Alexander, "They are not here to sell you insurance. They are here to give you money for your boss's wife death. She put a lot of money in Simpson Insurance and wants to give you the money since the boss is her beneficiary." Mr. Alexander tells Sherry from the intercom, "Send them in." The door knocks and Alexander tells the person, "Come in." The door opens and it's Billy and Gary who enter the office. Billy is carrying the briefcase and Gary closes the door. Billy and Gary sit down in their chairs and Billy puts down his briefcase. Mr. Alexander tells Billy and Gary, "So, Mr. Wallace, Mr. Rodriguez, I am Mr. Keith Alexander." Billy tells Alexander, "It's a pleasure to meet you, sir." Billy shakes Alexander's hand and let go. Gary also shakes Alexander's hand and let go. Gary tells Alexander, "It's also a pleasure to meet you too." Alexander tells them, "You guys are here to give my boss his life insurance check that his wife made a claim. Is that true." Billy tells Alexander, "Yes, it's true sir. But we are going to mail in your boss's insurance check in a week. Is he your boss Waldo Cooper is in his office today, so he can sign on the dotted line on an insurance forum so we can mail him, his insurance check." Gary tells Alexander, "We are going to do it in a one-day delivery system. I thought we could mail the check to his office. By the way, where is his office?" Alexander tells Gary, "This is in his office, I am filling in for him. He had a business meeting with one of our clients in Phoenix and he will be out for the week. But he said that any signature of any money transference or authorization will go to me. I'll oversee the week, and I can make legally give you guys my signature to get his insurance check." Billy tells Alexander, "Okay since Mr. Cooper leaves you in charge and gives you full authorization. I'll let you sign it." Billy sees his briefcase and grabs the briefcase. Billy opens the briefcase and takes out a full authorization forum. Billy closes the briefcase and puts the briefcase down on the floor. Billy gives the authorization forum to Alexander and looks at it for a minute. Billy tells Alexander, "I guess Mr. Cooper must really trust you to run his business here." Alexander tells Billy, "I worked hard for ten years here in this company. I had an MBA at George Washington University, and I took an internship there while I was taking business classes in G.W. He took me under his wing and after I got my MBA. He made his junior executive. I worked my way up to the top of Executive Vice President." Billy tells Alexander, "I guess why Mr. Alexander trust you." Gary tells Alexander, "Here's a thought, do you know Mr. Cooper who has a doppelganger names Waldo Rudy who served in the Marines for ten years while he was attending law school in George Washington University. Isn't that where you went, Mr. Alexander?" Alexander tells Gary, "Yes, that is where I attended." Gary tells Alexander, "He was in the Marines ROTC and got his law degree in 1997 after he got his commission. I heard he served in Iraq and Afghanistan after 9/11. He was in the marines for ten years after he died stepping on a detonator. He died on November 14, 2005, and I think our Mr. Rudy faked his death when he was recruited to join the NSA. Since Waldo's real name Waldo Rudy Carter before the NSA changed his name to Waldo Rudy" Alexander looks suspicious when they ask about Waldo Cooper. Gary tells Alexander, "He did a lot of work for the NSA and guess what, I heard that he was a best agent he had." Alexander tells Gary, "Is that so. That Mr. Carter has a doppelganger out there." Billy tells Alexander, "Something more about that doppelganger, But I heard he left the NSA three years ago because he fell in love with a woman he met while he was doing political business in China and got married and run his father-in-law's company. But I heard she passed away last year in Cambodia while she was doing charity work there, and I think she got

Malaria. But I have no idea what the name of the company was." Gary tells Alexander, "I think Mr. Carter doppelganger was building weapons for the NSA and made contacts with them. It was funny that Rudy was also the advisor to the US senator Joe Robinette last year and help him get elected as President of the United States that he won and President elect Robinette was about to be sworn in as President a week ago and it was a lot funnier that he was assassinated by Rufus Stonewalk who was also an ex-NSA agent who left the agency two weeks ago when he was questioned by some missing weapons in a top secret warehouse that Rudy picked to guard the weapons, since the weapons that this company was building Remington Model 700 rifles and grenades were stolen two weeks ago. Billy tells Alexander, "Mr. Alexander, it is a lot funnier that company was building those weapons wanted to get stolen when they were about to deliver to an army in Cambodia to protect them from an Armenian Terrorist group that was planning on invading the country. But since it was stolen two weeks ago, I think there might be a rumor that the company stole their own weapons and try to sell it to that Armenian Terrorist Group to invade Cambodia. It was not coincidence that President-elect Robinette was assassinated by Stonewalk, before Robinette was going to begin his peace treaty with Cambodia and Armenia to stop the invasion after he was about to be sworn in. I guess that plans changed, since the weapons are still missing and probably it will hand of Armenian Terrorist group. But like I said, it was just a rumor. I don't think Mr. Cooper's company would have anything to do with stealing their weapons and using it to sell it to a terrorist group and killing the president-elect to stop the peace treaty. Even if the new President-elect Robert Chavala would still do the peace treaty with Cambodia and Armenia. But he probably would have mess it up." Gary tells Alexander, "Besides Mr. Chavala is practically incompetent to pull of this peace treaty and called off this investigation since Stonewalk acted alone in Robinette assassination." Alexander tells them, "Yeah, I guess so." Alexander grabs his pen on his desk and is about to sign the approval forum. Alexander tells them, "I signed it, and the insurance check will arrive tomorrow?" Billy tells Alexander, "First of all, we have sent out the forum to our boss and he will write the check. He will mail to your company in one or two days. Since he is doing one-day delivery." Alexander tells them, "Sounds great, I'll be looking forward to get the insurance check for Mr. Cooper and make sure his insurance will be in good use." Billy tells Alexander, "Okay, that's it for today. It's a pleasure meeting you, Mr. Alexander." Gary tells Alexander, "We are sorry that we never had a chance to see Mr. Cooper. Maybe someday we will get to see him one day." Alexander tells them, "I sure he would love to meet you someday. Gentlemen, it was pleasure meeting you, bye!" Billy and Gary tell Alexander, "Bye!" Billy grabs his briefcase from the floor and opens it. Billy puts the Authorization forum in his briefcase and closes the briefcase. Billy and Gary get up from the chair and head to the door. Gary opens the door and exits Alexander's office and Gary closes the door. Outside Alexander's office Billy and Gary headed to the elevator. Billy tells Gary, "You think he bought it." Gary tells Billy, "Maybe in a few hours, but sooner or later he is going to find out who we are and kill us." Billy tells Gary, "Before he finds out that Mr. Cooper is not going to get his check anytime soon before we end up sitting ducks." Gary tells Billy, "Me too." Inside Alexander's office where Alexander looks at Billy and Gary and not buying that they are insurance salesman. Alexander picks up the phone and answers it. Alexander makes a call to one of his associates on the phone and tells the associate, "Martin, I need a favor. Do you have security footage in my office. I need to see the DVD, because I think the boss needs to see this." Outside Cooper Industries when Billy and Gary exit Cooper Industries and sees Ron waiting for them in the limousine that is parked right in front of Cooper Industries. Ron tells them, "How did it go?" Billy tells Ron, "It went well, Ron. Except Waldo Carter was not in his office, but his acting CEO Keith Alexander was their filling in for him. So, either Waldo Carter who is the mastermind behind this or we were wrong that Keith Alexander is the mastermind behind this." Gary tells Billy, "No Billy, you were right at first. It is Waldo Carter, mostly I think Alexander gave us the slip that Carter is doing a business trip in Phoenix, so he won't come out of the shadows before his real business deal with the Armenian Terrorist group." Billy tells Gary, "Thanks for listening to my theory and supporting it, Gary. It means a lot." Gary tells Billy, "You're welcome." Billy tells Ron, "He bought the act after we questioned him for a minute." Gary tells Ron, "Yeah, but I think sooner or later he is going to find out who we are and that we are working for the President before he kills us and Bobby." Ron tells them, "If we can find his operation and where he is going to make the drop aka when Carter sells his weapons to the Armenian Terrorist team." Gary tells Ron, "It could be anywhere?" Ron tells them, "Me and Mr. Chavala don't have any sources help us find it." Billy tells Ron, "You don't but I do. He's in D.C. Follow me." Ron tells Billy, "Where are we going?" Billy tells Ron, "If we are going to find Carter's operation where he is hiding the stolen weapons that he is going to use sell it to the Armenian Terrorist Group and a location where he's going to make the drop at with his clients. I know a guy who can help us and let's say he's owed me one." Ron tells Billy, "Well, I hope your guy can help us find Carter's operation and drop." Billy tells Ron, "Trust me, if anyone can find anything or information on anyone. My friend is the only can help us." Ron opens the limo door and Ron; Billy and Gary enter the limousine and Ron closes the door. The limousine exits Cooper Industries and heads to the place where Billy, Gary and Ron are going to meet Billy's friend at. Inside a top-secret warehouse where Alexander's boss men who are hiding the guns and grenades in flour in crates. The garage door opens and it's the limousine that enters the middle of the warehouse and stops for a minute. The limousine door opens and it's Alexander who exits the limousine and closes the door. Alexander is carrying a long yellow envelope in his left hand. Ernie comes down the stairs from the warehouse office and goes over to Alexander and talks to him. Ernie tells Alexander, "Mr. Alexander, the boss is here. He's just arrived 40 minutes ago." Alexander tells Ernie, "We better hurry, we don't want him to keep him waiting." Alexander and Ernie head to the stairs and go to the warehouse office where Alexander and Ernie's mysterious boss arrived. Inside the warehouse office, Alexander and Ernie's boss is working in his office and he is lurking in the shadows, and no one knows what he looks like. The door knocks and the boss with a raspy voice tells the person from the other side of the door, "Come in." The door opens and it's Alexander and Ernie. Alexander and Ernie enter their boss's office and Ernie closes the door. Alexander is still carrying a yellow envelope in his left hand. Alexander tells his boss, "Hello sir, I got something to show you." Their boss who's in the shadows with a raspy voice tells them, "Let me see it." Alexander and Ernie go over to the boss's desk and the boss exits the shadows and sees his real face, that is Bobby's presidential advisor Waldo Carter. Carter speaks with a normal voice and tells them, "Okay Alexander, what is the emergency you want to tell me, when I had to leave my mansion. I spent a long time, covering my tracks, you called me out of 20 story mansions to tell me there is an emergency, what is the emergency?" Alexander tells Carter, "Well, Mr. Carter, our business deal with Davit Group is going smoothly and the mission is a success. We are way ahead of schedule with our client Gor Aida and his men the Davit Group." Carter tells Alexander, "Hiring Stonewalk to steal our weapons from your company before the NSA was delivering it to our army to protect the Cambodian people from Aida's group and move it to this top-secret warehouse and killing Robinette to keep him away from a peace treaty with Cambodia and Armenia and arms deal with so he can invade Cambodia and make the people surrender." Ernie tells Carter, "The NSA paying more money to your company to build the weapons for the military. Except we are selling the weapons to Aida's terrorist group." Carter tells them, "Exactly, I am proud of you, Ernie for killing Stonewalk. If he stayed around, sooner or later he would have gotten caught by the FBI or Secret Service and he may spill the beans on us. Why I ordered you Ernie to kill him, he outlived his usefulness to us and cover his tracks." Alexander tells Carter, "You've been working with President Robinette your whole life to help him became a congressman to senator and to president of the United States. You are the one who got him here." Carter tells Alexander, "With my connections from the Marines and the NSA and my late wife's company who helped finance our operation and get him elected in office. That is the main reason why I want him dead, so we can block the peace treaty with Cambodia and Armenia." Ernie tells Carter, "What about our new president-elect Robert Chavala. Do you think he would be a problem." Carter tells them, "I wrapped Robinette around my little finger, and I will also wrap Chavala in my little finger too.

Since he is too incompetent and too weak to run the country. Except after my arms deal with Aida's team, we will get one of Aida's men to kill him. After that, the speaker of the house to be sworn in." Alexander tells Carter, "What happens if the Speaker of the house could be the problem." Carter gets up from his chair and goes over to Alexander and tells him, "Alexander what kind of sport does Michael Jordan used to play in the Chicago Bulls?" Alexander tells Carter, "Why is that important, sir?" Carter tells Alexander, "Answer the question, asshole!" Alexander is a little nervous and tells the Carter, "Basketball, Mr. Carter why." Carter tells Alexander, "Because I can do this!" Carter kicks Alexander in the groin and Alexander is soaring right now. Carter gives Alexander a round house kick to the face and Alexander falls on the floor and drops his yellow envelope. Ernie laughs a little that Carter is mad at Alexander and not him. Carter sees Ernie laughing a little and he is upset. Carter punches Ernie in the face and knees him in the stomach. Ernie is soaring a little and tells Carter, "What was that for Mr. Carter. I did not say anything." Carter tells Ernie, "That just in case, if you were questioning my authority and I'm keeping you losers in line. Get up dickweed and what were you going to tell me when you came in here." Alexander sees his yellow envelope on the floor and grabs it. Alexander and Ernie are still soaring, and Alexander gets up from the floor and tells Carter, "Mr. Alexander, there is something you should see. Can I use your laptop sir?" Carter nods his head for Alexander to go ahead. Alexander sees Carter's laptop and Alexander opens the yellow envelope that has a DVD of security footage of Billy and Gary talking to him in Carter's office. Gary turns on the laptop and opens the DVD-ROM and places the DVD inside the laptop and starts playing. Carter, Alexander, and Ernie see the security footage of Billy and Gary talking to Alexander at Carter's office. Carter looks at these two and tells them, "Who are those shitfaces?" Alexander tells Carter, "Well, Mr. Carter they told me they were insurance salesman, and their company Simpson Insurance was sending us your wife insurance check this week. Since I already did some checking there is no Simpson Insurance and your wife didn't die of Malaria last year. Since we ordered Stonewalk to kill your while she was in Cambodia for a charity work their while she was getting suspicious about our illegal activities with our clients Davit Group run by Gor Aida." Carter tells Alexander, "She was looking around my files at my office, why we had to eliminate her before she finds out what we were doing. She has always been weak, never figured out how to make real money. Instead of earning money legally, I found a way to take the money no holds barred." Ernie looks at footage of Billy and Gary and tells them, "Who are they, are they FBI or Secret Service. Mostly Mr. Carter covered our tracks well to keep the feds out of our business." Carter goes over to Ernie and grabs him by the neck, "Why are two little dorks are asking Alexander questions about my arms deal with Davit Group and my dead assassin who killed the president-elect Joe Robinette and why we killed him." Carter lets Ernie go and punches him in the stomach. Carter is upset and tells Ernie, "First rule, Ernie. Never question my authority again." Ernie fears Carter and tells him, "I am sorry, sir it will never happen again." Carter tells Ernie, "It better be, Alexander call Luthor and tell to identify the two losers who were asking you questions about my arms deal with Davit Group." Alexander tells Carter, "Yes, Mr. Carter." Carter goes to the office phone and picks up the phone and makes a call to Luther. Carter tells Luther on the other end of the phone, "Luther listens, I need a favor. I need you to identify a couple of guys who were in Mr. Carter's office today. Okay, thank you." Alexander hangs up the phone and tells Carter, "Luther will fax us the information in an hour." Carter tells them, "I guess we will have to wait until an hour." Inside Hank's sports bar where Billy, Gary and Ron enter the sports bar. Ron tells Gary, "Who do you know, that can help us find Carter's operation and his drop." Billy tells Ron, "Somebody that owes me a favor?" Gary tells Billy, "How do you know this guy?" Billy tells Gary, "Xander Osbourne was my friend in college and he and I were study buddies in English class. He owns the bar" Ron tells Billy, "Billy, I have two questions I have to ask you?" Billy tells Ron, "Go ahead, Ron." Ron tells Billy, "What favor did you do for him that he owes you and how can he help us?" Billy tells Ron, "I tutored him for his English final and got him a good grade for him to graduate. So, he owes me. His Uncle Ted is the deputy director of Homeland Security and has access to DOJ and every federal branch in the US. If want to find something or lose something, Xander is your guy to find anything. He helped me out a lot of cases when I was in L.A." Xander is tending bar right now. Billy, Gary, and Ron see him and go over talk to Xander. Billy tells Xander, "Hey Xander!" Xander sees Billy, Gary and recognizes his friend Billy. Xander tells Billy, "Hey Billy. It's good to see you, buddy." Billy shakes Xander's hand and let's go. Billy tells Xander, "Xander, these are my friend Gary Rodriguez and Ron Simpson." Xander shakes Gary and Ron's hands and let go. Xander tells Gary and Ron, "It's a pleasure to meet you guys." Gary tells Xander, "It's a pleasure to meet you too Xander." Ron tells Xander, "I'm not just Ron Simpson. I'm…?" Ron takes out his US Secret Service badge out of his left pants pocket and shows it to Xander. Ron finishes telling Xander, "I'm Agent Ronald Simpson US secret service." Billy tells Xander, "He works for the presidential unit and that badge is real, unless you want to show him his gun." Xander tells Billy, "No thank you, besides I can tell from a badge or I.D. that is real or fake. Trust me, that badge is real." Ron puts his US secret service badge away from his left pants pocket. Xander tells Gary, "He works for the President of the United States." Billy tells Xander, "We all do, that is why me and Gary are here in D.C. The President gave us an important case that we were hired to solve. If you help us, not only you are helping us. But you are also helping the President, if you do a good job, he can put in a good word for your uncle if you help us out." Xander is excited that he is working with the President of the United States. Xander tells Billy, "I said I owed you, maybe when I help you guys out the President will owe me a favor too. What is the favor you need?" Billy tells Xander, "Remember this case we are working on is top secret. We can't let anyone know." Xander tells Billy, "Hey no problem, I didn't see nothing or hear nothing." Billy tells Xander, "Anyway you heard about the former president-elect Joe Robinette was assassinated a few days ago." Xander tells Billy, "I heard about that, why no one caught the assassin who killed President Robinette." Billy tells Xander, "Actually the current president-elect Robert Chavala figure out the assassin who killed Robinette and his name is Rufus Stonewalk. He was an ex-Marine Sniper who was killed in grenade explosion on January 10, 2007. But the feds faked his death since he was recruited to working for the NSA. He was also hired by another ex-NSA agent to kill the presient-elect Joe Robinette. The guy who hired Stonewalk killed him to silence him if he ever got caught by the feds, he would drop a dime on the person who hired him." Gary tells Xander, "The person who hired Stonewalk is Waldo Rudy who is an NSA alias whose real name is Waldo Carter. Who was Robinette advisor when he was a US senator and use his NSA contacts to help him get elected as President of the United States." Xander tells them, "Why did Carter hired Stonewalk to kill Robinette. What was his M.O. to kill the president?" Ron tells Xander, "We found out that Carter's wife owns a defense company called Cooper Industries and he took over the company when his wife died last year. His company was building Remington Model 700 rifle guns and grenades for the US army. They were going to ship the weapons to Cambodia where the US army will need to protect the people of Cambodia who is being invaded by Armenian Terrorist team. But the weapons were stolen two weeks ago from a top-secret warehouse in the NSA. The only person who knew that warehouse inside and out was an ex-NSA agent who was supervising the warehouse and one of the weapons that killed Robinette was…?" Xander interrupts Ron for a minute and tells him, "Remington Model 700 rifle gun that was missing and was the one that killed the president. Let me guess, one of the Ex-NSA agents who was supervising that warehouse is Stonewalk." Ron tells Xander," Exactly, the same person who was hired to steal the weapons and who was hired to kill President Robinette was Waldo Carter. The reason why he wanted to kill Robinette, because after Robinette gets sworn in a week. He was planning a peace treaty with Cambodia and Armenia that can stop the war and bring down the Armenian Terrorist." Billy tells Xander, "That is why we need your help, Xander. Carter is going to sell his own stolen weapons to an unknown Armenian Terrorist group to invade Cambodia and force them to surrender. While Armenian Terrorist are terrorizing Armenia and other countries that can make Cooper Industries a lot of money for the defense department. We need you to find Cooper's operation where he's hiding the weapons and find out who is the Armenian terrorist group is and who is their leader." Gary tells Xander,

"Where they drop is. When Carter is going to make the arms deal with the Armenian Terrorist Group." Xander tells them, "No, problem. I can help you guys find it. I will make a call to my uncle and you guys will have your information tomorrow morning." Billy tells Xander, "Thanks Xander. I appreciate what you are doing for us. Now, I owe you one." Xander laughs a little and tells Billy, "It's okay, Billy, I owe you one. Ron makes sure you tell the president to put in a good word to my uncle since he is helping you guys out." Ron tells Xander, "Sure thing!" Ron takes out his card that has Bobby's phone number on it in his right pants pocket and gives it to Xander. Ron tells Xander, "Call the president tomorrow with this number and he will answer it after you get the information from your uncle." Xander tells Ron, "Sure thing. Bye guys!" Billy, Gary, and Ron tell Xander, "See you!" Billy, Gary, and Ron exit the bar and Xander looks at the card with Bobby's phone number on it. Xander takes out his cell phone from his left pants pocket and makes a call to his uncle. Xander tells his uncle on the end of his cell phone, "Hello, Uncle Ted, listen I need a favor." Back in the warehouse office where Carter, Alexander and Ernie are sitting down in their chairs and the phone rings. Alexander answers the phone and tells Luther on the other end of the phone, "Hello. Hey Luther. You got it, thanks a lot." Alexander hangs up the phone and tells them, "Luther is faxing the information on those losers in two seconds." The fax machine started and getting out the information on Billy and Gary. Ernie gets up from his chair and goes over to the fax machine and picks up the information on Billy and Gary. Carter tells Ernie, "Who are those ass-wipes who were sticking my nose in arms deal with Davit Group before they guys catch a bullet when I fired my favorite gun on them." Ernie is reading the information on Billy and Gary. Ernie looks practically worried and tells Carter, "Well, Mr. Carter they are not feds. But they are LAPD cops." Alexander tells Ernie, "Why are bunch of silly LAPD cops who are a thousand miles away sticking our nose on arms deal." Ernie tells them, "They're names are Detective Sergeant William Wallace and Gary Rodriguez who works in Narcotics. Detective Wallace is on suspension for messing up a drug bust that he and Gary made. Rodriguez resigned from the force and works as a Campus Security guard in USC.

Their friend Brian Scott is the one who got him the job, since he is Dean of Students in USC. Mostly they only reason they are here is because of the Current President-elect Chavala sent them and his friend Scott here to work on a top-secret case. Carter and Alexander get upset and exit their chairs. Carter and Alexander go over to Ernie and see the file on Billy and Gary. Ernie gives the file to Carter and Carter grabs the file and looks at it for a minute. Carter tells them, "So Chavala sent Wallace. Rodriguez and Scott to stopping us to make are arms deal with Davit Group." Alexander laughs a little and stops. Alexander tells them, "So our incompetent president sends in two cops like Wallace and Rodriguez to find our stolen weapons and arresting us and the Davit Group. Man, Chavala is pathetic sending in amateurs to prevent our arms deal with Davit Group." Ernie tells them, "What are we going to do, sir about Wallace and Rodriguez." Carter tells Ernie, "Simple, tomorrow morning you are going to find them and kill them. Since I know every move that Robinette makes. I know every move Chavala makes. If Chavala hired Wallace and Rodriguez to find our weapons and take us out. He's got another thing going." Ernie tells Carter, "How are we going to find them in the morning, they could be anywhere." Carter is upset and punches Ernie in the stomach. Ernie is soaring a little. Carter is still upset and tells Ernie, "First rule, Ernie never questions my authority. Second, since I know they are working for Chavala. He is probably accommodating them. I think they will be staying in the white house. I think they will take the presidential limo. Since I have known every move the secret service makes, I may figure out who is working with them and where they are taking them. So, we don't have to find them, they'll find us." Alexander tells Carter, "How are they going to find us?" Carter tells Alexander, "Because one of the secret service agents is working with Wallace and Rodriguez. All I need to do is send out a memo from the director of the secret service that the president orders Wallace and Rodriguez to meet them in a secret place. Tell them some more information on Robinette's assassination. This is top secret and not a word to anyone." Alexander tells them, "Once they meet the president in a secret place, we ambush them and kill them. After we are done with them, we hire another assassin to kill Chavala before he finds our arms deal with Davit Group and sticking our nose in our business." Carter tells Ernie, "You'll be in the charge leading our men to kill Wallace and Rodriguez and their secret service agent in our secret place that I will give you." Ernie tells Carter, "Yes sir!" Carter tells them, "Luckily, I have access to all the presidential memos so I can write one and so I can type one in and fax it to the director of the Secret Service. Come on gentlemen we have a lot of work to do." Carter heads to his desk and sits down in his chair and opens the presidential memo and types in a top-secret meeting from the president. Inside the Book Guys headquarters on the third floor at the DC Public Library where Brian is waiting for Bobby and Laura to return and Billy, Gary, and Ron too. Inside the study room on the second floor, it is empty. Bobby and Laura get up from the floor where they were getting laid, and their clothes are untucked. Bobby tells Laura, "That was a good twenty minutes. I know we told Brian that we were getting some diet pepsi's in the lounge for a few minutes." Laura tells Bobby, "I think he will ask questions what took us to get the diet pepsi's at the lounge." Bobby tells Laura, "I really like you, Laura. Even after me and Joe got elected. That you were a good friend to us. I know you like me back too. I know it is weird that my secretary and acting presidential advisor is my girlfriend right now." Laura tells Bobby, "I know even if we do get married, it will be weird that president's secretary is going to be the First Lady of the United States. I have no idea, how the public would react having a secretary becoming the First Lady of the country." Bobby tells Laura, "They will accept you if they can't accept you. I don't care, I chose who I want to be with. I chose you." Laura tells Bobby, "I want to ask, how come you don't have a girlfriend or not married." Bobby tells Laura, "Relax I never slept around and knock anyone up. Since I am a 41-year-old virgin. The dating department was not in the cards for me. Since I was always busy with my book tour and writing new novels. I have been working non-stop since I was an author, my Governorship, and my potential vice-presidential ship to presidentship. I never had any time to be in a relationship or date." Laura tells Bobby, "I guess when I got to know you. I fell in love with you at first sight and knew you were a good man." Bobby and Laura make out for a minute and stops. Bobby tells Laura, "We better get back to Book Guys headquarters because Brian is worrying about us. But first we must stop by the lounge to get the diet pepsi's first." Laura tells Bobby, "I know, let's go." Bobby and Laura head to the Study Group door and exit the study Group area. Back inside the Book Guys headquarters on the third floor where Billy, Gary, and Ron enter the headquarters and sees Brian sitting down in his chair on the table. Brian tells Billy, Gary, and Ron, "Hey guys, how did it go?" Billy tells Brian, "It was fine, but Carter was not there but his acting CEO and his executive president Keith Alexander was there when we ask him questions and I think he bought it for now when we asked him about Stonewalk and the arms deal that Carter is going to have with his Armenian Terrorist clients." Billy, Gary, and Ron sit down in their chairs and Brian tells them, "If Carter was not, they're in his office, maybe he is clean." Ron tells Brian, "What do you mean?' Brian tells Ron, "That Carter had nothing to do with hiring Stonewalk to steal his own weapons and hide it some top-secret warehouse and killing Robinette with one of his guns that he stole from an NSA warehouse so he can use it to sell it to an Armenian Terrorist group that they were planning on invading Cambodia." Gary tells Brian, "I don't think so, Brian. Besides even if Stonewalk was there we would have figured it out when someone is lying and someone playing us. I think Carter is in D.C., but he is hiding in the shadows and letting Alexander cover for him." Billy tells Brian, "I don't think Carter is going to come out hiding until the arms deal starts. Once he is finishing the arms deal, he will kill Bobby and us soon." Ron tells them, "When you guys interrogated him, he would have figure out you guys are cops, and he might send a crew to kill you guys. Not right now, but soon." Bobby and Laura enter the Book Guys headquarters on the third floor at the DC public library. Bobby is carrying a box of 12 diet pepsi's. Laura tells them, "Hey guys, how is it going?" Billy, Gary, Ron, and Brian tell them, "Fine." Bobby puts the box of 12 cans of diet pepsi on the table. Brian tells Bobby, "Bobby, we wanted 5 cans and not 12 cans." Bobby tells Brian, "Well, Brian since we might be here all day. I thought we could have some sodas to keep us awake all day. But I forgot we have a refrigerator here. Ron, can you put the rest of the sodas in the fridge." Ron tells Bobby,

"Sure thing, Mr. Chavala." Bobby tells them, "Okay guys, help yourself." Bobby, Laura, Billy, Gary, Ron and Brian grab their diet pepsi's and six of them are out of the box and Ron puts his drink on the table and grabs the box and puts the rest of the sodas in the fridge. Everyone starts drinking diet pepsi and Bobby and Laura sit down in their chairs. Bobby tells Billy and Gary, "Okay guys, what's the report and how did it go with Carter. Is it the same guy who is my presidential advisor?" Gary tells Bobby, "Actually when you showed a picture of him. He was not there; his acting CEO and executive Vice President Keith Alexander was them was filling in for him when we questioned about Stonewalk stealing the weapons from the NSA from his boss's company and one of them was used to kill Robinette and planning on selling the weapons to an Armenian Terrorist group." Laura tells them, "So Carter had nothing to do with killing the president and stealing the weapons from the NSA warehouse and selling it to an Armenian Terrorist." Bobby tells them, "Actually Laura, it is still Carter. Even if I went to that company, he would have recognized me in a heartbeat if I questioned him. He is not stupid enough to show his face in the company and lied to me that he was visiting his sick mother in Phoenix while we were in a crisis." Billy tells Bobby, "Well Bobby when we asked Alexander about where Carter was. He was at a business meeting with one of his clients in Phoenix and I hardly doubt that is his sick mother." Bobby tells Billy, "So, it is him. You were right Billy, like I said I did believe you. Anyway, if Carter went off the grid. I know he won't emerge out of the shadows until the arms deal. If we can find him, the stolen weapons, and the Armenian terrorist we have enough to put them behind bars. All we must do is find the drop." Ro tells them, "But first we must find Carter's operation first. If we can find the operation, we might figure out where the drop is when he sells the weapons to the Armenian Terrorist Group." Laura tells Brian, "Brian did you find anything on these Armenian Terrorist Team?" Brian tells them, "Actually I could not find anything about them, I checked into Interpol computer there is no Armenian Terrorist Group. So, either they don't exist, or somebody erased their records in the computers to cover their tracks." Billy tells Brian, "That's because somebody high up must erase their records or rap sheets about them. That must be somebody who must work for the NSA. That would be Carter since he was an ex-NSA agent." Bobby tells them, "So, it is impossible to find them." Billy tells them, "Not impossible, I have a friend who can identify them and help us find Carter's operation and his drop. If Carter erases their records from Interpol, but that doesn't mean my friend Xander cannot find it. Luckily, his uncle has a lot pull with MI6, who might have back up records in case any of their system was hacked into. Luckily MI6 has the backup records that Interpol in case if they were deleted or hacked into to help identify them." Bobby tells Billy, "That's great, Billy. When does Xander give out the information on our Armenian Terrorist Group and Carter's operation and drop?" Billy tells Bobby, "Tomorrow morning, Bobby. Xander is call Laura and he will fax the information here in 9 am in the morning." Bobby tells them, "I guess that's it for today, there is nothing we can do today. So, we will come back tomorrow morning and wait for Xander's response. Billy, Gary, and Brian will take you to the white house and we will show you to your room. Everyone we will meet back here 8:30 in the morning." Billy tells them, "Let's go!" Bobby, Billy, Gary, Brian, Laura, and Ron get up from their chairs and exit the Book Guys headquarters. Outside the white house where it is morning, everybody starts to wake up. Bobby is in his presidential room sleeping in his bed. The presidential door is knocking, and Bobby hears it. Bobby tells the person on the other end of the door, "Come in." The door opens and it's a Secret Service agent who enters Bobby's bedroom and needs to talk to him. Bobby gets up from his bed and wearing his pajamas and exits his bed. Bobby tells the Secret Service Agent, "What is it, Seymour?" Seymour tells Bobby, "Mr. Chavala the director of the Secret Service faxed me today that there might be security risk that somebody might try to kill you and risk your safety." Bobby tells Seymour, "What security risk that Devlin told you about, why he hasn't text or fax me the information to himself?" Seymour tells Bobby, "Well Mr. Chavala. Devlin got an anonymous tip that there might be an explosion somewhere around the white house or somebody is trying to kill you. There might be a mole in the white house, and I know you have this top-secret mission you are doing. So, Mr. Devlin's orders for your safety that you and your men must go in separate limousines so that way won't see you. We will put in an undercover SUV van and one of your team will be the decoys for you in the presidential limos that way we can figure out if anyone tries to attack you or put in a bomb in the limousine, they won't if you are not in the limousine." Bobby tells Seymour, "Okay, but if we were going to be separated possible there might be a mole trying to kill me. I need one of my men to come with me. It will be Mr. Scott who will accompany me to the van and Mr. Wallace, Mr. Rodriguez, and Agent Simpson will go to into limo to weed out the threat to Book Guys Headquarters so that way we don't have to risk their safety or mine." Seymour tells Bobby, "Yes sir." Bobby tells Seymour, "Let me get dressed and get started and call the rest of the crew and tell them what's going on." Seymour tells Bobby, "Yes sir." Seymour exits out of Bobby's room and closes the door. Outside the second floor of the White House, where Billy and Gary are dressed in jeans and t-shirts and jackets are exiting the white house with Ron who is wearing a suit. Billy tells Ron, "Morning Ron, why are we hurry to leave, we barely had breakfast." Ron tells Billy, "We don't have time to have breakfast right now. Because we must head to the library soon." Gary tells Ron, "What's the rush?" Ron tells them, "My boss told me that there might be a mole in the white house and a possible assassination or explosion scare somewhere in the white house and I need to get you guys to safety back to headquarters that way no one will be harmed." Gary tells Ron, what boss, is it Bobby?" Ron tells Gary, "No, it's Director of the Secret Service Lonnie Devlin, he got an anonymous tip that there might be an explosion scare somewhere in the white house or mole in the white house who is trying to kill you guys. I need to take you guys to the library without the white house mole suspecting anything and we can eliminate the explosion before it detonates." Billy tells Ron, "Anything for our safety. What about Bobby and Brian, are they coming with us?" Ron tells Billy, "We are going to take separate cars. You guys will be with me in the limousine as decoys so that way the mole can't find us and that way the rest of the secret service can find the mole and figure out where the explosives are. So, you guys will be with me, and Mr. Chavala and Brian will be in an undercover SUV to head to the library. Will meet them their soon. But Director Devlin gave me a top-secret tip that the mole from our White House might not be there, but he told Devlin to meet you guys at a top-secret place who might give you the information about where the explosive is at and if you guys don't show up, he will kill the president." Billy tells Ron, "It sounds kind of weird, that Devlin gave us a tip that there is a mole in the white house who is trying to kill us or put an explosive somewhere around here. Now he wants us to meet him in a top-secret place where the explosive is in the white house so we can stop it and lure himself out of hiding so we can arrest him so we can find Carter, his terrorist clients and the stolen weapons. It is kind of weird, I think this could be a trap." Gary tells Billy, "What do you mean, Billy?" Billy tells Gary, "It sound like a trap, our mole wouldn't just give out a tip of an explosion scare in the white house or possible assassination attempt on Bobby. The mole wouldn't tell us to meet him in a secret place where the explosive is in the white house so we can shut it down and arrest him. I think this might be a trap, but not to the president. It might be us." Ron tells Billy, "If this is a potential ambush, we better be prepared. In the meantime, let's meet our mole and find out if the explosion scare is true. Outside the White house where the Presidential limousine exits the white house and there is a van parked right across the white house. Inside the limousine and where Ernie is using his binoculars to see the presidential limousine exiting the white house. Ernie gives the binoculars to one of Carter's men 1 in the passenger seat and grabs it. Ernie takes out his cell phone from his left pants pocket and starts dialing his cell phone. Carter makes a call to Alexander and tells Alexander on the other side of the phone, "Alexander, they just left. Alright I will call you when I am done with the mission, bye!" Ernie hangs up his cell phone and starts the van and exits the street right across the white house. The presidential limousine parks right outside an abandoned parking lot. The back of the limousine door opens and it's Billy, Gary and Ron who exits the limousine and sees an abandoned parking lot. Ron closes the door and sees the abandoned parking lot. Billy tells them, "I think our mole is a little bit late if he wanted us to meet him here." Gary tells Billy, "Maybe he was stuck in traffic. You know how tough traffic jams are." The

White Van enters the parking lot near Billy, Gary, and Ron where the presidential limousine is at, and it stops. The White Van is parked near them. The front door opens from the White Van and it's Ernie. Ernie exits the White Van and closes the door. Ernie goes over to Billy, Gary and Ron and talk to them. Ernie tells them, "I heard you guys want to see me. Let me introduce myself I am Ernest Roland; I am the guy who is the mole in the white house who gave the tip to Director Devlin about a bomb scare and possible assassination on President-elect Chavala." Gary tells Ernie, "If you are the mole who are you and why are we here to meeting you?" Ernie tells Gary, "I was going to give you a tip where the bomb is and possible to call off the dogs when we plan to kill your president-elect. Since my employer hired Rufus Stonewalk to kill your former President-elect Joe Robinette and I killed Stonewalk to silence him in case if he ever got caught by you guys. I know he would drop a dime on us, like I said no witnesses." Billy tells Ernie, "You lured yourself out of hiding and told us where the explosive is in the white house, and you were going to turn yourself in so you can give us information about your employer and his clients. I always have the urge; this could be a trap. Because I don't think there is any explosives in the white house. I know a guy like you would not send in a tip to director of secret service about a possible threat to the white house or the president and lured yourself out of hiding. Unless you are springing into a trap for us. You didn't want to lure the president out, you wanted to lure us out to kill us." Ernie tells Billy, "Wow, give Sherlock a cookie. You're right, I did send a tip to lure you son of bitches out of hiding to kill you guys. But we are not going to kill President Chavala right now. We are going to kill you first, then he's next when he joins you guys in the afterlife. Kill those little sons of bitches." Ernie snaps his fingers and takes out a Smith& Wesson 5904 out of his right jacket pocket and aims his gun at Billy, Gary, and Ron. The rest of Carter's five men exits the van and carrying Smith& Wesson 5904 guns and aims their guns on Billy, Gary, and Ron Billy, Gary and Ron didn't lure Ernie into this trap, they lured Ernie and Carter's men into this trap. Billy tells Ernie, "You didn't lure us into a trap, we lured you here in our trap. Billy, Gary, and Ron takes out their Beretta 92FS guns out of the back of their pants and aims their guns on Ernie and five of Carter's men. Ernie fires his gun; two bullets comes out of his gun and hit the road near Billy and misses him. When he drives down on the left side of the road before the two bullets hit the floor and Billy fires his gun and two bullets comes out of his gun. The two bullets hit Ernie in the chest and dies. Billy dives down the road to the left. Four more bullets comes out of nowhere and Gary and Ron dive on the right side of the road. Ron fires his gun, and three bullets comes out of his gun and hits Carter Man 2 in the stomach and dies. Billy, Gary, and Ron hit the road and rolled over to the other side of the limousine where five bullets came out of nowhere hit the near Billy, Gary, and Ron and missed them. They reach the other side the limousine and gets up a little where they see the rest of Carter's men. Carter Man 4 fires his gun, three bullets comes out of his gun and hits the back of the limousine door. Gary aims his gun and Carter man 5 and fires his gun. Two bullets comes out of Gary's gun and hits the road near Carter Man 5 and misses him. Carter Man 5 jumps a little and is upset. Carter Man 5 fires his gun again and two more bullets comes out of his gun and hits the back of the limousine door. Ron fires his gun; two bullets comes out of his gun and hits Carter Man 1 in the chest and dies. Gary fires his gun, and three bullets comes out of his gun and hits Carter Man 4 in the chest and dies. Billy fires his gun; one bullet comes out of his gun and hits the road near Carter Man 5 and misses him. Ron fires his gun and three bullets come out of his gun and hits the road near Carter 3 and misses him. Billy fires his gun; two bullets comes out of his gun and hits Carter Man 5 in the chest and dies. Ron fires his gun, and one bullet comes out of his gun and hits the road near Carter Man 3 and misses him. Carter Man 3 jumps a little. Gary exits the back of the limousine and aims his gun on Carter Man 3 and fire his gun. Two bullets come out of his gun and hits Carter Man 3 in the chest and dies. Billy and Ron gets up and exits the back of the limousine and goes over talk to Gary. Ron tells Billy, "I knew you're planned worked, Billy!" Billy tells Ron, "We didn't bring any guns with us before we arrive, so luckily you stored your weapons in a hidden trunk before we left." Gary tells Ron, "Ron call Bobby and tell him, that our fake mole and explosives were neutralized, and we are out of harms way for now." Ron tells them, "I'll call him and tell him what's going before we head back to the library." Ron takes out his cell phone from his left pants pocket and puts his gun on top of limousine trunk to make a call to Bobby. Back in the Book Guys warehouse in the DC public library on the third floor. Bobby, Brian, and Laura are sitting down in their chairs and Bobby is on his cell phone with Ron. Bobby tells Ron, "Okay, thank you Ron. Bye!" Bobby hangs up his cell phone and puts his cell phone on the table. Bobby tells them, "I got a call from Ron, there was no explosion scare or threat against us. The fake mole and explosive was a scare tactic to lure Billy, Gary, and Ron out of hiding so they can kill them since we were questioned Alexander and Carter." Brian tells them, "They figure out we're onto them, since Carter posse is dead. He'll send another team to kill us." Bobby tells Brian, "I don't think so, Brian. Since Carter is busy with his arms deal with Armenian Terrorist group. I don't think he has time to send out more troops to take us out. After the arms deal, he'll finish the job. Anyway, we still must find out where Carter's operation and where his drop is." Brian tells Bobby, "Who are the Armenian terrorist group that Carter selling the weapons too." Laura's cell phone is ringing and takes out her cell phone from her right pants pocket and answers it. Laura tells the person on the other side of the cell phone, "Hello, hey Xander. It's great to meet you. Hold on." Laura takes the cell phone out of her ear for a minute and tells Bobby and Brian, "It's Xander, good news he's found Carter's operation and who the Armenian Terrorist Group. He's going to fax us in a couple of seconds." Brian tells Laura, "Sounds great." Bobby tells Laura, "Tell Xander, we appreciate it." Laura gets back on the cellphone with Xander and tells him on the cellphone, "Thanks Xander for everything, bye!" Laura hangs up her cellphone and tells them, "Xander's going to fax the information to us in two seconds." Bobby tells Laura, "Laura go to the fax machine and grab the information that Xander fax us, and we will have to wait for Billy, Gary, and Ron to arrive so we can tell them everything we know." Laura tells Bobby, "You got it." Laura gets up from her chair and heads to the fax machine. Inside the warehouse office where Carter and Alexander are sitting down in their chairs waiting for Ernie's progress report on the deaths of Billy, Gary, and Ron. The door opens and it's Luther. Luther enters the warehouse office and closes the door. Luther goes over talk to Carter and Alexander. Luther tells Carter, "Mr. Carter we have some bad news sir?" Carter tells Luther, "What is it, Luther and where's Ernie." Luther tells Carter, "Ernie's dead sir, Wallace, Rodriguez and their secret service bodyguard Simpson is still alive, sir." Carter is upset right now and gets up from his chair and goes over to Luther and talks to him. Carter tells Luther, "Luther you ever heard of the expression of don't kill the messenger." Luther is kind of frightened that Carter is going to kill him. Luther tells Carter, "Yes sir. But sir, please don't kill me sir. I am just the messenger if you want sir, I will find them myself and kill Wallace, Rodriguez, and Simpson myself if you still want them dead sir." Carter tells Luther, "Relax Luther, I am not going to kill you or beat the snot the snot out of you. Just for being the messenger." Luther tells Carter, "Thank goodness, sir. I thought you would be upset." Carter and Luther start laughing for a minute, until Carter stops laughing and knees Luther in the stomach and gives him a round house kick in the face and falls on the floor. Luther is soaring right now. Carter tells Luther, "I said, I wasn't going to kill you or beat the snot out of you. That doesn't not mean I can't give you a roundhouse kick to the face. Get Up!" Luther gets up from the floor. Carter tells them, "I can't believe those morons escape our clutches." Alexander gets up from his chair and tells Carter, "So, what are we going to do now boss. We can send out another reinforcement to kill Wallace, Rodriguez, and Simpson." Carter tells them, "We don't have any time right now, our clients Gor Aida and the rest of Davit Group is expecting our weapons in three days. We got three days before our weapon deals to start." Alexander tells Carter, "What about Wallace, Rodriguez, and Simpson sir?" Luther tells Carter, "What about Chavala, sir. Are we still going to kill him after we finish Wallace, Rodriguez, and Simpson sir." Carter tells them, "Once our arms deal Aida and the rest of his Davit Group is done. We will find Chavala and the rest of his crew and eliminate him. Chavala is still incompetent as president-elect. Once the deal is done and kill his crew. Chavala will be next and my favorite guy, the Speaker of the house who I have under my control will do everything I say, since he is afraid of me. I took down Robinette because he was totally weak when as a president, after I got him elected with my connections and when he tries to start a peace treaty with Cambodia and Armenia that looks bad for my defense company. I also made Chavala, the acting president and when he tries untangling my arms deal and trying to pick up where Robinette left off with Cambodia and Armenia peace treaty. After we are done with the Arms deal, Chavala will be next and so is the rest of the crew. Like I said, we kill his crew first and then him. After he sees how much of a failure as a president since he protect his own people or his team. Come on, gentlemen we got work to do." Alexander and Luther tells Carter, "Yes sir!" Carter heads to the door, opens it and Carter, Alexander and Luther exits the warehouse office and Luther closes the door. On the first floor of Carter's top secret warehouse where Carter, Alexander and Luther supervises him men who are still hiding the Remington Model 700 rifle guns and grenades into boxes covered with flour. Back in Book Guys headquarters in the DC public library on the third floor. Bobby, Laura, and Brian are reading the information that Xander sent about the information on Davit Group and Carter's operation and his drop. Billy, Gary, and Simpson enters the Book Guys headquarters and goes over talk to Bobby, Laura, and Brian. Billy tells them, "Hey guys!" Bobby, Laura, and Brian gets up from their chairs and talk to Billy, Gary, and Ron about what happened. Bobby tells Billy, Gary, and Ron, "Are you guys, okay." Billy tells Bobby, "Yeah, we're fine. Luckily, we are well prepared before Carter's guys ambushed us when he lured us into a trap." Ron tells them, "I can't believe he put in a fake bomb threat and a mole of the white house to lure us out of hiding and kill us." Gary tells them, "We know one of Carter's men killed Stonewalk before he ever got caught from the feds if he spills the beans of him for ordering the hit on Robinette and that was Carter who ordered the hit." Ron tells them, "His name was Ernest Roland who worked for Carter and just like Stonewalk who was hired by Carter to kill Joe Robinette and Carter hiring Roland to kill Stonewalk too before he ever got caught by the feds. Bobby tells Billy, Gary, and Ron, "Well good news, Xander called us, and he's got the information on where Carter's operation and who is clients are." Billy tells Bobby, "What did you guys find out?" Bobby tells them, "Let's have a seat, will tell you everything we know." Bobby, Billy, Gary, Brian, Laura, and Ron sits down in their chairs and Bobby grabs the information on Carter's operation and the identity of Armenian Terrorist group that Carter is selling the weapons too. Bobby tells them, "We know Carter is selling his stolen weapons from that was stolen from the NSA warehouse that he ordered Stonewalk to steal and use one of the Remington Model 700 rifle guns to kill Joe so, he can stop his attempt to begin his peace treaty with Cambodia and Armenia. We know Carter's real plan to sell the weapons to Armenian Terrorist so they can use it to invade Cambodia and make more money for his Defense company. His bigger plan after the arms deal with him is to kill me, so the speaker of the house can over my presidency. Since Carter has the Speaker of the house wrapped his around finger since the Speaker is afraid of him." Laura tells them, "The name of the Armenian Terrorist Group that Carter is selling the stolen weapons to is the Davit Group led by Gor Aida. They are the Armenian Terrorist group that are top war criminals to invade not just Armenia, but also take over Cambodia to make them surrender. There are Interpol Top Ten most wanted but they could never find them or has any evidence to bring them down. The main reason why Interpol has nothing on them, since Carter is an NSA agent who hacked into their computers and erased shreds of evidence of them. There were rumors that the Davit Group might be in D.C. in three days. But Interpol or MI6 don't know where it is or who their clients are that are buying the weapons from." Billy tells them, "Let me guess Aida's client is none other than Waldo Carter who owns Cooper Industries." Bobby tells Billy, "Correct. Why the FBI and CIA, could never link Carter or his company to Davit Group from the arms deal. But the bad news we can't find the drop it could be anywhere where Carter sell the stolen weapon to the Davit Group. But there is some good news." Gary tells Bobby, "What's the good news?" Bobby tells Gary, "We found Carter's operation at. Is at 679 West Dale in D.C. It's an abandoned warehouse that is owned by Cooper Industries and why that warehouse is never used. But he has a top associate who Carter trusted and that is Henry Luther who works for Carter. If we can find him, maybe he can make him tell where Carter drop is at." Ron tells them, "Any idea how to find Luther? Bobby tells them, "Luther manages a night club on Friday night at 7:00 pm at Club Carrie that is owned by Cooper Industries. Billy tells them, "Friday night at 7:00 pm, that is three days away. The same time Carter is going to make his arms deal with Aida and the rest of the Davit Group." Brian tells them, "But Carter's warehouse is practically useless. A search warrant could take days and Carter has guys everywhere who can tip him off that the feds are investigating his warehouse. By the time we get there he'll move the operation somewhere else. The only we can bring him down is to find the drop, if we find the drop we find Carter, the stolen weapons, and Davit Group to bring them down." Bobby tells them, "Brian's right, finding the operation is practically useless. So, I have an idea. Billy, Gary, Ron, you guys go to Club Carrie on Friday night at 7:00 pm and find Luther. When you find Luther, do whatever you can to ask him Carter's drop is at." Billy tells Bobby, "Sure thing, what happens if that doesn't work, Bobby?" Bobby tells Billy, "We go with Plan B. Brian, Laura, you will go to Cooper's warehouse at 7:00 pm in 679 West Dale and put a tracking device on Carter's car. He is going to head to the deal, he's probably going in style like his limousine. Mostly he must park his limousine right in front of his warehouse. When you see his limousine, tape the tracking device behind the bumper of his limousine. Once you guys are done, get back into the car and call me so I can start the tracking device on my laptop and I will call Ron, tell you where to go and it will help you guys find the drop." Laura tells Bobby, "Sure thing." Bobby tells them, "Laura, Brian once you are done, come back to headquarters after your job is done." Brian tells Bobby, "Sure thing." Bobby tells them, "Once we find the drop, I call the FBI and the rest of the Secret Service to give them the location of the drop. Billy, Gary, and Ron when you find where the deal is and if you see Carter and his men and Aida and his men. Stall them if you can, before the feds arrive to take them down." Billy tells Bobby, "You got it. But one thing we don't have a tracking device." Bobby tells Billy, "We do, Billy. Laura, can you get it." Laura tells Bobby, "Sure thing, Bobby." Lnda gets up from her chair and sees the box of items that the CIA built and goes over to the box that in the computer section and takes out a four post it from the box. This is no ordinary post it, because this post it has a red button on top of the post it. Laura grabs the four post it and heads back to the table and put the four post it down. Bobby looks at the post it and grabs one of the posts it and shows it to them. Bobby tells them, "Guys, this is our tracking device." Brian tells Bobby, "It looks like a post it." Bobby tells Brian, "Well Brian, this is ordinary post it. This post it is a display, see the red button on top of the post it. If you click the red button on once, the tracking device will start and if you click button twice the tracking device will turn off, and we can the use the post it to follow Carter and the rest of his posse to their drop." Brian tells Bobby, "That is practically neat." Bobby tells them, "Luckily being the president-elect has some good perks when you have connections to the CIA." Brian tells Bobby, "What about the rest of Post it?" Bobby tells Brian, "Those three posts it what you see there are explosives like grenades. If you click the red button once, the post it will explode in ten seconds. Billy, Gary, Ron takes them with you in Club Carrie in case of an emergency." Gary tells Bobby, "Wow, neat!" Bobby tells them, Billy, Gary, Ron take the limousine, Laura, Brian you take the white SUV van with you in Carter's warehouse." Laura tells Bobby, "Sure thing." Bobby tells them, "We got three days until the drop starts. It's time we go into training. Everybody let's get started." Bobby, Billy, Gary, Ron, Brian, and Laura get up from their chairs and put their fist together shake. Billy tells them, "Let's do it." Outside the D.C. Public Library in the main entrance of the library where Laura is carrying a post it and presses the red button and, she is carrying her cell phone in her right hand and calling Bobby. Inside the book guys headquarters Bobby is practicing with his laptop and giving Laura a thumbs up while he was on the cell phone on his right hand with Laura. Inside the book guys headquarters training area section where Billy, Gary, and Ron are their training clothes and Billy is wearing his boxing gloves and punching the punching bag hard. Ron flips Gary on the training mat. Bobby is on his laptop, and he is carrying his cell phone in his right hand. Gary is kicking the practice dummy hard. Billy is flipping Ron on the training mat hard. Gary and Ron are shooting six bad guys in a harbor in a computer game with their video game guns.

Brian and Laura are across the street of D.C. Public library and Brian is carrying the post it. Brian pushes the red button and nods at Laura. Laura is on her cell phone with Bobby on the other end of his cell phone. Inside the book guys headquarters Bobby is sitting down in his chair with his laptop and is on the cellphone with Laura and gives her a thumbs up. Billy and Gary are taking eight bad guys in a warehouse in a computer game with their video game guns. Ron is wearing his boxing gloves and punching that punching bag hard. Gary flips Ron on the training mat hard. Ron gives Gary a thumbs up. Ron and Billy took out five bad guys in an alley in their computer game with their video game guns. Billy is kicking that punching dummy hard. Gary is also wearing boxing gloves and punching that punching bag hard. Billy and Ron are taking eight bad guys to a construction site with their video game guns. Brian and Laura are on the first floor of the D.C. Public library and Laura is carrying the post it. Laura presses the red button on top of the post it and Brian is on the cell phone with Bobby. Bobby is sitting down in his chair at the Book Guys headquarters on the third floor. Bobby is on his cell phone with Brian and Bobby sees them on the laptop and gives them a thumbs up. Outside of Club Carrie where the limousine is parked right across the street from the club, the back door opens and it's Billy, Gary, and Ron who exits the limousine. Ron closes the door. The three of them head to Club Carrie right across the street. Billy tells them, "We got to find Luther and do whatever we can and tell us where the drop is?" Gary tells Billy, "Billy, what makes you think Luther is going to tell where the drop is. Mostly guys like him are usually loyal to guys like Carter." Ron tells them, "Even, with my secret service badge and my glare is not exactly enough to get him to talk." Billy tells them, "Whatever we do, we gotta try. Because time is running out." Inside Club Carrie where Billy, Gary, and Ron enters the club and sees a waitress going over to him. The waitress tells them, "Hi, can I help you gentlemen?" Billy tells the waitress, "We are looking for Henry Luther, Mr. Cooper sent us. He said we need to talk to Mr. Luther about the progress report on the club. Believe me, Mr. Cooper is not a good mood right now and he wants to know how the club is doing right now." Waitress tells them, "Are you sure, Mr. Cooper called you guys. Because how come he is not here himself to talk to Mr. Luther." Ron tells the Waitress, "Mr. Cooper has an important engagement today, so he sent us talk to Mr. Luther about how the club is doing and we need to see the books if this company is making money or Mr. Cooper will have to shut down the place if we don't see Mr. Luther right now." Waitress is kind of frightened a bit that she might lose her job and tells them, "I don't want this club to be shut down or lose my job. If this important for Mr. Cooper, then I can tell you Mr. Luther is in his VIP booth." Waitress points to the right of the VIP booth where Luther is at. Waitress tells them, "Right over there." Waitress puts her hand down. Gary tells the Waitress, "Thank you, you been a good help. We will put in a good word with Mr. Cooper." Waitress tells Gary, "Thanks, I appreciate that." Gary tells the Waitress, "You're welcome." Billy, Gary, and Ron makes a right to the VIP booth where Luther is at. Billy tells Ron, "Wow, you're good Ron. How do you do that?" Ron tells Billy, "Well Billy, you want to get in places sometimes you need a little white lie to open the door or a sale a product. Besides time was running out, we need to find Luther anyway." Billy tells Ron, "I got it hand to you, buddy. You're good." Ron tells Billy, "No problem." Inside the VIP booth where Luther is having a drink with three pretty girls and five of Carter's men in the booth with them. Billy, Gary, and Ron looks at Luther and goes over talk to him. Billy tells Luther, "Hey Luther, I thought we can sit down and talk and catch up for a minute." Luther recognizes Billy, Gary, and Ron and tells Carter's Men, "It's them, shoot them." Luthor and five of Carter's men take out their SIG-Sauer P229 E2 guns from their right jacket pocket. Luthor fires his gun, one bullet comes out of his gun and hits the wall near Billy and misses him. Billy, Gary, and Ron takes out their Beretta 92FS from back of the pants and everyone starts to panic, and three attractive women exits the VIP booth. Ron fires his gun; two bullets comes out of his gun and hits Carter Man 1 in the chest and dies. Carter Man 3 and 4 fires their guns and four bullets comes out of their guns. Billy, Gary, and Ron dive down to the floor to the left before the bullets were fired. The four bullets hit two drinking glasses to the right. Billy, Gary, and Ron roll down on the left floor. They roll over to the right of the floor to the

VIP booth on the right. Five bullets comes out of nowhere and hit the floor near Billy, Gary, and Ron and misses them. Billy, Gary, and Ron roll over to the right across the VIP table and stops. All three of them hide under the VIP booth and two bullets comes out of nowhere and hit the table and misses them. Gary fires his gun; three bullets comes out of his gun and hits Carter 2 in the chest and dies. Carter Man 5 fires his gun, and five more bullets comes out of his gun and hits the wall near Billy, Gary, and Ron misses then. Billy fires his gun, two bullets comes out of his gun and hit the drinking glasses near Luther and misses him. Billy fires his gun again and three bullets comes out of his gun and hits Carter Man 4 in the chest and dies. Carter Man 5 fires his gun, and three bullets comes out of his gun and hits the table again and misses Billy, Gary, and Ron who are hiding under the table. Gary fires his gun; two bullets comes out of his gun and hits Carter Man 5 in the chest and dies. Billy tells them, "We got to get out here!" Gary tells them, "I have an idea, "I'll stall them for a minute." Gary aims his on the floor near Luther. Luther is still upset and fires his gun, and three more bullets comes out of his gun and hit the table again and misses Billy, Gary, and Ron. Gary fires his gun, and one bullet comes out of his gun and hits the floor near Luther and misses him. Luther jumps a little. Billy, Gary, and Ron stalls Luther for a minute and gets out of the VIP booth and exits the club. Outside of Club Carrie where everybody is panicking from a shootout and leaving the club. Billy, Gary, and Ron head to the limousine and Ron opens the back of the limousine door and all three of them get into the limousine. Inside the limousine where Billy, Gary, and Ron are sitting down back of the limousine and Ron tells the limo driver, "Dan, move move now!" Dan who is driving the limousine and hears Ron screaming and tells Ron, "Yes sir!" Outside of Club Carrier where Billy, Gary, and Ron limousine exits the Club Carrie and heads to the highway. Luther and Carter Man 3 exits the club too and sees Billy, Gary, and Ron's limo leaving the club. Carter Man 3 tells Luther, "They're getting away." Luther tells Carter Man 3, "I know where they're going, follow me." Outside the highway where the limousine gets out of Club Carrie as fast as they can, and the limousine slows down a little. Inside the back of the limousine, Billy,

Gary, and Ron are pacing for a minute. Billy tells them, "Did we lose them?" Gary tells Billy, "I don't know, I think I lost my lunch back there." Billy, Gary, and Ron hears some bullets hitting the trunk back of the limousine. Gary tells them, "I guess not." Ron tells them, "Instead of chasing Luther, now he's chasing us!" Billy opens the limousine window and looks outside and sees Luther and Carter Man 3 2020 Land Rover Range Rover Evoque van right behind them. Carter Man 3 is driving the van and Luther has his passenger window and he is carrying a Norinco Type 56 rifle gun. Outside the 2020 Land Rover Range Rover Evoque van and Luther fires his gun and Four bullets comes out of his gun and hits the trunk of the back of the limousine and misses them. Inside the limousine, Billy has his Beretta 92FS gun right next to in the back seat and grabs it. Billy hears two more bullets out of nowhere and the back of the trunk again and misses them. Billy goes over and sees Luther's van and fires his gun. Three bullets comes out of his gun and hit Luther's van. Luther fires his gun, and two bullets comes out of his gun and hit the road near the limousine and misses them. Billy fires his gun again; three more bullets comes out of his gun and hits the road near Luther's van and misses him again. Luther fires his gun again and one bullet comes out of his gun and hits the taillight in the back of the limousine and misses Billy, Gary, and Ron. Back inside the limousine where Billy gets back inside the limousine while stuck in the window. Billy tells them, "We got to lose them." Ron sees a road closed sign in the right side of the highway and tells Dan, "Dan make a right now!" Dan tells Ron, "Are you nuts, the road is closed." Ron tells Dan, "Do it now!" Outside the limousine they see the road closed and where the construction site is at. The limousine makes a right and crashes into the road closed sign. Inside the limousine where Billy and Gary are upset with Ron and Billy tells Ron, "Of all the god damn roads in D.C., you had to pick this one!" Ron tells Billy, "We have to lose them, this is only place to do it!" Luther's van follows the limousine to the construction site and Luther is still carrying his Norinco Type 56 rifle gun and fires his gun and five bullets comes out of his gun and hits the taillight again back of the limousine. Inside the back of the limousine, Billy and Gary are upset with Ron and trying to get them killed. Billy tells Ron, "We're sitting ducks. If I don't make it, I going to put a bullet in your ass!" Ron takes a five exploding post its from his right jacket pocket and gives it to Billy. Billy grabs the five post its and tells Ron, "Now, it's not a good time take notes!" Ron tells Billy, "Remember Bobby told us, these are no ordinary post its. They explode when you turn on the red button on. Do it now!" Billy puts his gun down on the back seat and heads back to the window. Outside of Luther's van where Luther fires his gun again and two bullets comes out of his gun and hits the road near the limousine and misses them. Billy hits it outside on top of the window and carrying five exploding post its and Billy presses the red buttons on all five of them and throws it. The five exploding post hits Luther's van windshield. Inside the back of the limousine, Billy, Gary, and Ron are panicking. Gary tells them, "We are going to die! Either we are going to lead or fall to the end of road! Because we are going to die!" Billy voiceover tells them, "I got it!" Ron tells Dan, "Dan, break now!" Dan puts on the break hard. Outside the highway the limousine slows down a little and Luther's van is almost ganging up on them and Luther is about to fire his gun until he sees the five post its on his windshield and tells himself, "What the hell!" The five post its explodes and Luther and Carter man 3 van explodes including them. Luther and Carter Man 3 are dead when their van explodes. The limousine stops and parks for a minute. The back of the limousine door opens and it's Billy, Gary, and Ron exits the limousine and Ron closes the door. Billy, Gary, and Ron sees the van explode with Luther and Carter Man 3. Billy tells them, "How would like your steak, medium or medium well." Ron and Gary tells Billy, "Medium Well." Billy, Gary, and Ron laughs a little and Gary tells them, "I guess Plan A went up in smoke." Billy tells them, "I hope Plan B, we need to find that deal. We don't even have a Plan B." Ron tells them, "I hope Laura and Brian could do a lot better than we could." Outside Carter's top secret warehouse and the White SUV van that parked right across the warehouse where Brian is driving the van and Laura is in the passenger seat. Inside the White SUV van and Brian tells Laura, "You know where Carter's limousine is at?" Laura sees Carter's limousine right across the main entrance of Carter's warehouse. Laura is carrying a post it and black scotch tape. Brian tells Laura, "Okay, you know what to do?" Laura tells Brian, "I tape the post it in the back of the limousine trunk and press the red button and tracking device start." Brian tells Laura, "You better hurry up, Laura. Carter and his men will be out of the warehouse soon." Outside the White SUV van where the passenger door opens and it's Laura. Laura exits the white SUV van and closes the door. Laura sneaks into the back of Carter's limousine trunk as fast as she can before Carter arrives. Laura tapes the post it with black scotch tape and presses the red button. Laura sees someone coming out of the warehouse. Laura gets out of there as fast as she can. Laura heads back to the white SUV van passenger seat and opens and closes the door. Inside the SUV van where Carter and his men are exiting the warehouse and heading to the drop. Laura tells Brian, "Okay, Brian I got the tracking device on. I call Bobby and tell him to track down Carter's limousine." Inside the Book Guys headquarters on the third floor at the DC Public Library where Bobby is sitting down in his chair and his laptop on the table. Bobby is waiting for Laura and Brian's call. Bobby's cell phone is on the table too and his cell phone rings. Bobby answers his cell phone and tells the person on the other side of his cell phone, "Hello, hey Laura. You got it. Okay, hang on." Bobby puts the cell phone back down on the table and turns on the tracking device on his laptop. Bobby grabs his cell phone and tells Laura on the other end of his cell phone, "Okay, I got the tracking device on. You and Brian go back to the library. Your mission is over. I will call Billy, Gary, and Ron and tell them where the location is at. It will be up to them to stop that arms deal before the cavalry arrives. Bobby hangs up his cell phone. Bobby sees Carter's limousine location is at. Bobby makes a call to Billy's cell phone. Outside the highway where Billy, Gary, and Ron are about to head back to the limousine. Billy's cell phone rings and tells them, "It's mine. Billy takes out his cell phone from his right pocket and answers it. Billy tells the person on the other end of his cell phone, "Hello, hey Bobby. Okay, got it. Hang On!" Billy takes the cell phone out of his ear for a minute and tells Gary and Ron, "It's Bobby, Laura got the tracking device on the back of Carter's limousine. Bobby know where he is going. Let's go!" Billy, Gary, and Ron head back inside the limousine and Ron opens the back door of the limousine and all three of them enters the back of the limousine and Ron closes the door. The Limousine exits the construction site. The highway where three black SUV vans and Carter's limousine are in the highway heading to the deal. Inside the back of the limousine and Billy is on his cell phone with Bobby and tells Dan, "Dan, turn right on southeast." Inside the Book Guys headquarters Bobby sits down in his chair on the table and tracks down Carter's location of his deal on his laptop. Bobby is on his cell phone with Billy, Bobby tells Billy on his cellphone, "Go three miles and turn left is Southeast!" The highway where three black SUV vans and Carter's limousine are in the highway are still in the road. Inside the back of the limousine and Billy is on his cell phone with Bobby and tells Dan, "Dan, go two miles and make a left in West Avenue." Inside the Book Guys headquarters Bobby sits down in his chair on the table and tracks down Carter's location of his deal on his laptop. Bobby is on his cell phone with Billy, Bobby tells Billy on his cellphone, "Two more miles and go to West End." Bobby sees the location on his tracking device on his laptop where the drop is. Bobby tells Billy on his cellphone, "I know where the drop is at. It's 651 West Road. It's an abandoned hangar. That is where Carter is going to make the deal with the Davit Group at." Inside the back of the limousine Billy is on his cell phone with Bobby and tells Dan, "Bobby, knows where the drop is at 651 West Road. Dan, go to 651 West Road, it's an abandoned hangar." Gary tells himself, "Best place to make a business deal as an abandoned hangar!" Inside the Book Guys headquarters Bobby sits down in his chair on the table and tracks down Carter's location of his deal on his laptop. Bobby is on his cell phone with Lonnie, "Okay Lonnie send two SWAT vans and one helicopter and get the FBI on board. Thank you!" Outside the hangar where Billy, Gary, and Ron limousine enters outside the hangar and parks his car near Carter's limousine is at. The back of the limousine door opens and it's Billy, Gary, and Ron exits the back of the limousine and Ron closes the door. Billy, Gary, and Ron looks at the hangar and Ron tells them, "Carter is going to sell the stolen weapons to Aida and his possess the Davit Group in a few seconds." Billy tells Ron, "How long can the FBI or Secret Service will arrive?" Ron tells Billy, "It's going to twenty or thirty minutes to get here. The arms deal will be done, before they arrive." Billy tells them, "Will have to stall them, until they arrive." Ron takes out the car keys to the limousine from his right pants pocket and opens the trunk. Ron takes three berretta 92X rdo guns from the back of the trunk and gives the two guns to Billy and Gary and both grab it. Ron grabs another berretta 92X rdo gun from the trunk and puts it on the back of his pants. Ron closes the door and tells them, "Who's going to stall them first?" Ron and Gary looks at Billy for a minute and Billy tells them, "What?" Inside the hangar where Carter, Alexander and nine of his men with Aida and six of his Davit Group ready for the arms. One of Carter's crates is on the floor near the table, Carter grabs the crowbar and opens the crate. Carter takes out a Remington Model 700 rifle gun from the crate that is covered with flour and shows it to Aida. Aida is impressed and Aida nods his head to Davit Group Man 1. Davit Group Man 1 is carrying two briefcases and put them on the table. Davit Group Man 1 opens the two briefcases and see five million dollars each on the briefcase. Carter is happy that his deal is a breeze. Carter's arms deal is about to be finished until a voiceover tells them, "Hey!" Billy enters the hangar and goes over talk to Carter, Alexander and the rest of his men and Aida and the rest of the Davit Group. Billy sees them and tells them, "Is this is a party, and nobody invited me. I was kind of lost, I was about to head to the Lincoln Memorial for a tour of our nation capital. I kind of got lost, this is not much of a party here, must be a swap meet. If you guys are buying here, I wondered if I could get a deal on a watch here. Can you tell me where the watches are?" Carter, nine of Carter's men and Aida and the rest of the Davit group are upset that Billy is trespassing are in their arms deal. All of them take out their SIG-Sauer P228 from their right jacket pockets and aims their gun at Billy. Billy tells them, "Is this a bad time, I come back tomorrow and get a new watch." Carter tells Billy, "Kill that little son of a bitch." Carter fires his gun; two bullets comes out of his gun and hit the floor near Billy and misses him. Billy dives down to the left of the floor before the two bullets hit the floor near Billy. Billy dives down to the left of the floor near the barrels and hides. Billy takes out his berretta 92X rdo gun behind his pants and fires his gun. Three bullets comes out of his gun and hit Aida in the chest and dies. Carter Man 3 fires his gun, four bullets come out of his gun and hits the wall near Billy and misses him. Billy fires his gun, and three bullets comes out of his gun and hits Carter Man 3 in the chest and dies. Ron and Gary enters the hangar carrying their guns. Gary fires his gun, and two bullets comes out of his gun and hits Davit Group Man 1 in the chest and dies. Gary and Ron dive down to the floor to the left near the boxes and hide behind the boxes. Ron fires his gun, and two bullets comes out of his gun and hits Carter Man 2 in the chest and dies. Gary fires his gun, and two bullets comes out of his gun and hits Carter Man 4 in the chest and dies. Billy fires his gun; two bullets comes out of his gun and hits Carter Man 8 in the chest and dies. Carter fires his gun, and two bullets comes out of his gun and hits floor near Billy and misses him. Billy fires his gun; three bullets comes out of his gun and hits Davit Group Man 6 in the chest and dies. Davit Group Man 4 fires his gun, two bullets comes out of his gun and hits the wall near Ron and Gary and misses them. Billy fires his gun and two bullets come out of his gun and hits Alexander in the chest and dies. Gary fires his gun; three bullets comes out of his gun and hits Carter Man 9 in the chest and dies. Ron fires his gun, and two bullets comes out of his gun and hits Davit Group Man 3 in the chest and dies. Carter is upset that his best friend and right-hand man Alexander is dead. Carter fires his gun, and three bullets comes out of his gun and hit the wall near Billy and misses him. Billy fires his gun, three bullets come out of his gun and hits Davit Group Man 3 in the stomach and dies. Ron fires his gun, and three bullets comes out of his gun and hits Carter Man 7 in the chest and dies. Gary fires his gun, and two bullets comes out of his gun and hits Carter Man 6 in the stomach and dies. Billy fires his gun, and three bullets comes out of his gun and hits Davit Group Man 2 in the stomach and dies. Gary fire his gun and three bullets comes out of his gun and hits Carter Man 5 in the chest and dies. Ron fires his gun, and two bullets comes out of his gun and hits Davit Group Man 5 in the chest and dies. Billy fires his gun and three bullets comes out of his gun and hits the floor near Carter and misses him. Carter jumps a little. Billy is out of bullets and tells himself, "I'm out!" Billy takes out the gun chamber and gets a new one in the back and take it out. Billy reloads his gun and fires his gun. Three bullets comes out of his gun and hits the floor near Carter Man 8 and misses him. Billy sees Carter and he knows what to do. Billy tells Ron, "Cover me, I'm going in!" Billy comes out of the barrel and is about to tackle Carter. Billy starts running as fast as he can. Three bullets comes out of nowhere and hit the floor near Billy and misses him. Ron fires his gun and hits the floor near Carter Man 1 and misses him. Carter Man 1 jumps a little. Billy is running as fast as he can, and two more bullets comes out of nowhere and hit the floor near Billy and misses him. Billy starts tackling Carter from the table and the table and Carter and Billy both fall on the floor. Billy and Carter both drop their guns on the floor. Billy gets up first and so does Carter. Billy punches Carter in the stomach and his face. Billy knees him in the stomach and grabs him by the shirt and tosses him by the right side of the other hangar. Billy throws Carter on the floor of the right side of the hangar. Billy goes over to Carter, until Carter kicks Billy in the groin. Carter gets up from the floor and Carter punches Billy in the face and gives him a round house kick to the face again and Billy falls on the floor. Ron fires his gun, and two bullets comes out of his gun and hits Carter Man 1 in the chest and dies. Carter Man 8 fires his gun, and three bullets comes out of his gun and hits the wall near Gary and misses him. Ron fires his gun, and two bullets comes out of his gun and hits Carter Man 8 in the chest and dies. Carter kicks Billy in the stomach twice. Carter picks up Billy and punches him in the stomach twice. Carter punches Billy in the face again and Billy falls on the floor. Davit Group Man 4 sees he is being outnumbered and tells himself, "Figure it out, I'm being outnumbered. I'm going back. Outside the back of the hangar where Davit Group Man 4 tries to escape and stops when he sees Two FBI SWAT vans and Brian and Laura carrying their berretta 92X rdo guns and five FBI SWAT members are carrying Heckler& Koch MP5A2 guns aimed Davit Group Man 4. Davit Group Man 4 is about to fire his gun and even if fires his gun away out to escape. Brian tells Laura, "Ready, aim and Fire!" Brian and Laura fire their guns and four bullets comes out of their guns. Two bullets came out of Brian's gun and two more bullets came out of Laura's gun. The four bullets' hits Davit Group Man 4 in the chest and dies. Gary and Ron gets exit out behind the boxes and Ron tells Gary, "I better go help Billy." Bobby's voiceover comes out of nowhere and tells Ron and Gary, "No, I got this one." Carter still kicks Billy in the stomach. Carter sees his gun being dropped on the floor and goes over to his gun and grabs it. Billy is still hurt and moaning. Carter grabs his gun and aims his gun at Billy. Carter fires his gun, and one bullet comes out of his gun and hits Billy on top of his left chest and Billy is soaring. Billy tries to cover his gunshot wound. Carter goes over to Billy and gives him a round house kick to the face again and Billy falls on the floor. Carter tells Billy, "You think you and loser pals can come over here and ruin my arms deal." Carter is upset and kicks Billy in the stomach again. Carter tells Billy, "You're pathetic Wallace. I always knew Chavala was always an amateur president. Sending you and Rodriguez to do his dirty work. Thinking he can ruin my arms deal and cost me a lot of money. I may kill Robinette and Chavala becomes president. He won't be president for now, because after I finish you Wallace and Chavala's next. After I am done with him, I will kill the rest of loser crew who thinks they can interfere in my arms deal. Guess what, I will still exit out of here untouched and unharmed. There will be always going to be other arms deal with another terrorist group and after I am done killing you Wallace and Chavala will be next, and I will still run this country wrapped around behind my finger. This is what our amateur president gets sending an another amateur to do his dirty work. Guess what Wallace, your party is now over." Carter aims his gun at Billy, until he sees his gun slipping right across him and Carter is about to fire his gun, until he hears green paint hit in the back. Carter jumps a little and Billy gets up from the floor and grabs his gun and aims his gun at Carter. Billy tells Carter, "Guess what Carter, my party is not over it just begun. Consider your deal with Davit Group is off!" Carter tells himself, "What the…?" Billy fires his gun; and two bullets comes out of his gun and hit Carter in the chest and dies. Billy is still hurt and soaring. Billy sees Bobby out of nowhere and carrying a paintball gun. Billy tells Bobby, "Bobby what are you doing here. I always though you were going to stay neutral on this." Bobby tells Billy, "I did, but I wasn't going to miss out the action and let you have all the fun." Bobby goes over to Billy and grabs him since Billy got shot. Bobby tells Billy, "Come on, Billy. I will buy you a donut. You owe one, helping me out here and now I owe you one." Billy tells Bobby, "For this and saving my life." Bobby tells Billy, "Oh no, this isn't your favor. But this is a bonus favor, you're really favor just begun. Come one, I'll buy you a donut." Billy tells Bobby, "Make sure you get the glaze. I always love a glaze." Bobby tells Billy, "So do I!" Outside the hangar where firemen and police cars and FBI are here to clean up the hangar and the rest of the arms deal. Billy is in the ambulance with a bandage of his wounded shot. Bobby, Laura, Gary, and Ron goes over to Billy sitting in the gurney inside the ambulance. Bobby tells them, "I am proud of you guys for helping me out in this mission. The weapons are confiscated, by the FBI and the NSA will will have a chance to deliver the weapons to the US Army on time to help the people in Cambodia. Once I get sworn in, I will start my peace treaty with Cambodia and Armenia. Just like Joe wanted. Gary tells Bobby, "Sounds great!" Bobby tells them, "Billy, Gary, Brian you guys will be heading back to L.A. in a week after I award you guys the and Ron and Laura the President's medal of Freedom for your services for this mission. Don;'t worry Billy and Gary, I will send a recognition and recommendation to your boss to lift your suspension and get your promotions and a raise for you guys that the LAPD stiffed you guys from." Billy and Gary tells Bobby, "Thanks Bobby!" Bobby tells Billy and Gary, "You're welcome. I gave you a temporary job as my senior presidential advisor. Guess what you are no longer my secretary, you are now my full-time presidential advisor and if you want...?" Bobby gets down on his knees and takes out a engagement ring box out of his left pants pocket and opens the ring box with a huge diamond engagement ring. Laura Wilkins, will you marry me and be my First Lady." Laura is very touched, and she is in love with Bobby. Laura tells Bobby, "Yes, I will marry you. I love you, Bobby." Bobby puts the diamond engagement ring on Laura's right ring finger and Bobby gets up from his chair and makes out with Linda for a minute and stops. Everyone starts cheering for Bobby and Linda. Bobby's voiceover tells the people from his Presidential Inauguration, "Tomorrow I had to say goodbye to old friend." Inside Joe's hospital room where his wife Joan and Joe's young son and daughter with Bobby and Laura are there to say good-bye to Joe and the doctor pulls the plug on Joe's life support. Everyone starts mourning to the president. Bobby's voiceover continues and tells his people in his Inauguration, "Joe had a lovely funeral where he was buried in Arlington cemetery." Joe's coffin is about to be buried in Arlington Cemetery with an American flag covered in Joe's coffin and ten thousand showed to say good-bye to President-elect Robinette and Five US Army soldiers give a 21-gun salute to Joe and amazing grace on bagpipes are playing. Bobby's voiceover continues when he is speaking to the people in his Inauguration, "I awarded my friends the President Medal of Freedom to them, and I helped Billy and Gary reinstated back in the LAPD and got them raise and promotions for them as I promised." Inside the White House East Room where Bobby is awarding the President Medal of Freedom to Billy, Gary, Brian, Laura, and Ron for their services of mission with Bobby. Inside the LAPD headquarters where Billy and Gary returned as cops, they are back as detectives and sitting down in their detective offices and promoted to Detective and Lieutenant of the LAPD. Bobby's voiceover continues when he is speaking to the people in his Inauguration, "Me and Lura are going to have our wedding in three days after I get sworn in and begin my term as a full fledge President of the United States." Outside the capital building where Bobby is sworn in as President of the United States when he finishes taking his oath of the presidency from the Chief Justice of the Supreme Court. Billy, Gary, Laura, Ron, Brian, Joan, and Joe's kids are sitting down in their chairs at the presidential inauguration area. Chief Justices finishes his Presidential Oath to Bobby, "I Srinivas Robert Chavala, do solemnly swear (or affirm) that I will support and defend the Constitution of the United States against all enemies, foreign and domestic; that I will bear true faith and allegiance to the same; that I take this obligation freely, without any mental reservation or purpose of evasion; and that I will well and faithfully discharge the duties of the office on which I am about to enter: So help me God." Bobby tells the Chief Justice of the Supreme Court, "I Srinivas Robert Chavala, do solemnly swear (or

affirm) that I will support and defend the Constitution of the United States against all enemies, foreign and domestic; that I will bear true faith and allegiance to the same; that I take this obligation freely, without any mental reservation or purpose of evasion; and that I will well and faithfully discharge the duties of the office on which I am about to enter: So help me God." Chief Justice of the Supreme Court tells Bobby, "Congratulations, Mr. President!" Bobby shakes hands with the Chief Justice of the Supreme Court and let's go. After getting sworn in and Bobby finishes addressing the public in his Inauguration speech and tells them, "Thank you, ladies and Gentlemen and I will do best I can for this country. I will also do my best to help each and every one American in this country. God bless you and God bless America." Everyone was touched hearing Bobby's speech and Bobby looks at the crowd and says that he will someday change the world and he will. Bobby tells himself, "That's for you, Joe!"
The End.

THE GERBER FAMILY
BY BOBBY CINEMA

SYNOPSIS:

Kaia Jordan Gerber is the youngest detective and sergeant of the NYPD. She is 21 years old and starts her case in a drug bust. But the drug bust went bad and her captain chewed her out for it. Right now, her boss has given her a two-week suspension. Kaia is a child prodigy who graduated high school at age 10, graduated from Columbia and Columbia Law school at age 17. She did a two-year stint serving in the US army green berets as ranked as Captain when she joined ROTC in Columbia. Luckily, she got discharged at an early age 19 and let her be in the reserves. She fought 6 missions in Iraq. After she left the army, she joined NYPD academy and after two years she just promoted to Detective and Sergeant after a convenience store bust. Her older brother Presley Walker Gerber is in his first year as a deputy D.A. and needs her help on a case and it might be connected to her drug bust that failed her. Presley was trying to convict a drug lord, but the search warrant fell through, and all the evidence fell through. Somebody tipped off the drug lord about the evidence that the D.A. was going to investigate. Their might rumors that the D.A. might be working with this drug lord. But they don't have any evidence and needs her help. Presley and Kaia comes from a very successful family, his father Randy own a chain of nightclubs and their mother is a famous supermodel, Cindy. Since Kaia is on suspension, her captain decide to lift her suspension and give her a two-week vacation. Kaia decides to go to L.A. to find the drug lord who might be the mastermind of the drug bust that she tried to stop in New York when the person she was after is in L.A. Presley teams up with her little sister Kaia and Presley friend Bobby Dawson who is a college buddy of his to help them out. Bobby is the head librarian in the Malibu Public Library, so all three of them are working together to stop this drug lord making a huge heroin deal with an international terrorist who are they going to sell the drugs too. Can they do it, only time will tell.

204

Final Word

Thank you for reading Bobby Cinema's Third Librarian Detective Series. I hope you enjoy reading them. In my next detective series I will write the new detective story The Gerber Family. This is my Third Librarian Detective Series. See you, next time and remember readers, the library is always open, good-bye!.